Here's what people are saying:

"I cried, prayed, laughed, ached, and rejoiced through every page. It was a privilege to review this work; it is the best of its genre that I have read. I pray that *"Forgiven Much"* will reach the masses who so need a story like this to illustrate the depth of the grace and love of our Savior, Jesus Christ."

Kristen Johnson
Opine Publishing

"*Forgiven Much* is a story of hope shared from someone who has experienced the forgiveness and restoration only God can offer. Through this riveting account of a woman who has experienced all kinds of abuse and abandonment, we feel the despair and hopelessness and even identify with her poor choices. It's a story that will tug at your heart strings for a long time! And, it will be a definitive moment in your own healing process! As a wounded healer, Leslie reminds us that we all have a story to tell, and that God will use our obedience to bring healing to others who are walking where we once walked."

Lynette Wright
Director of Outreach Ministries

"In *Forgiven Much,* Leslie Dean has uniquely brought the major current abuse issues to a Biblical setting. Then and now seem merged into one seamless time. The reader finds himself in the time of Jesus…or is it that Jesus is brought to our time? We can be convinced that Mary of Magdala was the lady at the end of our street, the one we gossiped about, but neither knew nor understood.

This writing will minister to all sorts of abused and abusing people. The abused will learn that Jesus himself still reaches out and says, "Trust me." Abusers may be led to recognize their abusive ways and come to Jesus for healing and forgiveness. Millions of mothers, and no doubt fathers, will find hope of meeting an aborted child at the feet of Jesus in heaven.

The writing is imaginative, but much more than imaginative. It is real and it is Biblical. Real: The characters, the situations, and the healing come from the writer's own experience. Biblical: Scripture comes alive, and deepens our understanding of its practical application. These two halves are integrated skillfully into a convincing novel. The result is a grand view of the care and healing of Jesus in our lives."

Norm Smith
Teacher/Software Developer

"Reading *Forgiven Much* was like reading my life in print. I was astounded how Leslie was able to put into words the feelings of any abused or addicted person. From the earliest years through the healing process, she is thorough, but not grossly graphic. Although this story is about a woman, I believe that anyone who has suffered abuse, abandonment or addiction would benefit greatly by reading this book. I read it just as I was going through my healing and it strengthened me, inspired me, and sometimes made me angry with the lead character... because she was me. It is an awesome story! This book may be fiction, but it was all too real for me. Leslie has, with God's help, been able to give us a special gift with her writing talent. In the hands of hurting people, this book could be a real life saver. AMAZING pretty much sums it up!"

Amy Jefferson
Abuse survivor

"Leslie weaves her life into the fabric of God's redemption story, an invitation He extends to each of us. *Forgiven Much* will be a helpful and potentially healing read for those with wounded hearts."

Pastor Pat Lloyd
Support & Recovery Minister

"Leslie Dean's book *Forgiven Much* really impressed me with her ability to portray the lead character during biblical times. What especially impressed me was her knowledge of the scriptures. She made the bible stories come to life. At first, I wasn't quite fond of the character because I wanted her to make better choices instead of looking for love in all the wrong places. Yet, I know, due to her past rejection and abuse, she didn't know how. Her choices represented a cycle of abuse she was powerless to control.

When she met "the lover of her soul" and experienced His forgiveness, it made me realize how I had judged her. I condemned her choices solely based on my own experiences in life. Thankfully, Christ doesn't treat us the way our sins deserve. And thankfully, her painful life experiences were not without a purpose, for now she can forgive with the same depth she received it and help others who have been rejected and abused."

Loretta McWilliams
Maternal/Child Health

Forgiven Much

Leslie T. Dean

Dedication

To my children, Michael, Taylor, Matthew and Rachel.
Your love is more precious than diamonds.

To my children, Mary Elizabeth, Joshua David, Angel and
Jesse.

I will hold you in Heaven.

To my Savior. *Thank you.*

Table of Contents

Acknowledgments...................................... xi

Prologue xv

1 – Hidden Things.............................17

2 – Safe Places 29

3 – Trusted Friends...................................49

4 – Night Visitors 73

5 – Abandoned 89

6 – New Alliances 107

7 – Loss of Innocence 127

8 – Numb the Pain....................................141

9 – Secrets Revealed 161

10 – Life Taken 177

11 – Till Death Do Us Part......197

12 – Blackout......217

13 – Set Up!......237

14 – Forgiven Much......257

15 – Denial......277

16 – Life Given......289

17 – Reunited......305

18 – Loved Much......325

19 – Forty Days......343

20 – Wounded Healer......357

Epilogue......371

Acknowledgments

This book was a journey for me. A journey through my own past and the written past of my Savior. Had I not met Him, this book would never have been written. For it was the miracle of His salvation and grace, that gave me the ability to write it. The same salvation and grace granted to the woman crying at his feet. The first time I read her story, I connected with her. I understood her depth of gratitude. I understood that measure of love.

This is not a book that I wanted to write. By profession, I am a Registered Nurse, not a writer. But because God put it in my heart and sent people into my life to tell me I had a book to write, I finally gave in and was obedient to the call. I would like to take this time to thank those people.

First, my aunt and uncle, Larry and Judy Taylor. They prayed for me for many years as I wandered in the world. Seven years ago, they told me I had a book in me just waiting to come out and they encouraged me to write it. I wasn't ready.

My cherished friend and mentor, Lynette Wright. She walked with me through many of the experiences I have shared on these pages and she listened as I rehashed the rest...and still loved me. That was something I had never known. As a new Christian, she was Jesus' arm when I needed a hug, his mouth when I needed encouragement (or correction) and his love when I felt unlovable. That has not changed over the years. As Godmother to my children, she is also family (something else I had never known). She, too, told me I should write a book. I still wasn't ready.

My dear friend, Sherri Mohnkern. She has been an endless resource of help and encouragement. She has had many friends who have helped me, to whom I also owe much gratitude. When I felt the task was unbearable, Sherri prayed with me and encouraged me to "let the people know." I had spent two years struggling through writing a few chapters, and finally shared them with her. She too, encouraged me to write the book. I decided it was time.

The oldest of Sherri's eight kids, Aubree Mohnkern, is my next blessing. Even though she is a full time college student, she took the time to read and edit for me, offering me wisdom well beyond her years. Her perseverance and loyalty has been a gift from the Father's hand. When she read the few chapters I had worked on, she told me I *had* to write this book. So I did.

Norm and Florence Smith, who have been invaluable in helping me edit. And even more importantly, they have helped me understand people who, like themselves, have never lived through the horrors of the world. Their patience and understanding have been a blessing.

And without the love, patience and help from my family, I could never have written a single page. My husband Paul survived the hills and valleys associated with digging up old wounds-even if those wounds are healed. Our wonderful children, Mike, Taylor, Matt and Rachel were vigilant in daily asking me how the book was going or giving me spur of the moment hugs when I didn't want to go on- with a whisper in my ear, "You can do it, Mom!" I love them all more than words can express and so much appreciate their sacrifice.

Most of all, I dedicate this book to My Lord and Savior, Jesus Christ. I walked through these pages with Him. My gratitude grew exponentially as I remembered the things of my past and what He has done in my life. He showed me the way from my darkness into His light. He took me from death and gave me life. Eternal life. With Him… I can't wait.

Prologue

This is a fictional work based on real life events. Though I have taken some liberties with the lives of those mentioned in the Bible, I have done my best to portray the love and character of our Lord and His deep desire to help us heal. There are a few graphic scenes that some may find hard to read. But life in the world without Jesus is much harder than anything you will read on these pages. *And sometimes our choices make it even worse.* Obviously, to cover so many years, numerous details had to be left out and the most horrible have been omitted. To understand the enormity of the miracles that take place, you must understand the character's immensely dysfunctional life.

A life, not of joys and sorrows, but of abuse and pain and wounds so deep that you wear them like garments. A life where criticism, discouragement and neglect are the norm. Where understanding, compassion and most of all, love, are given out sparingly, if at all. A life where what you do and how well you do it determines your worthiness of attention. And if you don't do a job well, then prepare yourself for the wrath or sometimes worse, the silence. Days go by without a word—ignored—as if you don't exist. If you try to speak during this time, you will only hear, "Go away! I want nothing to do with you! You are an embarrassment! You are good for nothing! I disown you as my daughter!" Then there are the nights. Never feeling safe because you don't know who might come into your room. Or what they might do. The shame and fear are devastating.

How does a little child endure that kind of pain? What does she learn that she carries with her into adulthood? What coping mechanisms does she integrate into her personality so that when she becomes a woman, she can put on her mask and pretend she is "normal?" The answer lies deep inside the recesses of the brain— a place many of us consider "safe" because it's where we escape the anguish we experience in our lives. A dark, hidden, secret place where "all is well" and where the birthplace of denial and codependency are found. A place I hope to take you.

My prayer is that you may hear some morsel of familiarity that would cause you to seek the one who can release you from that place. The *only* one who can bring you back.

The one who knows no darkness, but is willing to rescue you from yours.

The one who allowed himself to be wounded long ago so that he could understand how you acquired your wounds, and more importantly, why you won't let them go.

The one who is...The Way, the Truth and the Life.

1

Hidden things

Today had been a memorable day for those of us in Bethlehem. Caesar had called for a census and everyone who was a descendent of David had come to be counted. All day, people had been arriving at my father's inn and he loved it. He was a man who worshiped money and had been saying for weeks, "an opportunity such as this comes about once in a lifetime." He was determined to take advantage of it!

I had worked hard all day and was so tired I came to bed early. I also had one of my headaches. I can't remember when they started; I only knew I was getting them more and more frequently. As I lay in my bed and reminisced about the events of the day, I thought about what had brought us here to Bethlehem. When my father purchased this inn four years ago, he volunteered my mother to be the caretaker of the kitchen and dining room. We all shared in the responsibilities of keeping the rooms clean and the mats turned and when I was old enough, the expectation was that I would help with my mother's jobs as well.

The inn and my mother were not on good terms, however. She had not wanted to move here away from her family. She felt that my father spent entirely too much time with the guests and not enough with us. He also went on numerous trips, usually to Jerusalem, to let people know about his inn. My mother felt his trips had another motive. The inn was a constant source of contention between them.

The last two days had been much busier than usual, preparing for the influx of people that my father had expected. My parents had been bickering and arguing the whole time. My mother was exhausted, but my father would not let up. I watched their exchange. "Naomi, you didn't get the dining area clean enough. This is the biggest night we have ever had and presentation is everything. What is wrong with you? Don't you care what people think?"

My mother had sat holding her head in her hands. I knew *that* was a bad sign! When she had looked up at him, there was hatred in her eyes. "Bartimus, I could care less about your guests! I know you probably have some of your little trollops coming here, too. You think you are so slick, but I know what you do!"

That was always the beginning of the battle. In my short twelve years, I had learned the signs. I immediately looked at Father's face, anticipating the smile. He always gave my mother a condescending smile that inferred he must have patience with this "poor, sick woman." It hurt my feelings when he directed that smile at me, but when he did it to Mother, she would become furious!

As I watched his face, I saw the smile forming and he slowly licked his lips. With calculated slowness, he said, "Naomi, you are so simple-minded! I'm very worried about you! I truly think there is something wrong with you! I'm beginning to believe that what all our friends say might be true. I think you are mad!" I knew it would get ugly after those comments and I quietly slipped out of the room. I never

18

feared them missing me. The only time I was missed was when I had not done one of my chores! Mother complained about Father having no time for the family, but *she* never had time for me! And besides all the work my father expected of her, she also had to care for my new little brother! Since he had been born, I had felt almost invisible! It made me miss my sister all the more.

I also hated the inn. Some things had been happening at night, but I couldn't talk about them. I had tried to a few times, but I found the safest thing was to keep my "secret" a secret. The scary part was I never knew when the man might show up at my door. He would just stand there. Sometimes he would go away. But on a few occasions he didn't.

As I felt the first heaviness of sleep in my eyes, I heard shuffling in the hallway outside my room. I was immediately wide-eyed and could feel my heart pounding in my chest. Not tonight, please! I was so tired! I listened intently as I heard the steps getting closer. I hoped that maybe they were just cutting through to the courtyard. But I knew this hall was supposed to be off limits to guests. I lay there motionless, barely breathing. Then the shuffling stopped and I knew he was at my door. I thought about screaming, but knew my mother had gone to bed early with my brother. She was so worn out; I didn't dare wake her. She would get really angry and it would end up starting another argument.

I had no one to protect me and nowhere to run. I was too tired to worry if he would leave or stay; my head was hurting so much. I knew I needed to go to my "safe" place. I found this beautiful refuge years ago when the visits to my room started. Sometimes I even drew pictures of it! Tonight, I needed to be there. No arguing, no work, no rejection, no tears, no pain! Just escape. I closed my eyes and pictured the huge mountains, the lush green grass and my big, beautiful tree. I loved my tree! It was tall and the branches almost reached the ground! I could get behind them and hide! It grew next to the small river that ran through the center of my special place. Listening to the water as it ran gently over the smooth stones gave me such a safe feeling. And when I was here, I *was* safe and aware of nothing else.

I awoke during the night because of some noise coming from outside. I sat up to look out the small window of my bedroom. I could see no one around, but noticed there was light coming from the stable down the hill. I decided I'd better go check that none of the patrons were down there with torches. Some of the men who were here at the inn were drinking quite a bit. I heard them getting louder and louder. My father's laugh mingled with theirs.

As I got up to get dressed, I noticed my bedclothes were partially removed and it reminded me of the man who had been at the door. Before I could even let myself think about him, I shook my head and decided not to consider anything except getting to the stable. I loved the animals there and one of my favorite chores was feeding them each morning. We had cows, donkeys, chickens and many sheep. My father got his sheep from the shepherds that lived nearby. They kept their sheep in a field a little down the road from us. He detested them because he thought they were just stupid, lazy farmers, but he was very nice to them when he wanted to buy their sheep! And he always got a good deal.

We also had horses, but we kept them in a cave that my father had found in the side of the hill behind our inn. That gave them the whole pasture at the foot of the hill, separate from where the other animals grazed. He said the sheep ate the grass down to the root and it was too short for the horses to graze. My favorites were the horses and I enjoyed spending my free time grooming them. Sometimes my father would let me ride by myself, but often he rode with me. Those are some of the best times I've had with him. We'd race across the fields and I loved feeling the wind and the horse's mane whipping my face! I usually won the races, but I think it was because my horse was younger. My father is not the kind of man who would just let me win.

I snuck down the hall and heard my father snoring and I knew I could get out without being heard. I noticed it had gotten chilly, so I grabbed a shawl as I went out the back corridor that led to the well. This was a shortcut to the stable that also kept me from being seen as easily. By the noise coming from the inn, I knew there were some people still awake and they sounded pretty rowdy. The night air was crisp and clean. It seemed especially dark to me and I had to take great care as I made my way down the stony path to the stable. I wish I had brought a torch! I looked up at the sky and there seemed to be a million stars and the fingernail moon, but little light came from them.

Approaching the door to the stable, I froze! There were screams coming from inside! In my twelve years, I don't think I had ever heard a woman in this much pain. Well, maybe once...

"You have to do something! I can't take the pain anymore. I feel like I'm going to split open!" My mother's screams were piercing. I didn't understand what was wrong and I was terrified. I was afraid she would die! The baby had been trying to come out since daybreak and the midwife was getting tired and frustrated. She was getting impatient with my mother, too.

"Naomi, you need to stop screaming! You are not helping yourself or the baby! Now calm down!" My mother looked at her with disdain. *"You trade places with me if you think this is so easy! I can't take it anymore! Bartimus, please do something!"* She tried to get some control of herself and lay back after the contraction ended and took some deep breaths. I went to her and wiped the perspiration from her brow, but she pushed me away. *"Bartimus, get her out of here! She doesn't need to see this and I don't want her around!"*

21

My father came running in from outside, grabbed my hand and yelled at me, "I thought I told you to stay in your room! Do what you are told! Don't you see you are upsetting your mother even more! Now, get out!" I ran out and started for my room when I heard her scream again. I couldn't stand it! I turned and ran down the corridor to the back of the inn. I ran and ran until I got to the cave where the horses were. I could still hear her, but it was much fainter.

I stayed there for what seemed a very long time, petting and grooming the horses. This was truly my favorite place in the world! I loved all our horses, but especially the little black gelding that I rode. He had a beautiful, long, black mane and tail and a big blaze on his face. I had named him Joshua, from a story that Joanna's mother told me. While I was here, at least for a little while, I could forget about my life.

After a while my father came to find me. He called for me and as I went out to meet him, I saw a huge grin on his face. "Mary, you have a new little brother! He is a big boy, but I think your mother will be all right. The midwife seems to think so anyway." I began to walk toward him and that smile was forming on his face; the smile that scared me.

He caught my arm as I tried to pass him. "Your mother isn't happy that it's a boy. I think she wanted another daughter, you know, to replace Salome. It's too bad you couldn't seem to do that for her!" He always knew what to say to shatter me, so he continued. "Why did you run up here to the horses? If that screaming bothered you, it's time you get used to it. You're going to hear it a lot if you become a midwife!" He shook his head in disgust. "You and your high-minded notions!" I shook his hand off and kept walking, saying nothing. I wanted to see if my mother was really all right. Sometimes I felt that he wouldn't mind if she weren't. Sometimes I felt that he wished she and I would just disappear.

When I went to my mother's bedside, I thought she was asleep, but when I pushed her hair back from her forehead, she opened her eyes. "You look worried, child. I'm okay. Did you see your little brother? We named him Bartholomew. I really had hoped for a little girl. You know how I have felt since Salome died." I shook my head and looked over at my brother. He seemed so helpless and small. I immediately thought about what he would have to suffer as a member of this family.

My thought was interrupted by my mother's voice. "Your father was gone most of the time, of course!" She sounded so disgusted. "He showed up for about the last hour so he could tell all his friends he was around when his son was born! Your father is never here when I need him." I knew she wanted me to agree with her, but I had learned a long time ago to stay out of their quarrels. If I did not agree, I took the chance of being ignored for days, but I think this time she was too tired to care. "Why don't you go make something to eat and let me rest?" I leaned over to kiss her, but she turned her face away as if she didn't see. I saw tears slip down her cheek and she quietly whispered, "I miss my Salome."

Silently, I left the room. Salome! It was always Salome! She had been my older sister and my mother practically worshipped her. For everything Salome did right, I managed to do two things wrong. All the love I desired from my mother was lavished on Salome. But my sister had become gravely ill last year, running an extremely high fever. She was always in pain, holding her stomach. Toward the end, her belly became swollen and rigid and she would scream in pain if you touched it. None of the physicians we took her to could tell us what was wrong or help her. One day she went to sleep and never woke up again. She died in my mother's arms and Mother has never gotten over it.

*My mother had become pregnant almost immediately after Salome died. She talked frequently about how much she wanted this baby to be a girl. Once, when my parents were arguing, she told my father that she **needed** to replace*

Salome and that my father should know why. That was one time he didn't give her that smile. He just left and ended up sleeping in one of the rooms at the inn for over a week. I didn't know what she was referring to when she said my father "should know why." I thought she wanted a girl just because he wanted a boy so badly. Maybe I was wrong.

I tried so hard to fill the emptiness I saw in my mother, but she would not accept anything from me. It hurt knowing she wanted to replace Salome. I would be glad to volunteer for that role! I would love to receive all the attention she had given Salome! Maybe I would get some now. She sure didn't seem too happy that she had a boy! And since this totally thrilled my father, I knew this would be yet another situation where they would argue and fight. And it would be my new brother and I that would have to suffer through it. I made a silent oath that night that I would protect my brother from all the fighting and screaming; the way Salome had tried to protect me.

The memories of that time were pierced by another wail from the stable and I was jolted back to the present. She sounded in great pain, not unlike my sister's cries in the days before she died. Then came another, but this seemed to be more of joy and relief instead of pain! Almost immediately, I heard the sound of a baby crying!

I stood there, outside the door of the stable and realized I was crying! I desperately wanted to see this beautiful sight! I have always thought the birth of a baby was a miracle! Being a midwife was my life dream, just so I could experience it every day. At that very moment, my thoughts were interrupted by a great noise in the distance. What had been the darkest of nights was now illuminated as if by fire! It was the brightest light I had ever seen! I knew this was the area where the shepherds kept their sheep and I couldn't imagine why they would be building a fire that large in the field. It would surely scare the sheep! My father would laugh when I told him about this!

As I continued to stare, I realized this light, though it glowed as fire, looked like it was up in the sky! I tried to make sense of what I was seeing, and then heard a man's voice coming from the stable. "Mary, I am so proud of you! You've done a wonderful job! Look at our beautiful son! I love you so much!" Then I heard a girl's voice answer, "Yes, Joseph, he is perfect! And his name is as beautiful as he is - *Jesus!*"

I completely forgot about the events outside and felt compelled to see this amazing wonder in our stable! The picture I saw when I entered took my breath! The girl looked no older than my sister had been. The man was gazing at them with such love; love that I had never seen before! And the baby! Oh, the baby was beautiful! I remembered my friend Joanna telling me how ugly her little sister had been and I had secretly thought the same about my little brother. But this baby was incredible! Something strange was happening to me inside. I felt a relaxing of my muscles and a smile so big, it felt awkward! Smiling was something I rarely did. I was tingly and giggly and it felt wonderful! This little baby was somehow making me feel something that I had never experienced! Peace.

This couple was so enveloped in each other that I felt embarrassed. I cleared my throat so they would know I was there. When they looked up, I quickly said, "I hope you don't mind me coming here. I am the daughter of the innkeeper and I heard some noise from my room. I was worried someone might be in the stable harming the animals. As I came closer, I heard the screams and was afraid until I heard the baby cry. Please forgive me for bothering you. I don't even know why you are here in the stable instead of the inn." I cleared my throat. "I just want to know if I can do anything for you."

The man looked at me gently, "Your father had no room for us in his inn, but he was kind enough to let us stay here."

I nodded in agreement but knew that what had probably happened is that my father had sized them up and knew they could not afford his prices; so he said there was no room for them. The inn *was* full, but I'm sure if it wasn't, they would still be out here. I was actually surprised that he suggested the stable! I couldn't ever remember it happening before this. He must have been drinking plenty of wine to make such a generous offer!

The girl spoke softly and told me her name was Mary and then introduced her husband, Joseph. "Could you bring us some water? My husband is tired from the journey. We had to get here before the baby came and he walked all the way to Bethlehem while I rode our donkey. I know my baby is hungry and I need water to drink so I can nurse him. We would be so grateful." I gladly agreed and ran from the stable.

I went up the hill to the courtyard. I realized it was dark again and when I looked toward where I had seen the great light earlier, there was nothing. "I must have imagined it." My father was always telling me that I was imagining things. Maybe he was right. As I approached the back door, I heard some of the men inside. I realized that fear had replaced the special feelings I had in the stable. I was afraid of these men when they sounded like this.

I silently went to the room where we stored the water jugs, grabbed the closest one and hurried out to the well, watching that no one was following me. I ran back to the stable as quickly as I could without spilling too much of the water and quietly went in. It was odd, but I wanted to be around these three strangers! I usually shied away from people. My dad always said I was scared of my own shadow. But the peace I felt earlier; I wanted to feel again ...desperately!

As I walked in, I saw Joseph caressing Mary's hair and gently holding her as they looked at the baby. He was doing for her the things that I knew my mother longed to receive from my father. But that would never happen. For years, he had found others on which to lavish his attention. I poured Mary some water and sat down with them. I felt so good! Just sitting here in their presence! Mary took the cup from me and asked, "Would you like to hold the baby?" I was so excited I could hardly answer as she put him in my lap. I felt such joy as I held this beautiful baby and when he smiled at me I began to cry again! "His name is Jesus," Joseph said. I had not heard that name before and I asked what it meant. Joseph began to answer but then stopped and looked at Mary. She looked up at him and I saw a silent exchange between them and then Joseph nodded with a slight smile. Mary looked at me and with tears welling in her eyes she said, "He will be a special person to everyone he meets. No one will ever forget him...or his name." I did not know why Mary was crying, maybe they were tears of joy. Holding him surely made me feel joyful! As I stared down at his little red face, I felt a warmth inside me that was unfamiliar. He was amazing!

When Joseph put his hand on my shoulder, it startled me and I jumped. I felt so embarrassed! I quickly handed the baby back to Mary and apologized. Joseph said, "I'm sorry! I did not mean to scare you. I just wanted to be sure you were okay. You have some blood on your lip." I touched my mouth and felt the dried blood and the slight swelling. Hot tears of shame stung my eyes. I had not realized that my father's slap, earlier that evening, had caused my mouth to bleed. I should not have told him I was tired. The slap had come swiftly and then, "My patrons come first!" I had finished my work and then gone to bed without washing up.

I jumped up and started for the door. "You don't have to leave," cried Mary. Joseph got up and came to me with concern in his eyes. "Your arms are bruised. Has someone hurt you?" I looked into his eyes and was drawn to the compassion I saw there. But at the same time, I feared it. I turned to leave again and Mary said, "Please tell us your name before you go. You have been so kind to us." I looked at both of them. Their eyes were filled with love! But that love couldn't be meant for me. All the special feelings I had earlier were gone. All I felt now was dirty and shameful for the way my father had hurt me and for what might have happened in my room earlier. I felt tears begin to sting my eyes. I couldn't bear to stay near them any longer. I opened the door to the stable and tried to leave quickly before they saw me crying. I paused and thought how nice they had been. I could at least tell them my name. I wiped my eyes and turned to look at them. "Mary," I said, "Mary Magdalene" and then I ran out into the night.

2

Safe places

I slowly made my way up the hill toward the inn. I couldn't bring myself to go back inside yet. I felt so ashamed. I also didn't want anyone seeing me cry. I stayed outside and sat down on the hill near the well. I could still see the stable down on my left. They were the most wonderful people I had ever met! And I had spent such little time with them to feel this way! I had never seen such love and compassion expressed in my life! Why couldn't I have had parents like the ones I had just met? Why did I have to live here? I had been so much happier in Magdala. I had my grandmother there and I stayed with her as much as I could to escape the fighting at home. She lived right on the water at the Sea of Galilee and I could swim all day! There was no place to swim here in Bethlehem. The only body of water near us was the Salt Sea and you couldn't swim there.

My father had moved us here when he bought the inn. He was always trying to find some way to make more money. He had not taken my mother's feelings into consideration at all. She had all of her friends and most of her family in Magdala and since we moved here, her angry fits came more frequently and with more intensity. She had been furious with my father when Salome got sick because she had no family to help her. Magdala is a journey from Bethlehem. And after Salome died, she had suffered alone. She started spending more and more time in her room.

Then when my brother Bartholomew was born, she again had no one with her except the local midwife (and she was not very friendly). I still felt guilty because I had not been there for her. I hardly ever saw her anymore. She stayed in her room and I was left caring for my brother most of the time.

I felt so alone. I had tried one time to talk to Mother about my bad dreams and the man I would see standing in my doorway at night. But she said I was lying; that I just wanted attention. I often found myself wondering what I had done to make her hate me so much. It was only on a couple of occasions that she even came to my room. She woke me up from a sound sleep and I could smell the wine on her breath. She told me my father had driven her to drink. I didn't understand because I knew how much she hated him drinking. She didn't seem to remember the following morning.

I thought again about the family in the stable. Mary and I even shared the same name! But I was sure that we had nothing else in common. I knew she had never done the things that I had done. When Joseph touched me, there had been that fleeting moment of pleasure. Then the thought that a man that was so kind would even want to touch me! Thoughts that were so confusing. Thoughts that were so strange. Thoughts that he might be attracted to me!! Why had I felt so guilty?

I tried not to think about the times the man had touched me; he hadn't hurt me. The things my body felt were not always bad feelings— it was almost like my body responded to his touch. And I noticed the older I got, the more I responded. I would pray for my body to be numb because I felt bad for liking it. I would feel guilty after he left and perplexed by the feelings. How could I enjoy any part of it? I always thought there must be something wrong with me.

That's how I discovered my "safe place." When I went there, I seemed to almost float away and not remember what happened. Sometimes I could pretend nothing ever did. I felt so isolated and had no one to talk to except my friend Joanna. She really could not understand my feelings, but she listened. I bet Mary would listen, too. She and Salome looked to be close in age, and Salome always listened and seemed to understand. But Salome warned me not to tell anyone. She said no one would believe me. It was almost as if she knew herself. Like it had happened to her. One night when she was tucking me in, I asked her if the man ever came to her room, but she didn't answer and told me to go to sleep.

I thought again about talking to Mary. I was so drawn to her! I wanted to go back and see her, but I knew she needed rest. Just thinking about the baby helped me feel better. Jesus! What a beautiful name! I loved just saying it- *Jesus, Jesus, Jesus.* The peace began to come back. I felt my body relaxing and I found myself smiling. Mary was right! He would be special and I knew *I* would never forget his name! I felt that I could go to sleep now.

As I stood and turned to go back to the inn, I noticed something strange down the hill. It looked like several men, carrying torches, and they were walking toward the stable! I thought my eyes must be playing tricks on me (they were burning so badly from the crying I had done). I watched to see where they were going and, yes, I was right! They were headed for the stable! I panicked! What if they tried to hurt the family there? They had torches and could set the hay on fire that I had put out that morning for the animals!

I ran down the hill as fast as I could. They looked like shepherds, but surely, even the shepherds wouldn't be out so late and abandoning their sheep! I approached the stable and realized they *were* shepherds! I startled one of the younger boys, grabbed his arm and breathlessly asked, "What are you doing here? There is a family in this stable with a newborn baby! I'll go get my father if you don't leave!"

One of the older shepherds turned to me and said, "Hush, child. We were told to come here. Come and look." As I wriggled through the many bodies, I saw the most incredible sight! Mary was holding Jesus and all the shepherds in the stable were bowing down to worship him! The stable was full of shepherds, men and boys. Many had brought their baby sheep with them. I could hear one of them talking to Mary and I strained to hear what he was saying.

Mary was looking at him intently and encouraging him to tell her again what he had said. He was older, maybe my father's age and I heard him say, "My brothers and I were sleeping in the field and we heard this loud noise, like horns. When we opened our eyes, the sky was lit up as if by fire!" I listened in amazement as he described exactly what I had seen earlier and was unable to explain!

"Then we saw such an incredible sight! An angel appeared in the sky! We were so afraid and some of us began to run! But then he spoke!" The shepherd paused and shook his head in disbelief. "I still cannot believe what happened!" Mary waited patiently and gently touched his arm. "Please tell me again what the angel said."

The shepherd looked down and when he raised his head to look at Mary, there were tears in his eyes. With a heavy voice he spoke, "The angel said, 'Do not be afraid. I bring you good news of great joy that will be for all the people. Today in the town of David, a Savior has been born to you; He is Christ the Lord. This will be a sign to you: You will find a baby, wrapped in cloths and lying in a manger.' Then, suddenly, there were angels everywhere, thousands of them, and they were singing, 'Glory! Glory! Glory to God in the Highest! And on earth, peace to men on whom his favor rests.'"

I looked at Mary and silent tears ran down her face as she looked at her son. It almost seemed that there was sadness in her eyes mixed with the joy of the shepherd's story. It was as if she were pondering what had been said and trying to take in all that had happened on this eventful night.

The significance of what the shepherd had just said did not sink in right away. I was so happy to hear that someone else had seen what I had in the sky! I wasn't crazy after all! And this shepherd had just told her something that was unbelievable! He said he saw angels that told him exactly how to find this baby—the Savior! This little baby was the one that Joanna's mother talked about coming! I guess I had expected something different. She made me think it would be a great king, certainly not this little baby!

The shepherd began to speak again. "We must go. There are many that must hear this great news! We have waited many years for this night and we can't keep it to ourselves! Thank you for letting us see this magnificent child! Rest now. You have had a difficult night. We will bother you no further." Mary assured him it was no bother and allowed those that were still outside to come in and worship.

I backed out of the stable, not wanting to bother Mary either, but bumped right into Joseph. I felt my face flush and was glad for the cover of night. He knelt down and looked at me intently and said, "You have witnessed a great miracle tonight, my child. Go home, get some sleep and come see us tomorrow." I didn't know if he was upset with me and I stammered, "I did not mean to come back and be a bother, but I saw the men and their torches and was afraid they would hurt you." Joseph smiled. "You are very brave to come down here and attempt to take on all these men. I will be sure to tell Mary of your courage! Now, go. Get some sleep, child."

I walked back to the inn and quietly tiptoed to my room. As I passed my parents room, I heard my father still snoring. I never could understand how my mother slept through that!

I went to my room, changed my clothes and lay down. I wondered about all that I had experienced this very long night. I wondered why my father was so stingy and made a pregnant girl and her husband sleep in the stable. I wondered what a Savior was! I made a mental note to ask Joanna's mother tomorrow. I wondered how angels came to be in a field talking to people that my father felt were so lowly. As I began to drift off, I realized this was the first time since I could remember that I felt safe. I thought about the baby they called a "Savior." And I went to sleep. I had a smile on my face, peace in my heart and his name on my lips. *Jesus.*

The next morning I awoke to my parents arguing. I knew when I didn't see the sun in my window; I had overslept by more than an hour. My mother was screaming that she could not get any sleep because Bartholomew had cried all night. My father was saying, between clenched teeth, that she needed to shut up before the patrons heard her. I got up, ran to their room and picked up my brother. He had been crying so hard, he had a hitch in his breathing. "Why do you two do this around him? You are upsetting him!"

The slap stunned me, and I had to catch my balance to keep from falling. I felt the warmth of the blood flow from my nose and lip. He had hit me in the same place. My father grinned at me through gritted teeth. "Who do you think you are? Don't ever talk to us that way again or next time I'll knock a few teeth out, too. Then you won't be so arrogant! No man will want you if you have no teeth!" I tightened the hold on my little brother in case another slap followed. My mother wasn't as obvious. She usually backhanded me. Today, however, she looked too tired to even get off the bed.

"Where have you been, Mary? You know I need you here first thing when the cocks crow. I have to fix breakfast for all these people and I haven't slept at all. You were very inconsiderate to sleep this late!" My father glared at me. "Maybe she needs to fix the breakfast this morning! Maybe it will get

34

her head out of the clouds! She seems to be too full of herself these days! I think she needs to stay away from that Joanna and her family. They fill her head with all those stories I'd sooner forget!"

He took Bartholomew from me and my brother began to cry. My father was not a gentle man when he was angry. I knew better than argue and went to the kitchen to begin the meal. I always dreaded this. Making the meals also meant serving the patrons. Some of the men made comments to me and touched me in ways that made me uncomfortable. Sometimes it was just rubbing my back or patting me on the shoulder. Others patted me on my backside and I hated that. I tried to serve them quickly and then stay close to the families. If I was near the larger groups and pretended to be especially engrossed in what they needed, I could avoid the others.

Someone had already made the bread dough so I stoked the fire and placed the bread inside the clay oven. I ran out back to collect the eggs and looked down at the stable. *They must be hungry, too*, I thought and suddenly I just wanted to get done so I could go take them breakfast. I ran back to the kitchen with the eggs, being careful not to break any. That would be another painful confrontation with my father. My mother had made cheese from the goat's milk and I collected some grapes and pomegranates.

As fast and as carefully as I could, I prepared the breakfast and set it out on the serving table in the dining room. Only a few had shown for the meal so far. Some were packing and others had gone early to get their names reported to the census takers. As I finished putting the food out and was turning to go out the door, I felt a gentle pinch on my bottom. I could feel the heat rising in my face, but I kept walking. "Come here little one! You are looking as delicious as the food you put out! Where is your father? Did he decide to give us a little time alone?"

His laugh was almost as awful as my father's, and I felt my cheeks flush and knew if I said anything, this could become worse. I ignored him as if nothing had happened and continued to walk away. I heard him laughing again as I went out the door and passed my father in the courtyard. "Where are going, Mary? Get back in there and finish feeding everyone!" I paused briefly but didn't turn around, and I heard the other man say, "Leave her alone, Bartimus! She has set a wonderful meal before us! Your daughter is becoming quite a little woman, you know! You better keep an eye on her!" My father laughed and replied, "Yes, Festus, and you would be the one I would have to watch the closest!" They both laughed and that sick feeling started in my stomach.

I ran back to my mother's room to see if she needed anything before I went to the stable. She and my brother were both sleeping; I looked at him in his cradle. He still had a little hitch in his breathing, but was finally sleeping peacefully. I would give anything to take him away from all of this. No one, especially a baby, deserved to live like we did. I suddenly had a desire to take him to meet the family in the stable. I gently picked him up and went over to check my mother. Even in her sleep, she looked troubled. Why can't the three of us get away from here and go back to Magdala?

Memories of my mother in happier days. There were times when I could even remember her laughing with my sister and me. During those times, it felt that she loved me as much as Salome. But something changed between my third and fourth birthday. I have so few memories of that year. Actually I have very few memories of anything when I was younger, but in particular, that year. I only know on my third birthday my mother was happy and loving and on my fourth birthday she was distant and cold. I can't even remember her hugging me that day. That was also when the long periods of silence started. If she got upset with me about something, it would sometimes be days before she would talk to me again.

She would totally ignore me as if I wasn't even there. Then, one morning, it would all be over, like nothing had ever happened.

During those times of silence, my father was always very attentive to me. I noticed that she would not be talking to him either and so we would do things together. He and I would ride our horses and go on trips to places where he did business with different people. I enjoyed those times with him. It was as if we had a bond between us because Mother wasn't speaking to us. I miss those times with him. We don't seem to do much together anymore. He is always too busy.

I have always tried to remember if I did something wrong that may have caused the changes in my parents. I loved my mother and father and hated it when they would fight. Father would come to me and tell me things about their marriage that I didn't want to hear. Then Mother would come to my room to sleep and tell me all the bad things he did to her. I was afraid to take anyone's side for fear that they would get mad at me. I always felt like I should be the peacemaker.

Salome used to stand up to him. She would not allow him to say anything about Mother. And he would never hit her. It seemed to me sometimes, that he was afraid of her. I always felt she had something she held over his head, some secret. I didn't even feel that he was that sad when she died, but I convinced myself I must be wrong. Of course he loved his daughter! What father would be glad for his daughter to die? These were the times that I thought Father was right when he said I was imagining things and that I must be possessed by demons. For me to think such terrible thoughts, he was probably right!

My father often said those things to me. He said them even more frequently to my mother. She would accuse him of staying overnight in Jerusalem to be with a prostitute and he would laugh and tell her, "Naomi, you are possessed! I don't know what puts such ideas in your head!" My mother would

37

argue with him and he would give her his condescending smile. That infuriated her and the rages would begin. A few times she got so angry, she pulled a knife out from under their mat and threatened to kill him. But he would just shake his head and smile again, thinking she wouldn't do it.

But I was never that sure. I would get in the middle of these quarrels and try to stop them. My father would leave and my mother would go to her room and not come out for a few days. During those times, Father would sleep in one of the rooms in the inn. Then, after two or three days, Mother would come out and act like nothing had happened. I would go to her and say we needed to get away from this, and she would look at me, bewildered, and say, "Why would I leave your father here alone?" When I would remind her of what had happened and that he had cheated on her again; she would look at me with disdain and say, "I don't know what you are talking about! I love your father! Quit trying to start trouble!" She would walk away and I would be left standing there, convinced I was the one that was possessed.

Suddenly, Bartholomew cried out in his sleep and I was abruptly brought back to the present. I reached down and stroked my mother's hair, kissed her and whispered, "I love you, Mother. I wish I could fix things so you could be happy." I looked at my little brother's upturned face. He was awake now and he smiled at me. I hugged him and said, "I wish the same for you and the life you will come to know." I hugged him again and felt the sting of tears in my eyes. "I have someone I want you to meet, Bartholomew. I want you to feel what I felt last night!" I touched my mother's hair again and then tiptoed out. I wrapped my brother tightly in his blanket, grabbed my cloak and headed down to the stable.

The morning was crisp and with the wind gusts it was very cold. I ran as fast as I could, holding my brother as close to me as possible. As I approached the stable, I remembered the animals got fed very early and they sometimes got pretty rowdy when they were hungry. My father had someone deliver hay to both stables every morning and then I spread out the hay and fed them the grain mixture. I knew that Mary and Joseph had only the hay to sleep on, and I was worried that even with the new hay, they would be left with little comfort.

When I entered the stable, Mary was lying down on a large bed of hay that my father's worker had brought. Joseph must have spread it out and made a soft place because she looked comfortable as she lay there nursing Jesus. Joseph was lying beside her with his arm around her shoulder. He seemed to be sleeping. I quietly went to Mary and sat beside her. She looked at me and smiled. "Good morning, Mary! Who have you brought with you? Oh, such a beautiful baby!" I smiled with pride and said, "This is my brother, Bartholomew. My mother did not sleep well last night so I am watching him. I also wanted him to meet you."

Mary looked down at my brother and then at me. She gently touched my knee and said, "You are like a breath of fresh air for me. I have been praying you would come soon because I need a few things for Jesus. I'm afraid I am an inexperienced mother and did not come well prepared." She blushed slightly, smiled at me, and asked, "Did you sleep well? I know it was a very long night for you!" I smiled remembering all that had happened and how peacefully I had slept. "Oh, I slept better than I ever have. But this morning I was worried about you because I knew the animals could get pretty rough when they are hungry, but I can't believe how calm they are! Didn't they try to eat any of the hay last night?"

"No, Mary. In fact, their bodies kept us warm as they slept next to us. It seemed as if they knew who my son was. We also slept very well." I looked at Joseph, who was softly snoring and smiled. "It looks like Joseph still is!" We both giggled and quickly covered our mouths so as not to wake him, which made us laugh even harder. Joseph stirred and groaned loudly. Mary and I could contain it no longer! We laughed out loud! Joseph sat up on his elbow. He looked at us with his eyes half open and said, "Are you girls having a good time this morning? Mary, I don't think I have heard you laugh like that since you entered your ninth month!"

Joseph looked down at my brother as I held him in my arms and said, "I see we have another young visitor this morning!" Mary had tears in her eyes from laughing so hard and Jesus was having a hard time nursing! "Yes, Joseph. This is Mary's little brother, Bartholomew. Someone for Jesus to play with!" Jesus looked up at us and smiled and we all began to laugh. I felt that wonderful peace inside my heart again.

Joseph looked at Mary and smiled. "I planned to stay up with you last night, Mary. I'm so sorry I fell asleep. I guess I did not realize myself how exhausted I was from our trip here. I did manage to get up and spread the hay out without waking you this morning. I was trying so hard to stay awake, but it was a futile effort. How was your first night as a new mother? Did Jesus keep you awake much?"

Mary lovingly caressed his arm. "You shouldn't worry about staying awake. You needed your sleep. Jesus and I slept very well. During the night, he only awoke one time to be fed, then again this morning when Mary arrived. Just as I prayed, she has come to see if we needed anything." Joseph smiled at me and said, "You are like an angel that God has placed in our lives to help us! Praise His holy name! My wife, I'm sure, is hungry and I'm famished... and she said she needed some things for Jesus. Can we get food and supplies at your father's inn?"

I started to say yes and decided that Father would probably charge them outrageous prices since he made no money from them for their stay. "Anything you need, I can bring for you. I made the breakfast at the inn this morning and can bring you lots of food. What things do you need for Jesus?" Mary pointed to the pile of cloths and blankets in the corner of the stable. They were wet and blood stained. "I'm afraid I did not come prepared with enough swaddling cloths and material to diaper our baby. I will need to wash those, but need some warm things for him while those dry. Do you think you have anything we could use?"

I knew my mother had many scraps of material from making things for the inn and from the clothes she made for us. "Oh, yes! Let me go and get you some blankets and cloth first and then I will bring breakfast." Joseph stood to go with me. I did not want my father to be reminded that they were still here. "No, Joseph. I will go get the things. But it would be a big help to me if you would hold Bartholomew while I go. You can stay here with Mary."

I wrapped my cloak around me and ran up to the inn. Most everyone had gone to the census and the inn seemed deserted. I walked through the courtyard and heard laughter coming from the kitchen. I peeked inside the dining area and saw my father sitting at one of the tables talking with a young woman. She seemed to be standing much too close to my father and I couldn't hear what they were saying.

I waited quietly and their laughter came to me again. I saw my father reach for the woman as she laughed louder and pushed him. She appeared to be trying to walk away. Father grabbed her and I heard him say something about "teasing him" and pulled the woman onto his lap. Now they both laughed and he was touching her in a way that made me wish my mother would walk in and catch them. I felt my face flush and my cheeks were burning! I was so angry! How could he act that way with Mother in the next building?

I backed out into the courtyard and ran to the room where Mother does her sewing. I considered for a moment that I should wake her and tell her what I saw—encourage her to go see for herself, what he was doing. But I knew the first thing she would want to know is where my brother was. She would yell at me for taking him, then leaving him with strangers. How could she understand, without meeting them, why I trusted them so much? Yes, the hope of having my father get caught was swallowed up by the reality of my own troubles.

I dismissed the thought and began to go through my mother's baskets of materials she used for our clothing and bedding. Everything was small and did not seem useful for swaddling Jesus. The scraps would be useful, however, for diapering him, so I grabbed as much as I could hold and began to walk from the room. As I did, I saw a leather trunk in the corner that I had not noticed before. I went back and opened it. I gasped at the beauty of the cloth inside! It was beautiful, seamless, white linen! I immediately recognized it as the material my mother had bought when Salome was a small child to use for her wedding gown! There was a great deal of it and it would suit Mary's needs, but I knew I would be in the deepest trouble I had ever known.

I suddenly heard movement in the hallway and I knew someone was coming! I had to get out of here! I quickly considered the consequences and decided to take the material anyway. I shoved it beneath my arm, hiding it under my cloak and slipped behind the door. I saw no one in the hall so I ran out the back corridor that led to the kitchen.

I was out of breath as I started down the hill to the stable, some from running, but mostly from fear. Not just from getting caught with things I had not asked for, but fear of what would happen when they found out I had taken Salome's wedding linen! My mother worshiped her, and I knew this beautiful linen was not being saved for me! As I stopped to get my breath, I thought how I have never gotten anything from my parents except punishments and beatings! Or if they needed someone to yell at or blame for something! "Why should I care what they think," I thought out loud. That was all I needed to rationalize what I had done so I would feel better. I continued down the hill to the stable.

When I arrived, Joseph was feeding the animals, and Jesus and Bartholomew were sleeping next to each other in the feed trough. Mary was awake and lying back on a bed of hay that Joseph had made for her. I placed the material I had brought on her lap. I was careful to place the beautiful linen under the other pieces so I would have time to think up a story about it while I went to get them breakfast. "See if these will work for you and I will run and get some food!" She looked up at me and smiled that beautiful smile of hers. She reached up her arms as if she wanted a hug. I tentatively leaned down, not sure what to expect and she hugged me. It was such a warm feeling; I knelt so I could hug her back. It felt so good to be held like this, but it was uncomfortable too, because it was so foreign to me.

I pulled away first and looked at Mary and she had tears in her eyes. "You have so much love to give, child. I feel that you long to release it and be loved in return. You seem so sad, for a child your age. But I sense so much kindness in your heart." I felt tears in my eyes and quickly stood up. It was as if she looked into my very soul! "I must run and get your food. I'll be right back." I went back up to the inn and it seemed deserted. I did not see my father or the woman, so I went into the kitchen and found two large bowls and filled them with the leftover food and fruit from breakfast. I filled two baskets with the flat bread I had baked that morning and placed them inside the bowls. I went out the back door and finally found one of the goats that hadn't been milked that morning. I filled a large jug for my new friends.

I carefully balanced the jug on my head and started back down the hill with the bowls and baskets of food in the other arm. When I came in the stable door, Joseph exclaimed, "You have brought us a feast! Mary, there is enough food here to last us all day! Thank you so much!" I felt embarrassment well up in me as Joseph and Mary complimented me on the how delicious the food looked. Compliments were not something I heard very often.

Mary looked at me and smiled, but it seemed to be mixed with concern. I immediately thought of the material I had brought and knew I had little time before the subject came up. I noticed I was getting a lump in my throat and it became difficult to eat.

As I sat and watched them finish their meal, I thought how I would love to live with them no matter where they went! Maybe just as their house servant! Anything would be better than my life here! I looked over at Bartholomew. He was sleeping so peacefully next to Jesus. His life would be so much better with them, too. Mary, softly asking Joseph if he would let us talk alone for a while, interrupted my fantasy.

"Oh boy, here it comes!" I thought. I had not come up with a good explanation yet for the white linen. The voice in my head continued to nag me. *"Come on, Mary, you mean you have not come up with a good lie yet? What are you going to do? Lie to the only people you have ever felt safe with? You are exactly what your father and mother say you are! Good for nothing! Go ahead! Think up a good one! Then they will hate you, too! You are such a disappointment. But, then again if you tell the truth, they will make you take it back and you'll have done nothing to help them. Then they won't like you anymore because you have disappointed them. Such a dilemma! Better think quickly!"*

I shook my head hard and told the voice to shut up. It was apparently loud enough for Mary to hear because she looked at me with a bewildered expression. *Great, now she will think I'm mad, too.* She continued to look at me with concern and said, "Mary, are you all right? You look frightened. I just wanted to talk to you for a little while." I looked away in fear that she might be able to read my eyes. "I'm fine," I lied.

Mary moved close to me and I felt that uncomfortable feeling begin to come over me. I was worried that Joseph could hear and I looked over my shoulder just in time to see him sit beside the manger and gently caress the babies lying there. His eyes were so intense and full of love. I hoped my brother could sense it. My attention was brought back to Mary when she took my hand. I wanted to draw it back! I did not want her to touch me. I felt dirty again and did not want her to be near me. So much had changed just because I took that stupid material! I wanted to run, but Mary's gentle words spoke to my heart.

"Mary, I see how troubled you are about something. I told you, I think you have such a beautiful heart, but I feel it has been wounded somehow and you are afraid of being hurt again. It is difficult to trust people sometimes. But, Mary, there is one you can trust and He will never let you down. I feel that I should share something with you."

"Nine months ago, an angel appeared to me and told me I would bear a son and that He would be called the Son of the Most High. I was 14 years old, not married and still a virgin. I could not comprehend how this could happen. The angel also told me of my barren cousin who was already pregnant. I knew this was a miracle because she was old in years and had been so ashamed to not have borne a child for her husband, Zechariah."

"Then the angel said, 'For, nothing is impossible with God.' Mary, I know the God of whom he spoke. Joseph is my husband, but has never touched me and without ever knowing a man, I gave birth last night, right here, and the shepherds came and confirmed the glory of my son. This same God loves you, Mary! I do not know what troubles you so, but I do know that He will help you."

I listened intently to Mary's words, trying to believe they applied to me. It was difficult when I was also trying to come up with a good lie about the material! Why did I struggle with this so much? Mary smiled at me and gently said, "Mary, I want to thank you so much for the material you brought us. The pieces for diapering were perfect. But I was truly amazed at the beauty of the white material! I know this is a very expensive piece of linen, something you would use to make a wedding dress. I want to be sure it is acceptable for us to have it. Does your mother know you gave it to us?"

I swallowed hard and said, "I promise that my mother had no intention of ever using that material as a wedding dress for me! It will be put to good use if you take it." *There. I didn't lie entirely!* In fact some of it was the truth! Mary looked deep into my eyes and it was with all the effort that I could muster to not look away. She seemed to be studying my face to see if I was telling the truth. Then the moment passed and she smiled and said, "Thank you so much, Mary. It will be an honor to swaddle Jesus in it. It is a large piece, though, and I will not cut it. Joseph was right, Mary. You are like an angel sent by God!"

I almost choked with guilt, but managed to smile and allowed her to hug me. Maybe she could teach me about God. My father wanted nothing to do with God and hated it when I spoke of Joanna's "Jehovah." But right now, I didn't want to think about anything. I felt relief mixed with sorrow. I had gotten away with giving them the material without having to lie outright, but I also knew I had not been completely honest with this wonderful person. She represented something to me that seemed out of my reach! How could I ever be worthy of the God she spoke of? How could I even be worthy of her friendship?

My stomach began to hurt. It felt twisted. I wouldn't think about these things now. I looked at Mary. She had walked over to Joseph and her hand rested on his shoulder. He still sat gazing at the babies. She was now doing the same. "Oh, God, if you are truly there, can you tell me— will someone ever look at me with that much love?" I sat and waited as if expecting to hear an answer. There were no words, but that incredible feeling of peace was returning! I didn't think I deserved to feel this good, but I could do nothing to stop it. I closed my eyes and let the feeling wash over me. I took in a deep breath and slowly let it out and whispered, "Thank you."

3

Trusted Friends

I woke up to the sound of babies crying. Mary was holding Bartholomew and trying to quiet him and Joseph was holding Jesus looking despairingly at Mary as to what to do. I could see they were desperately trying to let me continue to sleep and I felt such love and admiration for them. I truly could not remember a time when anyone thought of my needs before their own.. I jumped up and took my brother. He stopped crying and started to nuzzle. "I think he is hungry, Mary. I better take him home so Mother can nurse him."

Mary had already taken Jesus and was trying to help him get comfortable. She smiled at me. "We tried to let you sleep, Mary, but there was no more putting off feeding time! She had settled down and when she pulled back her undergarment to begin to nurse, I saw on her neck the most beautiful necklace! She noticed me looking and her hand went to it. "It's lovely, isn't it? My mother gave it to me. It belonged to her mother and it has been passed down on the thirteenth birthday of each daughter, for many generations. I don't think it is gold, but it has never lost its luster. It was crafted by someone in our family long, long ago."

Just then, the necklace fell over where Jesus was nuzzling her, blocking him from nursing. Mary moved it and he immediately found his mark. We both laughed. I looked to Joseph and thanked them again and again for their kindness to me. Joseph came to me and smiled and Mary looked up shaking her head. "No, Mary, it is us that should be thanking you! You have done so much and we don't know how to thank you enough. Go now and take your brother. Then come and see us again as soon as you can. We must find another place to stay, so I don't know how much longer we will be here. Please thank your parents for all they have done." I opened my mouth to say something and had to push back a sarcastic remark. I just nodded as I put on my cloak and waved goodbye.

The day was still windy and cold and the sun was low in the sky. How could my brother have slept so long without eating? I ran up the hill with Bartholomew wrapped tightly and ducked in the back corridor hoping to avoid any confrontation with my father. When I went to Mother's room she was lying in bed and crying. I ran to her to see why she was upset. She grabbed my brother from my arms and looked at me, her eyes filled with contempt. She was so angry I could see the veins in her forehead. "How could you do this to me? Where have you been? I have been worried to death about him and had no idea where you would have taken him! He must have been starving! What is wrong with you?"

All I really heard was her concern for where *he* had been. There was no concern for my whereabouts. I opened my mouth to explain, but my father came in and started on me also, slapping me as he yelled, "Don't you ever touch that baby again! You are totally irresponsible and I wouldn't put it past you to do something to hurt him. You know he is the son that I have been waiting for! What is wrong with you?"

I looked at my mother cuddling Bartholomew and felt so much rage that I was being accused of things like this when I, too, loved him so much. The anger welled up in me and I yelled at her, "You have not even let me explain what..." I was unable to finish my sentence. The kick was hard and swift. My right thigh exploded in pain. It was so intense, I could hardly breathe. I sank to my knees, gasping for air. "You will not be disrespectful to us! You are good for nothing!" Because of the extreme pain I was in I could not get up and leave. I was totally at their mercy as he finished his tirade.

"I leave tomorrow for Jerusalem. You will take care of all the chores that need to be done. We made more money in the last two days than we ever have and a lot of work needs to be done to clean up. You worried your mother so badly that she will not be able to do anything except take care of your brother. Do you understand?" I shook my head and through gritted teeth he said, "You answer me when I ask you a question. Do you understand?" I looked up at him and his eyes were filled with disgust. "Yes, Father," I answered. He began to leave the room and then turned to me, "Oh, and by the way. That family in the cow's stable. I want them out by tomorrow afternoon." My heart caught in my throat as I heard him continue. "They have mooched long enough. I expect you to take care of telling them to leave. I don't have time to worry about a bunch of needy shepherds. Is that clear?" I had such a lump in my throat, I could hardly answer, but managed to say, "Yes, Father."

My father left the room and I was finally able to get up. My mother would not look at me. She was totally encompassed in nursing my brother. I left the room, tears streaming down my face. The throbbing in my thigh was unbearable as I walked back to my room. I wondered how I could possibly tell those wonderful people to leave. I lay on my bed and cried until there were no tears left.

Times like these I missed Salome the most. She was the only one who would hold me and listen to me when I cried. Now I had no one. I remembered Mary's words about her God. Could he help me with this? I felt embarrassed, but closed my eyes and said to my empty room, "God of my friend, Mary. I don't know you, but if you can show me how to help this family, I would be so grateful." I felt my face flushing as I waited for an answer and added, "And if you could help the pain in my leg, I would also be grateful." I felt the peace I had experienced earlier returning. This is such a wonderful feeling, I thought. I didn't understand how it could be, but it almost felt like I had arms around me...like someone was holding me and I drifted off to sleep.

When I awoke, it was dark outside. I was grateful that we had no patrons tonight. I still felt the pain in my leg but nowhere near as bad as it had been. I knew it would still be impossible to work. I lit the candle next to my bed and rolled over to look at my leg. In the candlelight, it was black from my knee to my hip and extremely tender to touch. There was not a sound anywhere and I sat up on the side of my bed. I suddenly remembered that Joanna's parents had a few houses that they sometimes bartered. People that needed a place to stay would exchange services for a home. Could they possibly have a place now where Mary and Joseph could stay? I was so excited I jumped up and was quickly reminded of the injury to my leg. I would not be going anywhere tonight, but tomorrow I could talk with them! This was exactly what I had prayed for! I looked up at the ceiling of my room and whispered, "Thank you!"

I was up with the sun the next morning and rushed to get dressed. I anticipated seeing my father at breakfast, but he must have left very early. I knew he usually traveled with two other friends of his and they had no wives or families. My mother was always quick to remind him that just because of their lack of responsibilities, it did not give him the right to forget he had a family waiting for him. That was another one of those long, heated discussions that usually ended with him walking out and my mother staying in bed the rest of the day, talking to no one. I quickly got all the chores done that had been left to me and silently thanked Mary's God for no one stopping at the inn last night.

As I was cleaning the last of the dishes, I realized I had not even thought of my leg this morning. I pulled up my dress to reveal a huge bruise that covered the whole side of my thigh, from my hipbone to my knee. But I truly felt no pain unless I touched it and even then, not what I had expected. "Again Mary's God has answered a prayer of mine." I realized I was smiling as I said it and I found myself humming a tune I had heard at Joanna's house one day when I was there playing. Her mother hummed it all the time and I liked it. I could hardly wait to get to her house today! I must do an especially good job with my chores so Mother had no reason to keep me home.

After double-checking all my work, I grabbed several loaves of the day old bread and some fruit that were left over and placed them in a basket for Mary and Joseph. I thought I could stop by with the food on my way to Joanna's. I was so excited at the thought of seeing them! I just knew I would be able to help them find a place to live! I went down the back corridor to my mother's room and she was not there. I continued searching for her and found her in the sewing room. My heart sank in my chest as I dreaded the thought of getting caught for stealing Salome's wedding linen. I cautiously walked into the room, not knowing what kind of mood my mother was in today. The days when Father left were usually not good ones.

"Good-morning, Mother. I'm so sorry for yesterday. Can you please forgive me for not letting you know where I was?" I waited tentatively for the answer and when it came, it took me by surprise. My mother turned to me, put down her sewing and held out her arms. I ran to her and kneeled in front of her as she hugged me. I felt her chest heaving and realized she was weeping. "Mother, what's wrong? Are you all right? Is Bartholomew sick?" She just held me tighter and

cried harder. I felt uncomfortable but was enjoying the attention…especially being held by her.

Eventually the heavy sobbing stopped and she pushed
me back from her chest and looked at me. "Mary, Mary,
Mary. I do love you. I know I don't tell you or show you
enough, but I do. I know, in my heart, you wouldn't do
anything to hurt your brother. I was worried about both of
you and knowing your father was leaving was heavy on my
mind. You know how much I hate being here alone. It feels
like we are out in the middle of nowhere. I sometimes think
he brought us out here so he could make me miserable. I
was thinking about us taking a trip to Bethany and seeing
my brother. Would you like that?"

I was so shocked by the offer, I didn't know what to say!
I would love to go see my aunt and uncle and my cousins! I
felt good when I was with them and Mother was happy when
she spent time with her family. But I also needed to help
Mary and Joseph find a home. I took a chance and decided
to confide my plan. "Mother, you know the family in the
stable that Father spoke of? Well, they are very fine people
and they have just had a baby. They have nowhere to go and
I hoped maybe Joanna's parents could help. I would like to
go there and talk with them and then I could come home and
help you pack. I'm excited about going to Bethany again!"

I waited for the usual "no" response to my request, but
instead my mother smiled and said, "You are so considerate,
Mary. Yes, go and help these people. I am certain your father
will not be happy if they are still here when he returns tonight.
I will finish sewing and begin to get our things ready." I
thought my heart would burst, not only from my mother's
permission to go, but also the compliment she paid me! She
and I got along so much better when Father was away. I gave
her a huge hug and promised to be back soon.

I grabbed the food, ran down the hill as fast as my leg
would allow and breathlessly burst into the stable. Joseph

and Mary looked startled and I realized how unwise it was for me to barge in like that, especially with a baby here. "Here are some bread and fruit for breakfast. I am on the way to a friend's house to see about finding a home for you." I shared briefly that I was going to talk with Joanna's parents and Joseph immediately volunteered that he was a carpenter and would gladly barter some of his talent in exchange for a home. I promised them I would return with an answer soon.

As I was walking from the stable, I heard one of the horses whinny, and it occurred to me how much quicker and less painful my trip would be if I rode. I knew this was not a good thing without permission, but was afraid to push my mother. I ran as fast as I could up the hill and got Joshua from his stall. I was grateful that I had groomed the horses before the people had arrived for the census. It saved me a lot of time now. I slipped the bridle over his head and in a burst of excitement hugged him as hard as I could! "We are going on a great mission, Joshua. I need you to run like the wind and not let me fall off. If I fall on this leg, I may lose it." I laughed out loud at the remark, but wondered, by the look of the bruise, if it was far from the truth. It looked horrible. But riding Joshua would spare me any more discomfort. *As long as I don't get caught.*

We set out for Joanna's house and Joshua did fly! His mane whipped my face until it hurt, but I didn't care! The road was dry and dusty and it felt like Joshua's hooves barely touched the ground. We passed several traders along the way and they shook their fists at me as I galloped past. I'm sure the dust and dirt were flying! Riding was always such an exhilarating experience for me. No one bossing me around, putting me down or yelling at me. Just me and my horse and it felt good to be in control! That was something I liked feeling! This may be the only time I felt in control of anything! I also liked feeling the power of his muscles as

I rode. I could feel them bunching up with each lift of his hooves and then stretching out as he prepared for another.

My mother used to always tell me girls should not ride horses because it would ruin something. I never knew what she meant, she didn't give any explanations and I really didn't care. Every time Father took me riding, she would bring up the subject. He would just shake his head and give her that look and walk away. It didn't come up much anymore.

We rode just a little further and I saw Joanna's house. It was a big farm and kind of isolated. They did not have to worry about travelers always passing their house like we did. My mother hated that. She had liked the quiet that we had in Cana and especially in Magdala. Though it was on the Sea of Galilee, we had lived more towards the mountains so it was less populated. She had even been happy in Hebron. Again, because we had lived in a less populated area. But the constant influx of people where we are now annoyed her. The inn is on the road between Jerusalem and Galilee. Lots of travelers, lots of traders and lots of money for my father. I had to agree with Mother. Out here where Joanna lived was so much more peaceful.

I slowed Joshua to a walk so he would cool down. Joanna's parents were so nice and I loved being here, but my father hated me to spend time with them. He said they put silly ideas in my head about God. I made the mistake of telling him about a wonderful dinner I had with them, the Passover feast. He said he had given that up a long time ago because they had too many rules. He also said they expected too much money; he wasn't going to give a "tithe" to people he didn't even know. Mother had told me once, the real reason he turned from his religion was that his mother had died giving birth to him. His father blamed God for it. She said Father had grown up believing Jehovah hated him for killing his mother. One time, I tried to talk with him about it, but he just got angry, so I never tried again.

As I approached the house, I wondered if I should tell them about all that happened over the last two days. I decided I shouldn't. They would probably think I was mad. I even found myself wondering if everything I had heard was true. I steered Joshua to the back of the house and jumped down. I gave him another hug. "Thank you for getting me here so quickly! You must be tired. I will get some water for you. I know you're a thirsty boy!" His coat was wet, but not lathered so I knew he was not too overheated. I drew water from the well and took it to him. I petted him while he drank and as I did, silently asked Mary's God to please let Joanna's father have a home available. I also thanked him for my safe trip. I heard one of the horses in the field whinny and Joshua answered. I removed his bridle and watched as he ran out to play with them.

The door was open and I heard Joanna's mother, Deborah, humming a tune. The smell of fresh baked bread made me take in a deep breath. My stomach immediately began to ache and I realized I had not taken the time to eat anything today. I leaned my head in and said, "Anybody have some bread for me?" Joanna came to the door. "Mary, it's so good to see you. I have missed you." She gave me a big hug and pulled me into the room where her mother was. "Mother, look who's here. Mary has come for a visit."

Joanna's mother turned and a big smile covered her face. She was a large, robust woman and when she hugged you, you knew you had been hugged! She held out her arms to me. "Come here, you precious thing. How have you been? We were just saying this morning how long it has been since we have seen you! How are your parents and that new little brother? I have wanted to go see Naomi for two months, since I heard about his birth."

I was thoroughly enjoying this wonderful hug and found myself not wanting to let go. This was one of the few safe places I had and I felt guilty that I could not tell them the truth. Father always says that what happens in our house is no one's business but ours. I finally let go and looked her in the face and lied. "Everyone is fine and happy. Father and mother are enjoying Bartholomew. He is growing so fast. Father is in Jerusalem today and mother said I could come, so here I am."

Deborah had a round, gentle face, without the lines that you might expect for a woman her age. Her eyes were large and kind. They did not reveal that she believed my lie. She looked down and shook her head and then hugged me again. "Well, I am glad you are here and that you arrived safely. Even if it takes Bartimus leaving for the day so you can come! We'll take all the time with you we can get! Right, Joanna?" Dramatically, Joanna nodded her head.

Deborah walked over to a table full of food and asked, "Would you like to eat with us?" The aroma of the fresh bread was overpowering all the other smells, even the lamb stew, but it all looked delicious! I could not refuse such an invitation! "I would love to eat with you, but do you have a minute that I might be able to share something with you? I need to ask a favor."

I began to tell them about the family from the stable. I explained how they needed a place to stay because my father was kicking them out today. I was careful to leave out the part about the shepherds and the great light in the sky and the things about the baby being the Savior. I did mention that they shared the same God, Jehovah. I thought that might help! Joanna spoke up first and volunteered that someone had just moved out of one of her father's houses and he was at a loss because the man was the only carpenter he had to work for him!

This was too good to be true! I was so excited! I looked at both of them and said, "The man, Joseph, he is a carpenter! And he said he would be glad to barter with someone for a home. They feel they should stay here for awhile...and they are so nice. They came here from Nazareth." Deborah's eyes lit up and she smiled. "I have heard there are very good carpenters in Nazareth! We will have to talk to your father when he gets home, Joanna."

While Joanna and I reclined at the table, Deborah went to wake her younger daughter, Lydia. When she saw me, she came running in with arms wide open and gave me the biggest hug her little arms would allow. Lydia was four years old and she loved the times when I came to visit. She settled in my lap and whispered loudly, "Mary, I have missed you so much! Did you bring me anything?" Her mother immediately gave her a look of disapproval. I chuckled. "It's all right. She knows I always bring her date or pistachio cakes. But, I'm sorry, Lydia. I brought nothing today. I was in a hurry."

She shrugged her shoulders and started to eat some bread from the basket. "Lydia, you know we have not blessed the food and your father is not here yet." Joanna interrupted and said, "I think he is now!" She jumped up and ran to the door with Lydia close behind. I heard Lydia cry out, "Abba, you are home! Did you bring me anything?" I looked up at Deborah and we both burst out with laughter. Deborah chortled, "She is consistent! You have to give her that!"

Joanna's father, Benjamin, came in with Lydia in his arms and Joanna at his heels. He looked at me and smiled, "Hello stranger. It's good to see you again!" He walked over and gave his wife a hug with his free arm as Lydia wrestled to get down. Deborah pushed back the hair from his forehead and said, "You look tired. Did you have a lot of customers today?"

She helped him take off his cloak after Lydia had finally wriggled her way out of his arms, and he sat down. Deborah immediately got a basin of water and began to wash the dust from her husband's feet. He quietly thanked her and said, "Yes. It was very busy. There were people from the census who stayed in Bethlehem and wanted a cart to get around. I was amazed how many people walked here. It made for a busy day. I do wish we had been able to get the new stable finished before that carpenter moved on. That would have allowed me to hire someone to help me in a different location. I turned away quite a few today." He looked so forlorn that I thought I would burst before someone told him about Joseph!

Deborah looked at me and smiled. She saw my enthusiasm and winked at me. She finished with Benjamin's feet and we all reclined for dinner. Benjamin blessed the food and as soon as he finished she said, "I have something I would like to ask you about, Benjamin. If you could find a carpenter, say... today, to replace the last one, would you let him move in the house right away?" He looked up in amazement. "Woman, you shouldn't tease your husband like that! You know how heavy this has been on my heart!"

Deborah smiled. "I don't jest with you! Mary knows a family that needs a home and they need it today. The husband is a carpenter. They came for the census and his wife had a baby boy in Bartimus' stable. They have nowhere to go. And Benjamin," she looked at him with a twinkle in her eye, and added, "he is from Nazareth!"

I thought Benjamin would choke on his lamb! "Mary, is this true? Do you know how I have prayed for this?" Deborah interrupted him and chuckled. "We will all praise Jehovah, Benjamin!" He threw his arms in the air. "Oh, God of Abraham, Isaac and Jacob! You have truly blessed us. Thank you so much!" He turned to me and asked, "Mary, do you think they would come today? As soon as we eat, I could take the wagon and help them move in. The house is very close to your father's inn. Only a short distance from the olive groves. You could easily walk there!"

I was as happy as Benjamin! "Oh, I'm sure they would be glad for your help. They are wonderful people and they are so kind! Yes, this is just perfect!" Deborah looked at me and winked again. She leaned over and touched my arm. "Mary, I have taught you about Jehovah. He loves you, too.

And this blessing for our family is also a blessing for you!" I looked at her thoughtfully. I sifted through the things that had happened to me over the last few days, remembering, more than anything, the peace I had felt. I knew that living close to them would be a *very* good thing. Yes, I believe she's right! This is an incredible blessing for me, too!

After we ate, I ran out to the field and called Joshua. I could barely make him out among the other horses, but when he heard his name I saw him lift his head. He was such a majestic looking horse, with perfect confirmation. He immediately began to trot toward me. As he approached, I put out my hand to touch the big white blaze on his face and he stopped and nuzzled my chest. "We continue our mission, my beauty! Now we go tell Joseph and Mary they have a home. And they'll live close to us! We'll be able to visit every day!"

I heard footsteps and turned to see Joanna approaching. "Father is going to take the rest of the family in the wagon. I was wondering if I could ride with you?" "That would be fun, Joanna! Are they ready to go?" We both turned in time to see Joseph helping Deborah into the wagon. He then lifted Lydia to her and looked toward us. "Joanna, are you riding with us or Mary?"

"We will ride Joshua together," Joanna answered. I jumped on and then pulled Joanna up behind me. We walked over to the wagon. Benjamin was checking that everyone was settled in the wagon and then looked up at me. "We will follow you, Mary. I am praying for a miracle!" He had a huge grin on his face.

The ride back took a little longer than the one that had brought me to Joanna's, but it was filled with anticipation. I realized that everything I had prayed for last night in my room had come to pass. I knew I was going to talk to Mary about her God. I had questions for Joanna's mom, too, but felt afraid to ask them because of my father's warnings. I did know one thing, however! I felt, deep inside, that there was something special about this God that my father wanted nothing to do with. I would find out more!

When we arrived at the stable, I jumped off Joshua and held up my finger to Joanna's family to let them know that I would only be a minute. I knocked gently on the door and heard Mary softly say, "Come in, please." Afraid of waking Jesus, I quietly opened the door. He was lying in the manger wrapped up in Mary's cloak. Joseph was napping next to him. Mary was folding the pieces of cloth that I had given her. She looked up at me and said, "Mary, it's so good to see you. Thank you so much for the food this morning. My night was not as good as the first and Joseph and I got little sleep. I had terrible cramps and Jesus did not sleep as well. But as I was lying here resting, I just knew you would come back."

She reached over and embraced me. I smiled and whispered, "Mary, I have wonderful news! My friends are here to take you to a house not far from the inn. They are looking for a carpenter that can barter work for rent. And they are really happy to learn you are from Nazareth. It seems perfect for the three of you and I am excited because you will be close to me!" I could hardly restrain the exhilaration I felt inside!

Mary looked as if someone had pinched her! "That is wonderful, Mary! I can't believe it! I have been praying ever since you told me you would help us. I knew my God would provide; I just didn't expect it so quickly! I must wake Joseph. He will be so happy!" She got up and walked over to the manger. She leaned over and gently shook him. "Joseph! Joseph, my husband. I have amazing news for us!" He turned slightly and opened his eyes. "How long have I been sleeping? I don't even remember falling asleep." He sat halfway up and then saw me and smiled. In a sluggish voice he said, "Thank you, Mary, for the food this morning. It filled the large hole I had in my stomach. I think those five days walking from Nazareth took more out of me than I realized."

Mary couldn't wait any longer and interrupted him. "Joseph, Mary has found a home for us! The people are outside, right now, to help take us there! Isn't that wonderful? Joseph, are you hearing me?" Joseph looked at first like he was daydreaming and then he looked at me and said," Mary, how will we ever repay you for all you have done?" I put my head down as I felt the blood rise to my cheeks. Mary continued. "And Joseph, they want to barter your carpenter skills in exchange for the house. It's such a miracle!"

Joseph got up and asked me, "Can you introduce me to your friends?" I was on my feet in a second and went to the stable door with Joseph right behind me. We went out and I saw that Benjamin was already out of the wagon and waiting. The two men approached each other. I introduced them and they immediately began to talk about the details. I saw that Joanna had already gotten down from Joshua and had joined her mother and sister. I went over to them and asked if they would like to go into the stable and meet Mary. They all jumped down from the wagon without a word and we went into the stable.

Mary had picked up Jesus and was sitting in the hay with him when we came in. It almost took my breath at the sight of them, among these animals, with the dust from the hay in their hair and the smell of dung all around them. In the midst of all that, her face glowed as if a torch was lit in the room. Her smile, so gentle and inviting, was full of love. Oh, how I wanted to be like her! I came to where they were sitting and said "Mary, this is my friend Joanna, her sister Lydia and her mother Deborah." I turned to Joanna and said, "This is Mary and her beautiful baby is Jesus." Deborah came over to Mary and took her hand. "It is such an honor to meet you. You seem to be just a baby yourself! How old are you, child?"

I could see Joanna blush. Her mother was always so blunt and it embarrassed her. I looked quickly at Mary but it did not seem to affect her at all. "I am 15 years old. Yes, I am young, but I am learning a lot of useful things from our friend Mary." Deborah looked at me and said, "Oh, yes. She is a special girl," and they both shook their heads in agreement. Joanna came to me and said, "See, I'm always telling you how special you are." I was so self-conscious that I turned away from them and asked Mary if I could get her some water.

Deborah came to me, put her arm around my shoulder and said, "See that smile on your face. You like it when we say nice things about you even if you don't feel comfortable. The more we do it the better you will feel!" I leaned into her side and hid my head in her cloak. She was right. It did feel nice. I just needed to get used to it! Mary looked up at Deborah and said, "You know, I think I am going to like you very much." We all laughed and started picking up their things to prepare to leave.

In a few minutes Joseph and Benjamin walked in and announced that they were ready to go. Joseph had a big smile on his face and a twinkle in his eye! I was overjoyed. But a dark cloud suddenly passed over my happiness. "I won't be able to help you, Mary. My mother wants to go to Bethany to see her brother and his family and she wants to leave today while my father is away. But I promise I will come see you as soon as we get back. You will be in very good hands with Deborah and Joanna to help you. They aren't as close as I will be, but I know they will come if you need anything." Deborah grinned at me and spoke up, "Oh, you won't have to worry about them. I will be at the house every day with food until she is back on her feet. She needs to rest. She has been through a lot for a young girl."

We all walked outside and Benjamin helped Joseph put the few things they had in the wagon. Joseph went back into the stable to get their donkey. Deborah instructed Joanna to get in the back of the wagon where there was some hay, so she could hold Jesus. We then helped Mary climb in. Lydia was clapping her hands saying, "Me, mommy, I want to hold the baby!" Deborah shook her head and promised she could another time. Lydia crossed her arms over her chest and stuck her bottom lip out in a big pout. Deborah ruffled her hair and said, "That is all right, my angel. Patience is a blessing!" Lydia climbed in the front seat of the wagon, followed by Deborah. Joseph came out of the stable with their donkey and he and Benjamin went to tie it to the back. I prepared to mount Joshua and had to pull up my tunic to get my leg over his back. I heard a loud gasp and thought someone was hurt. When I turned to see what had happened, I saw Mary and Deborah staring at my leg.

Deborah gasped, "Mary, what happened to your leg? It looks dreadful! What happened, child?" I panicked! I was not prepared at all! I hated the thought of lying to either of them, but what could I do? I quickly thought of the monologue I had earlier with Joshua and said, "I was riding yesterday and fell off my horse. It was a pretty bad fall." I looked at Mary and could not read her face, but I knew Deborah did not believe me. I decided I had no more time to tarry. "I will see you all when I get back. Enjoy your new home, Mary." I looked at Deborah and smiled. "Thank you for being as kind to them as you've been to me." Mary looked at me with grave concern and I felt she wanted to say more, but only replied, "Thank you for introducing us to these wonderful people and helping us so much." I nodded a reply and with that I was off up the hill to put Joshua in the stable. I would feed and water him and give him a good brushing before I went back to see Mother. I knew I should be excited, but I had such ambivalent feelings because I wanted to stay and help my new friends, but also wanted to see our family.

When I got to my parents' room, Mother was almost packed. She was in such a good mood and the anger I had expected for taking so much time, was replaced with smiles and anticipation. "I have packed as many of your things as I could think of; if you want to bring something else please get it now. We have only a few hours of daylight left." I assured her that I would be fine. By the number of bags she was taking, I began to worry how long we would be gone. I didn't want to say anything that might ruin her mood, so I cautiously asked, "Mother, do you know how long we might be gone? I want to be sure to take enough clothes." She looked at me thoughtfully and said, "I don't know, Mary. Long enough for your father to realize he misses us!" I nodded my head but thought, *that could be a very long time.*

We piled everything into the wagon and I made a bed for Bartholomew and myself in the back. I told Mother we could take turns resting, but she felt the oxen were too temperamental for me to drive. After remembering the last wagon ride we took to Jerusalem, I agreed. I climbed in and she handed Bartholomew to me and got in herself. She turned to me and smiled, "Are you ready?" I nodded with a smile and she clucked to the oxen and we were off. Almost as an afterthought, she looked over at the inn and said "Good riddance!"

We spent almost three weeks at my Uncle Reuben's home. It was a fun time and my mother was incredibly happy the whole time we were there. I had only heard her laugh like that when Salome was alive. Her brother's family was like Joanna's; they were proud of their Jewish heritage. I could talk freely to my cousins about the little bit that I knew and ask them lots of questions. They all seemed to know that a Messiah was coming, and my uncle even mentioned that he had heard some ridiculous rumors that some shepherds were spreading about the Messiah being born in a stable in Bethlehem only a few nights before. Mother didn't put it together that it was our stable and I didn't volunteer anything.

I prayed every night that the time would pass quickly and that Mary and Joseph were doing well. I also prayed that I'd be able to spend lots of time with them. So much of what had happened to me since I met that family had been good! I didn't want it to end! I even gave Jehovah thanks for the changes in my mother. If she stayed this happy after we went home, life would be so wonderful. Maybe a miracle could happen for Father, too.

The time soon came for us to go back home and it was a sad time for us. Mother and my aunt held each other and cried and my cousins and I cried. My mother's tears didn't stop the whole way home. I started dreading the inevitable battle that would ensue when she was faced with the daily routine of the inn and my father's indiscretions. I realized my hopes for a permanent change in them had not been very realistic. The ride back to Bethlehem was a quiet one.

When we pulled into the courtyard, Bartholomew was still asleep so I jumped down from the wagon and began to unhook the oxen. Mother was slowly getting down and I noticed for the first time just how slow she was moving. She started to take some of the bags out of the wagon and I ran to her. "I'll get them, Mother." I reached up to help. She didn't look up, but quietly said to me, "No, Mary, I will get them. You water the oxen." Her voice sounded depressed and distant. I did as I was told and then led them out to the field to eat. The sun was setting and the stars were beginning to appear in the sky. I lingered and watched the sky paint a picture of twinkling lights with muted pastels over the mountains where the sun was setting. It was truly beautiful! My enjoyment was interrupted when I heard a horse come into the courtyard. It was Father! I ran back to see what was going to happen between them.

He was already off his horse and questioning her about where she had been. She quietly told him, but he kept up his tirade about how stupid she was for leaving him to care for the inn by himself. She continued to take the bags from the wagon and then called me to get my brother. My father was getting angrier with each passing minute because she would not respond to his accusations. I went to get Bartholomew and he tried to stop me, but my mother looked at him and said through gritted teeth, "Leave her alone and leave me alone! I don't care if this place burns to the ground! And if you don't shut your mouth, I will leave again! For good!"

With that she took my free arm and pulled me toward the inn. I feared what may come next, but nothing did. I helped Mother get my brother to bed and then she came to my room to tuck me in- something she had not done in a long time. She leaned over to kiss me and said, "Mary, I want things to be different for us. It may mean leaving someday. But he is not going to take everything I have worked so hard to get and give it to some young whore that he thinks will replace me! If we leave, my things go with me!" She looked very determined and I felt so much love for her. "Mother, I will go with you wherever you go, but let's just go! Our lives will not change here and the things you have are just that! Things! They are not as important as happiness! We can get new things. Let's just take Bartholomew and go!"

She looked at me with great consternation and said, "Mary, you do not understand. I will not let him get away with what he has done to me for years. If something ever happens to me, you and your brother will have nothing! I can promise you that! He cares only for money and women and I can at least get his money!" She kissed me again and I knew it was best to say nothing else. She walked from my room and I was left wondering if she realized that money held just as important a place for her as it did for Father.

That night, the shuffling steps returned outside my door. This could not be happening! After three weeks of peaceful sleep, I had to return to this! As the foot steps entered my room and got closer to my bed, I could smell the strong odor of wine. I had not visited my safe place for over three weeks. I decided it was time again.

The next morning, I was in my room bathing, when my father walked in, unannounced. I grabbed my tunic to try and cover my nakedness. He looked at me and said, "I'm your father. It's nothing I haven't seen before. I need you to help with breakfast; your mother is not coming out of her room." He left as quickly as he came. *It's not bad enough that I have to suffer the humiliation of last night...* I shook my head. I had woken with one of my headaches. I got dressed and promised myself I would get the chores done quickly so I could go see Mary and Joseph.

I rushed through the breakfast ordeal; it did not take long because we only had eight guests. Then I went to my mother's room. Her door was shut and I gently knocked. "I don't want to be bothered," came through the door. "It's me, mother." I heard her softly say, "What is it, Mary?" The smile I had seen for the last three weeks was gone. In its place were sadness and tears. "I was wondering if I could go see my friends... unless you need me to do something for you." I silently prayed that she wouldn't need me, but at the same time felt bad about leaving her alone. She was holding Bartholomew and looked up at me and whispered, "Go. Have fun and come back when you want." I went to the bed and hugged her and thanked her. "Mother, I love you." She nodded and said, "I love you, too.

It took me less than ten minutes to get to the little house on foot. It was nestled back in the olive groves, on the outskirts of Bethlehem. They would see very few travelers coming through here. Only local people going home. Benjamin wanted it that way so that his olive groves would stay in tact. That was a source of income that would always be lucrative for his family. I knocked on the door and when Mary saw me, she threw her arms around me and wouldn't let go.

"It is so good to see you again, Mary! We have missed you so much! Come in and look at our beautiful home! It is so much nicer than the home we had in Nazareth. We even have a front door and a little oven inside. I love it! And Deborah has been here three times every week. She said it's a short trip to get here. She has brought me food and clothes and more material for diapers. She even showed me how to make better diapers than I had been making. She is almost like a mother to me!"

She finally took a breath and laughed and I laughed with her. Her joy was contagious! We went in and sat down next to where Jesus was laying. I gasped! "Mary, he has grown so much! I have only been gone three weeks and he looks so much bigger!" Mary looked at him and added, "And drinking so much more!" She smiled at me. "Tell me, how was your trip? Did you have fun?" She leaned over to cover Jesus' legs where he had kicked off his blanket.

"Oh, I had a wonderful time and my mother got so much rest. Her brother believes in Jehovah and I got to ask lots of questions. Mary, there is so much I want to learn from you about your God. I just need to keep it from my father. As long as he thinks I come just to visit or help with Jesus, it will be all right. My father and mother are both Jews, but he has never let us practice the traditions; something that happened when he was young. He does not let me see Joanna very much because I told him they were teaching me things about their God."

Mary glanced at me and reached over and took my hand. "I would be honored to teach you about the God of Abraham, Isaac and Jacob. I would love to teach you about *them* also! He is a wonderful God who is real! He is not a piece of stone or wood. He wants a relationship with all of us and I know he especially wants one with you. You come as often as you can and bring your little brother if your mother will let you; it is never too early to teach children about his love. God has a special purpose for your life, Mary."

Her eyes were so soft and gentle and I knew she was speaking truth to me. "I will Mary. I will come every day that I can. And I will learn as much as I can. Thank you for being my friend. Oh, I brought you a present." I pulled the pouch from under my mantle and removed a small wooden dove.

"My uncle is a woodcarver. He does beautiful work and after I told him about you, he gave this to me to give to you." She took it from my hands and admired it. "It is beautiful Mary! Thank you so much. I will keep it in a special place." Her hand went to her neck and began to remove her necklace. "I know how much you admired this and I would like..." I stopped her. "No, Mary. That's a family heirloom. I couldn't take it. You don't have to offer me anything. Just teach me about your God. That is the best gift you can give me."

4

Night visitors

The next two years proved to be some of the happiest times of my young life. Though nothing much changed at home, Mary and I became good friends. She was only three years older than me and that made it easy to talk to her. I shared about my life and she shared about her God. Though my parents were Jewish, my father's anger kept talk of God forbidden. I told about my sister and how much I missed her, my concerns for my mother and I carefully evaded her questions about my father. She told amazing stories about men and women I had never heard of before. Stories of Moses, Jonah (I loved that story—the thought of living in the belly of a fish was exciting...and scary!), Joshua, Ruth, Esther (I really liked that story; she was so brave!) and so many others. King David was remarkable to me. He had done such bad things, but God still loved him and considered him a man after his own heart. Mary could not believe that I knew so little of David. I tried to tell her how isolated we felt from moving all the time, but I think it was difficult for her to understand. My father's search for riches at the expense of his family was hard for many to understand. Her tales of courage, faith, trust, obedience and sometimes failure and heartache, were teaching me truths that I had never known. For the first time in my life, I was learning about my creator and how much he loves me.

Remarkably, my parents allowed me to visit Mary and Joseph almost daily, as long as my chores were done. I volunteered nothing of Mary's spiritual teachings for fear my father would keep me from seeing them like he had done with Joanna's family. I think it was good for my parents to have me out of their hair; I know it was good for me. They even allowed me to bring Bartholomew sometimes. He and Jesus grew to be friends, too. They learned to eat solid food together, crawl together, and even walk together. Though my brother was a few months older than Jesus, they seemed to be on the same milestone schedule. As the boys learned to talk, toward the end of their second year, Mary taught them how to pray, just as she had taught me. It was so cute to hear the two of them trying to pronounce the words as she said them! I felt so blessed that we had this opportunity. I loved my little brother and my desire to protect him grew as he did.

One evening, my father was throwing a huge party for some people from Jerusalem. I dreaded the thought of all the work that would need to be done. After the expected argument between my parents over the type of people that my father entertained, my mother came to where I was cleaning and pulled me into my bedroom across the hall. She got very close to me and raised her hand and for a brief second I thought she was going to slap me. I flinched, waiting for the blow, but instead, she touched my face gently and held my cheeks between her two hands. Her face looked red and I could see she had been crying. The lines around her mouth seemed deeper and formed an almost permanent frown. My heart went out to her for the pain I knew she lived with everyday. She reached up and touched my hair and said, "Mary, your friends that live nearby, the ones with the baby, can you go there and stay tonight? I don't want you here among these men your father is bringing here. There will be much drinking and things will be said and done that you shouldn't be exposed to. Could you do that for me?"

At that moment, I would have done anything for her and I quietly answered, "Of course, Mother. I'm sure it will be all right. I'll pack up some things and go. Can I do anything for you before I leave? You look so sad." She shook her head and tears began to flow down her cheeks. "No my sweet Mary. No one can help me." She turned away from me and wiped her eyes and then helped me find some clothes to take. "Now, you are very sure they won't mind?" I nodded and she said, "Please tell them how very grateful I am. You have changed since you have been going there, Mary. I know I have not told you before, but I have noticed. You are happier and calmer, more patient. I appreciate whatever it is they are doing for you."

I had been waiting for this kind of opportunity to share with her. "Mother, they tell me such wonderful stories of Jehovah! He is our creator and he loves us very much. They have taught me how to pray and I have been praying for you. You can have the same..." My sentence was cut off by her quick interruption. "I don't want to hear anything else, Mary. You know how your father feels. I can't handle any more problems and if he finds out that they are filling your head with these things, he won't let you go back. Now, be on your way and forget we had this conversation." My heart sank in my chest. Not only did I ruin this rare moment I was having with her, but she also rejected the hope I had for her. I turned to leave, but she surprised me by hugging me again. "I love you, Mary. This will be our secret."

She watched as I went down the back corridor and slipped out into the dusky night. It was twilight. The sun was just slipping behind the mountains in the distance. I loved this time of the evening. It was the time when I could see the full moon rising, though tonight it was not yet full. The stars had just begun to show themselves. But there was something very odd about the sky tonight. A new, huge star was shining in the sky and it seemed to be glowing right over the area where Mary and Joseph's house was located. As I continued down the hill toward the stable, I thought about that bright light I had seen just two years ago. But that had been the angel heralding the birth of Jesus. It had been the beginning of an amazing journey with the family I had made my own.

My walk became a skip that soon broke into a run as I realized that my first impression was true. The closer I got to their house, the closer and brighter the star seemed. As I approached their yard, I saw Joseph, Mary and Jesus outside the house looking up at the brilliant star. I startled Jesus, who when he recognized me, came over and gave me a big hug. "Marwy, look at big light! See big light!" I laughed at the cute way he said my name and marveled as his huge eyes sparkled in amazement. I picked him up and went over to the place where Mary and Joseph were standing. "What do you think it is?" I asked them. Joseph's eyes never left the star, but Mary looked at me and smiled. "I don't know, but we are surely enjoying another of God's wonders. Jesus certainly likes it. We have been out here for some time and it seems to be getting brighter." Mary always had a way of giving God all the glory for everything that happened. I wanted to be like that! I wanted to recognize all his miracles and thank him like she did.

She looked back at the sky and then suddenly turned to me. "I just realized you're here… and it's late! Is everything all right?" I nodded and explained my mother's request. "I told her it would be all right. It is, isn't it?" For the first time since I left my home I thought that maybe I shouldn't have been so presumptuous. But my worries were quickly allayed by Mary's gentle voice. "Of course, Mary. You're always welcome here. Anytime night or day. Are you going to spend the night?" Her beautiful, gentle smile proved to me that I had no worries of intruding on them and I said, "If it's all right with you and Joseph."

Joseph's eyes were fixed on the star. Mary tapped him on the shoulder, but he seemed oblivious. She turned to me, laughing, and said, "I'm not sure with the interest he has in that star if he would even know you were here!" She looked to him again and said, "Joseph, my beloved. Can I have your attention for a moment? Mary would like to…" Mary's words strayed off as Joseph held up his hand as if to stop her. He looked at both of us and said with amazement, "That star! I believe, as I have been staring at, I have been able to see it move ever so slightly. It seems to have gotten just a hair closer to the one that is on its left. Do you see that?" Mary looked up and so did I, but in the short time we observed it, we noticed no movement. "No, Joseph, I'm afraid I don't see what you do. I am going in now to bathe Jesus and get him to bed. Will you be in soon? May I bring you a cloak? It's getting chilly. And do you mind if Mary stays with us tonight?"

Joseph and I started laughing as Mary realized how many questions she had just fired at Joseph. She shook her head and began to laugh with us. Joseph came over and hugged her. "I'll stay out here a little bit longer…and I would like my cloak…and of course Mary is always welcome. Did I cover everything?" We all laughed, and as Jesus watched us, he broke out into giggles, too. Joseph gently kissed Mary and promised to be in soon. The rest of us went into the house. Mary put some water in a small pot that she hung over the fire in their fireplace. "Will you help me bathe Jesus? He loves it when you help because you play with him more than I do. You are truly wonderful with children Mary! I love watching you with your little brother. I hope I can do as well as I get more experience."

I blushed from her words and thanked her. I picked Jesus up and started to undress him. Mary sat next to me and started going through the clothes she had washed to find something to put on him after his bath. I could sense her looking at me. "Mary, is everything all right at home? Is there a reason your mother wanted you to come here tonight?" Her concern for me always touched my heart and I could feel tears begin to form. "Yes, my father is having a party tonight and she was afraid for my safety, I think. They can get pretty wild and she felt I should be somewhere safe. She likes you both and is grateful for the changes in me since I have been coming here."

Mary hugged me. "Your mother loves you very much, though I know you don't feel it sometimes. But I'm curious, has another of your father's friends hurt you or done something that would make her feel this way?" I stiffened in her arms and felt sure that she knew something. "I need to check the water. We don't want it to get too hot." I jumped up and went over to the fireplace. Of course, the water had not had time to get hot, but I stared at it hoping it would quickly. I heard Mary get up and come over to me. She took my hand and I tried to pull away, but she only squeezed harder. "Mary, someday you'll need to let go of these things and share them with me. You will feel better if you will talk about them. You know King David wrote a psalm that talked about how God shines his light in the dark places. These are dark places for you and God can heal them if you'll let him." I turned to her and my tears were flowing now. "I'm not ready, Mary. Father has always said we must keep everything in our family a secret. I'm just not ready." She wiped my tears with her apron and held me until I felt safe. She then looked me directly in the eyes and said, "When you are, I will be here for you and I will pray for you…and God will heal you." Her words penetrated my soul and I knew they were true. I shook my head and promised her I would also pray about it.

We took the water down and poured it into a basin and sat Jesus in it. He immediately started splashing and playing. I tickled him and played with his toes and Mary and I sang songs to him. She knew several of the songs that Joanna's mother knew. The more I played with Jesus' toes, the louder his squealing got. Joseph came in the door with a broad grin on his face. "What are you doing to my son? He sounds as if you are torturing him." Jesus splashed and laughed loudly at the sight of his father. "Mawry tickle me, Abba. Mawry much fun. I wuv Mawry."

My heart felt like it would explode. Though the months spent with him had made me so much more relaxed, at times like these I remembered who he *really* was and I felt so unworthy. I quickly recalled the words Mary had taught me about God's love for me. After wrapping him up, I picked Jesus up and hugged him tightly. I walked over and offered him to Joseph. He kissed him on the forehead and said, "Son, I will be in shortly, I promise. I am so amazed at that star!" He handed Jesus back to me and with that he went back out to leave Mary and I to dress Jesus.

As I was cleaning up, Mary sat and began to nurse Jesus as she always did before his bedtime. When I had finished, I slowly looked around the room. This was such a wonderful evening! The beautiful, clear night outside with the miraculous star in the sky! This small, quaint little house with the soft glow of the fire playing on the walls. And most of all, me here with my friend, as she nursed her baby. I could not imagine a better night! I sat and basked in the peace and love that I was feeling. *This is what life is supposed to be like.* I had just sat down, when Joseph came in. "Mary," he said a little louder than I would have expected. When I looked up, his face had a mixture of concern and amazement. "What is it, Joseph?" she asked. He came over to us and said, "Mary, we have visitors. There are three men here, riding camels and dressed like kings! They say they have come from a long way off and they have been following the same star we have been watching. And it led them to us. They said it was as if the star came to rest over our home! That it was supposed to lead them to a King! To Jesus!"

Mary and I looked at each other and did not know what to say. Joseph kept on talking. "They said they have come to worship him and have brought him gifts. I didn't know what to say to them and offered, 'Yes, I told my wife that the star was moving.' That was such a ridiculous thing to say—they are kings!" Joseph was so excited he was pacing. Mary looked at him and said, "Joseph, calm down. This is God's will for us and we must treat these men with the respect they deserve. Jesus is still awake. Invite them in." Joseph walked to the door without a word and Mary asked me to get some cups of water and to fill the basin with water to wash their feet. As I was filling the basin, I heard the rustle of heavy material. I turned around and saw the first king come into the room. He had to bend over as he came through the door for he was a big man! His clothes were made of velvet and satin and he had much gold hanging from his neck and arms. His crown had many jewels, rubies and sapphires and other stones I did not recognize. He was a large man, in height and width and his presence seemed to fill the room. I found myself hoping the others were not as big or they may not all fit in the house. He had long gray hair and a graying beard and carried a gold walking stick. He looked at Mary and Jesus and immediately bowed down on his knees and put his face to the floor.

I then saw the second man come in. A much slimmer man though just as tall, his clothes were as richly made as the first and had just as much gold and inlaid jewels. He seemed younger than the other and his skin seemed to be darker in color. His hair was brown and he had a much shorter beard. His had chiseled features and he seemed quite focused. He too began to bow down, as I saw the third king come in. This man had a skin color I had never seen before, almost yellow in color, and odd shaped eyes. His hair was very black and he had no beard. His clothes, though a different style from the others, were as rich and lovely as theirs. He too bowed down with his face to the floor. I did not know what to do, so I did nothing except stare in amazement! Joseph had also come in and we were awestruck by the scene being played out before us. All except Jesus. He was trying to reach over and grab the crown off the first king!

There was total silence in the room as we waited for them to rise from the floor. Then I heard them speaking in a language I had never heard. They were all speaking at once, as if they were praying. This went on for some time before the older one sat up on his knees. The others followed suit and as I watched each of them sit up, I noticed they all had been crying. The older one spoke first in a deep voice with a thick accent that reminded me of some of the men that stayed at my father's inn. "Forgive us for intruding on your family at this late hour. We have studied this star for almost two years. We began to follow it many months ago and we knew when we found the place where it rested, there would be a great king, such as the world has never known. Yes, a king of the Jews that would free the people from more than the hold that Rome has on the land...this is a freedom of the heart and soul."

The slimmer man interjected, "We don't even understand all that we feel and to try to express it in words is impossible, but we knew we must bring this magnificent king gifts that would represent his majesty and his future. We have little time to tarry. We stopped in Jerusalem six days ago and talked with King Herod. We asked where we might find this one who had been born king of the Jews. He looked troubled and told us he would check with his holy men and get back to us. After waiting three days, we were going to leave and continue to follow the star without his help. That morning he sent a messenger to ask us to secretly come to him and he would give us the information we wanted. When we arrived at the meeting place, he had great interest in the exact time the star had appeared to us and he told us to come to Bethlehem. He asked us to make a careful search for the child and return to tell him where he was so that he may come and worship also. We thanked him and left. "

The older man began to speak again, "We decided that it was too late in the day to begin our travel so we packed up our things and made ready to leave early in the morning. That night, he (pointing to the third man) had a dream that we must not go back to Herod. We do not know why, but we will obey the dream. We would like to present our gifts now."

I looked at Mary and she looked troubled. She looked at the older man and said, "Sir, before you do, let us offer you some refreshment. And allow us to wash the dust from your feet. Please, you have traveled so far." Mary's eyes were almost pleading and I felt there was more to the offer than just kindness. But all three men were shaking their heads. "No. We must give the gifts and go," said the thinner man. "Your hospitality is appreciated but we must not stay. We had wanted to share our names with you and tell you how to find each of our different countries, so that you may bring the king to visit us, when he is older. But we feel now that we should not." The larger man added, "For your safety. We do not want to alarm you. We are only doing what we believe is right." The large, older man came to Mary and presented her with a beautiful box with jewels embedded all over it. I gasped at the sheer beauty of it! When he opened it, it was full of gold! He placed it at Mary's feet and said, "This represents his king-ship." The second man came and presented her with another bejeweled box. He opened it and the room was filled with a wonderful fragrance. He said, "This contains frankincense. It represents his divinity." He laid this at her feet also.

The third man, the one that had the dream, but had not spoken a word, seemed hesitant to come forward. He looked at the other two and they nodded for him to come forward He slowly came with his box almost hidden under his robes. Before he opened it, he bowed very low and held the box up to Mary without raising his head. His was a plain wooden box and when he opened it, we also smelled a pleasant fragrance, but did not know what it was. The older one said, "This is myrrh. Someday you will understand the meaning this has for him."

Mary looked at him and said, "Please sir. Tell me now whatever it is you need to say. I must know what this box represents." Her hand went to Jesus' head and she began to rub it gently. He lay against her chest and looked as if he would soon be asleep. Her eyes sought the face of the older man and then the slim man. "I beseech you, tell me everything." His eyes looked sorrowful and he slowly shook his head. "The myrrh represents that he is destined for death before old age takes him. We were given the knowledge for these gifts by a power that even we do not understand."

"When we first noticed the star and began a quest to understand it, each of us felt in a place deep inside," he placed his hand over his heart and abdomen and then continued, "that this was a special star, representing a special man. We are merely men ourselves, but this burning in us got so strong that we had to venture out and follow this star to see where it would lead. On our journey we were given the knowledge that this star would help us find the baby that would grow to be the King of the Jews. I can tell you no more than this, for I have no more knowledge myself." They all nodded their heads in agreement.

Mary had tears in her eyes and looked down at Jesus. He had fallen asleep with his head resting on her bosom. She stroked his hair and as she did, it became wet with her tears. I wanted to go to her and hold her like she held me, but I knew this was not the time. She eventually looked up and a smile had replaced her tears. "Thank you for your wise words. Thank you for your beautiful gifts. I will treasure them and ponder the things you have shared with me. Are you sure we can't get you some refreshment?" She looked at me and nodded toward the cups I had filled. I quickly gave them each a cup and they drank down the water and gave the cups back to me. "Thank you child," the larger one said. "Now we must go. We have a long trip and we must find a route that bypasses Jerusalem. You have been so kind to allow us this time to worship. Thank you and we will pray for your safety."

They all turned and one by one they filed out of Mary and Joseph's little house. A thousand things were going through my head, especially how I could not wait to tell Joanna! Joseph went out with them and helped them get their camels watered. He stayed outside until they had mounted and begun to ride away. When he came in, he looked reflective. "The star has lost its brightness. You can still see it, but it seems to blend in with the other stars now." He shook his head and looked at Mary, "This has been quite a night, my dear. How are you feeling?"

Mary looked at him and then looked down at Jesus. "I don't know what I feel, Joseph. They seemed to fear Herod and you know the terrible things we have heard about him. I also look at these gifts and think how special they are... except the one. That one makes me wonder if God picked the right woman for this job. I don't know if I can handle what his future holds." Joseph was at her feet before she even finished the sentence. Taking her hands in his, he gently said, "Mary, don't you ever question what God has done. You are the perfect choice, exactly who our son needs. I know the messages you have heard since Jesus' birth have been a burden on your heart. Simeon's words were very difficult to hear. Tonight, the meaning of this myrrh was hard to hear. But don't ever forget that God is in control of all of this and we have nothing to fear."

Mary looked up at him and placed her hand on his face gently. "And you, Joseph. You are the perfect father for Jesus. God could not have chosen anyone better for his earthly substitute. I am such a blessed woman to have you as my husband." She reached up and hugged his neck. I looked away in embarrassment. These were not things I saw at home. I felt uncomfortable. I picked up the cups and took them outside to rinse them off at the well. I wanted to give them time to talk about all that had transpired. The night was still and cool. Joseph was right. The star had faded considerably.

So much had happened tonight and the wonder of it all was more than I could embrace. Being around Jesus so much, especially watching him play with my little brother, I forgot about his divinity, his kingship, his purpose. He was just a little boy that I loved dearly. But tonight had been a clear reminder of who this little child really was. I felt so honored to be part of his life! To be part of this family! I prayed that nothing would ever take them away from me.

As I was finishing up the last cup, I heard a noise in the distance, like a horse galloping. We seldom saw people on the road after dark and even fewer in this area near the olive groves. I stood and listened a little longer…I was right! There was a rider coming very fast and he seemed to be headed this way. Panic immediately struck my heart! Could this be something to do with those men? I heard my name! "Mary, Mary! Is that you?" The horse came to a sliding stop, only a few cubits in front of me. The rider had dismounted before the horse was completely stopped. At that moment Joseph came out of the house. "What is going on out here? Mary, are you all right? Come over here and get behind me." I ran behind Joseph and as I did he addressed the rider, "Who are you and why have you come here this late at night?" When the man answered, the voice was immediately familiar to me. It was one of the men who helped my father with the animals. A very kind man named Thaddeus.

"I'm most sorry to alarm you and your family, but I have come to get Mary. Her mother is very sick. Her father sent me to get her." I peeked out from behind Joseph's cloak. Thaddeus continued, "Mary, Bartimus needs you to come home so you can help with your brother. Your mother is too weak to even hold him. She has been throwing up for over an hour." He looked up at Joseph and apologized, "Sir, I am sorry. I have been rude not to introduce myself. I am Thaddeus. I work for Mary's father. Again, I am so sorry to have alarmed you."

I had gone in to get my things even before the man finished talking. I went over to Mary who looked very worried and knelt at her feet. "Mary, please pray for us. I don't know what's wrong, but I must get home right away. My mother is very sick. I'm a little afraid because the men, whom my father is entertaining at the inn, are not nice people. That is why my mother wanted me to come here." Mary's face was grieved and she quietly asked, "Have any of those men hurt you, Mary?" I was not prepared for the directness of Mary's question…or the shock that I felt. It wasn't so much the question, as the feelings that it put into motion. Trepidation. Anxiety. Fear. I couldn't answer…because I didn't know!

My stomach was in knots and I felt pressure in my chest that made it hard to breath. She didn't push me for an answer, but instead said, "Do you need Joseph to go with you? He'll be sure you're safe." I briskly shook my head. "Oh, no, Mary! That would not be a good thing at all! I greatly appreciate the offer, but Father never wants anyone knowing his family's business. He would be furious!" Mary continued, "I understand how he feels, but your father is not our concern. You are. If you are in danger, we want to help you." She looked into my eyes, searching for a place that would help her understand the ambiguity she was hearing.

I looked down and tears began to sting my eyes. "Mary, my father would be angry with me if Joseph came. He does not want me sharing anything about our family with anyone! As for the men? I can't answer you, because I don't always remember everything that happens at night. Someone has been hurting me, but I don't have time to talk about it now.

But when Mother gets better, I will come see you and tell you everything. I think you're right; I will feel better if I get this out in the open. But right now, I have to go. Please pray for all of us, especially my mother." I leaned over and hugged her and reinforced the promise I had made. "As soon as I can, I will come back and tell you everything." Mary took my hand and squeezed it hard. "I will be praying for your family." She paused and touched my face. "And I will be praying for your safety. Go now."

I hugged her and started for the door as Joseph came in. "Mary, is this man a person you trust? If not I will take you, myself, to your parents' home. I want you to be honest. It is no trouble for me." I smiled at the way he tried to protect me. "Yes, Joseph. He is a very nice man and I feel safe with him. But if you would pray as I have asked Mary to pray, I would be so grateful." He nodded his head and followed me out. The man had already mounted the horse and I walked over to him. He pulled me up behind him and I wrapped my arms around his waist. Joseph looked up at him with a stern face and warned, "You take very good care of her. She is precious cargo. I will find you myself, if anything happens to her." He winked and flashed a smile. His face became serious again. He looked at me and with genuine sincerity said, "We love you Mary. We will be praying."

5

Abandoned

When Thaddeus and I arrived at home, Father was outside with his friends and they were quite drunk. When I got down from the horse, one of his friends said to him, "Bartimus, who is this beautiful young thing? Have you supplied us with entertainment tonight?" He began to walk toward me, but Thaddeus dismounted quickly and placed himself between the man and me. My father, who was standing near the doorway, yelled out to the man, "Artemis, don't get any ideas! That is my daughter. She is here to take care of Naomi and my son. I told you Naomi was sick." His words were slurred and he almost fell when he started to walk toward us.

As he approached, Thaddeus, in a low voice said, "Bartimus, don't you feel that you should send these people home. I don't like the way they're looking at Mary." Father stumbled as he put his arm around me and I almost fell with his weight. He looked at Thaddeus with a sneer and said, "Do you think that I can't take care of my daughter? Have you forgotten your place? Maybe you would like to find yourself another situation? What I do with my family is none of your business!" He enunciated his last words by pushing his finger into the other man's chest.

Thaddeus did not back down, but addressed him calmly. "Bartimus, I'm not trying to get into your business, but these men are drunk and I wouldn't want things to get out of control and I know you wouldn't want that either." Father seemed to relax and said everything would be fine, that the men were leaving soon. He pulled me close to him and whispered, "How about a little kiss for your old father?" At that moment, I loathed him! I pulled away from him and ran into the corridor that led to Mother's room.

She was lying on her mat and had a foot basin next to her that she was using when she got sick. She was holding her stomach and her face was very pale. I went to her and touched her forehead to see if she had a fever. She opened her eyes and murmured, "Mary, I'm so glad you're here. I think I've thrown up everything that I ate over the last month. I've never felt so bad." I took her hand and held it to my face. "Do you know what's wrong, Mother? Do we need to get you to a physician?" My voice trailed off as I heard someone stumbling down the hall. It was a shuffling walk, one that was familiar to me. I shuddered and held my breath as the footsteps came to my mother's door. It was Father. He stumbled in and looked at me and said, "There you are! I wondered where you went in such a hurry! I'm glad you're here with your mother. Do you know what's wrong with her?"

Before I could answer Mother screamed at him, "You know what's wrong with me! That fool, Artemis! You say he's such a good friend!" My mother's voice was dripping with sarcasm. Father looked confused and then laughed. "Oh, Naomi! He was playing around! You take things too seriously." He began to give her that smile and slowly shake his head. I could feel Mother trembling with rage. "That simpleton threw me over his shoulder and carried me around and you did nothing but laugh! Well, I didn't think it was funny! What kind of a husband are you?" I patted her shoulder, hoping she would calm down, but she shrugged off my hand. "You need to get out of here before I tell all your little friends what you really are and how you spend your spare time!" This time it was Mother who had the smile on her face and vengeance in her voice. I looked up at Father and watched as the smile melted from his face and was replaced with a look of apprehension. My mother knew she had the upper hand now and she didn't stop, "If you don't leave right now, I will tell Mary everything, Bartimus. Don't test me!" Her eyes held his until he finally looked down. He looked defeated. He turned and slowly left the room.

I didn't know what to say or if I should say anything. Mother began to weep and I asked her what she had been referring to when she said she would "tell me." She was looking at her hands in her lap and shook her head. "That Artemis! He was drunk. I had been in the sewing room and he kept coming to the door asking me to join them and I ignored him. Later, I was getting up to use the latrine, and he grabbed me in the corridor, threw me over his shoulder and carried me out to the courtyard. I was furious! And your father stood there and laughed. Just laughed! I was so humiliated! Then all the other men began to laugh! I ran back here to my room."

I looked at her and wondered if this had anything to do with her feeling sick. I knew how shame could make your stomach feel. "Mother, do you think that is what made you sick?" She wiped her eyes and slowly shook her head. "No, Mary. I did a stupid thing. I got so mad; I decided that I would be as big a fool as your father and embarrass *him* for a change! I went into the room where he keeps the amphorae of wine and poured out a jug for myself. Then I came in here and proceeded to drink the whole thing. I knew Bartholomew would probably not wake up, so I threw care to the wind!" I realized for the first time that my brother was not here with her. "Where is he, Mother?" I did not trust any of those men outside. She looked at me and smiled. "Don't worry. He is in your room sound asleep. I passed out at some point and when I woke up, I was sick. I don't think I stopped for thirty minutes. Your father drove me to that, Mary."

I grabbed both her hands and pleaded. "Mother, please let's leave. We could go stay with your brother or we could go back to Magdala. Anything! You don't need to live this way and neither does Bartholomew! I could help you pack and we could leave in the morning." I was practically begging her to end this madness that we lived in! She looked at me shaking her head. "I will not leave all my things so he can bring some trollop in here and benefit from my hard work. Never!"

I knew it was useless, we had been here before, so I dropped the subject, picked up the basin and headed for the latrine. On the way, Artemis and another man I didn't recognize passed me. I had to step out of the way to keep from running into them. I heard one whisper something and then I heard tittering. I felt such revulsion for both of them and then, "Mary, why don't you come out and dance for us. I bet you can really move!" More laughter. The blood had rushed to my face, not with embarrassment but with anger. I turned and walked back to them and shoved the basin in their faces. "Do you know what that is? If you don't want to be wearing it, I would suggest you don't talk to me or my mother the rest of the night." The shock on both of their faces was priceless and I heard one of them say, "Leave her alone; let's go!" I was starting to feel some of what my mother had felt earlier and when they turned to walk the other way, I volunteered, "Good choice, gentlemen!"

I dumped out the basin and went to the well to rinse it out. I thought I'd better get some fresh water for Mother to drink, surely my father would not remember. I fetched a water jar and filled it for her and headed back to her room. My brother came to my mind again and I decided to check on him first. In my room, my mother had left a candle burning for him and he was sleeping soundly. I thanked God for that and knelt down to kiss him. I covered up his little body and quietly whispered, "We must both pray for our mother to have the wisdom of Solomon and take us away from here. We will go to Mary and Joseph's tomorrow and seek their advice. I love you Bartholomew."

But there would be no going anywhere for the next three days. Father was on a rampage! It was non-stop work from morning till night. Every time I thought I had my chores done, he would find something else for me to do. I could not get any help from Mother either. They had argued relentlessly since the night of his party. She had lost her adamant tone from that night and had become apathetic. She didn't come out of her room at all and I was left to care for my brother as well as the chores. I longed to spend time with Mary and tell her what happened the other night. I was kind of proud of myself for standing up to those two men. Even more, I'd become excited about unloading all my past and I longed for the relief that Mary had promised me. I diligently prayed for Father to run out of things to assign me.

The sun was beginning to set. It had been another long day and I thought there was a thread of hope to leave in the morning and visit my friends. Father had been sleeping in one of the rooms on the upper level for the last three nights and tonight he was in the courtyard drinking wine. He was not in a bad mood, at least from what I could judge. I asked him if I could go visit Mary and Joseph under the pretense that they wanted me to help with Jesus. I bravely added that it would be fun for Jesus if I could take my brother. "I don't care, Mary. Did you ask your mother?" I shook my head and he said, "I better go ask her then. I haven't seen her since this morning." I didn't think it was wise to bother her, but when I suggested this to Father he said, "I don't know if it is or not... and I honestly don't care!" With that he got up and headed for their room.

I sat on the bench and waited, silently praying there would be no objections. Within minutes my father was running toward me and yelling for our servants. "What is wrong, Father?" I cried. He looked worried. "I don't know Mary! I can't wake up your mother! We need to get her to the physician in the city!" One of the servants had come into the courtyard and said, "The only physician in Bethlehem has moved and has not been replaced. You will have to take her to Jerusalem."

My father ran his thick fingers through his hair and ordered, "Get the wagon and the oxen. Mary, pack up some things for all of us. Enough for a couple days at least. I don't know how long we will be gone. I will get your mother." My heart was pounding... I was scared! What could be wrong with her? I went to gather things to pack for the trip. I had wanted to visit Jerusalem, but not under these circumstances! I also thought that it would be another few days before I could see my friends. *That's a pretty selfish thought; your mother and brother need you right now.* I shook my head and continued packing.

When I had finished packing, I ran back down to the courtyard. Father already had her in the wagon on some hay with lots of blankets. Bartholomew was asleep next to her. "Father, what is wrong with her? Did she get hurt somehow?" I was leaning over the side of the wagon trying to see her face. It was covered with her hair. As I tried to move the hair from her eyes, he grabbed me and pulled me into the back of the wagon. The smell of wine was strong on his breath. "I don't know what is wrong with her." His voice sounded more disgusted than worried and I knew to say nothing else. I scooted down as close as I could get to her and pulled my brother onto my lap. As I bent down to kiss her, I thought I smelled wine. I sniffed closer to her mouth and I was right! She reeked of it! I couldn't believe she had drunk again! And so soon after her last sickness! This worried me even more.

My father got in the front of the wagon and turned to look at me. "Get yourself comfortable. It is going to be a rough ride and I'm not stopping." With that he turned and clucked to the oxen and we were off. I moved some of the blankets around and made a bed for my brother and myself.

I was so worried. Mother and I had been so much closer since we went to her brother's a few years ago. There were still some tense times, but she was more protective of me now. She felt I had changed. She was right! My time with Mary and her family had transformed me into a new person. I also got to see a lot more of Deborah and Joanna because they often came to visit when I was there. I had learned so much about Jehovah and had begun to accept him as my own.

I was perplexed about the drinking. What could have happened that would make my mother drink wine again? It had made her so sick only a few days ago and I couldn't imagine her doing it again. I also didn't understand why she wasn't throwing up like the last time. I wanted to ask my father, but I knew it wasn't wise, not now. I still found myself wishing I could see Mary before we left. It was selfish, but I was so close to getting it all out. I just wanted to do it!

My thoughts went back to the three men who had come to visit Jesus. It was amazing to me that they'd studied that star for such a long time and then ventured out to follow it without knowing for sure where it would lead. Mary had been quiet, her face revealing a mixture of joy and sadness. It was the same look she had the night Jesus was born after the shepherds came. I saw it one other time when she shared with me about Simeon's words, when they took Jesus to Jerusalem for dedication and circumcision. She said she had tucked these things away in her heart.

I snuggled up close to Bartholomew and began to pray for my mother. I knew that whatever it was, Jehovah could take care of it. My mother stirred in her sleep and I reached over and gently rubbed her head. "I'm here, Mother. I'll take care of you." I continued to caress her, combing her long, black hair with my fingers until I started to drift off. The last thing I remember saying was "I love you, Mother."

I awoke to sounds like thunder. I looked up at the sky and the stars and moon shown brightly, so I didn't know what the noise could be. The covers had slipped off Mother so I covered her up and I also covered Bartholomew completely, even his head. His little cheeks were cold and I did not want him getting sick. I tucked the blankets under Mother so he would not roll out and I sat up in the wagon and asked father what the noise was. It was getting louder and louder. He yelled at me to lie back down; that some riders on horses were coming. Before I did, I noticed him pulling a large club out from under a blanket on the seat beside his. He pulled it closer to him and covered it again with the blanket. I lay there with my heart pounding! I knew Father carried the club in case of any trouble. The traders and caravans along this road could be dangerous. I was grateful for Mother being asleep. She would be terrified.

The noise was getting louder until I had to put my hands over my ears. Then, I saw soldiers riding by on each side of the wagon; they seemed to be in a great hurry! The line of riders looked endless! Soon the noise decreased and I thought they had all passed, when I heard a voice ask us to stop! Now I was really afraid! What if they tried to hurt Father? I couldn't protect us!

We came to a slow stop and I craned my neck as far as I could without actually sitting up. I saw the soldier removing his helmet and lean over to say something to my father. I heard laughter and then, "Bartimus, I did not expect to see you on the road tonight. In fact I was going to give you some business. We are on an urgent mission from Herod." He paused and with disgust in his voice added, "He would not let us leave in the morning, so I knew we would have to bunk down tonight. We will need plenty of rest for the work we must do tomorrow." He leaned down from his horse and confidentially added, "I was hoping you might find some young women for my soldiers after we were finished." My father shook his head and pointed to the back of the wagon. The soldier nodded his head and continued, "Where are you going at this hour?"

Father explained everything to him and then asked what he was doing for Herod. The soldier shook his head and said, "Nasty work, Bartimus. If I'd known I would have to do this kind of thing as a soldier, I would never have enlisted." He was obviously not going into any more detail. Father explained that he didn't know how long we would be in Jerusalem. "But if you want to take your men to stay at the inn, you can leave the usual amount for me in the empty amphora in the corner of the room where you usually sleep. We can settle up later if there are any additional charges. And as to the other matter..." I heard my father chuckle, "I can't help you this time, but next time I promise your money's worth." Both men laughed this time and I felt sick to my stomach. I pulled myself closer to my brother and almost covered his body with mine. I was not totally sure I understood the conversation, but I got the gist of it. Here my mother is sick and he is talking about other women! I heard them whisper something else to each other and laugh again and then I saw the soldier riding past me.

I heard father cluck to the oxen and we started off again. He said something to me, but I pretended to be asleep. For some reason, memories of my nighttime "visitations" had surfaced. I usually never thought of them anymore since they had stopped a few months ago, but as I remembered them, my body was reacting in a way that was confusing to me. I did not want to feel this way, but it was out of my control. I immediately began to pray. "Please take away these feelings. I don't want to feel them, especially because I sometimes think they feel good. I want to be pure, like Mary taught me.

Please make them stop." I lay very quietly and continued to pray and soon fell asleep.

We stayed in Jerusalem four days. After we arrived, the physician examined Mother and was able to arouse her. He said she had admitted to ingesting some opium and the combination of that with the wine explained her sound sleep. He made us wake her and keep her awake for many hours, forcing her to drink water every few minutes. She was not very happy with us, but I was willing to face her wrath if it would make her better. The physician said she would not be strong enough to travel for at least three more days. I knew that put a thorn in my father's side and he wanted to make sure my mother paid for it.

As soon as she was lucid, my father reamed her about drinking wine. His tone was one of disgust as he said, "Only whores drink wine, Naomi. Not a wife of mine. What kind of example have you set for your daughter? You are possessed and hopeless!" I prayed that he would stop and leave her alone. She looked so haggard. I did not know what this "opium" was or how Mother had gotten it. I especially did not understand why she took it. I hoped she would talk to me after Father left to go the market.

When we were alone, I asked her about what had happened. She explained she was tired of dealing with all of Father's adultery. She had found evidence of yet another woman that my father had been with and when she confronted him, he had said the usual—Mother was crazy, it was all in her head and she was possessed! I again wanted to ask her to leave him, to end all this pain, when I realized... that is exactly what she had tried to do! How could I help her? I wanted so badly to talk to Mary and ask for her advice and prayers. Mother needed to meet them and learn the things I had learned so she could have peace, too. I came out of my reverie when she asked where Father was. I explained he had gone to the market to buy things to take back with us. She nodded and then asked for Bartholomew. I pointed to a mat across the room where he was playing with some things the innkeeper had provided for him. He seemed to not have a care in the world and I was glad for that! Mother said she would like to rest some more until Father came back, so I went to play with my brother and continued to count the minutes until I could get back to my friends.

When my father returned, he hastily got our things together and instructed me to get my mother and brother into the wagon while he hooked up the oxen. We were walking down the steps of the inn when Mother muttered, "Look! I guess my sickness didn't affect him too much." In the back of the wagon, cushioned between bags of wheat and grain, were several amphorae of wine. I never understood why they were made the way they were with such a skinny base and a wide body. Father had said it had something to do with being able to sink them in the sand and keep them cool. I only cared that they didn't fall on us during our trip home. We all climbed in, with me helping Mother. She was still very weak. Father finished with the oxen and climbed in. He didn't even turn around, just slapped the reins and we were on our way. As Mother and Bartholomew slept, I promised myself I would see Mary and Joseph tonight if I had to wait for everyone to go to sleep before I left! I silently prayed, thanking Jehovah for my mother's recovery and then added my request: that nothing else would get in the way of me seeing my friends!

I fell asleep next to my little brother for the short trip home. When we arrived, Father climbed down and gave me orders to take care of the animals and he would unload the wagon. He didn't even try to help Mother down. He immediately went to the amphorae and began to carry them into the room where he always stored his wine. I went to the back of the wagon and helped my mother and brother down. She stopped to hug me and thanked me for helping her so much. I blushed and asked, "Mother when I get the oxen watered, may I go see my friends. I left them praying for you, the night you got sick and they'd probably like to know how you are. Would it be all right with you?" She nodded and gave me another hug and whispered in my ear, "Yes, and take Joshua so you can get there faster. Don't worry about your father. I'll take care of him." I hugged her as tight as I could and said, "Thank you, Mother. Thank you so much."

I arrived at their house in no time. Joshua wanted to run and I was more than willing to let him. When I jumped down and led him around to the back of the house to give him water, I realized that Mary and Joseph's donkey was gone. I thought that was strange and I considered that Joseph may have gone into the city to get supplies. I finished watering Joshua and walked around to the front door. Though my heart was filled with anticipation, I knocked first. There was no answer. I knocked again. Nothing. My heart seemed to stop beating and when it began again it was pounding in my chest. This was silly. What was I afraid of? I pushed the door open and said, "Mary! Didn't you hear me…?" I stopped in mid-sentence. The house was empty! Not a single thing was left! What was going on? The afternoon sun was streaming in the side window and I saw something sparkle in the sunlight. I walked over to the mat where Mary and Jesus usually sat. It had been the only item in the house when they arrived. On the mat was Mary's necklace! My chest began to tighten and I felt a lump forming in my throat! Where were they? I picked up the necklace, put it around my neck so I would not lose it and ran outside.

I decided to head for Joanna's to see if her family knew anything about their whereabouts. I didn't think there had been foul play because all their things were gone, things that would not be valuable to a robber. No, I believed they had left and I had to find out where they had gone! I rode Joshua hard, apologizing the whole way. He seemed to sense my urgency and gave me all he had. I barely slowed enough to stop when I arrived at their home and Benjamin, who was outside working, yelled out, "Whoa, there, Mary! What is wrong? Is someone hurt?" I jumped off Joshua and breathlessly asked him, "Where are Mary and Joseph? I just came from their house and they are gone! The only thing left was this necklace that belonged to Mary!" I held it up for him to see.

Benjamin looked perplexed. "We have not seen them for over a week. There have been terrible things happening here and I have not been working. Here, come in the house and let's talk with Deborah also." We walked in and Deborah came over to greet and hug me. I dodged her and repeated everything that I had said to Benjamin. "I'm really upset because, if something bad had happened, there would be some of their things still there. But there was nothing except this." I showed Deborah the necklace. By this time Joanna and Lydia had both come into the room. Both of them tried to embrace me and I pushed them away. I was sorry after seeing the hurt look on their faces, but I had to find out where Mary had gone! There was audible silence in the room.

Deborah spoke first. "Let's sit down and talk, Mary. First, we have been very worried about you and your family as well as Mary and her family. Some things have been happening that I'm sure you're aware of, in the city and on the outskirts." I shook my head and explained that we had been in Jerusalem because Mother was sick. I noticed her exchange a look with Benjamin and I felt my anger building. She began again. "So, you know nothing of the soldiers coming to Bethlehem?" My thoughts immediately went back to the night we met the soldiers on the road and I told them what had happened. Deborah's eyes became slits and her voice dropped. I didn't think I had ever seen this woman upset, but this looked like anger. "You mean to tell me that your Father put these animals up while they did their abhorrent work for Herod! He deserves to be…"

Benjamin interrupted her, "Deborah! That's enough! We don't know the whole story and Bartimus was with his family." She had not calmed down yet. "He has no reason to even be doing business with them! Nothing means anything to him except money!" Benjamin gave her a look that finally caused her to back down. I was so confused; I did not know what to think. "Could someone please tell me what happened here," I pleaded. Just then, a woman came out of one of the sleeping rooms, looking as if she had just been awakened. "Is everything all right, Deborah? I heard yelling and I woke up." Deborah got up and went to her. "Yes, Esther. Go back to sleep. You have not slept in days. Everything is all right." The woman looked at me and then turned to go back to the room. I soon heard weeping.

Deborah started to say something and Benjamin held up his hand. "I will tell her what happened. Mary, you can count it a great blessing that you were in Jerusalem. Herod sent the soldiers that passed you. He had ordered them to kill all the babies two years old and younger. We think it must have been only boys, because they went to Deborah's sister's home and spared her daughter who was 9 months old, but…" Deborah had begun to cry. "Well, they killed her son. He was almost two. That is Esther, Deborah's sister in the other room. The soldiers came here just before she arrived and questioned if we had any sons. When Esther got here and told us what happened, for the first time in my life, I was glad God had only blessed me with daughters! Esther is a widow and will probably stay with us for awhile."

I could hardly breathe! Bartholomew could have been killed if Mother had not gotten sick! Then it struck me! "What of Jesus," I cried. Benjamin nodded. "I don't know, Mary. Let's take the wagon and go to the house and see if we can find anything that may explain what happened." I nodded in agreement, jumped up and went outside to get Joshua. He was lathered up pretty good and I had not given him water.

"While you get the oxen hitched up, may I water my horse?" Deborah answered, "Of, course, Mary." She started to say something else, but I turned away. I had such a mixture of emotions swimming in my head right now; I didn't feel like being friendly to anyone! Not even Joanna could comfort me, though she tried. I just wanted to get to the bottom of this whole thing!

I finished watering Joshua and asked if I could give him a rest by tying him to the back of the wagon. They were happy to have me ride with them and I was sure Joshua didn't mind. The ride to the little house was a quiet one. No one spoke a word. When we pulled up into the yard, even Benjamin shook his head. "I believe you are right, Mary. They have gone. The pieces that I had asked Joseph to fix for me are here, completed, and I never paid him. If someone came here to rob them, they would have taken these pieces. He was supposed to bring them to me this week." We all went inside and found nothing that could give us a clue of their whereabouts. Benjamin spoke up, "I'm sure they went before the soldiers arrived." Sadly, he shook his head. "I will have a hard time replacing Joseph. He was the best carpenter I have ever had work for me."

I was becoming irritated with what I considered small talk. The lump in my throat felt like it was going to strangle me and I was doing everything I could to hold back the tears. "Where are they?" I yelled. I startled Lydia, who began to cry. "I have to find them. Mary said she would never leave me and she would always be here for me. Where is she?" I started pacing around the room and nothing that any of them said relieved the pressure in my chest. Benjamin tried to comfort me. "Mary, I'm sure they will return in time. I know they were happy here and I know Mary feels about you as you do for her. She always prayed for you and..." I spun around in disgust. "I don't want to hear anything about prayer! And I don't want to hear anything about how much she cares about me! If she did, she wouldn't have left!" I saw the shock on everyone's face, but I couldn't stop. "And if you cared about me, you would have stopped them from leaving! I don't want to see any of you again!"

I ran past all of them and went outside. I was sobbing so hard, I could hardly see. Joanna came out and grabbed my arm. "Mary, please listen..." I shook her arm off, ran to the back of the wagon and untied Joshua. I jumped up and before I could leave, Joanna was at my side. She grabbed Joshua's reins and looked up at me. "Mary, I know you are hurt. But nothing has changed. Mary does love you. The whole family does. None of us know what happened, but we should be grateful for their safety! Mary, you must know that Jehovah loves you and so do we." I yanked the reins from her hand and leaned over and through clenched teeth said, "I want nothing to do with your Jehovah! I want nothing to do with your God! I want nothing to do with you!" I turned and galloped away as fast as Joshua could carry me. I cried the whole way home.

My mind was saturated with thoughts of the last two years. They had been the most meaningful and happy days of my life. The time we spent together, however, obviously meant nothing to them! Then the voice. *Did you really think you meant something to them, Mary? They don't think you are worth the dirt on their feet! Why do you always fill your head with such notions? And this Jehovah that you have wasted your time learning about? Can you see him? Can you touch him? Do you hear him speak to you? He is a fantasy. A delusion. A false hope for hopeless people who have nothing else to do all day than dream about a god that they believe loves them. A god has more important things to do than want a relationship with us! There are too many people in the world to think that he has the time for each of us. Those are the musings of mad men. Mary, face it, your father is right! Gods are for the weak and feeble. Why do you think he has so*

*much money? He doesn't buy into these lies! Just remember.
The only important thing is you. Living for you and making
yourself happy! No one else ever will!*
I shook my head hard and realized I was getting one of
my headaches. I had not had one in quite a while. The voice
in my head had said many things I did not want to believe.
But I also felt there was some truth in those words! I shook
my head again. I didn't know what to think right now. My
eyes were burning terribly and I needed to let Joshua cool
down. I slowed him to a trot and then a walk. I could not stop
the tears. I felt totally empty inside. Rejected. Abandoned.
If they cared about me, Mary would have left a note. She
had taught me how to read and write. Even if they had been
in a hurry, she could have written enough to explain *something!* No, the voice was right. I was just a tool for them to
use until they had finished with me and then they could toss
me away. I was sure wherever they went they would find
someone else just like me!
I saw the inn masking the setting sun and felt empty
inside. I didn't recognize until today, how totally dependent
I had become on Mary. She had been my lifeline to something better. I had wanted so desperately to tell her about
my secrets, but now I would have to keep them to myself. I
would, eventually forget in time. I would just not think about
them anymore. Actually, I realized, I had thought about my
troubles a lot less *before* I met Mary! Maybe her friendship
had not been as good for me as I thought! I walked Joshua
to the stable and spent a lot of time brushing him. No matter
how hard I tried to make Mary out to be a bad person, the tears
kept coming! I thought about that night, two years ago when I
had first met them and all the magical events that surrounded
it. *That's all it was, Mary. Magic. Let it go. Let them go. Move
on with your life!* I realized my headache was getting worse
and I kissed Joshua's blaze and bid him goodnight.

I went to the well and pulled up enough water to wash up. While I was rinsing off my face, my fingers touched the necklace. I had forgotten about it! Why would Mary leave her family heirloom? If there were anything I thought she would be sure not to forget, it would have been that! *Well, at least you got one thing out of the time you spent with them.* I felt such bitterness with that thought, it actually scared me! I began to walk back to my room. I started to pray that my parents would be asleep and promptly stopped myself. "Praying won't be necessary anymore," I said out loud. Everyone was asleep and I was grateful. I wanted no inquisitions tonight. I changed my clothes, lit my candle and lay on my mat. I wanted to write something, but I had nothing with which to write. I lay there and words started forming in my head. I just let them come and as they did, I recited them over and over until I finally fell asleep.

Most things can be broken only once.
Some can be mended.
The heart is an exception to this rule.
The difference is the heart can't be mended.
It just goes on breaking into smaller and smaller pieces.
Until nothing is left, but some remnants of love.

6

New alliances

Many, lonely months passed. My fifteenth birthday came and went with a small celebration that amounted to the immediate family having a special lamb stew, my mother's favorite fig and pistachio cakes and a gift of a new bridle for Joshua. It was a stark realization of how few friends I had. I didn't grasp the extent of my emotional connection to the two families I had come to know and trust, until they were out of my life. Without having that outlet, the monotony of the routine at the inn began to get me down and I became introspective and resentful. My mother even noticed the change and asked me why I did not visit my friends anymore. I answered with a simple, "They moved." She seemed concerned about me because I had become so quiet and told me I did not seem happy anymore. She even suggested I go see Joanna. She volunteered to cover for me with Father. But I declined stating we had "grown apart." I knew that I had said things to Joanna's family in anger that were not true and were not fair. But I also saw them as a reminder of the betrayal I felt by Mary.

This became a reality when Deborah, Joanna and Lydia came to see my mother and me for a visit. It appeared to be a visit so Deborah could spend time with Mother, but I felt it was more of a visit to see how I was doing. That would normally have been a good thing, but now I seemed to resent them in my life. At first, I felt excited to see them when the wagon pulled into the courtyard, but that feeling was soon replaced with memories of happier times that could no longer be.

Joanna and Lydia jumped down from the wagon and came running toward me. Lydia held her arms open as she always did and hugged me with all her might. "Mary, I have missed you so much! Are you still angry with us?" Joanna came up behind Lydia and smiled at me and then told Lydia that it wasn't nice to ask questions like that. Lydia looked at her with confusion on her face and said, "Why not? You and mother say it all the time!" I couldn't hide my chuckle. Joanna smiled at me. "It's good to see you again, Mary. It's good to hear you laugh. We've all worried whether you were still upset; we've missed you." I looked down and patted the top of Lydia's head and continued to hug her. I refused to look at Joanna. "I have missed all of you, too. I'm sorry for the things I said. I was deeply hurt and I still am. I don't understand what happened and I probably never will, but I have to move on with my life. Seeing you... it just brings back the pain of them leaving me." I fought the tears that were trying to creep into my eyes. I had become very good at swallowing my emotions.

"I'm sorry, Mary. I know that you're hurt. If you could just..." I looked up and held up my hand and stopped her. "I don't want to hear anything else, Joanna. I'm doing a lot better than I was and I did it all on my own with no help from anyone. I have a lot of chores I need to get done." I saw Deborah beginning to walk our way and I did not want a confrontation with her so I gave Lydia another quick hug and then reached over and hugged Joanna and turned to leave. I heard Deborah call out my name, but I kept walking and turned into the corridor that led to my room. I don't know how long they stayed. I never went back outside. It had to be this way so I could emotionally survive.

Not long after that visit, my father hired a new servant that would live across the courtyard from our quarters. We had only two other servants that we provided lodging for and they were both men. This was the first woman we had provided a home for and she had a daughter my age. Father said we needed more help because Mother was doing less and less. This was true. She spent more and more time in her room sleeping or sewing or going places with Bartholomew. In the process, Father and I seemed to do more things together. We had been riding horses a lot and he took me on some of his trips. As long as I kept my distance when he was drinking, I felt somewhat safe. I hated when he drank wine because he always asked me to kiss him or sometimes he would just do it. He also talked about how my breasts were getting larger. But it only seemed to happen when he was drinking.

I met the new servant and her daughter at the well just a few days after they moved in. They both seemed really nice and introduced themselves to me. The mother's name was Tamar and the daughter was Elizabeth. They both looked very thin and unkempt. I was not sure if Elizabeth was going to be a potential friend or not. She said nothing and did not even look at me when I said hello. I told them that I was glad they were here to help us. Tamar thanked me, took her water and left. I watched as they walked away and noticed they didn't speak to each other either.

The next several months went quickly. The volume of people coming through the inn was fairly steady, with big crowds that usually coincided with a pilgrimage to Jerusalem. Elizabeth finally opened up a little and I found out that her father had died when she was two and her mother had no other family, so she had been virtually shunned. They were Jews that had little to do with the people anymore. Her mother had to go to work to support them and sometimes the work had not been pleasant. Whatever job she did, she had to keep Elizabeth with her and that reduced her opportunities dramatically. Elizabeth shared that she spent many nights alone.

One day we had finished our chores and I asked her if she would like to go riding. She hesitated and I said, "You'll love it, Elizabeth! There's so much power in it! You feel free!" She smiled at me and nodded and we headed up to the stable. Even though she and I had become friends, she was still very quiet. Having a conversation with her was difficult. I had been a little concerned because on a couple of occasions, I thought I had smelled wine on her breath. I dismissed it because she was only a year older than me. But it nagged at me and I decided that today I would ask her about it. We pulled out Joshua and the little chestnut mare that my sister used to ride and brushed them down. I asked her if she had ever ridden and she said only a few times, so I knew that the chestnut was a good choice. Salome had been a tentative rider; she really rode only because my father forced her.

After I reminded her how to mount and control her horse, we rode around in the pasture until she felt comfortable. Then we headed east toward the mountains and just walked and talked. I shared a little with her about my sister and how different things had been when she was alive. She told me about her life of traveling with her mother and how many awful things had happened to them both. The first job her mother got after her father died had been working for a stonecutter, cleaning his house. One night he came to the room he provided for them. He had been drinking and started saying things to her mother that scared her and before she knew it, her mother was being raped. Elizabeth saw the whole thing. Not long after that her mother had started working as a prostitute and Elizabeth spent almost every night alone. When she was eleven, one of her mother's regulars came to their house to find Tamar. He, too, was drunk and when her mother was not to be found, he had his way with Elizabeth.

"That's terrible, Elizabeth! What did your mother do?" Elizabeth slowly shook her head and answered, "Nothing, my mother could do nothing. A prostitute has very few friends and her word is dirt. This man held a high place in society and no one would have believed her anyway. After that, she gave up being a prostitute and only worked during the day. The money was not as good, so we had to move every few months. I started finding ways to forget the embarrassment of our lifestyle." She looked really sad and I thought I saw tears falling behind the long hair that seemed to always hang in her face. I understood her need to forget painful things. Though the man did not come to my room anymore, I had still found going to my safe place comforting. But even that was not working these past few months. To make it worse, many things I hadn't remembered until now were beginning to surface. I didn't know what to do with all the shame that I was carrying and had become more and more depressed. I decided to share some of these things with Elizabeth and find out what she did to forget.

"Well, when I was eight, I started trying the beer and wine that my mother always had. She sometimes traded for them instead of for money. There was a Samaritan man that would bring her large jugs of beer and a Persian man gave her wine every time he would travel through Jerusalem. At first I thought it tasted nasty but then I realized how giddy it made me feel and it was worth the bitter flavor. Soon, though, I began to like the taste and found it helped me stay numb." I interrupted her to ask what she meant. "Mary, it's hard to describe, but I guess it feels like my problems are far, far away... at least temporarily. Nothing has really changed when I wake up the next morning, except for a sick stomach and headache. The pain is still there, but for a time, I can escape the shame attached to it."

Elizabeth mused. "I had to start watching how much I drank so my mother would not miss it. She was usually much worse off than I was, and I only got caught on two occasions. One of those was pretty bad. My boyfriend had spent the day with me while she was at work and she came home early. She caught us... you know, together... and beat him the whole way down the street! Then she came back and did the same to me. I didn't drink for a while after that. But then I ...." Her voice trailed off and I had to lean in to hear what she was saying. When she didn't start talking again, I asked if she was all right.

She seemed to ignore my question, but said, "Mary, could we stop for a while? There's a group of trees up ahead and I would like to rest in the shade." Her voice was barely audible. I agreed and we trotted up to the little oasis and dismounted. I led the horses to the small pool of water and left them drinking. I returned to where Elizabeth was sitting with her back against a palm tree and looking off into the distance as if she was daydreaming. I sat down next to her and realized for the first time that she was truly an attractive girl. Her hair was off her face and blowing lightly in the wind and her features were more visible. She had high cheekbones and olive skin not unlike my own. Her eyes slanted up slightly, a little like a cat's would. She seemed oblivious to everything around her and did not seem to notice when I leaned back against the tree. It was peaceful here and it made me think of the feeling I got when I was around Jesus and Mary. *Oh, I missed them so much! Why did they have to leave me? Would I ever see them again?* I felt the tears begin to flow that I had kept pent up for many, many months. Elizabeth reached over and took my hand and began to speak.

"Something bad happened, Mary, which I just can't get out of my head. I started to tell you that I stopped drinking after my mother caught the boy and I together. But then I found out I was pregnant. She was really angry with me. I was only thirteen and she said she could not support both a baby and me. Because we had no family, she had no place to send me. She said she knew a midwife that could get rid of the baby. I begged her not to make me do it; I loved children. But she wouldn't listen. It was horrible, Mary. They gave me this nasty tonic to drink and then put some kind of leaves inside of me and it hurt so much. It made me have severe cramps. Then the pain became unbearable. I remember screaming for my mother and asking her to make it stop. She went and got the midwife and after a few hours, they told me it was over. I felt like my insides had been pulled out and stomped on. I bled for days after that and then... it finally stopped.

One night I asked my mother why I had to get rid of my baby and she told me she understood how I felt. I was crying and she put her arm around me and told me that she had become pregnant by that stonecutter and had to do the same thing. I had looked at her in horror and said, 'But that would have been my little brother or sister!' I still remember her face...it looked shattered and then she got up, looked down at me and said, 'Yes, and you would have had my grand-child.' She just walked away and we never talked about it again. But she drank a lot more after that and so did I. My baby would have been almost three years old this month."

Elizabeth put her head down and began to weep. I held her and cried with her. I couldn't understand how someone so young could have been through so much pain, but I knew how I felt when I lost Salome and I think I finally understood a little better, my mother's pain. After a time, Elizabeth straightened up and wiped her eyes. She pulled her hair away from her face and shook her head as if to clear it of some invisible spider web, then reached under her mantle. Hanging from her belt was a wine skin and she pulled it out and began to drink.

I was so shocked! "Elizabeth, aren't you afraid of getting in trouble? Won't your mother smell it on your breath?" She shook her head. "No, she drinks all day, so she can't smell it. But just to be on the safe side I keep this." She reached to her other side to a small pouch that had some dried herbs in it. She pulled some out and offered them to me. "If you just chew a few of these, it hides the smell. That's how my mother hides it from the people she works for," she chuckled softly and added, "including your father." I tasted them and they weren't unpleasant. I was very curious about the taste of the wine and, even more, the way it made her feel, that I decided to be brave and ask if I could try it.

"Elizabeth, do you think I could try some?" She didn't hesitate. As she handed me the wine skin, I realized my mouth was dry and I swallowed hard in anticipation. I was thinking about how my mother would kill me if she found out. I didn't even want to think about what Father would do. I took the skin and held it over my head and let the rich, red liquid flow into my mouth. It was tepid and had an acidy taste. I swallowed several times before returning it to Elizabeth. The warmness of the liquid slid down my throat and seemed to spread throughout my body. It was a strange, but pleasant feeling. Elizabeth looked over at me and said, "So what do you think, Mary? Is it what you expected?" I leaned back against the tree and just sat for a few minutes. Soon I felt so relaxed. I thought if it felt this good with a little, what if I drink some more! "I think I like it! It doesn't taste all that great, but I love the way it makes me feel. Can I have some more?" Elizabeth handed it to me and for the next several minutes we just passed the skin back and forth until it was gone.

We both sat there and said very little, enjoying the feeling. My head felt foggy and I wasn't able to concentrate on anything. My cares and concerns did seem far away. *Really, this is not that bad, certainly not what I had expected!* I had begun to perspire profusely so I removed my outer shawl. I shut my eyes so I could enjoy the feeling even more, but that was a mistake! Everything was spinning! I felt like I did when I was a little girl and would spin around in circles really fast. Then my stomach began to ache. I opened my eyes and changed my position, but could not make it go away. It soon turned to nausea and I lay down rubbing my stomach. "Are you all right, Mary?' I heard Elizabeth ask from somewhere far away. "I feel like I'm going to get sick," and with that, out came my lunch and my breakfast. I felt like my whole stomach would soon come out my mouth! Elizabeth was laughing and as I lay back down I wondered why she was laughing at me and then I remembered nothing else.

I woke up with water dripping in my face and when I opened my eyes I saw Elizabeth standing over me, swaying back and forth. "Mary, wake up! It's getting late! We need to get home to prepare dinner. Hurry and get up!" I tried to remember what had happened and where I was. Slowly everything began to come back. I rolled to my side and the smell from the wet ground where I had thrown up, was an immediate reminder and I sat up quickly. My head hurt and my stomach, though now empty, still felt funny. "Oh, Elizabeth! How long have I been asleep? I don't even remember falling asleep!" I looked off toward the mountains and realized the sun was low in the sky. It was certainly close to dinnertime! I looked over at Elizabeth and she had sat back down against the tree. She looked over at me and said, "You didn't go to sleep; you passed out. You drank too quickly and I didn't think to stop you because I also drank too much. I'm going to need a lot of help getting back, Mary. I am pretty unsteady on my feet." She was slurring her words so badly, I could hardly understand what she was saying. She sounded just like Father when he drank.

"I'll try to help you, Elizabeth." I tried to get up and the feeling started again in my stomach. Before I could finish standing, I had thrown up again. This time it was nothing but a yellow bitter tasting liquid that smelled horrible. How was

I going to help her when I needed help myself? How long would I feel this way? I asked Elizabeth for some of the herbs she had, hoping it would take this foul taste out of my mouth. We both chewed some and I went to get the horses. With difficulty, I helped her get on her horse and told her to be sure to squeeze her thighs tightly to keep from falling off. I think she may have heard some of what I said, but she didn't look like she cared much. Her eyes were mere slits and she was leaning from side to side as she sat on the chestnut's back. I thought again how glad I was that I had chosen the mare. She was so patient and gentle, just like her former rider.

On the way back, I led Elizabeth's horse and I thought about the things she had shared with me. She'd been through a lot, like me, but she seemed to be more in control of her emotions. Getting rid of your own baby- that was a tough one. As much as I loved children, I was sure I could never do *that*. I didn't think this drinking thing was the answer, but it sure seemed to take away her pain. My head still felt foggy and I wondered how she could feel this way every day and still function. Or maybe that *is* how she functioned. If she could get relief from her sorrow in this way, maybe I should give it another try. I looked back at her and she had her eyes closed, nodding her head and humming. She had not gotten sick and she still seemed to have that relaxed feeling I had before my stomach began to hurt. That numb feeling. Maybe it got better the more often you drank. I would ask her if we could do this again. I was ready for some relief, too. We soon got home and suffered through the dinner chores. We were both glad to get to bed that night.

Over the next several weeks, we had many such outings. My mother thought it was great that I finally had another friend and Father didn't care what I did as long as I got my work done. Tamar also seemed to be glad that we were friends, but Elizabeth felt it was only because she was out of her mother's way and she could drink more often. "She

really thinks I don't know. How stupid does she think I am?"
Sometimes I felt that my mother was glad for me to be out
of the way, too. It gave her more time with Barthomew. She
had also started taking trips to see her brother and his family
almost every month and with me out of way, she could just
go. She had stopped caring what Father wanted her to do.
Sometimes Mother would ask me to go, but I really didn't
want to hear anything about the God I had left behind. Mary
had told me I could have a wonderful life as long as I stayed
close to her God; that he would never leave me alone. *Of
course that didn't mean that **she** would never leave you
alone! Mary, Mary, Mary. Do you really think **anything** she
told you was the truth?* I shook my head to clear the voice.
Somehow, the notion of the life she had talked about did not
fit in well with the things I was doing now.

Elizabeth and Tamar celebrated my sixteenth birthday
with my family and me. It was more special with my
friends here. My parents gave me new clothes and sandals.
Bartholomew was four now and he gave me a little sack of
stones he had found. He was very proud of his gift and I
thanked him every time he reminded me of it. Elizabeth and
I were eager to celebrate in our own way, so after the party
we rushed to get our chores done and then went riding. We
frequently went for walks or rides nowadays and she always
had a full wine skin. I found the more often I drank, the less
problems I had with my stomach. I also learned that eating
bread before we went out helped a lot. We never got caught.
The herbs worked well and my mother wasn't able to smell
the wine on my breath. My Father sniffed around me a few
times, but that was only when he was sober. When he was
drinking, I didn't worry about him smelling anything, but his
overtures were still a problem. He kissed me on the mouth a
few times after coming home from his long trips, but I had
learned how to handle him gracefully. I didn't like it when

he did it in front of Mother, though. She would not speak to me for days afterwards.

One day we were out and I decided to show Elizabeth the house where Mary and Joseph lived. We stopped for a few minutes in front of the house, so I could tell her a little about them. A woman came to the door and waved to us. We looked at each other and we both shrugged our shoulders because neither of us knew who she was. She came out into the yard and waved to us again and said, "Come in and have some cool water. I have been looking for someone your age to help with my children. Come, I won't bite!"

She was strikingly beautiful and had a friendly smile. She wore more makeup that I had ever seen on a woman before, but it looked good. We both went in and she gave us some fig cakes and fresh water. We eagerly ate and drank as she proceeded to tell us she needed someone to help with her children. But the best part was she would pay us to do so. This was a wonderful opportunity for both of us and we enthusiastically agreed. While we sat and ate, she got up and went to the corner of the room where Jesus used to sleep and I saw four, large amphorae sitting there. I noticed as she walked over to them that she was not real steady on her feet. She was trying to tip one of them over to fill a jug and it started to fall. Elizabeth and I both leaped up and grabbed it before it hit the ground. The woman thanked us and said, "That would have been a mess! You girls saved me from a lot of work by being so quick on your feet. One good turn deserves another. Would either of you like some of what I'm drinking?" Elizabeth eagerly nodded her head. I also agreed, but wondered where this woman's children were.

She poured our wine into expensive looking stone cups. Her wine was much stronger than any I had before and Elizabeth asked her where it came from. "Oh, this is from Rome. I have a friend who brings it to me every time he goes to Jerusalem. He's one of the reasons I need someone to watch my children. The other reason is, I help out a friend in the city, a seamstress, and she needs me there three days a week to help her in the market." I looked around and then asked her, "Where are your children?" She stopped in the middle of pouring her drink and thought for a moment and then said, "They're with a friend. She took them to Bethlehem with her for the day. By the way, what are your names? My name is Salome."

I almost choked on the sip I was taking. What a coincidence! "I had a sister named Salome, but she died a few years ago. My name is Mary and this is my friend Elizabeth." She patted my arm and said, "I'm sorry that you lost your sister. I lost a brother when I was very young. It's hard." She smiled slightly. "But your sister had a beautiful name. It's also the name of my oldest daughter. My name has been passed down through numerous generations. We're a family of dancers and while in Egypt, I danced many years for many people. Then my family moved us here, to Judea. But that was thirty years ago." I was surprised! She looked so young!! "You don't look that old! How old are you?" She lay her head straight back and let out a loud laugh. "You are a charming girl, Mary! Such a compliment will get you many favors from old women like me! I am forty-one. And how old are you young ladies?" Elizabeth spoke first, "I'm seventeen and Mary is sixteen. Her father owns an inn just a short way from here. My mother and I work for him." The woman's face brightened. "You are Bartimus' daughter? Oh, yes, Bartimus and I go back many years. He's a very handsome man; you have some of his features, Mary!" The way she said it made me think there was more to their relationship than just friends. Fortunately, the wine had relaxed me so much, that I didn't linger on that thought.

I started to stand, but she pushed me back down and said, "You have just one more. Then I will let you go." I sat back down and thought that she was not the type of person that

Benjamin would have working for him or living in his home. Maybe I would ask her what she thought of her landlord. She took a long drink and then nodded, "I don't like him as much as the old one. I only knew that family for a few weeks before they sold it to Simon. He's a jackal. He wants no excuses for anything!"

My breath caught in my throat! Where had Benjamin and Deborah gone? "Do you know what happened to the previous owners? They were friends of mine. In fact that is how we came to be here today." Salome shook her head and laughed. "If they were friends of yours, they would have told you they were leaving, no?" She must have seen the crushed look on my face and then said, "I'm sorry. I know very little, other than they decided to move." I was shocked! Even if I had brought myself to be their friend again, now they were gone! And Salome's words drove home the truth of my situation! Abandoned by them, just like Mary and Joseph! I asked Salome for another drink and she gladly filled my cup. "Anytime you want to come by and have a drink you are welcome. Any daughter of Bartimus is a friend of mine." Then she chuckled and moved closer to me. "Just don't tell him I'm giving you wine. He might not like that! It will be our little secret." She winked at me and I promised her that I would never tell. I wasn't that stupid.

Elizabeth looked at me and signaled that we needed to leave. We got up and thanked Salome for her hospitality. We were both pretty drunk and I thought it was going to be a long walk home. I would not ride Joshua feeling like this. I needed the extra time to sober up a little; we would have to sit somewhere for awhile. Salome offered us a handful of the same spices Elizabeth always had. We both laughed and thanked her. She put an arm over each of our shoulders and said, "If you can start watching my two little girls next week that would be great. Salome is seven and Lois is five." We told her we were excited at the prospect and we promised to ask our parents.

We stopped in the olive grove and found a tree to rest on. Salome was the topic of our conversation. We both laughed and agreed that she could come in handy if we ever ran out of wine. Elizabeth became thoughtful. "She could become a good friend, Mary. Someone who can teach us a lot of new things." I was not entirely sure what she was talking about, but it sounded good so I nodded in agreement. We realized that we had quite a bit of time before we had to be home. There was a warm breeze and we were quite relaxed. We were quiet as we pondered the possibilities that a job could bring and didn't really notice the two donkeys coming toward us.

Two handsome men were leading the donkeys and as they approached I noticed Elizabeth's whole demeanor change. She brushed her hair back from her face and looked at me with a big smile. The boys stopped and she walked right up to them and said hello. I had seen many of the women Father flirted with move and walk seductively, just the way Elizabeth was doing. The boys seemed to immediately respond to her and then she introduced us.

The taller and more attractive one said, "Hello, I am Nathaniel and this is Joel. We are going to Hebron for our brother's wedding. We have come from Jerusalem and are looking for a place to stay, but we have little money." Elizabeth and I exchanged looks and then she said, "Mary's father owns an inn and I am sure we could put you up there and it won't cost you anything." I was shaking my head. I was not sure what she was up to because my father gave nothing away for free. She gave me a look that meant, "Be quiet!" and so I waited to see what her plan was.

She continued. "Do you mind sleeping in a stable? It's clean and I could be sure you are comfortable, Nathaniel." She winked at him and caressed his arm gently. The way she was moving her body against his, made me uncomfortable.

Joel looked over at me and he was blushing. I knew I was, too. Elizabeth and Nathaniel seemed to be totally enamored with each other and oblivious to us. Joel smiled and said hello and asked if it would really be all right to stay in my father's stable. I felt a warm rush of emotion I had not felt before and suddenly was quite sure that it would be fine.

We began to walk back toward the inn. Elizabeth and Nathaniel were arm in arm while Joel and I just talked. When we arrived at the stable, I showed them where they could sleep and a flood of memories came over me. This stable had represented the beginning of such meaningful and happy times in my life, but so much had happened in the last three years. Well, those were things I didn't want to think about right now. I felt a headache coming on. I had not had one in a long time, but the feelings I was experiencing from the memories and from being close to Joel were somehow triggering one.

Elizabeth and I instructed them to not leave the stable and then we left them to do our chores for dinner. We had more people than either of us wanted to serve, but we got it done and were free for the rest of the night. I promised Thaddeus I would take care of the animals tonight and in the morning. Elizabeth checked in with her mother and asked if I could sleep in their quarters for the night. She lied and said I had a fight with my mother and needed to talk. Tamar was already to the point of passing out and I don't think she cared what we did. I went to find my mother and she was in the sewing room with Bartholomew playing at her feet. I kissed her and said I was staying with Elizabeth. I used the same story Elizabeth used with her mother and it worked. She leaned over to kiss me and paused. I saw her sniffing and then she seemed to dismiss it. "All right, Mary. But don't stay up all night talking." I promised we wouldn't, went to my room and grabbed some blankets, then went to find Elizabeth.

She was waiting for me in her room and she had put on a beautiful tunic and some makeup. "Why are you dressed like that, Elizabeth? You look like you're going into the city or something!" I put my things down and she looked at me in alarm. "What are you doing? We are going to the stable. I promised Nathaniel I would come see him!" I looked at her to see if she was joking! I knew she wanted me to spend the night and I thought it was just to talk about the boys. I didn't think she would want to go see them! "I don't really know those boys, Elizabeth. We can't go down there!" She looked at me and I knew she was getting angry, but then a slow smile came to her face. "You're a virgin! You're a virgin, aren't you, Mary?" The smile had become a smirk, like she was making fun of me. "Yes, I am. I've never even kissed a boy. What difference does that make?" I felt offended and hurt. She had become my best friend and she was making a joke of my virginity. "Mary, you're missing so much fun! What if Joel wants to be with you? Are you going to say no? That will soon turn him away and you won't see him again."

That made no sense to me. I probably wouldn't see him again anyway and I told her that. She looked at me in disgust and said, "Never mind, Mary. You'll understand soon enough. Now take your blankets and let's go. She shoved her wine skin in my mouth and tipped it up and I took a long swallow. We drank half the skin and then she said, "Let's go!" She seemed determined and with the help of the wine, I was beginning to find the whole idea intriguing! We looked out into the courtyard and saw no one that would recognize us. We went out through the gate near the well. While we walked down the hill we drank most of the wine she had. Elizabeth was walking ahead, then stopped and turned to me. "You know, Mary, you are going to have to start getting some of your father's wine. My mother already said she knows I'm stealing from her." I shook my head and promised to fill the skin next time. It seemed that she could talk me into anything, even when I knew it was wrong.

We quietly knocked on the door to the stable and heard a hushed "come in." Both of the boys were sitting in the hay and Joel jumped up when we walked in and came over to me. Nathaniel didn't get up, but held his arm out to welcome Elizabeth and she went and sat next to him. I could tell she was really feeling the wine and was surprised to see her lean over and kiss him. I felt heat rising to my face and then Joel took my hand and we sat down on the other side of the stable from Elizabeth and Nathaniel. I was feeling a mixture of fear and excitement. He asked me how old I was and then volunteered that he was seventeen. We talked briefly, long enough for the wine to really hit my head. And then he kissed me. I was lost in that kiss! I had spent so many nights wondering what it would be like (and even sometimes using my forearm to practice). My body was responding in ways that reminded me of those nights in my room. It had been a sickening sensation that somehow, didn't feel so bad anymore. I was finally getting my first kiss!! This was the first time in my life I didn't try to stop my body from responding. Soon his hands seemed to be everywhere. I wanted him to do more, but he stopped.

We both heard the other two making noises that made us aware they had not chosen to stop. Joel told me that he was betrothed to someone in Jerusalem and he felt bad that we had done as much as we had. I told him I had never done this before and I was glad that he had stopped. He looked at me in disbelief. "You are a virgin?" I nodded and then he said, "I'm sure with the way your friend is acting, it is not her first time." I shook my head slowly. "No, it isn't for her. We have not been friends that long. But she thought you were nice and wanted to spend more time with Nathaniel." Joel chuckled, "Well, she succeeded." After a few more minutes, I saw Nathaniel get up and he walked over to us. "Are you two done? We have a long trip tomorrow and we need to get some sleep." I was embarrassed by the tone in his voice and knew that he wanted us out of there as soon as possible. I got up and went to Elizabeth. I asked her if she was ready to go and she looked past me to Nathaniel and said, "Are you sure I can't stay with you tonight? No one will find out and I can make you breakfast in the morning." He did not even turn around. "No! Just leave, please. We need to get some rest." I saw him look at Joel and roll his eyes. Joel handed him a small cloth bag and he in turn, tossed it to Elizabeth. When she caught it, he said, "I hope that will be enough!" We both looked at the bag, then said goodbye. Only Joel responded and neither of them came to the door with us.

Elizabeth was angry and crying as we walked up the hill. She opened the tiny bag and found close to twenty coins inside. We didn't even know what they were worth. "That jackal! He thinks he's too good for me. He got what he wanted and then paid me like a common whore." She sat down on the hill and began sobbing. "I just want to be loved, Mary. Why can't someone love me? I give all of myself and they just leave me alone." I said nothing, but thought about what she said. I understood being left and feeling unloved, but I think tonight was my first taste of how men felt about girls that were loose and I didn't relish the flavor. We consoled each other and then went back to Elizabeth's room to sleep, but it would not come easily tonight. The feelings that had been awakened in me were hauntingly familiar and I found myself hoping I wouldn't have to wait too long for it to happen again. Elizabeth lay next to me and by the hitch in her breathing I could tell she was crying. When I tried to console her, she pulled away and asked me to leave her alone. I felt bad for her, but thought tomorrow we would forget all this and ask our parents if we could baby-sit for our new friend. I thought maybe Elizabeth was right. Salome could become a very good friend.

7

Loss of innocence

Salome's offer was received well when we shared with our mothers. They thought it was a wonderful idea for us to take the new job and so we started the following week. Our days became quite interesting. We cared for the girls during the day and when Salome came home, she'd feed us and give us all the wine we wanted. Afterwards, Elizabeth and I would leave and walk along the road where we'd met Joel and Nathaniel. We found that we could meet some nice young men on this road and it became a regular habit for us. Some of these men had wine and some had beer (I didn't like that too much, but Elizabeth drank it). We would usually invite them to Father's stable, unless they had money, then they'd stay at the inn and we'd meet them in the stable, late at night. We knew we wouldn't see them again so we made up elaborate stories about our lives. We pretended to be the daughters of kings or rich travelers or whatever came into our imagination at the time. I'd always tell them I was a virgin, too. Most of them would stop if they knew that. A few got pushy, but my experiences with Father had taught me how to handle them.

One afternoon, we had no patrons at the inn and Father said we could have the day off. We could do what we wanted and we didn't have to rush back. We told our parents we would be at Salome's house. They all trusted her and of course we never told about the drinking. When we arrived, she wasn't at home so we decided to do our usual. Just to try something new, we went south, toward Hebron. We had never ventured this way and we shared the wineskin as we went. I had started filling it pretty frequently from Father's stock and just this morning heard him say to Mother that he better not find any of the servants in his wine. I had only filled the skin halfway today.

It was a beautiful day. The sky was a clear blue with only a few of the fluffy clouds that I used to like to find shapes in. It was cool and we didn't even break a sweat after drinking the wine. We were enjoying the day and neither of was particularly concerned if we met anyone. We agreed on a point in the distance where we would turn around and head back to Salome's. The breeze was refreshing as it blew our hair and we laughed as two jack rabbits ran across our path chasing each other. As my eyes followed the rabbits, I noticed a house a little ways up, on the left. It sat back off the road and had many olive trees around it. When we got a little closer, I realized the house looked quite a bit like the house where Salome now stayed. I wondered if this had been one of Benjamin's houses also.

I heard Elizabeth sigh and when I looked at her she said, "Let's head back, Mary. I want to see if Salome came back yet. We don't have enough wine for a whole afternoon of freedom! Besides, I need to use her latrine!" We laughed and I agreed. As we turned to head back, a man came out of the house. He waved at us and then another man came out. Elizabeth looked at me and I thought, *here we go!* She waved to them as they stared. Then another came out and joined them. They began walking toward us and I noticed they were older than the usual men we met. The first one to approach had black, greasy looking hair and a broad smile. He seemed very friendly, but I felt a catch in my breath as he got closer. Something wasn't right. The smile surrounded by his short, graying beard didn't match the dark, cold eyes. He smelled like wine and some kind of smoke that I didn't recognize. The second one was a huge man and he had long, dark brown hair and a full beard that went down the center of his chest. It looked like some of his breakfast was still in his beard. His smile wasn't as broad. The third one was very tall and thin. His hair was a lighter brown and he smelled like he hadn't bathed in a long time. He also smelled like that strange smoke and his eyes looked glassy. He didn't smile at all.

Elizabeth spoke first. "My name is Elizabeth and this is Mary. We've been walking for some time and we're very tired. Would you have some cool water we could drink?" I saw her looking from one to the other trying to size them up. She lowered her voice and said in a sultry tone, "Or if you have anything else to drink, we wouldn't mind that either." She smiled at the one who seemed so friendly. He winked at her and said, "Yes, we have fresh water. Come, we'll draw some from the well for you." The others said nothing. I couldn't shake the fear I had and tried in vain to get Elizabeth's attention. We followed them to the back of the house and found they had at least a dozen goats surrounded by a large fence. In the center of the fence was the well. Some of the goats were kids and we petted them while we waited for our water.

I noticed the man that offered us the water and the big man discussing something. The third man had gone to the gate and locked it. He was now leaning against the house and leering at us. My fear was mounting! I pulled Elizabeth toward me and whispered, "We need to leave. Now!" She shook her head. "You're just scared! Relax. I have this under control." She went up to the friendly one and seductively pulled back his mantle and asked, "Do you have some wine hiding under there? I'm really thirsty." He smiled and licked his lips. "I have something for you. Just wait." The two began talking again and this time I could hear what they were saying! They were arguing about which of us they were going to take in the house first! The reality of what they planned to do with us filled me with terror and I grabbed Elizabeth. She shook off my hand and asked them what they were planning! *Why was she trying to antagonize them?* I was petrified! I tried to pull her again and she just kept taunting them. I finally cried, "Please, don't do this! I am a virgin!"

Time seemed to stop. As if in slow motion, the smaller man turned to me and he had a sneer on his face. I could see spittle drooling from the corner of his mouth. "A virgin! I haven't had a virgin in a long time. That settles it! We take her first." Elizabeth called me a stupid cow and continued to curse at them and demanded they let us go. The bigger man looked at her and then me and when he did, she said something to him under her breath. He grabbed her arm so hard she cried out and through gritted teeth said, "No, this one needs to be taught some manners. I want to shut her mouth!" The other man grabbed her other arm and they dragged her into the house. I felt almost paralyzed! I looked at the third man. He was still leaning against the house. I quickly measured the distance between him and the gate and tried to determine if I had enough time to beat him to freedom. I could run and get Salome or if I had to, my father.

I heard Elizabeth scream and I knew I had no time to waste. I turned toward the gate and before I had taken two steps he was on me. He knocked me to the ground and got on top of me. I heard more screams from within the house and I struggled to get up. The sneer that seemed to be plastered to his face, never left. "I have a little friend I would like you to meet." With an ostentatious gesture, he pulled a huge dagger from his belt. "This is Balthazar! And Balthazar likes to do whatever I tell him to do!" He passed the blade by his mouth and kissed it and in a flash had it at my throat! "Now if you get any more ideas of running, Balthazar will show you what he can do! Do you understand?" With each word he pressed the knife deeper and deeper into my neck. I had never known fear like this! I couldn't breathe from the pressure of his weight on my chest or the pressure against my throat. I felt like my lungs were going to explode if I didn't take a breath soon! But I was afraid if I did, the knife would cut my throat. So I prayed.

Oh, God! I know I don't deserve to ask you, but please help me! I am so scared and I don't want to lose my virginity like this and I don't want to die. Before I finished all I wanted to say, he got off of me. I rolled over and took in a huge breath. I coughed several times and then rolled to my back. My hand went to my throat, I expected to feel blood. I looked at my hand. No blood! I rubbed my hand back and forth across my neck and felt nothing except Mary's necklace. It was lying across my throat where he had held the knife! It had prevented the knife from cutting me! I silently thanked God and then sat up. The man had gone back to the wall and was leaning on it, watching me. I heard nothing coming from inside.

Time passed slowly. It felt like hours went by before I heard the shuffling of feet. I looked up and saw the two men dragging Elizabeth through the door, her elbows hooked in theirs, her feet dragging behind her. She appeared to be unconscious. Her left eye was badly bruised and swollen. Her lips were puffy and bleeding and her arms were terribly bruised. The front of her tunic had been torn open. They lay her on the ground next to me. For a brief moment I thought she was dead. I watched her chest and saw the shallow rise and fall of her breathing and was relieved. Then a hand on my arm yanked me to my feet. It was the "friendly" man. His breath stank and so did his body. He leaned into my face and

I could see his yellow rotting teeth and I smelled that smoke again on his breath. "I am so excited about having a virgin! Would you like to see how excited?" Instantly, it seemed, he was on the ground. The large man had thrown him down! He leaned over, spat on him and said, "You do what I say, when I say it. Do you understand?"

He turned to me and terror ran through me like ice in my veins. Desperately, I grabbed the front of his tunic in both of my hands and pleaded, "Please, don't do this! I will do anything if you don't do this… please!" He looked down. He was a giant of a man. I was a tall girl but he towered over me. I had little hope that he would listen to me. I was aware of Elizabeth moving and groaning. I never took my eyes from his. He had cold eyes. Like the shark my father had described to me once. He said they had "lifeless" eyes. That is what this man's eyes were like. I closed my eyes and prayed. When I looked at him again, something had changed. His eyes had softened and his vice grip on my arms was relaxing. "I will let you go if you will kiss me. One good kiss." I thought I must be dreaming. There was no way he just said that. "A kiss?" I asked. He nodded his head. "Just one kiss." His eyes never left mine. I thought he may be trying to trick me, but wasn't about to take the chance. I stood on my toes and tried to ignore the smell and the food in his beard and kissed him the best I could. When I pulled my face away, his eyes were still closed. He slowly opened them and said quietly, "Now go. Take your friend and don't look back. Don't think about bringing anyone here, either. We are only here for tonight. Go! Get out of here!"

The man on the ground started cursing him and one look from the big man shut his mouth. I helped Elizabeth up and we slowly walked toward the gate. The man against the wall came over, opened it for us and we walked away from the horror of that day. We went to Salome's home and found her at home. Her children were asleep and I was glad. I didn't want them to see Elizabeth looking like this. Salome went straight to work cleaning her up. She didn't ask any questions. They had brutally raped Elizabeth and when Salome tried to clean her, Elizabeth stopped her. She took the cloth and in a weak voice said, "I'll do it." Salome didn't argue. She found her a clean tunic and after Elizabeth was done, we sat down with Salome. She had poured us all cups of wine and as we drank, we told her the whole story.

As I shared what happened, I saw Elizabeth wince as she tried to take a drink. Her lip was split pretty badly and the wine probably burned. I drank mine straight down and asked for more. After we were done, Salome solemnly told us that these men were probably part of a caravan. They travel from Jerusalem to Egypt and trade what they can along the way. She said I was very fortunate, because they feared no one and she was truly astounded that I had escaped unscathed. I was not feeling very fortunate, but then I would look at Elizabeth and realize that God had answered my prayer. "You know Salome, I prayed for God to help us and I think he did." Elizabeth looked at me with disgust and when she spoke, her voice dripped with sarcasm, "God *really* helped me! Didn't he, Mary? Just like he helped Mother and me when my father died! Don't talk to *me* about God!" I looked at Salome and she just shook her head in disbelief. I never gave another thought to my answered prayers... or to my God.

Salome suggested we stay with her until we could think of something to tell her mother. Elizabeth was afraid of jeopardizing her job. I assured her that we would think of something. We decided that I would go home and get the horses and bring them back and we would fake a riding accident. I was sure father had not checked the horses in some time; he left that to Thaddeus. It sounded like a good plan and it worked. Tamar was upset and said Elizabeth could not go riding again and my father said we could not go out together for a while. He felt that we could have hurt the horses riding them so hard. Neither of those punishments bothered us too much. We were not eager to take any more walks alone.

Elizabeth did not baby-sit anymore. In fact, she didn't do much of anything with me. This left me spending more and more time with Salome. The more time I spent with her, the closer we became. The difference in our ages seemed insignificant as we discovered how much we had in common. She loved to write, as I did and I shared many of my poems with her. She promised me some papyrus when her husband returned from one of his trips to Egypt. She would sometimes take me with her to Bethlehem and on a few occasions we went to Jerusalem. We celebrated my seventeenth birthday there with some friends of hers. I don't remember a lot of it. They had some of the best wine I had ever tasted! She knew lots of men and helped me meet quite a few. Her husband was never home. She said he traveled to far away, exotic sounding places and when he came home he brought her beautiful jewelry, the likes of which I had never seen in Judea. But I think she liked it when he was gone. He was more than twenty years older than she and when he was away, she enjoyed the attention of younger men. I made friends with some of them that were close to my age and she would buy us all the wine and beer that we desired. A few of them smoked opium and when I smelled it for the first time, I immediately realized this was the strange smoke I had smelled on the three men who had terrorized us.

I tried to share this with Elizabeth, but she didn't seem to care much about what I had to say anymore. I'm not sure she cared about anything anymore. She had become quiet and withdrawn, like when she first came to stay with us. Her mother had become the same way. One morning Father came running in looking for Mother, yelling that Tamar and Elizabeth had left in the middle of the night. Apparently, they took one of his wine amphorae with them. I couldn't believe they would steal from us, but I wasn't surprised that they'd left. Father tried to blame me for the missing amphorae. "If you hadn't become such good friends with them none of this would have happened!" Another notch in my belt of guilt.

My father had to hire someone to replace them and this time it was a woman and her son. The boy was nice looking and I was immediately drawn to him. His name was Matthew and a year younger than me, but neither of us cared. His mother was very sweet and a hard worker. Father had assigned him the stables and I was more than happy to show him the ropes. He was a quick learner and when we got done with our work for the day, he would bring the horses to the courtyard, pick me up and we would ride for hours. He was an experienced rider. His father had been wealthy; you had to be to own horses. Before he divorced Matthew's mother to marry another woman, he had raised horses for the chariot races in Rome. Matthew had things to teach *me* about horses.

Matthew also had things to teach me about life. He too was a virgin and one day after brushing down the horses, he kissed me. This kiss was different from all the others. There was a chance for a future with Matthew. A chance to be loved. A chance for marriage. A chance to have children. Yes, life with Matthew could be so different. No more fighting and yelling or beatings and pain. My children would never experience what I had with my parents and I would be the best wife and mother ever. We kissed long and passionately and my dream for a new life grew with every clandestine rendezvous we shared. This became a regular meeting place for us and soon we were doing more than just kissing. He would bale out the new hay every morning so it was always fresh. And every afternoon, we enjoyed the softness of it. I wanted him to make love to me; still we both held back. But I just wasn't sure how much longer we would be able to.

One day, I took him to meet Salome. She told him how much she liked him and that I was a lucky girl. He liked her compliments and when she invited him to come with me the next evening for dinner, he eagerly accepted. We got permission from our parents and took the horses and slowly walked them to her home. The night was cool and the air sweet with harvest. It was a magical night. When we got there, Salome's home was lit with candles, but there was no one else at home. There was a pot of lamb stew and jug of wine sitting on the table and a beautiful animal skin on the sleeping mat against the wall. Perplexed, I looked at Matthew and shrugged. "Where could Salome be? Why would she leave all this and go away?" I walked over to the mat and there was a piece of papyrus (the gift from her husband) with one word written on it, "Enjoy."

"It looks like she left this for us, Matthew. I don't think she will be back tonight." He looked at me and smiled and said, "I love you, Mary." I ran to him and wrapped myself in his arms and whispered, "Oh, I love you, too, Matthew. We kissed and kissed and eventually ended up on the mat. He was gentle with me and I was grateful that we were both innocents in this right of passage. There, with the musky smell of the animal skin, the soft glow of the candles and a sober mind, I gave him the gift I had promised to save for my husband. At the moment it happened, my thoughts were clear. *There. Now it's over. I've lost my virginity and I can't get it back. But he loves me! Finally someone really loves me and he will marry me and that will make everything wonderful!*

But he didn't stay in love with me. He didn't marry me. And everything wasn't wonderful. After four months together, he told me he was seeing someone else in Bethlehem. *A friend of the family.* Someone he had introduced me to a few months earlier, when he went to Bethlehem with Salome and me. And then to add vinegar to my wound, he and his mother moved to the city so she could work for the girl's family and he could be close to his *new love. Abandoned again. The pain and emptiness was sometimes more than I could handle. But, I knew ways to stop feeling like this. No, the problems and feelings never disappear, but I could temporarily numb the pain.*

My life became a blur of wine, beer and (if Salome had her way) lots of men. Though I didn't sleep with most of them, she couldn't seem to stop. I spent all my free time with her. She had found someone else to watch her children and we would go on frequent trips to Bethlehem and Jerusalem. She seemed to have friends everywhere and a room was always available for us at the local inns. She taught me how to get many nice things by what she playfully called her "five finger discount." She could steal from right under the nose of someone and never get caught. My abilities came quickly and we found ourselves filling our days with these excursions. We filled our nights with lots of parties and lots of wine. With my virginity out of the way, I had no guilt about giving myself to a few of these men. I would still tell them I was a virgin in the hopes that maybe one of them would love me. Maybe one of them would marry me. *Maybe one of them would save me.*

Salome became more and more interested in the young men I had made friends with and soon we were having parties that lasted for two or three days with all the wine we could drink and even a little opium if it was available. The white powder scared me because on the few occasions that I tried it, I was unable to control myself. It felt like everything around me was moving very slowly, almost like time itself was coming to a stop. I didn't like that feeling at all.

During one of these parties, I noticed one of the younger men watching me and smiling whenever I would look at him. I made a point of introducing myself to him. His name was Haman and he was very handsome. He had an accent and when I asked where he was from, he avoided my question. He seemed quite drunk but obviously wanted to be with me. We kissed a few times, but nothing more. I ran into him at several more parties and it was always the same. He seemed to really like me, but he never tried to sleep with me. That was confusing; I was certain they went hand-in-hand.

On a few occasions, Salome ended up sleeping with some of my friends. It never happened with Haman, but I still started to feel betrayed. They would laugh at her behind her back because of her age. But it didn't stop them from being curious about her sexual skills. Once, she and I were at her home, where we had been drinking most of the evening. Her husband and children were sound asleep. I was sitting on the mat and Salome was getting more wine for us. I said something to her about the comments the boys had made about her sensuality. She slowly walked toward me, stood over me, swaying provocatively from side to side, and said, "Well, Mary, you sound jealous! I could teach you what I know!" I was confused and asked what she meant. She smiled and sat down very close to me. She leaned over and tried to kiss me. I jumped up and wiped my mouth and said, "I'm, sorry, Salome. I can't do that." She looked hurt. I felt guilty because she was my friend. I felt disrespectful because she was my elder. But most of all, I felt betrayed because I had trusted her. I walked out. We never discussed it again, but I didn't enjoy being around her anymore and I started to find excuses not to go on the trips to Bethlehem.

Soon Haman started to visit me at the inn and my parents seemed to really like him. We had been intimate for some time now and we loved each other. He had even talked about marriage. So, I had little interest in Salome's party life anymore. I was totally consumed with him. I wanted to be with him all the time. I would cry when he had to go back to the city for work and he would tell me I was being silly. When he drank too much, he would get angry and tell me I was too possessive and a few times he even slapped me and told me to stop my whining. But the next day he would be so sorry, I would forgive him. I knew he loved me.

The day after my eighteenth birthday, my father announced he was going to sell the inn and move back to Cana. Some new opportunity had been presented to him and he was jumping on board. Mother was happy because this put her much closer to Magdala. She did not mind the fact that it was in the mountains, west of her hometown, she just wanted to be back in Galilee. It was quiet in Cana with little traffic and when we had lived there before, she seemed to like it. I was happy for her but I did not want to go.

Haman was here and I was sure we would be married. I had lived here on the outskirts of Bethlehem since I was eight and though there were many bad memories, it had become home. I still wanted to become a midwife and I had started training with a woman in Bethlehem. I did not know where I would work. I did not know where I would live. But I had Haman and that was all that mattered. If he were not ready to get married yet, I would talk to him about living together. That way I would have a place to live and I would always know what he was doing. It seemed the perfect arrangement.

8

Numb the pain

*T*here is a place, deep inside every little girl that longs to be loved and cared for by her father. She desires to be adored, to hear loving endearments, to feel precious. She wants to be the twinkle in her father's eye. When those things are absent, she develops a void. Add to that, abuse of any form— physical, emotional, mental or sexual—and the void grows. She desperately tries to fill it with substitutes that she hopes will make her feel less empty inside. Less meaningless. Less hopeless. Things that will temporarily numb the pain she is feeling. Substances that allow her to say and do things that she normally wouldn't do.

With each failure, she becomes needier and more desperate. She tries to find men who can fill the void and often jumps from one relationship to another in the hope of getting some relief. She rejects the men who are kind to her because they don't fill her need to suffer, to be the victim. She chooses the ones who treat her as her father did. But they fail to perform the needed exorcism from her bondage. She allows the name-calling, the beatings and the infidelities because there is an internal message that says she deserves what she gets. And when the man of the hour gets tired of her despera-

tion, he leaves and she replaces him with another who will do the same. Each man fails because no common man can succeed in filling the role of her father. No common man can succeed in filling her void. So her search continues...

A year passed before my father and mother sold the inn and moved to Cana. Part of me was glad to not have to be around the arguing and fighting anymore, but there was also a part of me that missed them very much. I also wasn't prepared for the grief I felt for Bartholomew. I wasn't sure I grieved because I missed him or that I wouldn't be there to protect him. I had made a promise that I would always try to keep him safe, the way my sister had tried to do for me. But as much as I loved my brother, I couldn't leave Haman. I needed him and he needed me. Or so I thought.

When my parents sold the inn, I helped Haman come around to my way of thinking, like how alone I was with nowhere to go. After much persuading, he finally agreed to live together. After all, I was finishing my apprenticeship as a midwife and I could contribute to the finances. We lived together for over three years. The first year was pretty good, but after that we seemed to argue and fight all the time. We had talked occasionally about marriage, but with each beating I received and each woman he slept with, my resolve grew weaker. I forgave him many times, but when it didn't stop, I decided to get even and do the same. Unfortunately, he found out and *that* beating left me unconscious and badly bruised. It was weeks before I could leave the house. Things got even worse after that. It seemed every few months, there was some reason that I needed a beating and it would be followed by his one-night trysts. Then the tears and apologies would come. I had become anesthetized to his excuses early in our relationship and I was just biding my time until I could find someone to rescue me from this living hell.

Earlier this year, my opportunity came when Haman had to go to Joppa to do business with some traders he had met.

From there they took a ship and made many stops on their way to Rome. He was gone for almost four months and while he was away, I met a wonderful man, Amos. I met him at the market in Bethlehem. He was a gentle man and was living in Bethlehem for a short time until his work was finished. He was not only kind, but respectful whenever he saw me and I found myself going to the market more frequently so I could run into him. After the second week, I invited him to my house and we talked for hours about things, pleasant things, things that I'd long forgotten. After that he came to visit me several times a week. The more time I spent with Amos, the more I realized how little I'd talked with Haman, how little I'd done with him. I had only been passing time... aimlessly wandering through life, like a castaway adrift in a small boat, lost at sea. Just before he left for Rome, it felt like the boat had capsized and I was worn out from treading water. I was going down for the third time.

With Amos I felt alive again! We took long walks and went on picnics and he brought me beautiful gifts. We had extensive conversations about what we wanted for our futures. I shared with him my love for children and that I wanted twelve of my own. He shared his desire to be a successful carpenter and the thought of twelve kids didn't seem to scare him. One night he told me that when he finished his work here, he was moving back to Nazareth so he could start his own business. He'd grown up in Nazareth and he hoped his time and experience in Bethlehem had helped his reputation as a fine carpenter. I felt tempted many times to ask if he knew Joseph, but never did. I wanted to leave that in the past. It was still very painful for me whenever my hand brushed Mary's necklace. A few times, I tried to throw it away, thinking I could forget, but I always put it back on. Amos noticed how much I loved the necklace and asked me what meaning it had for me. I wasn't ready to talk about that part of my life so I just said I found it. After that he started giving me pieces of jewelry. He gave me a lovely gold neck-lace for my twenty-second birthday, but I still wouldn't relinquish wearing Mary's. He asked no questions, but after that only gave me rings or bracelets.

The time grew closer for Haman to come home and for Amos to go to Nazareth. We spent almost every day together. We talked and talked and talked. That's all we ever did. And that was beginning to bother me. Amos knew about Haman and tried to talk me into leaving him. He said he was afraid for my welfare and safety. He was so nice to me that it began to get on my nerves! I kept waiting for him to do more than the little kiss on the cheek each night. I wanted him to give me a sign that he wanted to be with me. I felt like he really cared (after all, he told me he loved me) but if he really did, surely he'd want to know me intimately. I thought maybe it was because I was living in the house that I shared with Haman.

One night, I hinted that I would like to move out, but with my parents gone, I really had nowhere to go. He offered some ideas, but none of them included living with him. I knew I needed to do something soon, before I lost him, so in desperation I went to Salome for help. Even after all this time, she was willing to help me. Before Haman came home, Amos helped me move my things to her house. I didn't have much, so I took up little space. The following week, Haman returned home. He came by Salome's a couple of times on his way to and from Jerusalem, but she told him she had not seen me. It wasn't long before I heard that he had moved another girl into his home and fortunately, I never saw him again.

Salome had calmed down quite a bit. Her husband, Jethro, was getting quite old and he wasn't well. Because he didn't go on trips anymore, she was forced to change her lifestyle. She had sent her children to live with her sister in the region of Decopolis. This really surprised me because she seemed to love her family so much. I couldn't imagine having children and then just giving them away because they weren't convenient! But Salome had changed a lot. I talked to her about Amos, but she didn't even seem interested in getting to know him. While I was staying with her, I noticed she started drinking as soon as she got up in the morning and didn't stop until she lay down at night. Then she and Jethro would argue for hours. I felt like I was living at home again!

Amos and I had been seeing each other for over six months. He was getting ready to return to Nazareth and still had not made any move toward a sexual relationship. He didn't even seem to know how to have fun with me. I tried to get him to drink a few times, just to loosen him up. Though I hadn't been drinking like I did with Haman, I still liked to relax when I wasn't working and wine helped me do that. Not Amos! Except for an occasional cup of wine here and there, he said he "needs nothing to relax him except being around me." I even tried to seduce him a few times, but he was always the perfect gentleman. I explained to him I really needed that sexual closeness to believe he loved me. He told me that wasn't possible because he "respected me." He even started talking about religious stuff for the first time since we had been together. He was Jewish and his family members were staunch believers in Jehovah. It has been so long since I even thought about those things, that I found myself getting frustrated and impatient with him. It was hard to believe, but I was really getting bored with him and I found myself anticipating his departure.

Some of the midwives I trained with thought I was crazy for wanting to break up with Amos. One day I was sharing with them the ambivalence I was feeling, when Leah, the oldest and kindest midwife in Bethlehem said, "Mary, this is a man that will take care of you and love you. The men you have been with in the past have only used and hurt you. Don't you see the difference? You think he doesn't love you because he won't have sex with you. What you don't understand, Mary, is that Amos doesn't have sex with you because he *does* love you!" Her words poked at my heart. Did I deserve such admiration and love? Could this man really care for someone with a past like mine? He shared with me that he had never known a woman, that he was a virgin. So didn't he deserve a virgin for a wife? But he knew my past and loved me anyway. Maybe the things Mary had taught me were true. At least about this. I felt so confused.

What do they know? They know nothing about you and your needs! You need to get rid of that man and find someone who really loves you. After all, how can you truly love someone without sex? It is the ultimate expression of love! Remember the stories that Mary shared with you about Adam and Eve? What do you think God meant by 'be fruitful and multiply?' They weren't married, were they? If this man loved you, he would desire you and want to touch you! This Amos just wants a friend, someone he can talk to and spend time with. After all, Mary, how good could it possibly be with a man that is a virgin? I shook my head to stop the voice.

I politely listened to the rest of the women's unsolicited advice and then made an excuse to head home. We had five births that day and I'd assisted with four of them. It was late and I truly was exhausted. As I was leaving, Leah stopped me at the door and said, "Mary, think hard before you make any decisions that will affect the rest of your life. You told me once that you knew who Jehovah was and that your friend had taught you about him. It doesn't matter why you left him, he hasn't left you." In her face was such gentleness and for a brief moment she reminded me of Mary. Her words sparked a feeling I hadn't felt in some time, but it was short lived. *Silly woman! She believes in that same Jehovah that abandoned you, Mary. Don't listen to her! She lies like all the rest of them. Go home before she can say anything else.* I thanked Leah and gave her a hug and turned to leave. She began to say something else and I stopped her. "Leah, I'm fine. Please understand. I don't want to hear about Jehovah. I'm really tired and need to get home. Goodnight." I turned away from her and left.

On the way home, Joshua and I walked slowly. He was getting older and I thought he might have painful joints by the way he moved his legs when I mounted him. He was such a loyal horse; the thought of him dying some day was unthinkable. While we walked, I leaned over and hugged his neck. I felt the sting of tears and gently whispered, "Old friend, we've been through a lot together. I don't know how I could've endured without you to talk to when I was young." The tears flowed freely now. "My life is so messed up and sometimes I wish I could end it, but no matter what I try to do, I somehow manage to survive. I lived through all that pain with my parents to just do it all over again with the jackals I have picked. And now I have this Amos who gave me hope for something better, but I was wrong. Oh, why did Mary have to leave me? I loved playing with little Jesus and the long talks I had with Mary. I was so close to finally being happy." I hugged Joshua's neck harder and he stopped walking, seeming to know that I needed time to cry. We stayed like that, in the middle of the road to Salome's house, for a long time. I cried years' worth of tears. I cried until my chest and throat hurt. Then in the midst of my tears. *What are you crying about, Mary? You act as if you have had it so rough! You have had a good life compared to a lot of others. Look at Elizabeth and her mother! Your life is a lot better than theirs! And when are you going to quit grieving and mourning over that selfish Mary? She left you! And Jesus doesn't even remember your name anymore! Get over it!*

When I finally quieted down, Joshua began to walk slowly, as if he was waiting for me to start up again, but I'd decided the voice was right. I sat up and wiped my eyes, patted his neck and resolved that this was the last time I'd cry about these things. "Joshua, you are lucky to be a horse and not have to go through these painful trials." I patted him on the neck and thought more about Amos. I concluded that he probably just wanted to be friends. Even if it was more, I would never be truly happy with him. I'd be bored and I really didn't want to marry him without "knowing" him first. I'd just bide my time until he moved back to Nazareth and then begin scouting for someone else.

When I arrived at Salome's, Amos was waiting for me. He ran outside and hugged me and said, "Mary, I'm so glad you're finally home. I was worried about you." I broke away from him and walked in the house thinking about how smothering he could be sometimes. He followed me in and I said, "I'm sorry Amos. I was just talking with some of the other midwives. We didn't realize how late it had gotten. I'm sorry to have worried you." I tried to conceal in my voice the annoyance I was feeling. He must not have noticed because he smiled at me and placed his hands on my shoulders and said, "Mary, I want you to come to Nazareth with me. I want you to meet my parents. I'm sure they'd love you and I think you would like them. I think you'd like Nazareth, too! It's quiet there; 'quaint' my mother calls it! You could stay with us until you found work. There's always a need for a midwife!" He was so excited he didn't seem to notice me shrug his hands off my shoulders.

I looked over at Salome and she slowly shook her head as she walked toward me to hand me a cup of wine. I drank it down and went to get another. I tried to read what was on her face, but she didn't make eye contact with me. I turned back to Amos and saw the big hopeful grin on his face. His attitude irritated me. He was looking at me as if he had just offered me a thousand shekels of gold. I think he really believed that was what I had been waiting for or something! My aggravation with him was growing and I needed more wine. I gulped two more cups before I felt able to answer Amos. The warmth of the wine was relaxing me and I felt more able to deal with him. I didn't want to hurt his feelings, but I also needed him to go to Nazareth so I could move on with my life. "Amos, that sounds so nice, but I need to stay here and finish my training. I need to work with these women until I feel confident that I can work on my own. Maybe after a few more months, I could come and visit."

He looked disappointed, but never lost that hopeful smile. "I understand, Mary. I know how important this work is to you and I will wait as long as it takes." He smiled and gave me a hug and said he was going home to pack his things. He was leaving for Nazareth early the next morning and needed to pack his tools and clothing. I half-heartedly offered to help but he declined. He gently touched my face and said, "Mary, you've had a long day and you need to rest. I'd rather remember us right here with the candlelight sparkling in your eyes. Besides I don't want you to travel alone at night especially after you've been drinking." That was the last straw! I looked over at Salome and she rolled her eyes. I gritted my teeth and forced myself to hug him. He asked me to walk him outside while he bridled his donkey. I hesitated, but went with him and as soon as we were out the door, he hugged me again and for the first time he kissed me on the mouth. It was a soft, gentle kiss, the kind of kiss I hadn't experienced in years. But I was too angry to even enjoy it. When he pulled away to look at my face, he looked concerned, but it was quickly replaced with a smile. "Please take care of yourself, Mary. I will come see you when I can." He kissed me on the cheek, waved to Salome who was standing in the doorway and went out into the yard to get his donkey. When he was finally ready to leave, he turned again to wave goodbye. I put my hand up in a feeble gesture with a silent "good riddance" on my lips. I watched until he was out of sight.

The day after he was gone, Salome and I sat and drank some of her really good Roman wine. I actually missed Amos and felt bad for not going with him. I shared my feelings with Salome and she laughed. "You don't miss him! You're just bored! He's not exciting enough for you. Here, I have something that will spice up your life a little!" She got up and went to the bedroom and came back with a little cloth bag. The bag was filled with a pale yellow powder and she placed some in one of her husband's pipes. She got a small stick and held it in the fire until it caught and then brought it to me with the pipe. "You'll like this, Mary. They gave this to my husband for his stomach pain and after he smokes it, he feels nothing! Well, you know me! My curiosity got the best of me and I tried it. It made me feel so good! I felt like I was floating. I loved it! But you can't take very much if you've been drinking."

She leaned in toward me, but I was reluctant. She looked at me, rolled her eyes and sarcastically said, "Would you feel better if I went first?" She put the pipe to her mouth and then lit the powder with the stick. It was gone in only a few seconds. I looked up at Salome and her eyes were shut. She began to sway and then suddenly sat down. She sat there with this silly smile on her face saying nothing. She opened her eyes, looked at me and started to say something, but couldn't get it out. Then she started to giggle! I thought I definitely needed to try this powder. Salome never giggled!

I took the pipe from her and put in some of the powder. I held the fire to it and slowly inhaled the smoke. I immediately started choking. It tasted different from the opium I had tried and it hurt my throat. In seconds I felt dizzy, like I was going to pass out. I lay down on the mat and the room soon stopped spinning. I felt numb, like nothing could ever bother me again! Everything I tried to think about, including Amos, seemed in a distant dream. I sat up and noticed Salome was just sitting and smiling, humming a song. I started to say something to her when we heard a knock on the door. Neither of us could get up and Salome just yelled, "Come in!"

It was her friend, Sarah, and she looked like we felt. Sarah was probably Salome's age and she looked every bit of it. Her hair was long and almost gray. She also wore makeup, but didn't do as good a job as Salome. She wore lots of jewelry and too much perfume. It seemed to be a meager effort to cover a less desirable odor. She looked at both of us on the floor and started laughing. "You been smoking that stuff again, Salome? You look like you are falling asleep! Who is your friend?" Salome introduced us and Sarah sat down and asked her for some of the powder. "I wanted to know if you could come to a party with me tonight. A friend of mine is celebrating her birthday. It's not far from here, over the hill behind the inn." She had gotten the pipe from Salome and took a deep inhale of the powder. She didn't seem as affected by it as we were. I got the distinct impression this wasn't new to her.

"I'm sorry, Sarah. I need to stay here with Jethro. He's not able to get up to relieve himself anymore. I don't think it'll be long." I was shocked! This was the first time I had heard her talk about Jethro with any compassion. I had been living here for two months and had only seen him the two times I went into their bedroom to help clean him. Salome had been too drunk to turn him and he was dead weight after he smoked the powder. I hadn't realized until now, how close he was to death.

"You could take Mary with you. She'd probably enjoy herself. Mary, what do you think? Would you like to go?" I wasn't sure how I felt about Sarah, but the powder had relaxed me so much I had trouble thinking as clearly as I'd have liked. The one lucid thought I did have was this might be a great opportunity to meet someone new. It didn't take me long to decide what to do. "Yes, I would like to go if Sarah doesn't mind!" Sarah was taking another puff on the pipe. She nodded her head. "I don't care who comes with me as long as I go! All the wine we can drink! I hear it's that

good stuff like you get, Salome. I just want to get there."
She looked at me and offered the pipe. I declined so she took
another puff and said, "Are you ready, Mary? We are going
to have fun!"

Sarah had a donkey that she rode while Joshua and I
walked beside her. We talked very little along the way. As
we approached the inn, my mind was flooded with memories. I was amazed how clear they seemed, like it was just
yesterday! So many times I had taken this route home after
spending long days with Joanna and her family. Then I had
ridden home many nights after having wonderful talks with
Mary and Joseph. And after they left me, I had late nights with
Salome (though many of them were hard to remember.)

It was amazing to me the transition my life had taken
over the years. I no longer knew that young, vibrant girl that
rode her horse like the wind. She was someone in a distant
memory. Oh, I could still remember everything that happened
to me and often it was more than I wanted to recall, but I
couldn't relate to the innocence that I once possessed. What
happened to that wonderful peace I always felt when I was
with Jesus? When did things change so much and how did I
let it happen?

*You know when they changed, Mary. When that so-called
friend of yours left after promising to help you! She said she
would always be there for you. She said she would listen to
all your troubles and help you. Then she left you. Just like
Matthew and all the other men. Just like your parents. That
Mary is the reason you changed! Because she wasn't trust-
worthy... and she abandoned you. All those safe, peaceful
feelings you thought you had when you were around Jesus
were just a trick to make you think he was something special.
You felt those same things when you smoked that powder
tonight, didn't you? Don't get confused, Mary. You can only
trust yourself to find the peace and happiness that you desire.
And you need to find it any way you can!*

I looked around me as we were approaching the inn. It felt like I had lost time, like I had blacked out! But I was still awake! It was almost like I had been in a dream. I leaned over and asked Sarah if she had a wineskin with her. She stopped and removed one from the basket she had on her donkey's back. "I was getting a little thirsty myself. This is the same wine Salome has. It's very good." I really didn't care what it tasted like; I just needed the feeling that came with it. I began to take long drinks from the skin and then Sarah exclaimed, "Mary, slow down! You need to be careful after smoking that powder. The two don't mix well!" I remembered what had happened to my mother and handed the wineskin back to Sarah. "I'm sorry. My father used to own that inn and I was remembering some things that are probably best forgotten.

Sarah nodded and said, "I've got a few of them myself. The only problem is the wine and the powder, only work temporarily." I nodded in agreement and then asked, "Do you know what that powder is, Sarah? I've had opium before and it has a different taste. Tonight was the first time I'd tried this one and Salome never told me what it was." She chuckled and drank deeply from the wineskin before handing it back to me. "It doesn't really have a name. It comes from Persia and it has opium in it, but it's mixed with something else. Physicians use it for people that have severe pain. I used to give it to the women during labor. Sometimes they'd mix it with water or wine and drink it."

I looked over at her in surprise. "You're a midwife? I am too! I've never seen you with the others!" She took the skin back and drank again. "That's because I don't practice here anymore. I grew to like this," she pointed to the wineskin, "more than my job." She was quiet for a moment and then continued, "Besides, I guess I gave too much of that powder to some of them. A few babies were born dead. Nobody really knew for sure, but I think that's what happened. One woman that I interrupted was in so much pain, I gave her some of the powder in wine. I guess I gave her too much because she went to sleep and never woke up. I told the family it was a complication of the pregnancy that killed her. Fortunately, they believed me." She became quiet again.

I was bewildered by what she had just said. I had no idea what an "interruption" was. She looked absorbed in her own thoughts, but I decided to ask anyway. Her face became sad as she explained. "It's when a woman is pregnant, but she doesn't want to be; she wants to get rid of the baby. Maybe it isn't her husband's or maybe she is too young or maybe she was raped. They would come to us, secretly. There were only two of us who would perform the procedure. Afterwards, they would stay with family for a couple weeks, to recuperate. A few went bad. Within a few weeks, their bellies would get hard as a rock and they would have terrible pain and…" Her voice seemed to trail off, but I wasn't even listening after she described the symptoms. Her explanation sounded just like my sister before she died! I felt guilty because I had not thought of her in a long time and as clouded as my thoughts were now, it was hard to remember all the details. But the familiarity of the description Sarah gave, was awakening things long past. "Are there any other symptoms besides the rigid belly and pain?" I carefully inquired. Sarah, who by now was pretty drunk, looked up at me and in slurred, angry words said, "Like I just said, they run a really high fever. Weren't you listening to me?"

My thoughts were racing! I had so many more questions, but I knew better than ask anything else. My heart felt like it would pound out of my chest! I had questions for my mother, too. This could not be what happened to my sister! I asked Sarah for the skin and we kept on like that, passing it back and forth as we continued on our way. We said nothing else for the rest of the ride, but we persisted in our attempt to drink away our past. Neither of us realized we were being driven by an inner abscess filled to bursting with guilt, shame, rejection, abandonment... and the list could go on. A bulging, painful abscess that cries out for relief. Pleads for a merciful termination. Implores a lancing, so finally the massive amount of trash in our lives could pour out and we could, at long last, have peace.

The party in Bethlehem did birth a new relationship for me. This time with a man named Saul, the host of the party. He, like all the others, was handsome and before the night was over, I knew I wanted to be with him. Though he had been accompanied by another woman that night at the party, he made sure I knew that he wanted to see me again. He asked if I would have dinner with him the next time I was in Bethlehem. He put the woman he was with in her wagon and sent her on her way so he could spend the rest of the evening with me. He must have really liked me to do something like that and I bored Sarah to tears talking about him on the way home. I could not wait to see him again! Thoughts of my sister were lost in the excitement of a new love.

My next trip to Bethlehem came the following week. After I finished my training, Saul and I had dinner together. I ended up staying the night. Within a week, I was moving my things into his house. After packing my clothes, Salome hugged me, stuck a small cloth bag, just like hers in the palm of my hand, winked at me and told me to be careful. By the smell of her breath, I doubted that she would remember our conversation in the morning.

I justified moving in with him by convincing myself that I would have less traveling to do and it would be easier on Joshua. Saul had his own stable (which was rare in the heart of the city) and a horse of his own. I felt complete again. We had good times together. He liked to drink as much as I did, but he did it more frequently. He worked as a blacksmith and said he needed the relaxation after swinging the hammer all day. I knew he worked hard at his job because he was very strong and the muscles in his arms were huge.

After only a few weeks, I noticed that he wasn't coming home before dark and sometimes not at all. I knew he wasn't working so I began a nightly search for him at the inns and taverns. Sometimes I found him and sometimes I didn't. The times that I did, he was usually so drunk I had to find someone to help put him in the wagon so I could drive him home. There were a few times I found him when he got angry and told me to leave. When he looked at me like that, I didn't argue. It was also not wise to question him about anything, so I never did.

After several months of this, I began smelling perfume on him when he came home. The nights he wouldn't show up at all, I went to the taverns and asked the regulars if they had seen him. They exchanged looks and then denied any knowledge of his whereabouts. I knew they were lying and became more determined that ever to find out what he was up to. The first few weeks I had no success, but finally I found him, sitting in a tavern, hanging on another woman, kissing her neck. I was devastated! I watched through the window as they laughed together and she sat in his lap and played with his hair. She was rubbing his chest and with each circle she made, her hand got lower on his abdomen. I felt a red-hot rage fill my gut that I couldn't control!

I burst into the tavern and pulled her off him and started hitting her! I was consumed with jealousy and hatred for this woman! I didn't care if I killed her! Within seconds, I felt arms pulling me off her and then someone spun me around. It was Saul! He had hold of my mantle with one hand and my hair with the other, holding my head back at such an angle that I could hardly see his face. He looked at me with as much rage as I felt and shrieked in my face, "What do you think you're doing?"

At that moment he let go of my wrap and his fist connected with my nose and mouth; I felt an explosion in my head that nearly drove me to unconsciousness. There was no give with the punch because he still had hold of my hair and it felt like his fist crushed my face. Blood was pouring from my nose and mouth and it had splashed on his face as well. I ran my tongue over my teeth and felt the ragged edge of where my front tooth had chipped. When I saw him draw his fist back for another blow, I begged him to stop. The room had begun to spin and I knew I was going to throw up. I heard a voice from behind him say, "Stop! You'll kill her, Saul! Let her go!" Slowly he released my hair and I sank to my knees.

The pain in my head was horrendous and the spinning was getting worse. I leaned over and threw up. In the distance I heard some people laughing. I looked up and a few were looking away shaking their heads while others were trying to get a closer look. I was so humiliated! And to add insult to injury, I saw Saul helping that woman get up from the floor and begin to wipe her face. He was holding her and apologizing for me!

Another man came to me with a damp cloth and gently wiped my chin. He tried to wipe my mouth, but I cried out in pain. My knees were hurting and I sat down. He knelt next to me with the gentlest eyes I had ever seen a man possess. He did not look like he belonged in a place like this. "Let me help you home, Mary. You are badly hurt. I'm afraid for you to walk alone." I didn't know how he knew my name and I didn't care. I just wanted to get out of here. He helped me up and it seemed like no one even noticed us leaving. He walked me the short distance to Saul's house and helped me lie down on the mat. He lit a candle and continued his attempt to clean my face. I asked him who he was and he said, "Just rest now, Mary. Let me take care of you. Trust me."

Those were the last words I heard until the next morning when Saul woke me up, nudging me with his foot. My eyes would not open all the way because of the swelling and my head still ached, but it was tolerable. Saul stood over me with the sun coming through the window behind him. I couldn't make out his face, but I heard his voice. "Don't ever come looking for me again and embarrass me like that. Do you understand? You may not leave this house until your face clears up. I have a good reputation around here and you are not going to ruin it by showing those bruises and making up stories about me. Do you understand?" I looked up at him and said as clearly as I could through my swollen mouth, "You don't need to worry about me, Saul. I'll be leaving today. Do *you* understand?"

Before I even finished speaking, he was on the floor pulling me up to his face by my hair. "You won't go anywhere! If you try to leave me, I will kill you! Is *that* clear? I have friends all over Judea and if you try to run, I will find you and what you got last night will just be an appetizer!" He let go of my hair and I fell back down to the mat. The pounding had returned, mostly from fear that he would again hit my already disfig-ured and pain-filled face. He walked out and I was left there on the mat wondering how I could possibly stay with this man. I knew what I needed, if I could just get to my bag. I attempted to stand, but was unable to get my balance. I ended up crawling and discovered more injuries I didn't know I had. Both my knees were badly bruised and scraped. I guess I had fallen harder than I realized at the tavern.

I finally got to my bag and pulled out the powder. I had smoked what Salome gave me a long time ago, but had learned from one of the midwives how to get more. I smoked until the pain in my head became tolerable and then put everything away. Saul would not like what I was doing and I had to be careful to hide it well. I crawled back to my mat and wondered how I ever got to this place in my life. I began to cry. My hand went up to my face. My nose and lips were so swollen! I wondered how bad it looked. I laid there and cried for a long time. I was sobbing so loudly, I almost didn't hear the soft knock on the door. I turned to get up and heard, "Don't get up, Mary."

I looked in the doorway and there was a young girl with a basket of fruit. "Who are you?" I managed to get out before the throbbing made me lie down again. She knelt down and said, "My name is Leah. I saw you walking home last night and you looked hurt. I know Saul's temper, so I figured out what had probably happened. I brought you some fruit. I can cut it up in small pieces so you can eat it." I was amazed at her insight and thought she must have done this before. "Yes, that would be good and I'd also like some water if you don't mind." She brought me a cup of water and gently lifted it to my lips. "It's going to burn, Mary, be careful." I looked into her knowing face. "Yes, I know. I have been here before." She slowly nodded her head. "So have I, Mary. It used to be my sister he would knock around. I was always nursing her back after one of his beatings. She finally escaped and moved to Galilee. I haven't seen her in two years. She's afraid to come visit us."

I was desperately trying to get the water into my mouth without it running over the split in my lip, but it was a futile effort. I winced in pain as I took a few more sips and then Leah went to cut the fruit. I was feeling a little better and asked her how she knew my name. "I know a couple of the midwives fairly well and they told me. They said this had happened to you one other time, with a different man. I shook my head and said, "I wish it was only one other time. I kept the other times hidden from them. Especially from an older one who also has the name Leah. I am training with her." Leah nodded. "Yes, that's my grandmother. She's a very good woman and cares deeply for you, Mary. She prays for you all the time." I nodded. "Yes, that sounds like Leah. Last night was a complete surprise to me. I've seen Saul angry, but nothing like that! It was the first time he ever hit me."

Well, that was not exactly the truth! He had not hit me that hard, but this young girl did not need to know the details. I continued, "If it hadn't been for that wonderful person who helped me home, I don't know if I would have made it here. Leah, you said you saw me walking home. Did you know who the man was that helped me, so I can thank him?" Leah had knelt down next to me to help feed me. She looked alarmed. "Mary, I think you really need to rest for a few days. You're seeing things that don't exist!" Bewildered, I looked up at her. "What do you mean? There was someone who helped me! He brought me in and cleaned me up and told me I could trust him. I didn't dream that! You must have seen him walking next to me, holding me up!"

Leah looked worried. She gently pushed back my hair and said, "No Mary. You were leaning quite a bit while you were walking and I remember thinking that you were going to fall over any minute, but you never did. I promise you though, there was no one walking with you." I looked at her in disbelief. He had been so real and I *had* woken up this morning cleaned up. Even the clothes I had vomited on had been removed and replaced with clean clothes! In the condition I was in, how could I have done that myself?

Leah must be right. There had been more damage done to my head than I realized. I would take advantage of the time that Saul wanted me to stay indoors. I would rest and take time to re-group. I was twenty-two years old and I was not going to live like this the rest of my life. I would get my thoughts together so I could find a way to escape. The way Leah's sister had. If things got too tough, I had my wine and the powder. They numbed things temporarily. And I would bide my time. I would think of something. I always did.

9

Secrets Revealed

I suffered through six more months of Saul's temper before I finally found the courage to leave. I celebrated my twenty-third birthday alone. He never did stop seeing other women and I learned, quite painfully, not to try and stop him. My use of wine and opium had gotten so bad it was affecting my ability to do my work. I wasn't showing up and when I did, I felt so bad that I was little help to the other midwives. I was sure that if I could get rid of Saul, the pain would be gone and I wouldn't need to drink or smoke so much. But I was so afraid of his threats that I felt paralyzed to escape.

Then one day I was at the market in Jerusalem and whom should I run into, but Amos! He immediately wanted to hug me, but I pushed him away. While stealing furtive glances around me, I briefly explained my situation. "Mary, how could this have happened to you? I've tried to find you both times I've come to Jerusalem. Two times I went to Salome's. The first time, she was planning a funeral for her husband. She was grieving and I hated to question her, but I had to know what happened to you. And the second time…"

I interrupted him and explained we needed to go somewhere more private. "Saul has many friends, Amos. They keep an eye on me and then tell him what I do during the day. Even when I come here to Jerusalem! I think he knows everyone in Judea!" I glanced around again. "Do you know where the Bethesda Pool is— the Sheep Pool?" Amos nodded. "Meet me there in half an hour. No one that knows Saul would be there; it's mostly the poor and sick." I quickly looked around again and pointed south of the city as if I was giving directions, and then added as I walked away, "Please be there Amos, I need to talk to you." He nodded and walked in the direction I had pointed. I smiled and said a silent thank you for his wisdom.

When I arrived at the Pool, Amos was already there. As I approached him, one person after another held out their hand for something—anything—I might give them. I kept shaking my head and quickly sat down with Amos. I wanted to hug him to thank him for coming, but knew I better not risk it. "Amos, thank you so much. It is a miracle that you have come just when I needed a friend so desperately. But first, you were telling me about Salome's husband. He's dead?"

"Yes, he apparently died the day before I got there. Salome was not in good shape herself. She could hardly stand up straight while I was talking with her." I looked down at my hands and nodded. "That doesn't surprise me. She depended on him much more than she realized."

Amos continued, "She told me you'd moved to Bethlehem, but she didn't know where. I went there to try and find you, but no one seemed to know anything about you. I came back this week to get some supplies for my shop so I went back to Salome's to see if she'd heard from you, but the house was empty. Then I came back to Jerusalem to finish picking up my materials... and there you were! It's so wonderful to see you, Mary. I've missed you so much. How can I help you out of this mess you're in?"

Amos always had a way of grating on my nerves and his comment about my life being a mess did the job. But I knew he was right. My life was a mess! I just didn't want to hear it from him or anyone else that never had a tough day in their life! I swallowed my irritation and said, "I need to get away. I need to get my things and just go…sometime when he's not around. If he gets any inclination of my plan, he will kill me." Amos gasped. "Mary, we have to do this as soon as we can! Do you want to come to Nazareth with me? I've started a very fine business and I could help you find a job."

I shook my head. "No, Amos I need to go home to my parents. They are in Cana and I need to see them as well as my little brother. It's been almost five years; Bartholomew will soon be twelve. And Amos… I want to get my life straightened out. I can still see you. Cana is not far from Nazareth, just a little ways north. You could visit me." Amos nodded and leaned over to push my hair off my face. I had tried to keep it down to cover the bruise on my cheek. I noticed him looking at it, but he said nothing. "Whatever you want to do, Mary. I just want you to be safe. Let's figure out how we can get you out of his house without being seen. Tell me about Saul's daily schedule."

We talked for over an hour and I was very impressed with how Amos' mind worked. He proposed that we'd leave at night when Saul made his nightly rounds at the taverns. We'd have to begin as soon as it got dark and then head north to Jericho. It was a little out of the way, but Amos had a sister there and he was sure she would welcome us. We made our plans for the following night.

Except for Saul leaving later than usual that evening, everything went as planned. It was all I could do to keep my mouth shut about finally beating him at his own game. *To let him know that I was going to win.* All the verbal berating and black eyes and women had embittered me, and I wanted to get back at him. But if I said anything, he would get suspicious. So, I played 'nice' and fixed him dinner…and waited. The way he was flirting with me, I feared he was going to stay home and demand something from me. Occasionally he did that and the thought of being intimate with him was sickening. The few times that I gave in, I resorted to the safe place from my childhood. It was still available to me.

Finally, he left. Amos arrived just after dark and helped me pack up. Because I had been afraid to do anything that would alert Saul, nothing was ready for Amos to carry out. It took us over an hour to load Amos' wagon. I went to the stable and got Joshua and tied him to the back of the wagon and finally we were off. I got under an old blanket with my things and I stayed there until we were well out of the city. Even cover of night did not make me feel safe.

It took several hours to get to Jericho and Amos' sister was glad to have us. The trip to Cana took three days, partly because Amos had so many friends that we ran into along the way. Amos and I talked a lot and I found myself feeling what I had felt for him in Bethlehem. He had risked his life to help me and his gentleness was a welcome change after the brutal months with Saul. By the end of our second day, I began to wonder why I had not gone to Nazareth with him.

We stayed at an inn on the outskirts of Nain and as always, Amos got separate rooms for us. I felt so drawn to his tenderness that when he helped me down from the wagon, I kissed him. He hesitated and then kissed me back and it was with the same passion as the night at Salome's house. He tried to pull away, but I wanted more and he had to take my arms from around his waist and push me away. "Mary, we are not married and we are traveling together without a chaperone. We need to be prudent." I looked at him as seductively as I could and said, "I don't want to be a prude, Amos." My hand went to his face and I caressed his beard. "No one will know. We are in the middle of nowhere." Amos got very serious. "I will know, Mary. And my God will know."

I couldn't believe this was happening! This was why I didn't go with him to Nazareth! I rolled my eyes. "Where was your God when I was having my face smashed in by that jackal, Saul? I don't care what your God knows or doesn't know! He's not concerned with me!" With that I turned on my heel, untied Joshua and took him to the stable. Then I went to my room. I lay down on the mat and within seconds the tears came. What is wrong with me? How could I treat him like that?

Mary, nothing has changed with this man. He still doesn't want you. He has rejected you again. Saul may have beaten you, but at least he desired you. I covered my ears and screamed out loud to my empty room, "Shut up! Just shut up!" I lay like that for some time before taking my hands down. The voice did not come back and I began to pray for the first time in many years. "Please God, help me make it right with Amos. Let him forgive me for the way I treated him. And please God, let my parents still be in Cana. I need to get my life together. Thank you." A familiar feeling started to surface, one I had not experienced in a long time. *Peace.* I fell asleep almost immediately.

Amos did forgive me and took me the rest of the way to Cana. Along the way, I felt that he was a little distant and reserved. I prayed I had not ruined things between us. We found my parents and I introduced them to Amos. They invited him to stay the night, but he said he needed to get back to his business—he had a lot of work piled up. He promised to come back soon. We did convince him to eat the midday meal with us before he left. I walked him outside and he kissed me good-bye. It was a kiss on the cheek. When I tried to kiss him on the mouth, he backed away. He took my hand and smiled at me and said, "Mary, I think we need to slow down." Then he left for Nazareth. I watched him drive away and wondered if he would ever come back. I realized after he left that I hadn't even asked him about Joseph and

Mary. Surely the carpenters in town would know each other. I would remember to do that when—and if—he returned.

My reunion with my parents was strained. My brother was not here and I felt things may be better when he got home. He was with my mother's family in Magdala. My parents promised I could go with them when they picked him up. My first few days were tentative as I tried to hide the remnants of the bruise... and the remnants of my life. Neither of them asked any questions and I offered no history lesson. It didn't take long for my father to shake off his good behavior and begin his usual nagging and yelling. At least he was gone most of day. He delivered wine for a local wine-maker who, because he was crippled, was unable to deliver it himself. After a few weeks of my father's mouth, I started sneaking some myself.

Mother's conduct had not changed when Father started one of his tirades. She yelled and screamed back and then went to her room and talked to no one. It had been two months since I arrived and things were escalating between them. The argument of the day was about the long hours he was working and how late he was coming home. After he yelled his last insult and left, Mother went to her room. I found one of Father's wineskins and drank most of it. I didn't think I was going to need to do this after leaving Saul, but some things never change. Certainly, nothing has changed around here!

When Mother finally came out, she was quiet, so I chose to say nothing and just helped her with dinner. Father didn't come home, so she and I sat down to eat. During our meal, she talked about some of the things she had been sewing. I remembered the wedding linen I had taken and wondered if she ever missed it. I still had questions about how Salome died. I thought maybe this was a good time to ask. "Mother, there are some things I don't remember too well about Salome. Could I ask you about them?" She looked at me and said, "Yes, Mary. You know, she would have been twenty-six this year. She would have been married by now and I would have grandchildren." Tears were slipping down her face. "On her birthday, I went into my trunk to look for the linen we had bought for her wedding dress, but it was gone. I guess it got lost in the move. Or that woman your father had working for us may have taken it. I think her name was Tamar," she paused, "You know who I mean; you used to play with her daughter. She took one of your father's amphorae of wine; I guess she could have taken the material, too."

Did I ever regret this conversation! Not only did I make her cry, but also it brought up all kinds of memories that neither of us wanted to think about. There was one thing though, that I had to know. "Mother, if it isn't too painful for you, could you tell me again how Salome died?" I thought for a moment that she was going to get up and leave. I could see the internal struggle she was having as her memories of Salome surfaced. "Yes, Mary. I can tell you. I have never told you the whole truth because you were too young to comprehend. But now, I think your age and your work will allow you to understand." She looked squarely into my eyes. "Your sister was pregnant."

My shock was audible. "What? But she was so young, only fourteen if I remember correctly!" Mother nodded. "She was raped at the inn. I have always believed it was one of two men. Do you remember that jackal, Artemis?" I nodded. "I think it may have been him. Your sister told us she never saw who it was because he grabbed her from behind and threw her facedown on the floor. It was one of those nights that your father had his friends come to the inn and they would drink to oblivion! I had gone to bed to avoid seeing any of them. She told me she had gotten up to check on you. He grabbed her outside your room and pulled her into my sewing room. She was afraid to tell me what happened, and I believe it was because she really did

167

know who it was. She didn't want to start more trouble between your father and me."

Her face looked strained and I said, "Mother, who was the other person… or if this is too hard…" She held up her hand. "No, I want to get this out. I have held it in too long. A few months before she got pregnant, Salome told me someone had been coming to her room at night and messing with her." My heart felt like it dropped out of my chest! I could hardly breathe! I grabbed her arm and she must have read the panic on my face because she said, "What is it, Mary? You look like you have seen a ghost rise from the ground!" I felt like my throat was too tight to say anything, but I managed a whisper. "Did she tell you anything else about the man, Mother?"

Her eyes were searching mine and I felt like they were piercing my soul. "Yes, Mary. She said she heard a shuffling noise in the corridor just before he came into her room." I laid my head in my hands and cried. It was the same man! Salome had been through the same horrors I had experienced! That's why she was so protective of me! I looked up at my mother and asked what she had done after Salome told her about the man. Mother put her head down and started crying. "I did nothing, Mary! I did nothing! I told her it was her imagination; that no one was coming into her room! I told her not to talk about it anymore. Then, later, when she told me how she was feeling, I knew she was pregnant. I knew she had been telling me the truth. I knew I could have stopped it!" She was shaking all over as she sobbed. "I knew I should have listened."

My head was spinning. Salome never had a baby, so was the procedure Sarah told me about performed on Salome, as I had suspected? "Mother, what caused Salome's death? There was never a baby. Did something happen?" Mother's crying turned to wailing and again I wondered how wise it was for me to push her, but I had to know. She eventually quieted and whispered, "Your father told me he knew two midwives who could get rid of the baby. We did not want Salome to grow up with the stigma of having a baby out of wedlock. Some of the people we knew there would have wanted to stone her! Mary, you know what people would say! She would never find a husband and her life would be ruined. It was bad enough that she had lost her virginity! And she was so sweet, she did not deserve that!" Mother began to wail again. My thoughts went to the way Sarah had described the "interruption." I also remembered the things Elizabeth had shared with me. It had been awful for her! And that is what had killed my sister! I was so confused! Why didn't my mother send her to a relative, she had so many that I knew would have helped!

Finally, Mother calmed down again and, as if she had been reading my mind, said, "I wanted nothing to do with that idea of your father's. I told him we just needed to send her to my brother's… or Mother's… I didn't care where. She could have the baby and then the family could raise it as its own. Salome could come back to us and no one would ever know what happened."

Mother's voice became bitter. "But, no! Not your father! He would have nothing to do with any of it! He said the only sure way to keep the secret was that procedure. He also said he could never keep up with the inn without all of us being there. He was convinced I would be off visiting Salome every chance I got until the baby came and that I would take you with me. Then he would be left to do all the work. So the decision was made. But something went wrong. She had horrible pain during and after the procedure. She cried out to me as I held her! Then the fever came and soon her belly became hard and tender to touch. Nobody we took her to could help her. Oh, if only I had listened, maybe…" She began to wail even louder this time.

I got up and began to pace around the room. So many things were coming together for me. Like my mother's grief

Forgiven Much

for Salome and her anger with Father. She blamed herself—
and him—for Salome's death. My sister had told me not to
tell when the man came to my room, because she was such
a peacekeeper. She didn't want any problem to surface that
may cause more friction between our parents. So she became
my protector. How many times had she guarded me from that
man? Was she defending me the night she was raped? Why
was there so much friction between Father and Salome? Did
she really know who it was that came to her room? And was
this the secret that I always felt gave her power over Father?
So many questions that couldn't be answered. But there was
still one question that I thought Mother could answer. She
had quieted and I decided to ask again about the other man.
"Mother, who do you think the other man was?" She shook
her head as she held her head in her hands and then slowly
looked up at me, "First, you tell me why you reacted the way
you did when I told you about Salome."

I swallowed hard. What strife might this start? Well, I
had nothing to lose. Mother had never been more open with
me, so I felt it was safe to tell the truth. "The same man came
to my room, Mother. But he never raped me; he only fondled
me. I didn't know who it was either, because he only came
when it was very dark. He always smelled of wine and garlic
and had the same shuffling footsteps that Salome described.
I wanted to tell you, but Salome always told me not to. Then
after she died, I got scared. Once I tried to tell, but you said
I only wanted attention."

Mother looked up at me and she looked confused. "You
told me that a man came to your door! You never said he
touched you! I didn't do anything because I thought Salome
had told you about the man. I thought you were just repeating
what she told you. I also knew that Artemis had left for
Greece and would not be back for over a year. So who could
have been bothering you?" She seemed to be getting angry.
"Why didn't you tell me the whole truth? Do you realize if

170

you had come to me before Salome got pregnant, I would have believed both of you and none of this would have happened?" Her anger was escalating.

"Mother, calm down! When I was little, I didn't remember the details. I only remembered the man at the door. I knew something had taken place, because my bed clothing would be messed up or removed, but I couldn't remember any details of what had happened. Those memories did not come until I was much older and even then, they were sparse. But, you said Artemis was gone, so what about the other man?" Mother had gotten up and was pacing. She finally stopped and glared at me. "You know, Mary, this is your fault! If you had just been truthful, none of this would have happened! Even if you had mentioned the shuffling feet, I would have known Salome was telling the truth and I could have taken her away from the inn before she got pregnant." Her eyes held hatred for me. "Before she was violated."

Her words had caused my heart to sink. I felt my throat tighten and tears welled up in my eyes. It wasn't so much her blaming me, I was used to that. It was what she said about taking Salome away. She had not mentioned taking me with them! "Mother, what about me? Would you have taken me away, too?" My tears were coming like a flood. Old wounds had been slashed open and I was drowning in the truth of my mother's feelings. The things that happened to me did not concern her! My pain did not concern her! It was only Salome! "What about me, Mother? Would you have just left me there for that man to continue doing what he was doing to me? Is that…?"

She interrupted me, "That's not what I meant, Mary! Of course, I would have taken both of you! I love you, too. I just know that if you had told me, things would have been different. You could have…" I stood and held my hand up to stop her. "I don't believe you, Mother! You would have left me. It was always Salome that you cared about and you know it!" I was shouting now. "You said you would tell me the name of the other man. I need to know…was it Father?"

Her eyes shot a look of alarm at me. "Why would you say something like that? What are you thinking, Mary?" Memories were coming to me in torrents and I was trying to filter them. "Remember the night I came home from Mary and Joseph's because you were so sick? While I was in the room helping you, I heard the shuffling footsteps coming in the hall. I felt immediate fear, but when I looked at you, there was terror in your eyes. And then when it turned out to be Father, you lost control. You started screaming at him! Artemis was there that night and you were furious with Father about something Artemis had done to you. I think he had thrown you over his shoulder." I was crying so hard, I could hardly get the words out. "You said to Father that he needed to leave you alone or you were going to tell me the truth about everything. And the way he backed down, I knew it was something bad. Is that what it was, Mother? Was it Father's shuffling feet Salome and I heard in the corridor outside our rooms?"

As the words were leaving my mouth, Mother looked behind me in horror. Then I heard a loud crash as a clay cup hit the inside wall of the house. It was Father! I didn't know how long he had been standing there, but the rage that covered his face, told me he'd heard more than I wanted him to hear. He looked at mother in disgust and then looked at me. Through clenched teeth his words spewed out. "Get your things and get out of my house! You are nothing but a troublemaker and a little drunken whore. You think you're so slick! Do you think men don't talk? Do you know how embarrassed I have been when I hear men in taverns snicker as they mention your name? Then, you come here and steal my wine and start telling your mother lies!" He looked over at mother and yelled, "Naomi, go to your room! I'll help her get her things from the stable."

I stared at Father in disbelief! I thought my life had been kept far away from them. I thought I could come here and start over! But he seemed to know everything! And worse, he heard me accuse him of being the man that got Salome pregnant! What if I was wrong? This would alienate me forever! I watched Mother slowly get up and walk away. She didn't even look at me. First Amos and now my parents! I was an expert at messing up everything. I saw Father glaring at me so I turned to get my clothes from my room. As I was walking away, he snarled, "Don't tarry. I want you out of here." Then he went out the door.

After getting my things, I went to Mother's room and stood at the doorway. She was lying on the mat, silently crying. The candle flickered softly on her back. "Mother, I'm sorry. I just had so many questions. I never meant to start trouble. Please, Mother, talk to me." When I received only silence, I remembered more things...long past. So many times, when I was little, I had stood at my mother's door and had this conversation. The response was the same. Nothing.

I tried again. "Mother, I'm leaving. Please, talk to me." The candle still flickered on her back. The sobbing was audible now. She didn't turn over to look at me and she said nothing. I walked away as I had numerous times as a child. Unwanted. Unloved. Rejected. Tonight, I felt like that little girl again.

I went outside and my things had all been thrown into one of my father's wagons. He had hooked Joshua to it and was waiting for me. I was perplexed because I had no way to return the wagon. I didn't even know where I was going! "Father, I don't know how I can return the wagon to you and..." Before I could finish, he said, "I don't care about the wagon. It is an old one and I just want to get rid of you. And I don't ever want you to come back." He took my clothes from me and threw them on top of my other things. I remembered my brother and couldn't stand the thought of never seeing him again! "But Father, we were supposed to pick up Bartholomew next week. I haven't seen him in many years, and I miss him so much."

The smile that I knew so well, started to form on his face. In slow, controlled words, he said, "Well, Mary, I guess you should have thought of him when you were out drinking wine and entertaining men!" The smile became more evil. "You should have thought of him when you came here and decided to dredge up the past. I promise, you will never see him again, Mary!" He turned on his heels and left me standing in the yard with my heart in my throat. Never see Bartholomew again! I had promised I would take care of him. The way Salome had cared for and protected me.

Salome. Oh, I wish I could hold her again! She had loved children so much! It must have destroyed her to do what she did! Oh, God, how could all of these things have happened? Then the voice returned. *Didn't you pray to God and ask him to help you? Is this the way he helps you start a new life? By keeping your brother from you? By causing this big fight between you and your parents? By allowing your sister to get pregnant and then die? Why are you praying to this God? He will not help you, Mary!*

I shook the voice from my head and climbed into the wagon. I was alone. Totally alone. I didn't know where I would go. My first thoughts were to go to Nazareth and find Amos. But what if I found Mary and Joseph instead? But, in actuality, did I have any other choice? I clucked to Joshua and he began to walk. I noticed him hesitate and I knew his legs were getting worse. I worried that this load was too much for him, but I had no other way to get my things to wherever I was going.

As we traveled south, I thought about what a mess I'd made of my life. I'd been so sure when I left Saul and Bethlehem... and put them behind me... I would escape the sources of my pain. But, somehow, I had managed to find even more. What was wrong with me? The self-loathing I felt was almost too much to bear. Oh, I needed a drink! I wish I had filled my wineskin when I had the chance. I did have some opium with me, though. I pulled Joshua to a stop and found my bag. I knew I'd regret this in the morning; it always made me feel awful the next day. I sat and smoked until I felt better...until I felt numb.

I clucked to Joshua and we began our journey to Nazareth. I believed Amos was the one person who could help me now. It would mean some changes. The thought of meeting his family made me nervous. Putting up with his comments would be a challenge. His inexperience would be a test of my patience. Yes, there were many things he would need to change. But I could help him with that and I could learn to love him. And maybe, just maybe, he would even marry me.

10

Life taken

*Since the beginning of time, it has been a woman's deepest
joy to know she is carrying a baby—someone to love and
adore and also to feel her love reciprocated. Also deeply
settled in a woman's heart and soul, is her innate desire to
love and protect her baby. Women were created this way,
with this inherent need, so if any danger should threaten the
child's life, the mother would be there to protect him.
Even if that meant giving her own life in the process.
It was God's perfect plan that a wife share that joy
and responsibility with her husband and—together—
they love and protect their baby.
But because we live in a world where lies and deception
run rampant, God's plan doesn't always prevail. People
have sex without the protection of the marriage commit-
ment. Women get pregnant. Men get scared. Choices get
made. Irreparable choices. And marriage is not always
a safeguard against those things happening. The sanctity
of the marriage bed is not always respected. Busyness
happens. Extramarital affairs happen. Abuse happens.
Name-calling. Lonely days. Lonelier nights. Conversation
stops. Divorce proceedings begin.*

"If the relationship isn't working, is it really fair to bring
a baby into the world? Wouldn't it be easier—more
convenient—to just not have the baby? After all, there
is plenty of time to have a family later, when everyone
is happy. When there is enough money. When the 'right
person for me' is found. When it's more convenient...."
Choices get made. Irrevocable choices. It is a woman's
deepest joy to know she carries a life, her intrinsic nature
to love and protect it. But when irreversible choices get
made, she then experiences a woman's deepest sorrow.

It did not take me long to find Amos. His carpenter skills
had given him quite the reputation in Nazareth. I had
driven all night and was exhausted, but was determined to
find him. After asking only two people, I was directed to his
home, just south of the city. When I pulled up in the wagon,
I saw him in the yard, working. He looked up and a huge
grin spread across his face. As I was getting down from the
wagon, he ran to me and hugged me. "Mary, you are here!
It is so wonderful to see you! Did you come for a visit?" He
was so happy to see me and it was exactly what I needed
after last night's nightmare.

"No, Amos, actually I am here to stay if you will have
me." I gave him a quick synopsis of the events of last night,
leaving out the unsavory details. He hugged me as tight as
he could. "Mary, I am so very sorry. I know how much you
wanted this reunion to be special. Of course you can stay
here. Come in and meet my parents." We went inside the
small house and he introduced me to Reuben and Hannah.
They were older and to my surprise, made me feel at home,
like I had known them all my life.

We ate together and then I told Amos I had to get some
sleep. I noticed a visual exchange between him and his
parents. I thanked them for the meal and then Amos and I
walked outside. He suggested I sleep in his workshop behind

the house. He slept out here on occasion because he said it was quieter. He chuckled. "My father could wake the dead with his snoring! You would sleep much better out here!" We both laughed and I told him I understood; I had the same problem with my father. I started to get my things, but he stopped me and turned me around. "Mary, I am thrilled that you are here. This is what I have prayed for. But you and I are not betrothed and my parents are not going to let you stay in their home unless we are. It would cause talk among their friends. We can work all these things out, but it will take a little time. I don't want you to get discouraged." He reached over and hugged me again and then helped me get the trunk with my clothes. I watched as he carried it to his workshop. I followed him and he showed me to his sleeping mat. He kissed me on the cheek and said, "Sleep well, Mary. I will wake you for dinner."

Amos left me there and went back to his work. I changed my clothes and lay down. I looked around his shop and thought how thoroughly organized it was. It reminded me of my father. *That's one person I didn't want to think about.* I sat up and thought about Amos' parents. I had mixed feelings about them. I felt they were judging me without even knowing me. I would probably never be good enough for their son! Would I ever just be accepted for who I was? Sleep was overtaking me quickly and I turned to my side and shut my eyes. As I drifted off, my final thought was how I didn't think this arrangement was going to work.

I awoke to a cock crowing. Disoriented, I sat up suddenly, not knowing where I was. I had been dreaming about wandering in the desert, with no food or water and that voice I always heard saying over and over, *"You're not good enough! You're not good enough! YOU'RE NOT GOOD ENOUGH!"* I looked around and slowly the events of the last few days sifted into my mind. The dream became more distant (for which I was grateful) and I sat and got my bearings. Amos was supposed to have awakened me for dinner, but now it was morning. I listened to see if he was working, but heard nothing. I got up and put some things together to wear. I badly needed to bathe and stuck my head out the door to see if anyone was in the yard. Amos had told me there would be some water behind the house and when I looked, I noticed several jugs. I ran over and grabbed one and brought it back to the workshop and proceeded to wash up.

I wondered why I heard no sound coming from the house. Surely they must be eating breakfast by now. After I was dressed, I went out to see where everyone might be. No one was in the house and the wagon and oxen were gone. My wagon had been moved to the back yard and Joshua was tied to a stake next to it. He was grazing and I went to him and hugged him. "You made it, old boy! I was worried about you. I wish I could say we have arrived at our permanent destination, but I don't believe that to be the truth. I think I will need to find my own place...and soon. Let me get you some water." I went to get the jug and noticed only a few houses along the road that led to Nazareth. I wondered how far I would have to go to find a place to live. As I was looking, I saw a wagon coming toward me. I hoped it was Amos coming home; I was famished!

It was their wagon and as they pulled into the yard, I noticed Amos was beaming. "Mary, I found a job for you with the midwife in Nazareth!" He jumped down from the wagon, helped his parents down and then turned to me. "I took my parents into town to the market where I saw Orpah. She is the midwife and she told me you could work with her! She was hesitant because she doesn't know you, but I promised that you would make a good partner for her. Also, Orpah said she knew of a place for you to stay. It's small and in the city, but I think it will be perfect for you until my parents get to know you better and we can talk of marriage." He was so excited, it was contagious! I wasn't sure how I felt about getting to know his parents too intimately. Mary had taught me a lot about my Jewish heritage when we were together, but time had taken away most of it. Having not been raised with the traditions, I feared embarrassing myself. I was very excited about the job and the house, however, and thanked him for all he had done. His mother stuck her head out the door and told us to come eat. Amos looked at me and said, "Let's eat and then I will take you to see your new home!" Maybe I had been wrong. Maybe this was going to work out after all!

As we got ready to leave, I thanked his parents and his mother asked me how soon I could return. I offered that when I was settled, I would come back and we could talk more. That was all I was willing to commit to at this point. Amos tied his donkey to the back of the wagon and we were on our way. As we went, I remembered about Joseph and Mary and tentatively asked if he knew them. "Oh, yes! Joseph taught me everything I know. Do you know them?" I nodded my head. "Yes, Mary and I used to be best friends when they lived in Bethlehem. We drifted apart after they left. I never found out where they moved."

Amos looked thrilled. "Why, Mary, they are right here in Nazareth! Let's go there now. Mary would love to see you, I'm sure." My hand went to the necklace. I was not ready to do that! A part of me would love to see them and especially Jesus. But I still had an awful lot of pain and anger. "No, Amos. That's not a good idea. It has been a very long time since I saw them and I don't feel like talking with anyone today. I would prefer that they don't even know I'm here." Amos looked at me with confusion and concern on his face, but said nothing. We traveled the rest of the way in silence.

When we arrived at the house, Orpah was inside removing some things and cleaning up. She apparently was the owner and allowed her helpers to stay here until they found something more permanent. Amos introduced us and she showed me the inside of the house. It was small, but I felt it would be perfect for now. She talked with me briefly about meeting her the next day and then left. I walked out to where Amos was and looked around. The house was situated in the city, but the back of the house faced the mountains with no other houses behind me. It seemed from my vantage point, that most of Nazareth was nestled in the foothills of Galilee. Some may have seen this as a disadvantage, but I was glad. I had not liked living in the heart of Bethlehem. I was used to being in the open. I had a small yard in the back with grass for Joshua. There was a small lean-to that looked as if it were about to fall. "I can fix that for you today, Mary. I brought my tools and a few nails should make it nice and sturdy for your horse." He immediately went to work and I got busy unpacking the wagon. I felt like this would truly be a new start for me, regardless of what happened with Amos.

After he finished, Amos took his donkey and told me he would be right back. He went to the market and bought some food for me and also brought me a large jug of water. When he returned with them, my heart was so full of gratitude, I kissed him. He gave me a hug, but told me not to do that again. "Mary, things are different here in the city. Someone is always watching. You must never show any outward signs of affection. We must be betrothed for a year before we can live together as husband and wife. After that year, when the harvest is in, we can be married. Until then, we must be discreet."

I was confused and a little put off. Was he asking me to marry him? "Amos, are you asking me to marry you? Is that why you're telling me these details?" Amos shook his head. "Mary, I want to marry you, but my parents have to be satisfied that you are the one for me. I am their only son and they are the ones who choose my wife. They have heard me speak of you for many months and I refused to marry another until I was sure of our future. Now I am sure! You are here! But, you must spend the time with my mother. You must do it for us."

I took in all he had said and still had doubts. Everything sounded conditional. Well, I wasn't going to think about it now. I thanked Amos again and asked if he wanted to stay for dinner, but he said he had work to do at home. He helped me move the wagon as I took Joshua into the back yard and then he said he would come see me the next day. I watched as he rode off on his donkey. I had such mixed feelings about that man! Well, there was plenty of time to decide those things later. Today I would just relax and enjoy my new home.

Days turned to weeks and weeks to months. I spent time with Hannah and allowed her to teach me to cook the things that Amos liked. Some things I already knew, but she had her own way and no matter how hard I tried, I never felt like I was doing a good enough job. I never felt that *I* was good enough. She was always kind to me and treated me respectfully, but something wasn't right. Also, my work was nowhere near as busy as it had been in Bethlehem. Probably the close proximity of Jerusalem had kept us on our toes, but here it was almost boring. That seemed to be how my life was now...boring. Work was boring and Amos was boring. All he kept talking about is that I needed just a little more time with his mother before we could get betrothed. I was at the point where I really didn't care anymore. I had not had a drink or used any opium since the night I left my parents. Until today, I had not even thought about it! I didn't want to begin to drink again; it had been difficult for me to stop. But I had begun to wonder if that was why my life was so boring now. Something needed to change.

One day after I had just returned from a particularly difficult day at work, Amos showed up at my house. His grandfather had died and they needed to travel to Jericho for the funeral. "We should be back within a few weeks. My mother wants to stay with my sister for a time and visit with the grandchildren. Will you be all right until I return?" I assured him I would and asked him to give my sympathies to his family. "I will return as soon as I can, Mary. Take care while I'm gone. You could always visit Mary and Joseph if you get lonely." I swallowed hard. "I'll be fine, Amos. You go and take care of your family, I'll be fine." He took my hand, said goodbye and left. I almost felt some relief. I had been entertaining the thought of visiting the tavern in Japhia, a local town. Nazareth was too small and I dared not take the chance of Amos finding out. I had heard another woman speak of Japhia while I was getting water at the well. Apparently her husband spent more time there than she liked.

I wasted no time the following evening. I put on my best clothes and with great expectation, jumped on Joshua and headed for Japhia. It was only a few miles and I enjoyed this time riding alone. I was amazed how little I did it anymore. I also wasn't quite sure how much time I had left to ride Joshua; his legs seemed to hurt him more and more. I found the tavern on the outskirts of the town as part of the only inn in Japhia. It was like my father's had been, but not as large. The wine was not as good, but it did the job. It seemed that most of the people here were transients, probably traveling south to Jerusalem. I started going to Japhia one to two times a week, even after Amos came home

Weeks passed and my disillusionment with Amos grew. I began to look for things to complain to him about and these always justified my visits to the tavern. I was getting lonely and bored with the life I had here and the future I saw ahead of me with Amos. Besides, the last two nights I had been at the tavern, I had noticed a man smiling at me. A very handsome man. On the third night, he came to me and asked if he could join me. His name was Thomas and we sat and talked for some time. He was from the region of Samaria and was looking for a home near Nazareth. He was a mat maker. We talked until it was very late and I was very drunk. He asked if I would like to stay with him at the inn and I did.

The next morning, I awoke with the sun and I could not believe what I had done! Surely, someone would find out about this and tell Amos and his family... or worse, tell Orpah. I got up quietly and slipped out. I found Joshua tied to the post and galloped the whole way home. I was bathing when Orpah showed up to tell me we had a woman in labor and I needed to come right away. I went with her and as we walked she said, "Mary, you know this is a small town and the women talk. The well is a breeding ground for gossip. People are talking about your trips at night. One of the husbands has seen you. You know that Amos and his family will hear. Does this bother you?"

I looked at her, trying to read her face. Trying to read judgment for my actions, but I saw none. "Orpah, truly, I don't love Amos. I only care about doing a good job for you and keeping this position with you." Orpah looked at me and smiled for the first time since this conversation started. "Well, you have no fear there. You are an excellent midwife and I have seen great wisdom in your difficult deliveries. That breech you handled last week should have been born dead, but your idea of manipulating and turning the baby early in her labor, saved them both. I just don't want you to ruin your reputation here. If you do, the women will not want you to handle them. Enough said." And that was the end of the conversation. When Orpah said her piece, she wanted no argument or explanation.

That evening Amos came over and I told him how I felt. At first he seemed upset, but then just touched my hair and said, "I will wait, Mary. I waited for you before and I will wait again." I shook my head, "No, Amos! You don't under-stand! I have met someone else!" He just looked at me and said, "There have been others before, Mary. I will wait." And with that he turned and left. I just stood there in bewilderment. This man was so hard to understand! I ate my meager dinner and got myself dressed and headed for the tavern. When I arrived, I saw Thomas talking with another woman and my heart sank! But when he saw me, he came and sat with me. I asked him who she was and he explained, "Oh, she is just someone who works here." I looked over at her again and could not remember seeing her before, but I let go of what was stirring in my gut.

I asked Thomas to stay with me this time. Maybe if he started coming to see me, I would not have to come here and take the chance of being seen at the tavern. He agreed and we walked our horses back to Nazareth, enjoying the beauty of the evening. We conversed so easily, it felt as if we had known each other for many years. It was much easier to talk with him because I didn't feel that he was judging me as I did with Amos. We talked so late, he ended up staying the night. In the morning, I awoke early. He was still sleeping, so I got up, built a fire in the small clay oven and started to make some bread. I cut some fruit and waited for the bread to bake. I felt so relaxed with Thomas and after only a few nights, I truly enjoyed his company more than Amos. I secretly hoped he felt the same way. I did, however, feel like I was betraying Amos and his family. *Well, after last night what else would you call it? You need to get rid of them and all their religious traditions anyway! This Thomas, he is more suited to you. Quit wasting your time thinking about Amos.*

When the bread was finally baked, I woke Thomas. He was surprised that I had made him breakfast and showed his appreciation by giving me a long, deep kiss. As we ate, he kept staring at me. It was making me so nervous, I could hardly eat! "Why do you keep staring at me? Is my hair a mess or something?" My hand went to my hair, but he took my hand in his and said, "You are so beautiful, Mary. Your eyes mesmerize me. I think I am falling in love with you!"

I almost choked! What was he saying? I could get no words to come from my mouth, so he said, "Let's live together! I could start a mat-making business here and you could continue with your work. And if things go well, later we can be married. What do you think? Let's do it, Mary! I love you and I know we will be happy." I could not believe what I was hearing and could believe even less my response. "Yes, Thomas, I think I love you too. Let's do it!"

Within two weeks, my whole life had changed. He went down to Sychar, in Samaria, to get the rest of his things and then moved in with me. My little house filled up fast and I was glad! I would not be lonely anymore and he seemed to really care about me. The only thing that could make things better would be marriage. I worried about my reputation after what Orpah had shared with me and hoped this would not jeopardize my standing in Nazareth. The next day she put my concerns to rest. "Mary, you have made your choice. The women will not know if you are married to this man or not as long as you keep your mouth shut. It is not an uncommon practice in Samaria, you know. But tell no one where he is from. I do not want to lose you, so please keep quiet!" I promised her I would.

At first, my life with Thomas was wonderful. I could not imagine being happier. He said and did nice things for me. His work was going well and I was certain at any time we would be talking about marriage. We already were talking about how much we loved children and how many we wanted. I even felt safe telling him about my family. My desire to drink had vanished and though we occasionally drank together, I didn't feel I *needed* it anymore. We did take trips together, but seldom went into Nazareth to the market. We tried to be as discreet as possible. At the well, no questions were ever asked. I never ran into Amos or his family and had, at one point, inquired if he was still living in Nazareth. I guess it was my good fortune that we never saw each other.

After a few years, things began to change between Thomas and me. I started to feel very insecure because I was getting older, twenty-seven now, and marriage was never discussed. On the few occasions I brought it up, he would say we would talk about it later. He stopped caring if he got home on time. The trips we used to make together to get his materials, he now wanted to make alone. During one of those trips, my curiosity about Mary and Joseph got the best of me. I asked Orpah if she knew them. "Why yes, Mary, I do. You know them?" I nodded and asked if she knew where they lived. She looked at me with curiosity, but asked no questions and gave me directions. They lived on the opposite end of the city and it took me some time to find their home.

As I approached their house, I saw two men in the yard, working on a wagon together. As I got closer, I realized one of the men was much older than the other. The younger man had a sparse beard and longer hair and was quite tan. I ventured a few more steps hoping not to be noticed, but at that moment the older of the two looked up. "Good day! May I help you?" It was Joseph and the other must be Jesus! I felt the heat rush up my neck and was grateful for the covering over my lower face.

"No, but thank you for asking. I am just taking a walk." At that moment, Jesus looked over at me and his eyes met mine. He flashed a broad grin that revealed beautiful white teeth that seemed even brighter against his tan face. I quickly calculated in my head and realized he must be fifteen now and so grown up! And when his eyes met mine, my heart froze! He raised his hand and waved, as if he knew who I was. Even Joseph looked bewildered and asked him if he knew me. Jesus shook his head and I thought I saw him looking at my necklace. I knew I must be imagining things, but quickly pushed it under my cloak. My eyes met his again and I felt, for a brief moment, that he truly did recognize me. The moment passed and after waving back, I hurried on. The whole experience had shaken me up and the unresolved feelings surfaced. I didn't think I would ever go back.

One night Thomas came home after it was dark and I could smell the rich scent of an expensive perfume. I tried to sound calm. "Where have you been, Thomas? You smell of perfume." He had been drinking and turned and tried to kiss me. The smell of perfume was even stronger. I pulled away and asked again. He rolled his eyes at me and slurred. "I was looking for something nice to bring you and this is what I get?" For a fleeting second I thought how much this sounded like Father... and then it was gone. I apologized and thanked him for thinking about me. I made his dinner and after we ate, he went to sleep. I sat and looked at him as he slept and remembered all the years I had thought my mother was stupid for believing Father's lies. How long had it taken her to stop? How long would it take me?

Four more years. Yes, it took me four more years of lies before I finally caught him. And to make matters worse, it was Michal, the new midwife Orpah had hired. I thought she had been a friend, a good friend. She was just a little older than me and had worked in Gerasa, in the region of Decapolis. She lived in Japhia, not far from the inn where I had met Thomas. She came into Nazareth everyday, even if we didn't have anyone in labor. She would often come and stay with me during the day. I enjoyed listening to the wild stories of her life.

I didn't think she was a very good midwife and I don't think Orpah did either, but we needed the help. She did not care at all about her reputation, and was the focus of the talk at the well. When I invited her for dinner, I should have picked up on the eye contact between her and Thomas, but I ignored it. I should have picked up on the way she brushed up against him at every opportunity, but I ignored it. I even ignored the late nights when I would want to go to sleep and he would walk her to her wagon and it would be a very long time before he came back. But the one thing I wasn't able to ignore was finding them together on *our* mat, when I came home early one afternoon.

I lost all control and bodily threw her out and then began to throw his things out the door. He looked at me like I was possessed and at that moment I felt like I was! If he had made one hurtful comment, I would have killed him! But he only got dressed, picked up his things in the yard and murmured, "I'll come back when you have calmed down." I just stared after him as he walked out the door and then I said, "Well, if that's the case, I may never see you again." I picked up his sandals and threw them at him as hard as I could. They found their mark.

A week passed and I didn't hear from Thomas. He came one day when I wasn't home and took the rest of his things. I heard from Orpah, that he had moved in with Michal. Orpah had warned her not to come back to Nazareth or she would make life very hard on her. Everyone knew that Orpah was one to keep her word and I never saw Michal in Nazareth again. Two months later, I found out I was pregnant.

I had all the symptoms and confirmed my suspicions with Orpah. After she examined me she slowly shook her head. "What are you going to do, Mary? Do you have family where you can go and have this baby?" I shook my head. "No, Orpah, I have no one. If I stay here, I will be disgraced. None of the women will let me work with them again! I also know that Thomas will not have me back." I sat down with my head in my hands. "Orpah, I want this baby! I love children, but I love my work here, too." She was very quiet for a few moments and then said, "There is another option." Horror struck me in the gut like a sharp, cold knife! "No, Orpah! I know what you are going to suggest! No, that is out of the question! That is how my sister died!" My insides were twisted and I felt nauseated.

"Well, Mary, I don't know what else to suggest. You have a lot to think about and choices to make. I will give you all the time you need if you decide to…well, you know. If you decide to keep the baby and leave Nazareth, I will miss you terribly. I don't want to lose you. Go home and think these things over and let me know your decision."

It turned out to be the longest night I had ever spent. Every fiber of my being wanted this baby. Someone I could take care of and love. And in return, receive the unconditional love I have always craved! But I was alone. I had no husband to take care of me. I had no family to take care of me. I was truly alone. I lay on the mat and fought the tears that had been trying to surface all day. I knew if I cried, it would all become real and I didn't want to feel any emotion. Not now. But my futile attempts failed and when I finally allowed the tears to flow, they came in torrents. I think I cried 31 years worth of tears. Absolutely nothing, with the exception of becoming a midwife, had happened in my life the way I had dreamed that it would. Here I was about to embark on the most joyful experience a woman can have, and I had to think about ending it. I rolled over on my stomach and sobbed. As hard as I could, I tried to stop the voice, but it was relentless.

You know you are getting what you deserve, Mary. For years you have been dishonest. It started back when you were a just a child, stealing from your own mother! You stole that wedding linen for Mary so Jesus could have something warm to wear. And even before that, you led those men on so they thought it was all right to come to your room. If you had been honest with your mother, Salome could have worn that wedding linen on her wedding day! You lay here like some poor victim and it is your fault that Thomas left! You kept him on such a tight leash, he had to escape somehow! And now you're pregnant! That was a brilliant move! Thomas doesn't want you, your parents don't want you and if you keep the baby, Orpah isn't going to want you either! You better start thinking, Mary! Don't make an even bigger mess of your life! You have a choice to make. And you already know what your choice is. I cried until I finally fell asleep.

I awoke the next morning groggy from the hours of sobbing. I knew what I had to do. After all, I could always have another baby later. This was just not going to be the best time. I bathed and dressed and went to Orpah's house. After I shared my decision with her, I asked when she could perform the procedure. She looked appalled! "Mary, I can't do that! It would ruin my reputation if someone found out! And what if something went wrong? No, you must go away for this. There is a woman I know in Gadara, on the other side of the Jordan River. For years she was in Judea, but she was forced out of there because of her drinking. I have heard she has straightened up and rumor has it that she still takes care of these types of problems. I will give you directions and I'll help you with the cost."

I had not even thought about it costing money. "Thank you, Orpah. I understand your position. It would be better for me to be in another region, far away from here. I will go pack and leave today if that is all right with you?" Orpah came and hugged me. "Mary, I wish there was another answer for you. I've watched how your eyes glow when you deliver babies and how tenderly you hold them and swaddle them. That is the reason you are so good at what you do. I know this is breaking your heart, but there will be time in the future, when you are married and happy." I slowly nodded. I wish I felt as encouraged as she sounded.

I went home and packed some things and loaded them onto Joshua. I made a quick sweep of my home and thought how different things could have been. "Stop, Mary!" I said out loud to myself. "You have made your choice and you need to stop thinking these thoughts." I backed out of my house and turned to Joshua. "Come on, old boy. We are on another journey together." We walked to Orpah's home; she was waiting for me. She handed me a bag of fruit and a wineskin full of water. She also gave me a small sack full of coins. This should take care of the cost of staying at the inn and the fee for the procedure. I will look for you in about a week."

I thanked Orpah and we hugged, then she followed me outside. I tied the bag onto Joshua and then mounted him. She looked up at me. "You may want to think twice about riding a horse. A wagon may be a better choice. The ride there might not be a problem, but coming back could be painful." I had not even considered the aftermath of what I was doing. "No, I will be fine. Joshua is not strong enough to pull a wagon and we have been through an awful lot together. I want to be with him." Orpah nodded and waved goodbye. As we headed west toward Mt Tabor, I patted Joshua on the neck. "I am glad I have you for this journey, my old friend. I promise you, we will only walk. I'm truly not in a great hurry. I need this time to say goodbye to my baby."

After I arrived in Gadara, I was able to find the local midwife quite easily. I was directed to her house on the northeast end of the city, near the Yarmuk River. I found it without difficulty and after tying Joshua to a palm tree in the yard, I went to the door. I leaned in and asked if anyone was home. No one answered. I called louder. Still nothing. I walked around to the back of the house and saw an older woman with long, white hair walking toward me with a jar of water in each arm. There was an air of familiarity to her stride. As she approached, I realized why. It was Sarah! The woman I had been with the night I met Saul! I could hardly believe it! This woman certainly had a great deal of experience, but she had relayed some pretty repulsive stories to me, also. And I knew how much wine and opium she used to use! Orpah had told me she had stopped that and I hoped it was true. As she got closer, she looked up at me, glanced at my belly and said, "Well, you don't look like you need a midwife. What do you want?"

Sarah's attitude had definitely not changed. "Hi, Sarah. I came to you because I need some help." She stopped when she got in front of me and put down the jars. She peered into my face and looked perplexed. She had aged a lot since I had last seen her. Her skin looked as old as the leather of my wineskin! Her voice crackled as she spoke. "Forgive me; you seem to have an advantage over me. You know me, but I don't seem to know you." She picked up one of the jars and carried it into the house and then came back out. I tentatively began my explanation. "My name is Mary. We met many years ago; I was a friend of Salome's. She was not able to go to a party with you and suggested I go instead. You and I went to Bethlehem together."

Recognition washed over her face. "Ah, yes. You are the one that moved in with Saul and then you disappeared. You know he's dead now? The girl that moved in with him after you? Well, he beat her badly and her six brothers came to look for him. People heard them arguing with him near the tavern and he challenged one of them. They went outside the city with him and that's where they found Saul's body the next day. No trace of the brothers or sister and no one knew where they were from." I felt a brief rush of anger and replied, "He got what he deserved. He was an awful man." Sarah nodded. "Yes, I heard he almost killed you." I felt a twinge of impatience with this woman. "It was a tough lesson for me. But that is not why I'm here. I'm pregnant, but I can't keep it. I need your help."

Sarah picked up the other jar and started for the door. "It's going to cost you a lot, Mary. More than I believe you are ready to pay." She did not look at me as I followed her into the house. The way she was talking, I had the impression she was referring to more than money. "I have money to pay you. Lot's of it." I pulled the bag Orpah had given me from under my cloak and handed it to Sarah. "Some of that is to help pay for a room and to get me back home, but the rest is for you." Sarah sat and dumped the bag in her lap. She carefully counted the coins and nodded. "Yes, this will more than cover the cost. Are you sure you want to pay it?"

Again that ambiguity in her words. I was loosing my temper. "I would not have come all the way to Gadara if I was not willing to pay! When can we get started? I have to get back to work next week." I was pacing the floor and stopped when I heard her say, "Tonight. We can start tonight. It is a two day process, so if I place the leaves tonight, we can finish tomorrow." I paused, surprised at the quickness of her decision. For some reason I thought she was going to try and talk me out of it... or maybe I hoped she would. I looked at her face and saw she was serious and said, "All right. I'll water my horse and get my things." I started for the door then remembered the powder. I turned to her and asked, "Sarah, when we talked that night, on the way to Bethlehem, you mentioned you sometimes used that powder before you did this, to help with the pain. Do you still use it?" There was a part of me that was desperate. Afterwards, I would remember little of what had been done. She shook her head. "No, Mary. I will give you a piece of wood to bite, just like a mother who is in labor." Her words stung. I nodded and went out the door.

The week passed quickly. Sarah allowed me to stay with her because I had lost a great deal of blood and she did not want me riding a horse. It also afforded her the opportunity to keep an eye on me and massage my stomach several times a day. We talked very little and that was fine with me. I didn't want to talk. I didn't want to think. What I did want was to get home so I could get on with my life and forget this whole mess. It had been worse than anything I could have imagined. The physical pain was dreadful, but what I was feeling inside was agonizing. I hated my life and the person I had become. I just wanted to escape, but how do you escape yourself? It had been a long time, but I knew I needed a little help to get through the first few weeks. Maybe on the way home I would stop in Nain and fill my wineskin. And maybe someone there would know where I could find some opium. I knew I couldn't do what I had done before. I had to keep my head clear for my work in Nazareth. I could control it. I promised myself it would only be for a few weeks... until I felt better. Just a few weeks.

11

Till Death Do Us Part

My journey back to Nazareth was long, lonely and painful. Orpah had been right. A wagon would have been a better choice. But the poignant agony I was feeling far outweighed the physical pain. I felt numb and cold. Like something in my emotions had been severed. My love for children and desire to have twelve of my own seemed disconnected, like it had been someone else's desire.

I didn't stop until I reached Nain. I found the inn and got a room. Ironically, the very same room I had when Amos and I stopped here. I immediately talked with the innkeeper about getting my wineskin filled. He eyed me suspiciously and I lied and told him it was for my husband. I then asked him where I might find the local midwife. He gave me directions and I set out hoping she could supply me with some opium. When I arrived at the house, an old woman came to the door—she looked older than Sarah—and informed me she never used the powder, but referred me to a local gentleman who supplied the men in town. It took little time to find him and he was more than willing to help me. There were several men sitting in his house smoking the powder when I arrived and they didn't even seem to notice me.

I went back to the inn, fed and watered Joshua, then headed for my room. There I sat and drank until my physical pain had numbed. Then I drank until the emotional pain was at a comfortable distance. Then I drank some more. But it wasn't enough. I could still feel the emptiness. I could still feel the loneliness. I staggered across the room and got the powder from my bag. When I poured it out of the little pouch, I discovered it was the yellow powder! It had been years since I had this! The old man had been generous and with only a couple puffs, I passed out.

The next morning I awoke nauseated with my head pounding. When I sat up I was unable to move fast enough to get to the little chamber pot. Because there was nothing in my stomach, nothing came up except that bitter tasting yellow fluid. I gagged until the muscles in my belly ached. Finally the feeling passed and I fell back on the mat and went to sleep. When I awoke again, the pain had eased, but my stomach was crying out for food. I slowly sat up and found my clothes soaked with blood. The straining I had done earlier when I was sick, had caused me to start bleeding again. I changed my clothes and girthed myself with some clean undergarments and went down to have breakfast. After I got Joshua ready to go, I went back to the innkeeper to get my skin filled again. He looked at me, shook his head and in a gruff voice asked, "Wouldn't you do better with some fresh water instead?" I declined saying my husband needed it. Under his breath he said, "Sure he does!" Nevertheless, he filled it for me and I was off again on this lonely trip. I knew the wine would come in handy.

I arrived home late that night. Even though my head was a little cloudy from the wine, the ominous reality of my empty house was overwhelming. The hopes and dreams I had shared with Thomas came flooding back. I had believed he would be my husband and we would have many children together. But he was gone and so was our baby. I lay on the mat we had shared and began to cry. What had I done? What had I done with my life? There were so many terrible things I saw my parents do to each other and I had promised myself I would never live that way. Yet, here I was. With all the pain I felt for my sister, I had still done this to myself! The questions kept cycling through my mind and then the voice. *Mary you have certainly messed up your life! Your sister would have been as ashamed of you as your parents are. If she had lived. If she had been allowed to have the baby. If you had just told the truth...*the voice was always there to make sure I knew how bad a person I really was. I cried harder as the consequences of my choices pierced my soul. Until finally... sleep brought me some relief.

The next several months went by quickly. I had become distant to Orpah's concern and compassion. I didn't want anyone to get to close to me. I didn't want anyone to worry about me. Well, maybe with the exception of a man. I needed to find another man in my life. I was desperate to not be alone... not with myself. When I was alone, I thought too much... remembered too much. Drank too much. I was desperate to feel something again. It seemed like I felt numb all the time now. I even felt numb without the wine or the powder. My joy at delivering babies was gone. I could hardly recall the way I used to feel. It seemed I had lost my desire to do anything. When I didn't work, I stayed home and slept. When I couldn't sleep, I used the wine or the powder, whatever I had available, to help me. We had become close friends.

One morning, I was awakened with someone frantically knocking at my door. When I opened it, I saw Orpah in a way I had never seen her before. She looked frightened and spoke quickly, "Mary, you must come immediately! We have an emergency! A crisis! I went with her to a small house on the opposite side of town, not far from the home of Mary and Joseph. She said nothing to me on the way there. I had never seen her act like this. I figured it must be a breech or some other difficulty we sometimes come across during childbirth.

As we approached the house, ear-piercing screams broke the quiet of the morning. Pain-filled screams. I had heard them before. In a distant memory, I had heard these same screams before. As it finally surfaced, so did the name. *Salome! I had heard this as I lay in my bed, late at night. I had listened to her pain, feeling helpless because I could do nothing for her. I had known better than ask any questions. As a little girl, I had covered my ears and tried to drown out the sounds that would haunt my subconscious into adulthood. And just a few days later, Mother had told me she was dead.*

Another scream brought me back to the present. Orpah was running now and I was close behind. I was unprepared for what I found. A young girl, maybe fourteen years old, with two women holding her down as she writhed in pain! Orpah turned to me, her face aggrieved. "Her uncle raped her. She is about three months pregnant. She and her family would have been shamed if she had the baby! I was trying to help them, but something went wrong. I need your help, Mary." I looked at her in horror! She was totally against doing this! She saw the reservation in my eyes and begged, "Please help me, Mary! Her mother is my sister!"

I took over the situation with a detached determination. It took several hours, but we finally finished and the girl rested quietly. Orpah and her sister thanked me profusely for my help. The mother was sobbing and wailing and repeating over and over, "Thank you, so much! Thank you for saving my daughter." I just nodded and walked outside. I needed a drink and I needed it badly. Orpah followed me out and stood next to me. She placed her hand on my shoulder. "Mary, I know this was really hard for you after what..." I shrugged off her hand and looked her in the face. "Your sister may thank me for saving her child's life today, but I can promise you that your niece will hate me for taking the life of hers."

Her eyes looked wounded and I thought she was going to cry. That was the last thing I needed to see this morning. I said goodbye and headed home.

When I got home, I drank and smoked more than I ever had. I remembered Salome and Sarah's warning about being careful when I drank wine and smoked the powder. But there was an internal message that encouraged me to keep going. And I did. My hope, as I spiraled down into oblivion, was that I would never wake up again. The last lucid thought I had was saying goodbye to my brother.

The next thing I knew, there was sunlight on my face and birds singing outside the window. My mind felt like I was slowly coming up out of a very dark hole and I opened my eyes. I was in my house. I tried to remember what had happened yesterday and reluctantly, my mind gave up its secrets. I wasn't supposed to wake up this morning. I had purposely tried to never see another morning. Then the memory of yesterday morning came back to me. How high could I pile the guilt on my shoulders? How many more things could I throw on the trash pile of my life before I finally collapsed under the weight? Well, it wouldn't be anymore from this town! I was going to leave. Leave the job... the mistakes... and the memories.

My head still felt hazy, but I was focused. I actually felt clearer than I should have and that surprised me. I could not even remember how much I had smoked. By the number of things knocked to the floor, I must have blacked out. My resolve to end my life scared me in the light of this new day. The shame that surrounded such an effort was suffocating. Yes, I had to get away from everything here. The fear of running into Mary or Joseph—and especially Jesus—and having them recognize me was ever present. That was a confrontation I knew I could not handle.

It took me only a few hours to pack up my things and place them in the wagon. I left a lot behind. The fewer memories the better. I went to get Joshua and hitched him to the wagon. "Old boy, I promise you, this is the last time you will have to pull this wagon. I'm going to start over and find a husband and a house and you will be free from any more labor. I promise you, Joshua, this is the last time. You are the only true friend I have ever had that has seen me through it all. I love you so much." I gave him a hug and put the last few things on the wagon.

I headed to Orpah's house. It would not be easy telling her that I was quitting, but she would have to understand. She was very upset and pleaded with me not to go, but even her tears had no effect on me. "Orpah, I must go! I have to find a new start. I have to find a husband. I have to find myself. I don't feel anything anymore. I have to go." She hugged me and I tentatively hugged her back. She held up a finger to gesture for me to wait and ran back into her house. It took some time for her to come out and when she did she had a letter in her hand. "Here Mary. This is a letter of recommendation for you. I know a midwife in Tiberias that needs help. She is by herself and has been very busy. A lot of people have been moving there to start businesses because they are on the Sea of Galilee. This letter will help you get work with her."

I thanked her and climbed up into the wagon. She came beside me and reached up and took my hand. "I'll always be here for you Mary. If you need anything, you can come to me. You will always have work here if you want it…and a friend. I owe you so much for your help last night." I looked deep into her eyes. Her sincerity was genuine. I felt only bitterness. "I hope you and your family feel that way ten years from now." She looked perplexed by my remark. I patted her hand then drove away.

I drove out of town, heading east, considering her offer in Tiberias. It was awfully close to Magdala and I didn't need to be running into any relatives. But after all, I had lived in the same town as Mary for many years and had never seen her, not even at the well. Maybe this would be a good choice. I loved the water and it could afford me the possibility of meeting a nice fisherman. As I was pondering all this, I saw a wagon approaching. When it got closer, I realized it was Amos! Of all the times to run into him! It had been at least a couple years. He saw me and started waving. I waved back and silently hoped that this would be quick. As his wagon approached, his smile turned to surprise and before he had stopped, he blurted out, "Mary, are you leaving? I didn't know! Has something happened with your work?"

I shook my head patiently and thought again how innocently this man viewed life. "No, Amos. Orpah is sad to see me go. It was hard to leave her, but I have to. I have too many bad memories and painful reminders to stay any longer." He pulled his wagon next to mine and had such a deep look of concern on his face that it almost made me think he could still be a possibility. But as always, his words irritated me. "Mary, have you thought this through? Is there anything I can do for you? Maybe if you come and talk with my mother, she could give you some good advice."

I tried hard to hide the edge in my voice. "Amos, I'm 32 years old. I'm a big girl now, old enough to make my own decisions. I appreciate the offer, but I think I'll pass. I am probably going to Tiberias to live. You are welcome to come see me anytime." I clucked to Joshua, but Amos stopped me. "Forgive me, Mary. Of course you can make your own decisions. I just want to see you happy and I wish I could play a part in that. I will always be here if you need me, Mary. Please take care of yourself." The gentleness in his eyes and compassion in his voice was a welcome relief to the voice that endlessly taunted me. As I looked at him, I found myself wondering if maybe someday...

"Thank you, Amos, for everything you have done for me. I am sorry if I have hurt you. I just need to get my life together. I have messed up so much. Maybe this will be the start I need." Amos looked at me tenderly, "I will pray that it is, Mary." Again, I clucked to Joshua; he was slow starting, but we were off. I had the sense that Amos watched me for a long time before he headed home.

It took only a few days to reach Tiberias. I had no problem finding the midwife, whose name was Ruth. She was an older woman who smiled little. I believe the days when she enjoyed her work delivering babies, were long gone. She spoke very highly of Orpah and hired me immediately after reading the letter from her. I asked her about living arrangements and she volunteered her brother's home. His house was vacant, because he had gotten married and was living with his new wife in Judea. I followed Ruth to the house and was very pleased with what I found! It was a nice little house, actually a little larger than the one in Nazareth. And it was near the water! I would be able to see the water from my yard! Surely this was going to be the new start that I wanted!

I was settled in my new home very quickly. It had been a good decision to bring only a few things with me. I loved the view of the Sea of Galilee from my door. It was only a short walk to the water and every night I went out and sat on the shore. I had done this in Magdala with my father. Those were good memories. So were the ones when we rode horses together. As an adult, I guess I can look back and realize it wasn't bad all the time. Someday, maybe I can tell him that.

I still fought the urge to drink. I resolved on the way here that I was going to quit all the destructive habits that were destroying my life. I had stopped before and was sure I could again. But the work was heavy and the days were long. With each delivery, my womb felt emptier. I would see the joy on the mothers' faces and my pain would return. With each passing day, it grew harder to keep the pain stuffed down. And to add insult to injury, Joshua was very sick. He had been lying down for two days and I didn't know what was wrong. He would eat only if I fed him and he drank little water. The next morning, I found him dead. I lay on top of him and held him and cried. For over twenty years, he had been my best friend. The only one who never left. Now he was gone, too. At least I had kept my promise to him—he would never have to pull that wagon again. After his death, my conviction to not drink was weakened. At first, I tried to drink only a little. But soon, I was going to sit by the water each night with a full wineskin and was not coming in until it was finished.

One night after work, I went to the tavern to get my wineskin filled. I lingered there for a short time so I could get a head start on my drinking. There was a man there that kept smiling at me and he eventually came over to sit with me. He introduced himself as Didymus and he was a fisherman. His words were very kind and inviting. "You said your name is Mary? You are very beautiful, Mary. I couldn't believe my good fortune when I looked across the room and saw you here alone. Please, tell me you're not married?" I felt the blood rising to my cheeks and I could feel my heart pounding in my chest! He was young, probably younger than me, but his flattery was sorely missed in my life.

"Why, thank you, Didymus! And no, I am not married. How about you? You're a very handsome man yourself and I would guess that you would be married." I looked at him hopefully, half expecting him to say yes. He laid his head back and let out a hardy laugh. "No, Mary. I was and thank goodness it is over. I gave her a bill of divorcement and got rid of that terrible part of my life. Since then I have been waiting for someone just like you to turn it all around for me! Could you be the one, my beautiful Mary?" I was giddy with embarrassment and I could hardly believe *my* fortune to have met him here tonight. We talked late into the night and then he walked me home. We passed his home on the way and he stopped in to get more wine. I escorted him down to the water and we talked even longer. Finally, I took his hand and led him to my house. We were both pretty drunk and my ability to think clearly was gone. And there for the first time in many months, I gave myself to a man. It was not wonderful, but it felt good to be close to someone again. We fell asleep almost immediately.

The next morning, we awoke famished, having not eaten dinner the night before. I had little food available and he invited me to his house and there over breakfast we talked of marriage. He was sure I was the one he had been waiting for and I felt the same way. And in less than three weeks after meeting him, I was finally married. Ruth thought I was foolish, but said little else except that she wanted my assurance that I would not be missing any work. Didymus and I did not have a big celebration. Our parents were not even present. His best friend came and so did Orpah, I think more to support me than to give her approval. It was not the wedding I had always dreamed of, and Didymus was not the husband I had dreamed of, (I don't even think I loved him) but at least I was married.

It took only a few months to discover all the things about Didymus that I should have known before I married him. He was not unlike Thomas in regard to his infidelities, except Didymus began his much sooner. One month after we were married I caught him down by his boat kissing a young girl. He apologized to me, saying that she had been an old girlfriend who didn't know he had gotten married and he was just saying goodbye. That seemed like a lame excuse but he was so sweet to me for the next several days that I finally forgave him.

His opium habit was a real concern to me. I had no idea when we married that he used so much. Every day that he got paid, he spent almost all of it to buy opium. He used the rest to buy wine. My money was all we had to live on and I started finding that missing, too. If I said anything to him, he said he was getting something for his boat. I found the safest thing was to hide the money and not divulge what I got paid.

One good thing came of this situation, however. Watching him pass out every night made my conviction to stop, much stronger. If I drank, it was rarely more than a cup at a time.

But the most devastating discovery about Didymus was that he didn't feel he was able to father any children. I had overlooked discussing this with him during our short courtship. If he had been an honest person, he would have volunteered it. He said he had been married for eight years to his first wife and she had never gotten pregnant. She had a child with her previous husband and after he died she had married Didymus. When they were unable to have children, she had constantly whined and nagged about it until he couldn't stand it anymore and gave her a bill of divorcement. This story also served as a silent warning to me not to nag and whine about children or he would divorce me too.

What had seemed a miracle in the beginning was now, yet another reminder of my life's failures. I had to stay married to him because I could not stand the humiliation of a divorce. I grieved the knowledge that I would never have children. And of course, this brought into stark awareness, my decision to not have Thomas' baby. If I had just controlled my anger that day! Maybe he would have stayed. But the truth was, had I married Amos when I first went to Nazareth, *none* of this would have happened!

But I didn't marry Amos because I thought he was boring and I would have to make the best of my situation now. As long as I kept my money hidden, I knew we could get by... and as long as he kept his promise that there would be no more women. I would have to learn to cope with delivering babies, by pushing the emotions attached to my poor choices, deep down inside. It was a hiding place like the one I used as a child, except I could remember the details. And when they surfaced, I pushed them away quickly before any feeling could be connected to them.

The next seven years proved to be worse than I could have ever imagined. His drinking increased. His use of opium increased. His infidelities increased. I continued to feel helpless to do anything. So I looked the other way. I detached. Every time I had tried to talk with him about any of it, it ended in an argument and I didn't want to end up like his first wife. So I passively suffered through my days of going to work, coming home, eating my dinner, sitting by the water, and then going to sleep. That was my life…my existence.

The morning after I turned forty, I woke up very sick to my stomach. I thought it might be a side effect from the night before. Didymus had remembered my birthday and had brought home some excellent Roman wine. I had not had good wine in a very long time. He brought me flowers and I felt so romantic that I drank all the wine with him. We had a nice evening together, for a change, and I didn't know why I had to suffer for it this morning!

Didymus was already gone and I moved to get up and got sick right next to the mat. I lay back down and decided I would not be working today. When I felt better, I got up and ate some bread and that seemed to help. I promised myself I would not drink like that again! Later on in the day, I felt fine and I was glad for that. I wanted to be at my best for Didymus. I hoped we could have another evening like last night—minus the wine! But he didn't come home. In fact he didn't come home for five days and every morning of those five days I woke up sick. After the third morning, I got a little apprehensive and felt my breasts. They were very sore! I was pretty sure I was pregnant! How could this be? Didymus must be wrong about himself! I couldn't wait for him to come home so I could tell him! He would never spend another day with another woman once he learned I was pregnant with his baby!

The night he came home, he was apologizing almost before he came in the door, begging for forgiveness. He was still a little drunk and hugging me with all his might. "Mary, I promise I will never do this again. I wasn't with a woman, I promise! I met some old friends and we went to Capernaum. I never meant to stay so long! I was in their boat and had no way to get home! Honest!" He pulled back to look at my face and I was smiling! He looked totally shocked, expecting, I'm sure, the silent treatment that he usually got. "You're not mad, Mary? I thought you would be furious!"

I guided him to the mat and we sat down. "Didymus, I have such incredible news! I could hardly wait for you to get home so I could tell you! I am with child! Isn't that wonderful? You are going to be a father!" I waited for the elation and joy that surely he must feel, but it never came. Instead, he jumped up from the mat and looked at me horrified. "You're what? You can't be! You whore! You lay with another man and get pregnant with his baby and try to pass it off as mine?"

My heart dropped in my chest! This was not what I had expected at all! Something had gone horribly wrong! This was supposed to be a wonderful time of joy and hugs and kisses! Not name-calling and accusations! How could he think I would be with another man? "No Didymus! It is your baby! I have not been with anyone else! I would never do that! You are the father!"

His look of alarm had turned to one of disgust. He walked over to me and I was sure he was going to hit me, but instead threw his cup at the wall. "You are nothing but a cheap whore, Mary! My first wife and I tried for eight years and we never had a baby! You and I have been married seven years and all of a sudden you come up pregnant! What else should I think? I can't believe this!" He was holding his head in his hands and pacing like a caged animal. Suddenly, he stopped in front of me and yelled, "I'm leaving and I won't be back until you're gone!" With that he went out the door and I was left sitting on the floor, totally crushed. What was I going to do now?

The next morning, even with my morning sickness, I went to work. I had Ruth examine me and she confirmed what I already knew. She was not real encouraging. "This is not very convenient, Mary. I suppose you are going to want to quit when the baby is born?" Her words felt so harsh. I looked at her and began to cry. Uncharacteristically, she came and put her arm around me. "What is it, Mary? I don't think I have ever seen you cry!" Through the tears and hitches in my breath, I told her about last night. She shook her head and said, "That Didymus is a scoundrel. He has had that reputation all his life. I hate to tell you this, but I doubt he married you for any other reason except you had a job that could support his drinking. If his father and mother had not died and left him that house, he would be living as a beggar. He had nothing before he met you, Mary." I knew her words were true. I remembered the way his house had looked that first night I went there. I wish I had not ignored it. "Why didn't you warn me, Ruth? I would have listened to you."

She shook her head with a knowing smile. "No, you wouldn't have, Mary. You came here with that intention. To find a man. I have seen many like you and they all have the same look. Hungry for love and attention. But now, you are in a tough situation. He's a fool because he does not believe that Jehovah can do anything. There have been many barren women over the years that suddenly got pregnant because our God blessed them. He is a God of blessings. You would do well, Mary, to trust in Jehovah. I think you will need him to get through this crisis." Her words rang true as I remembered the story Mary had told me of her cousin and even more remarkably, Mary's pregnancy as a virgin.

I nodded. "I used to believe, Ruth. I had a friend, the one who gave me this necklace, who taught me wonderful things about God. But she left me as everyone else has in my life. If this God loved me, he wouldn't let such bad things happen to me." Ruth surprised me by laughing. "Oh, I have heard these words many times before, Mary! You are far from the first. What you and many others do not understand about Jehovah is that he does not make our choices for us. Since the beginning, man has made his own choices and suffered his own consequences. But that is *never* Jehovah's choice for us. He wants us to obey him and if we follow his law, he will take care of us."

Her words reached a place inside that had been dormant for a long time. There was truth in her words and I wanted to hear more. "Ruth, maybe you are right. Maybe I need to listen more to you. Would you help me? I have been through so much and it will be hard for me to believe again, but I am willing to try." Ruth hugged me. "I would be glad to help you, and if you want to move back to that house you had before, it is vacant." I nodded and said, "Thank you, Ruth, but I need to preserve my marriage. Maybe he will trust Jehovah, too." Ruth laughed out loud. "I promise you, Mary, Didymus trusts no one. His trust lies in the bottom of a wine goblet. The best thing you can do is forget that man and allow him to give you a bill of divorcement and go on with your life."

I thanked her and headed back home. I was not going to leave him! If what Ruth said was true, and he only married me so I could support him, then he might not leave after he had some time to think about it. I had to convince him that the baby was his. Maybe he would talk to Ruth! I arrived at home and started picking up the broken cup he had thrown. I looked around at all the things I had bought to make this house comfortable—make it feel like home. How could I leave? No, I would stay here and stick it out! He would realize I was his only means to continue living the way he wanted to and he would have to come home. I was sure of it!

It only took a few days for him to come back. He was much calmer and I believe he was even sober. He apologized for the way he talked to me and informed me he had an idea that would take care of the 'problem.' "I have talked to some friends of mine and they told me there is a procedure you can have done. I'm sure you must know about it with the kind of work you do. If you did that, I would stay with you and we could remain married." Realization of what he was implying seeped into my consciousness and I felt like someone had cut my legs out from under me. I became light-headed and sat down hard. This jackal was suggesting I kill our baby! I put my head down in my lap and took deep breaths until my ears stopped ringing and my head felt clearer. I looked up and the hopeful expression on his face made me want to scratch his eyes out! I could feel my eyes becoming mere slits as I carefully controlled my voice. "Yes, Didymus, I know what you are talking about and I won't do it! This is your baby because I have been with no one else! You certainly can't say the same, can you? I will not be a married woman carrying my husband's child and then get rid of it. I won't do it!"

His eyes had also become smaller as his anger was building. "You will do it or I will divorce you and tell everyone in Galilee that you are an adulteress—and you know what they do to an adulteress!" His words stung. I didn't believe that he would do something that low. The consequences of his threat were far reaching and I could not outrun them. I decided to change my tack. "Didymus, just for a minute, have you considered that this could be your child? I swear to you that I have been true. I am not that naive to take a chance like a young, stupid girl! Think how wonderful it would be to have the child you have always wanted."

His expression didn't change. "I have told all my friends that you are barren. They thought my other wife's child was mine. I will not have that embarrassment brought to my name." I felt the anger welling up inside me. "You lie to your friends, so your precious pride will be kept intact, and I have to suffer for it. Plenty of women who thought they were barren end up pregnant! These women believe in Jehovah's blessings and he gives them children!"

Didymus began to laugh. He laughed until I thought he was going to lose his breath. I looked at him with revulsion. I wondered what I had ever seen in this man and why in the world I would want to stay with him. Finally he calmed down and between snickers, said, "Don't tell me you believe Jehovah would bless you? You, the one I found in a tavern? Do you believe I really thought you had never frequented those places? The only difference in you and the women on the street is—you were free!" He went off in another gale of laughter. I was seething inside. I knew at that moment that this man needed to die. If he died, I would just be a widow with child. No questions asked. No consequences. Yes, he needed to die. And I would help him.

The next day, after he left for the boat, I took a trip to Nain. I would get some more of that yellow powder. Now, I regretted that I had not saved mine. I had thrown it out for fear he would find it. In retrospect, that could have been the best thing that happened to me! He probably would have smoked it all and that would have been the end of him! But, I had tried to protect him and now I must get some more. I would be gone for only a few days. Let him wonder where I went! I needed time to make a plan.

The same gentleman answered the door. I couldn't be sure, but I thought the same men were sitting inside with him smoking the powder. I thanked him and went back to the inn where I had stayed before. At least this time, I had a different room. Nonetheless, I was amazed at the parallel between the last two visits I had made to Nain. Last time it was to numb the pain of killing my child and this time it was to kill the father of the child I was carrying. I desperately wanted a drink, but knew it would only make the morning sickness that much worse.

I lit the candle in my room and lay down on the mat. Memories from the past thirty years swam in my head. My conversation with Ruth had awakened hope in me! The conversation with Didymus had slashed my hope to shreds. I closed my eyes and began to cry. My hand went to my belly. My baby was in there! How could I do this again? How could I take the life of a miracle? *How can you not do it, Mary!* I shook my head. I did not want to hear the voice tonight. *Oh, but you will hear! If you don't get rid of that baby, you will be labeled an adulteress and you will be stoned. Then you and the baby will die anyway! Sure, life with Didymus has not been wonderful all the time, but he is the one person in your life who has never left you! So he has a few women on the side! It's always you he comes home to. He will leave you if you don't do what he wants. And then you will be alone again. And he will ruin you. Even if you travel far, far away, people will know what you are and you will never work again as a midwife. You have no choices, Mary. Be smart for a change!*

I sat straight up, shaking my head and screaming, "Shut up, please, shut up! That is why I am going to get rid of him. He will not be able to say anything to anyone." I lay back down and started to pray. I wasn't sure that God would even listen to me, but I would try. How could I pray that I would be successful in killing my husband? I felt so confused and as I finally slipped into sleep, the last word on my lips was *Jesus.*

Sitting in a stable. Next to me is Mary and she is holding a baby. It is Jesus! Mary is nursing him. Joseph is across from us sleeping. Mary is looking at me and smiling. Her face is almost angelic. She reaches over and takes my hand and gently says, "Mary, God loves you so much. He does not want any harm to come to you. Whatever your problem, he can fix it. This little baby I hold has been sent to free you from all your pain. But you must stop running. You have forgotten that nothing is impossible with God! Please don't do this thing you have planned! God will take care of you. He loves you, Mary. He loves you." I was looking at her, wondering how she knew and then I heard... "Trust me." I

*thought it was Joseph, but he was still asleep. I looked back
at Mary and then down at Jesus and I heard it again. "Trust
me." I was sure it was coming from him!*

I woke with a start! I looked around not knowing where
I was. My clothes were drenched with sweat and I smelled
the sweet, smoky remains of my candle. It had burned all
the way down and snuffed itself out. I had been dreaming of
Mary and Jesus! We were back in the stable the night he was
born! It had been so real that I was still not sure that I was
awake. Gradually, I remembered where I was and what my
plan had been. In my dream, Mary knew! And that "Trust
me." I had heard that before! But where? It was not a child's
voice that I had heard. It was a man's voice! Why would that
seem like it was coming from Jesus?

*Mary, pay no attention to that! It was only a dream! Why
do you have such silly notions? Need I remind you what
your father always said about you? You are sounding pretty
possessed right now—suggesting that there would be any
truth to this dream you had!* Again I shook my head and said
aloud, "That dream was too real to ignore. I don't understand
it, but I won't ignore it."

I got up and put my cloak around me. I could not carry out
this plan. I would take my wagon and head for Judea. It was
the one place I had not been in years. I could get a job there.
No one would know me after all this time. Saul had been
dead for many years. *But what about the baby? Who is going
to hire an unmarried pregnant midwife? If you say you're not
married, you will be stamped an adulteress. If you say you
are, they will want to know where your husband is! Quite a
dilemma, Mary! You know you have only one choice!*

The truth of Mary's words in the dream was still with
me in regard to Didymus, but they didn't seem to apply to
the baby—not in light of what the voice had said. Her truth
seemed to be segmented—compartmentalized—I couldn't
seem to discern if her words applied to everything in my

life. The voice drowned that out. I needed a new start and if I wanted that for my life, a baby was going to be in the way. It felt like an internal wall of large, heavy stones had been erected. I was on one side and the baby was on the other. Even the emotions and feelings of protection I had earlier, were distant… and worse...they were numb.

I hitched the ox to the wagon and climbed up in the seat. I knew it was not safe for a woman to travel at night by herself. I didn't much care, at this point, if I was safe or not. I had started heading south toward Jerusalem and abruptly turned to the east. First, I would head to Gadara and hope that Sarah was still alive and not too old to help me. I was focused. All my things were still at our house in Tiberias. *Along with all my hopes and dreams.* But I was willing to leave everything I had behind. I gently placed my hand across my stomach and rubbed it. *Everything.*

12

Blackout

"Oh, Lord you searched me and you know me,
You know when I sit and when I rise; you perceive my
thoughts from afar.
You discern my going out and my lying down; you are
familiar with all my ways.
Before a word is on my tongue you know it completely,
O Lord.
You hem me in—behind and before; you have laid your
hand upon me.
Such knowledge is too wonderful for me,
too lofty for me to attain.
Where can I go from your Spirit?
Where can I flee from your presence?
If I go up to the heavens, you are there; if I make my bed in
the depths, you are there.
If I rise on the wings of the dawn, if I settle on the
far side of the sea,
Even there your hand will guide me, your right hand will
hold me fast. Psalm 139:1-10 NIV

My time with Sarah was short. She was not working as a midwife anymore and age had softened her. She was in her seventies now and was as nimble as the day I met her. Her face however wore the lines that many years of sun and experience had carved. She welcomed my visit, but discouraged my choice. She told me I would regret what I was doing. After I shared my situation… and desperation, she resigned herself to help me. *Help me.* Isn't that an odd choice of words for what she was doing? I already held anger in my heart for this woman because of the last visit. Now here I was again getting her *help*. This time things went much smoother and I was on my way to Judea after only three days.

I was grateful to have the wagon. It was much easier on me physically, and I needed to take my time. The last time I had made a long trip it had been with Joshua. Tears slipped down my face as I remembered all our wonderful times riding together. I closed my eyes and I was on his back again, the breeze in my face causing tears to come to my eyes and his mane whipping my cheeks! I felt so free from worries when we ran like the wind. It was almost like I was running away from my problems. I opened my eyes suddenly and thought, "Oh, Mary, you are still running from your problems. Nothing has changed in all these years except your mode of transportation. When are you ever going to get your life straight?"

I nodded my head. I did need to do something positive with my life. I had sacrificed two children so I could have new starts. Last time I had messed everything up, but this time I had to do things differently. I placed my hand on my belly. I felt so empty inside. Like someone had carved out a piece of me and left it along the side of the road. I had to make what I had just done count for something. I made myself promise, this time it *will* be different.

It had been eighteen years since I had seen Bethlehem and it had been that long since I worked with Leah. I credited her with my abilities as a mid-wife. She had been an effective teacher and training with her was a wonderful experience. I would try to find Leah in Bethlehem and see if I could work with her again. No one had seen me since I left and I was certain my history with Saul had been forgotten.

Leah had been a Jew and that may be a good thing for me right now. Ruth's words had awakened something, even though I knew it was mixed with guilt right now. I still did not understand how Jehovah could have let my life turn out so bad, and since it had been so bad, why would he want to help me? The more I thought about it, the more troubled I became.

I took my time getting to Bethlehem. There seemed to be more people than I remembered, but I found that was due to the celebration of the Passover. The pilgrimage had arrived. I remembered from working at my father's inn, there were always a number of people that could not find a place in Jerusalem. So they stayed in Bethlehem and would travel the short distance into the city. The marketplace was packed with people, especially those buying animals for the sacrifice and food for the dinner. It would be hard to locate people I knew during this time. I hated being around a lot of people, but decided to take a chance and find Leah's house.

Her door was open so I just leaned in the doorway and called, "Leah. I am looking for Leah the midwife." At first I didn't hear anyone so I called out again. A young woman came to the door and said, "I am Leah. May I help you?" I knew this was not the Leah I was looking for and then I remembered the young girl who had helped me. "Hello, my name is Mary. I was looking for a much older woman who used to be a midwife here. But I am certain that would not be you." We both laughed and that seemed to break the tension. She cocked her head to one side and studied my face. "No, that would have been my grandmother. But you look very familiar to me. How do you know my grandmother? Perhaps I helped her deliver your baby?"

The gut reaction I had at her words was not expected. My knees felt very weak and I thought I was going to faint! She looked alarmed and grabbed my hand, pulled me into the house and helped me sit down. "Are you all right, Mary? All the color drained from your face and you looked white as a lamb!" I put my head down between my knees until I felt the ringing in my ears stop. Slowly the blackness faded and color returned to my surroundings. I brought my head back up and apologized. "I don't know what happened. I felt like I was going to faint. Thank you for helping me, but I don't think it's the first time you have come to my rescue."

She looked bewildered and I continued. "Many years ago, I used to live with a man named Saul. He badly beat me one night and a young girl came to help me. She told me her name was Leah, the granddaughter of the woman I was training with." Recognition came to her face. She reached over and hugged me. "Mary, it is so good to see you! None of us ever knew what happened to you! You just disappeared and our only hope was that wherever you went, you were safe." I shook my head. "I guess it was safer than living with Saul, but I haven't done that great a job with my life." I told her about my years in Nazareth and Tiberias, carefully leaving out the ugly details, like Gadara.

Leah shook her head sympathetically. "I'm so sorry, Mary. You know Saul is dead. I heard he was killed by some Egyptians." I nodded. She continued. "Of course, my family was not too broken-hearted. We were hoping you and my sister might come back after that. My grandmother and I prayed for you before she died." I took her hand and hugged her. "I'm sorry, Leah. I know how much you loved her. How long ago was that?" She looked down at her hands. I could tell the loss was still with her. "It has been six years and I have been working in her place ever since. I will never be as good. She thought you were an excellent midwife, too. Are you looking for work here, because I could really use you?"

Those were the words I wanted to hear! "Yes, Leah! I just arrived today and need to find a place to stay, but I will be ready in about a week. I have not been feeling well and need a little time to recuperate." It wasn't a total lie.

Leah's face lit up. "Do you have many things with you, Mary?" I shook my head. "No. I left everything I had in Tiberias. It's a long story; one I don't want to talk about right now." Leah was undaunted. She looked excited. "That's great, Mary! My sister has a house, but she is very crowded. If you had too many things, she wouldn't be able to help you. But since you have only yourself, this may work! Praise Jehovah!" It had been a long time since I had heard anyone praise Jehovah. Ruth talked about him, but in a much more subdued way. "I will talk with her today, if I can find her. Everyone is frantically buying food for the Passover. She lives with two other women. If I can't locate her, I should run into one of them. You can stay here with us until we work things out. I would love for you to meet my husband, Simon, and our three children."

Another gut reaction hit me. Not as severe as the first, but still there. Like someone had punched me in my belly. The thought of being around children right now was too painful. It was too soon. But I didn't know how to get out of it! Leah was still talking, though I had not heard most of what she said. "...and you could have Passover dinner with us." I nodded as if I had heard everything. I wasn't at all sure I would be able to handle a whole dinner. I hoped her sister's house was available today.

Good fortune was with me. Her sister stopped in to visit and quickly agreed to Leah's suggestion! Her name was Lois and she was as sweet and innocent as her older sibling. I followed Leah to her sister's home and met the other two midwives that lived with her. They were all younger than me and I was glad. I had been around the older ones all my life. The house was comfortable and they had extra clothes for me. I'm sure they thought it was a little strange that a woman my age had acquired nothing of material value in her life, but no one asked any questions. I had two undergarments, two bags, a mantle, a tunic and my cloak. Other than my wagon and ox, that was it.

I felt welcomed and loved here. They were Jewish and I was grateful now for my training with Hannah. I didn't do everything with them, but I understood what they were doing. They treated me with respect and that was a nice change. No one here drank wine so it was never a temptation and I seemed to have lost the urge. Even more important, no men! And I didn't seem to miss them! I always had someone here to talk to and never seemed to get lonely. Over the next three years, my life was better than it ever had been.

The day before my forty-third birthday, Leah came over and asked if I would come to her house for a birthday dinner celebration. I felt honored and said, "I would love to, Leah. That is so kind of you. Whose birthday are we celebrating?" Leah looked at me and laughed out loud. "There are times I worry about you, Mary! It is your birthday!" I felt the heat rising to my face. I wasn't used to anyone caring that much about me. I knew it was my birthday, but I didn't think she had remembered. "I am so embarrassed, Leah. Thank you so much for remembering. I would love to celebrate with you."

I arrived at Leah's house early. She was not inside but I heard her singing in the back yard. I walked out back and asked if there was anything I could do to help her with the dinner. She was busy beating the rugs and singing as loud as she could. I decided I better shout. "Leah, can I help you with anything?" She didn't miss a beat. "Oh, hello, Mary. Isn't it a beautiful day! I have planned such a special feast for your birthday! The children have made you presents, too."

I felt myself blushing. "Where are your children?" She beamed at me. "They are with Simon. He took them to pick out a lamb for our dinner tonight. But first I think he was considering taking them to the Jordan to hear the great prophet there. Have you heard about him? He preaches about a baptism of repentance for the forgiveness of sins. People are confessing their sins and he is baptizing them in the Jordan. His name is John. Some say he is the Christ!"

I suddenly looked up at her and started to say something, but bit my tongue. I knew this man was not the Christ! Jesus was the Christ! At least that is what the shepherds had been told. And that is what they had told Mary. And the wise men had come from a great distance to bring him gifts because he was a King. No, this John was not the Christ, but my curiosity had been piqued. I decided to go to the Jordan to see and hear this man for myself. I looked up at Leah and asked, "Do you know where this John is baptizing? I would like to see him, too." Leah smiled. "You will have no problem, Mary. There will be a large crowd there. There always is."

Leah and her family made my birthday very special. I couldn't remember having a birthday like that since I was a child. The dinner was divine and the little animals the children made from clay were very special. It was still uncomfortable for me to be close to them, to have them hug me and sit in my lap. But I felt it was getting better. With time, I believe it was getting better. During dinner, Simon said that he had seen John, the prophet that day and many had been baptized. He said he was wonderful to listen to and again made the comment that many thought he was the Christ. I expressed my interest in going, but was worried about taking the wagon. I knew I would have to cross the mountains so I asked if I could borrow one of Simon's donkeys to make my journey. He was glad to oblige.

Two days later, I traveled east, over the mountains and down to the Salt Sea. It would have been easier to go north and then east, but I wanted to be near the water. It had been three years too long since I had seen the Sea of Galilee. It took me a few days to reach the mouth of the Jordan. As I followed it north, I started seeing people traveling the same route. I assumed we were all looking for the same thing.

Soon, I came to an area where a huge crowd was gathered. Just off the shore, standing in the water, was a man preaching. He was rough looking with long unkempt hair and a long beard. But his words pierced my soul. His voice resounded in the valley. "Repent, for the kingdom of heaven is near." I wasn't sure what his words meant, but others must have. People were flocking to him and he was baptizing them in the water. Some were crying when they stood up from the river. I sat and listened for some time. The things I had done wrong were too numerous to remember. Surely, this "water baptism" was not going to help me.

Suddenly, I saw the baptizer's expression change. I followed his gaze to the east and saw a group of men walking toward us in fancy clothes. They looked a little like the wise men that had come to Mary's home except they were all dressed alike. They held their heads high and by the expressions they wore, they felt very out of place among the people here. They looked as if they were picking their way through bramble instead of men and women. They abruptly stopped when John's voice, much louder than before, echoed in the valley.

"You brood of vipers! Who warned you to flee from the coming wrath? Produce fruit in keeping with repentance. And do not begin to say to yourselves, 'We have Abraham as our father.' For I tell you that out of these stones God can raise up children for Abraham. The ax is already at the root of the trees, and every tree that does not produce good fruit will be cut down and thrown into the fire." The men stood aghast and some were walking away in anger waving off John as if he were a mad man. Soon they had all left except one and he stayed near the back of the crowd.

One man spoke up and said to John. "Why do you speak to the Pharisees and Sadducees like that? Are they not the teachers of the law and sons of Abraham?" Another spoke up. "What should we do then? How do we escape this punishment you speak of?"

John's voice softened. "The man with two tunics should share with him who has none, and the one who has food should do the same." Two men came forward. One of them spoke up. "Teacher, we are tax collectors. What should we do?" John smiled at them. "Don't collect any more than you are required to." Then some men stood up to my right. They looked like they may have been soldiers. "What should we do, teacher?" John replied, "Don't extort money and don't accuse people falsely—be content with your pay." Another man stood and looked around him as if he were embarrassed. His words came out haltingly. "Teacher, many of us have been here many times to hear your words and you speak with such authority that we have wondered if...you might be...the Christ."

John's eyes softened and with more tenderness than I had heard before, answered, "I baptize you with water. But one more powerful than I will come, the thongs of whose sandals I am not worthy to untie. He will baptize you with the Holy Spirit and with fire. His winnowing fork is in his hand to clear his threshing floor and to gather the wheat into his barn, but he will burn up the chaff with unquenchable fire."

The people were excitedly talking among themselves. Many that he had addressed had come down into the water for him to baptize. His words rang in my head! Could this other person he spoke of be Jesus? He had never actually come out and said it, but it must be! It still filled me with awe that I had been with Jesus as a child. I had played with him and changed his diapers! But where was he now? Why was he living as a carpenter in Nazareth? Had something changed or had his time not come yet?

I listened as each person came down and poured out their hearts to John. I had not heard any confessions that were as bad as mine would be. Maybe this was the thing I needed. Maybe this was what would finally change my life. I tentatively stood and began to make my way down to the water. There were many people there and a very long line had formed. I had almost reached the end of the line when a group of women came running down the hill to the water, wailing as loud as they could. They had ashes on their heads and were frantically screaming as they cried. They seemed to be leading one particular woman forward and as they did she fell into the water at John's feet. She looked up at him and between her cries said, "Teacher, my baby has died. I just gave birth and she has died. If I have done something, or my family has done something that has caused this, I must be forgiven. I could not live with myself if I did something that killed my baby!" She went off into another tangent of crying and the other women were doing the same.

That feeling in my gut—the one that made me feel like my legs had been cut from under me—was back. I had no business here! This poor woman did nothing to hurt her baby and she greatly feared her sin! I deliberately killed mine! What hope was there for me? As soon as I could, I moved away. I heard John tell the woman to repent of her sins and then he baptized her. I thought as I walked back up the hill that there wasn't enough water in the Jordan River to help me.

I headed back the same way I had come, walking by the water. The deep-seated pain I had been keeping at bay was consuming me. Tears slipped down my face as I thought about the woman at the river. How could I have thought I deserved forgiveness? All the lies I had told, the things I had stolen, the wine and beer, the men, the powder, the babies— it was all in my face. And I wanted a drink. No, I *needed* a drink. It had been a long time since I had even tasted wine. The days I had to deliver babies were very hard, but Leah was always there to encourage me. My ability to disconnect from my feelings also helped, but that had grown less and less successful in the last few months. The thought kept racing in my head, *you need a drink, you need a drink,* until I decided to give into it.

As I guided the donkey toward Bethlehem, I realized in the three years I had been living here, I had not come to see the inn where I grew up. Maybe I was afraid. Afraid of the memories. But today all those memories were there in my head anyway, so I might as well visit the place that I knew had wine—and lots of it. It might be nice to re-visit those days.

I came into the courtyard of the inn and stopped at the well. I watered the donkey and led him down to the stable. *The stable.* It seemed like an eternity since that night when I looked out my window and saw light coming from the stable and feared it was a fire started by one of the drunken men. Oh, how I used to fear them! (Or had I feared them because they smelled like the man that came to my room?) I gave the donkey some hay and started back up the hill. I thought about the times I had run up this hill to get food or something else for Mary and Joseph. I remembered how painful it had been after my father kicked me… so many memories.

I found the innkeeper and paid for a room. There was no way I could go back to Bethlehem after I had been drinking. As I walked across the courtyard to the steps that led to my room, I looked over at the innkeeper's quarters. The rooms Salome, and later Bartholomew, and I had used were over there. *Salome.* Had she been protecting me the night she was raped—the night that led to her eventual death? Why didn't Father let us share a room? It would have been more money for him and we would have been safer. I wondered how things might have been different for me if she had lived. And Bartholomew! What had become of him? Would our paths ever cross?

I climbed the steps and found the room. I had cleaned this room so many times. Mother and I had scrubbed these floors and beaten the mats and replaced the candles in all of these rooms, almost daily. It was dusk and the sun was just going down. I watched from my window and remembered how much joy I got from this as a child. It was one of my favorite things to do. I seemed to be void of that joy now.

I took off my mantle and cloak and reached into my bag to get money for the wine. My hand brushed something else and I opened the bag all the way and saw a little leather pouch. It was the pouch of powder I had bought at the old man's house in Nain! I had completely forgotten about it! I had not used this bag for a long time because I had not taken a journey anywhere since arriving in Bethlehem. There was a sense of excitement mixed with fear. I had promised myself not to do this again. I put the bag on the mat and decided I wouldn't touch it. I said aloud to myself, "I don't need that. The wine will be enough to take care of me tonight." I took the wineskin that I had used for water on my journey, and headed to the tavern.

I got the skin filled, borrowed a cup from the tavern and went back to my room. With great anticipation I took the first drink. The wine was sweet, bubbly and very strong. It burned as it went down my throat and it burned my stomach. Within minutes the warm feeling I used to know so well, traveled up my legs, across my torso and into my head. It was very strong! I couldn't remember it hitting my head this hard since that first time with Elizabeth! Now, there was a name I had not thought of in a long time. She may be one person whose confession would be worse than mine!

I continued to take drinks as I thought about the times Elizabeth and I had spent together. I allowed myself to heap on the guilt as I remembered the things we did—the boys we had met and had taken to the stable and that awful day with the three strangers. Even though I hadn't lost my virginity with any of them, I still did things I had no business doing. And I lied to my parents, stole wine and then drank it! And I certainly wasn't helping Elizabeth because she did have sex with those boys and drank the wine with me. She had been deeply wounded at such a young age. I had felt such pity for her and then proceeded down the same road myself! I drank another cup of the wine, straight down. I wondered if she was still alive. We could share some stories!

My head was foggy. The wineskin was half empty; I had not drunk like this in years. I knew I shouldn't drink anymore, but was compelled to finish it. After all, who knew when I would ever get to do this again! Thoughts of Matthew drifted in. My first love. I was going to be his bride! And he was going to be my savior! He was going to take me away from all the yelling and screaming at home. Tears began to fall in my lap as I remembered the day he left. After that, I seemed to fall apart, especially after I met Salome. She was just bad news altogether. I would never let a daughter of mine spend time with a woman like that!

A daughter of mine! One of those babies could have been a daughter! The tears were falling harder. Oh, if only I could hold one of them. Kiss their little faces. I poured the last cup of wine. I was crying so hard, I could hardly see what I was doing. This all started with Mary leaving me! If she had not abandoned me, my life would have been entirely different. It could have been like Leah's life. She was so happy! She adored her husband and her three children were precious. Yes, my life could have been like that if only Mary had been there for me. I felt the necklace and rubbed it the way I had for the last thirty years. Why had she left this for me? To haunt me with her memory? I yanked the necklace from my neck and threw it across the room.

Horrific memories were pounding away in my head and I couldn't take it anymore! I looked over at the leather pouch. I didn't have a pipe. What am I thinking? I promised myself I would never do that again! *Oh, go ahead, Mary.* The voice. I had not heard it since I came to Bethlehem. I had not been totally happy, but my life had been tolerable. And the voice had left me alone. But now it was back! *Go ahead, Mary. You know it will numb the agony you're in. You know it always does.*

I started to pick up the bag and hesitated. *You know, it's a good thing you didn't get baptized! What a fool you would have made of yourself! There were people there today that knew about you! People everywhere know about you, Mary! If you had been baptized publicly so everyone could see... and then they found out what you are doing here tonight, they would laugh you out of Judea! Go ahead, Mary! You might as well finish the job. There is no sense in leaving it half done.*

I grabbed the pouch and started dumping it into my cup. Only a little at first, but then as the words I just heard took root, I emptied it. I stirred it with my finger, paused for only a second and drank it straight down. The repugnant, bitter taste made my stomach reverse its flow and I had to swallow hard to keep it down. I looked across the room at the necklace. I crawled over and picked it up. My vision was so blurry I seemed to be holding three necklaces. One for Mary and one for each of my babies. *Oh... I miss all of you so much! I would do anything to hold any of you right now...*

Somewhere in my past, I remembered feeling like I was drowning and going down for the third time. That would be a good description of how I felt now. I shut my eyes and let my body begin to drift down into the water—deeper and deeper until when I looked up I saw nothing but darkness above me. And there was utter terror knowing that I eventually had to take that last watery breath. Then —-*nothing.*

I felt hands on my arms trying to pull me up. "Leave me alone. I'm too tired. Leave me alone, please." I don't think I'm talking out loud, or am I? A voice. Gentle. Calm. Tender. Filled with compassion. "Mary, wake up. Mary you must wake up! Let me help you walk back to your room. Mary, wake up!" No, I can't move. "Leave me alone. Can't you hear me? Let me sleep, please!" Somehow I know his voice. It sounds so familiar. But I can't get my eyes open! Who does that voice belong to?

This time arms picking me up from behind and dragging me. I try to open my eyes again. I feel like I'm being pulled up out of dark, murky water. I don't want to go, though. It is better here. But, the arms won't let go and I finally break the surface of the water. I gasp for breath and try again to open my eyes. It's almost light. Or is it almost dark? I can't tell. I look to my left and I see the well. There is water pouring in my face. I turn my head to the side and want to scream, Stop it! But I still can't speak. Then a shadow falls over me. It is a person, but I can't make out the face. "Mary, you need to get up and let me help you. I need to get you to your room. Can you hear me?" The voice is so familiar! I open my mouth and this time words come out, "Who are you?" I feel his hand touch my cheek tenderly. "Trust me, Mary. Trust me."

I feel his strong arms pick me up and half carry me up the stairs. He makes me walk back and forth for a time and then takes me to the room I had last night. At least I think it was last night! He gives me some cool water to drink and helps me lay down on the mat. I still have not gotten a clear view of his face, but I'm sure I've heard the voice before. He walks to the other side of the room and picks up something. It is the necklace. He carefully helps me sit up and fastens the necklace around my neck. "I thought I had broken that. How did you fix it?" I see him smile and then he says, "Mary, promise me you will drink all the water I brought for you and eat the bread and fruit. I must go now." And before I can stop him, he's gone.

I did as he said and then fell back to sleep. When I woke up my head felt completely clear. I was not sure how that was possible, but I wasn't going to complain. I tried to remember what happened last night and could only recall looking at the necklace before passing out. So how did I get down by the well? I heard footsteps in the hall and a then a knock at the door. "Miss, are you awake?" I quickly checked to make sure I was covered up and answered, "Yes, come in." A young girl, not much older than I had been when I lived here, came into the room with a dish of hot lamb stew. She brought it to me and asked if I was hungry. I had not thought about it, but I was famished! "Yes, thank you. It was very kind of you to bring me something to eat. Let me get my bag and I will pay you." She shook her head. "That won't be necessary. The gentlemen paid for everything. He said he wanted us to care for you until you felt better and if it was more than he gave us, he would return and pay the balance."

I was so confused! "Who was that man? Do you know?" She again shook he head. "No, we thought he was a friend of yours. After you finally stopped yelling out by the well — I guess you passed out — he came and sat with you until this morning." I was totally befuddled. "What do you mean I was yelling by the well? The last thing I remember, I passed out here in my room."

She looked at me in amazement, shaking her head. "No, miss. You were running all around the inn last night and you ended up at the well. You were calling out several different names. Salome and Mary and your parents. One time you were yelling at your father and then you yelled at God for a long time. My parents were glad we had only two patrons. Anyone who blasphemes God brings curses on themselves and they did not want that!" My head was spinning! What had happened? I must have completely blacked out! I could remember none of this. "Would you mind sharing with me what I was saying? I truly don't remember." She hesitated and I wasn't sure for a moment if she would tell me. Then she said, "You were asking him why he had taken away all the people that you loved and why he hated you so much.

Then you said something about your lost daughters. Did you lose two daughters?" Her innocence made me want to hug her. "No, I lost two babies." I figured that would be the best explanation for her. She nodded. "That happened to my mom between me and my brother. She was so sad. She cried about it for days. How long did you cry? Was it very long ago?" I nodded. "One was three years ago and one was eleven years ago. I am still crying about it." She looked thoughtful. "That's a long time. Who are Salome and Mary and why were you yelling at your father." Just then we heard someone coming. A woman's voice at the door said, "Miriam, are you in there?" "Yes, mother. Come in." A tall slim woman entered the room. "Miriam, you need to finish your chores. Right now!"

Miriam got up and waved goodbye to me and left. The mother turned to me. It was difficult to read her face, but not her voice. "The gentleman you were with paid us very well to help you, but you must understand we do not want the kind of reputation a woman like you could bring to our inn. We are not a well-to-do family and this is our only income. My husband is very upset and asked me to see if you were ready to leave yet. He has gone into Bethlehem to get some things and hoped you would be gone when he got back. We will give the money to you that your friend gave us."

Her words cut deep, but I still felt she deserved an explanation. "First, I am so sorry for last night. I never intended for this to happen. My parents used to own this inn when I was your daughter's age. I guess all the bad memories got to me." She looked at me bewildered. "Is that why you were cursing your father last night? I have never heard a woman talk like that. And you scared my little boy, running through our quarters crying for 'Bartholomew.'" I nodded in disbelief! I had acted like a possessed woman last night. "I'm sorry for the way I spoke and for scaring your son. I'm truly sorry. Bartholomew is my brother. I have not seen him in many years. It is a long story. My father and I did not always get along very well."

I looked down at my hands. "As for the man, I don't even know who he is. But I am grateful for his help." I could tell by the reaction on her face that my comment had been taken out of context. "Please believe me! I did not bring him with me. He just showed up and helped me." The woman was nodding knowingly. "Do you think you will be ready to leave soon?" I knew this would be the best thing for all of us and told her I would leave as soon as I ate. She offered me the money but I declined. "You keep it for the trouble I caused you."

The short journey to Bethlehem was a time of reflection. I still didn't know who the man was and I had possibly ruined my reputation with Leah. I had added more to my trash pile and this bunch was really putrid. I shook my head and hoped all that happened last night stayed at the inn. I approached the outskirts of the city and saw a bunch of women at the well. It couldn't be that late in the day! I looked to the horizon. It was true; I must have slept most of the day, because the sun was setting. I wondered if I would ever truly enjoy that beautiful sight again.

When I got closer to the women, I realized that one of them was Leah. Then I thought I saw Lois, too. I raised my hand and waved to them, but Leah put her head down, as if she hadn't seen me, and walked away. Lois and the other women followed suit. I was too late! The innkeeper must have told what happened when he came here today. Though it was only a short journey to my home it was the longest one I had taken since my trips to Nain.

When I got to my house, my things were outside in my wagon. Both Leah and Lois were there and they looked sad to have to do this. Leah was the first to speak. "I am sorry, Mary. We don't want to make you leave, but we can't keep you in our home anymore. What happened at the inn is all over Bethlehem! I know the women here will not allow you to touch them ever again. It would be best for you, Mary, to find work in Jerusalem or somewhere else. We are very sorry." Lois added, "We will give you a letter. Your work has been exceptional."

I knew they meant what they said and I knew I deserved what I was getting. I had a chance and I had messed it up... again. But I would not need a letter. I would never work as a midwife again. I would go to Jerusalem and I would find a man to take care of me. I had not been with a man for over three years and I guess it was time to start looking. Certainly, no one in Jerusalem would have heard about last night. I could make a new start. *Another new start.* I tried making it on my own and failed. It seemed that everything I tried had failed. Would I ever find whatever I was looking for?

There was one thing I knew for sure, I would never use that powder again...or opium. That was one promise I would not break. I didn't think I could make the same promise about the wine. If I had stuck to just the wine last night, I would have been fine. I thought I might need the wine to relax, but I would only use it for that purpose. Nothing else. And after I got a man, I could stop again. I would have to get that bill of divorcement from Didymus at some point. I didn't think he would give me a hard time about it. But that could wait. Everything else can wait. First, I had to focus on Jerusalem... and a new start.

13

Set up!

The Feast of the Tabernacles was in full swing. The celebration was one of the most joyous times of the year for it was a celebration of the final agricultural harvest and a new year. There were little "booths" or huts being set up all over Jerusalem commemorating the time the Hebrews spent in the wilderness. During the Succoth, as it was also known, the Jews would stay in these booths during their time in Jerusalem. As the celebration continued, dancing, singing and rejoicing would commence. This would last for eight days before everyone packed up to head back home.

It was only during such celebrations, that I would venture out of my little house to be sociable. My most recent lover, Nathan, had moved on and my heart felt so heavy that I could hardly stand it. He had been my fourth relationship since I moved to Jerusalem just a little over a year ago. I really thought he would be the last one, but it ended as the others had. In our last few weeks together, there had been constant fighting and his occasional slaps had become punches. His words had crushed me. "What is wrong with you, Mary? Everything I do to get money coming in to put food on the table, and all you worry about is where I am at night! It's none of your business where I go or what I do! All you need to do is worry about staying here and keeping the house clean."

I was seething at his arrogance and I looked at him knowingly. "Do you think I don't know where you go? You may say you're out drinking with your friends, but I know! I followed you and saw you with that whore!" The blow was swift and hard. I immediately tasted the saltiness of the blood in my mouth. He grabbed me by the throat and began laughing at me. "You think you can talk to me like that and get away with it? I'll have any woman I want any time I want and you will do nothing about it. Who do you think you are? You think you are some great catch? There are plenty of women in Jerusalem that would love to be with me!"

In the past I would have kept quiet out of fear, but I didn't care anymore. I really didn't care if he killed me. What kind of life was this? He was an animal and I was sick of him coming home drunk and wanting to "make love." There was no love in it! It was going through the motions until he would pass out on top of me and I could roll him off and begin to drink myself to sleep. As I looked at his sickening grin, I remembered another, with a grin like that.

"I told you to take off your clothes! Do it now!" "No, Father, please! I am 12 years old. Please don't. I am too old for spankings." He would grab me and put me over his knee and I would fight him. I always saw that grin on his face as he finally won the battle. I would scream for him to stop! I was so ashamed for my father to see me naked. This time my mother was in the room and when I saw her face, I froze. She was sewing and she was smiling also, as I struggled with Father. She tried to cover it with her hand, but I saw it. My heart sank in my chest. No one to protect me...

"You think you're a big man, hitting a woman! There might be other women who think they want you, but not after they spend one night with you!" His face changed in an instant from a grin to sheer rage. His grip tightened on my throat and the next punch dazed me. Everything began turning black and I went limp. He was pummeling me in the face, breasts, and stomach. I barely noticed when he let go of my throat. I fell, face down on the floor. "There! Now you got what you wanted! I'm out of this house and out of your life! You are nothing but a cheap whore! And you talk about *other* women!" As he walked by me to the door, he kicked me in the side and I remembered nothing else until I woke up this morning. Another day in the life of Mary of Magdala! I would not dwell on what happened last night. Now it was the Festival, and I would go "celebrate" with everyone else. Maybe I would even meet a *nice* man for a change. Someone who could take me away from this!

I got cleaned up and dressed as nicely as my aches and pains would allow. It seemed that every move I made was accompanied by pain. My body was covered with bruises - and my face! I would need to wear a veil. I found my wine-skin empty. I must have drained it at some point last night. I filled it to the top and slung it over my shoulder and went out into the day. I was grateful for the cooler weather. The last few days had been unbearably hot and I would have suffered with all the clothes I had to wear to cover my bruises. I was not in the mood to have to make up stories about what had happened to me.

As I walked through the streets and surreptitiously drank my wine, I found myself approaching the temple. Many people were gathered around and listening to someone talk. I heard them whispering things about the person before I even saw his face. "He is a good man." and "No, he deceives the people." I even saw some of those gaudily dressed priests hanging around. They always made me laugh! They were so full of themselves! Then I heard the man they were talking about say, "Yet not one of you keeps the law. Why are you trying to kill me?" The crowd around him exchanged looks and the man next to me said, "You are demon possessed! Who is trying to kill you?"

That got my attention! I used to hear that all the time at home! The man was speaking again, but I could not hear him over the crowd's yelling. They seemed to be getting angrier at every new thing he said. I managed to hear, "Stop judging by mere appearances, and make a right judgment." I could relate to those words. I strained to see who this man was and as I tried to push forward, I heard some in the crowd say, "Is this man the Christ? Why are they letting him speak publicly? Have the authorities really concluded that he is the Christ? But we know where this man is from; when the Christ comes, no one will know where he is from."

The Christ? Was this Jesus speaking? I pushed harder and finally was able to see him. It had been so long since the last time I had set eyes on him in Nazareth; he had been only a teenager. Now his hair was longer and he had a full beard, but somehow I knew that it was he. Then he stood and with great authority he cried out, "Yes, you know me, and you know where I am from. I am not here on my own, but he who sent me is true. You do not know him, but I know him because I am from him and he sent me." As he finished, there was a surge in the crowd. I felt they wanted to seize him and I found myself trying to block those near me. Jesus seemed to have no fear on his face though. He just walked away.

I saw the men in their fancy robes whispering to each other and one of them ran inside the temple. Within minutes, there were half a dozen temple guards patrolling the area. Jesus had moved away from the temple and was in the outer court, the place where women could gather. He was speaking again, "I am with you for only a short time and then I go to the one who sent me. You will look for me, but you will not find me; and where I am, you cannot come." The crowd was grumbling again, perplexed by Jesus words. He looked down at the ground - he seemed sad. I thought I saw tears in his eyes. When he looked up again, I knew it wasn't possible, but I thought he looked directly at me! I had a veil over my face to cover most of the bruises, but it still felt that he knew me. I held his gaze for only a brief second and then turned and hid behind someone next to me. When I looked up again, he was gone. I turned to go and saw the guards behind me, but they made no effort to follow him.

I had seen Jesus again! I would love to talk to him and share that I had known him as a baby. Ask how his mother and father were! But I could not do that. The condition of my face right now would take time to heal, and did I really want anyone to see us talking? Someone might tell him about my life and I could not bear for him to hear that or share it with Mary. I slowly walked home, draining the wineskin before I got there. I was feeling pretty drunk and relieved that I did not have to think anymore about how I had messed up my life. I crawled into my bedding without even undressing, and fell asleep.

I didn't venture out of my house for the next five days. I was afraid I would run into Jesus. But if I was to be completely honest, I also hoped Nathan would come back. How stupid is that? I confine myself to my house because of the beating he gave me, so I can wait for him to come back? My father was right about me. I am possessed! I drank most every night to numb the loneliness I was feeling inside. With Nathan gone, there was no money to buy food, and I was running out of wine. I had to get work, but was afraid to talk to the midwives. Some had made comments about me living with men I was not married to and others had heard about the blackout incident. At times like this, I found myself wishing I *could* get my hands on some opium, but I would not break the promise I had made to myself. I had already broken enough promises. Besides, the wine helped. My problems were still there in the morning, but at least it got me through the nights.

The morning of the sixth day, I decided my face was healed enough that I could go out. It was the last day of the Festival and many considered it the greatest day. I did not want to miss it all! As I ventured through the city, my curiosity got the best of me. I carefully walked toward the temple. I had finished half a jar of wine before I ever left the house and I had brought a full wineskin with me. My gait was unsteady, but I thought if I walked slowly, no one would notice. I sipped on the wine at every chance. I was not surprised to see Jesus speaking again. Another large crowd had gathered and I wove my way through until I could hear him. At just that moment, he stood and said in a loud voice, "If anyone is thirsty, let him come to me and drink. Whoever believes in me, as the Scripture has said, streams of living water will flow from within him."

The people around me were excited and whispering, "Surely this man is the Prophet." and "He is the Christ." I heard another say, "How can the Christ come from Galilee? Does not the Scripture say that the Christ will come from David's family and from Bethlehem, the town where David lived?" The men around him agreed with him.

But, he is from Bethlehem! I was there the night he was born! I spoke up and tried to tell them what I knew, but my words were slurred. The man who had said Jesus was from Galilee, looked at me. It was one of Saul's friends! With utter repulsion in his voice, he said, "What do you know? You are drunk! You are not even supposed to be this close to the temple." The crowd cheered him on and I found myself being half carried out of the courtyard. I kept arguing, "You don't understand! I was there and I saw everything! He is the Christ, born in Bethlehem!" Saul's friend, now behind me said, "Ignore her. She is that Mary of Magdala. The only knowledge she has comes after dark!" They all laughed and then pushed me from the outer court. I tripped and fell to my knees, cursing at them and crying.

The stones under my hands and knees were cutting into my flesh, but everything was spinning so fast, I was afraid to move. I shut my eyes hoping for relief but it made it worse. What the man said came back to me. I was there, wasn't I? Those things did happen, didn't they? My mind was so cloudy with the wine; I was unable to think clearly. I felt sick to my stomach and before I could get to my feet, I threw up in the street. The people looked at me in disgust and walked away. Those with children covered their eyes and shook their heads, moving away from me as quickly as they could. I had messed up again. Ridiculed again! How would I ever be able to work in this city? I wiped my face and looked up. All but one had left me alone. Amazingly, it was one of the chief priests. He actually came over and helped me up! I was so embarrassed, and immediately started making apologies. He shook his head and smiled at me and said, "Mary would you like something to eat? I can take you to my home and give you a wonderful meal." I was too shocked to answer right away! How did he know my name? After emptying my stomach, my head was a little clearer than it had been. I desperately wanted something to eat. I looked up at him and said, "Yes, thank you so much. You are so kind!" He glanced around him as if he was making sure no one else was looking, and then had me follow him to his home just outside the city.

When I entered his house, I was astonished at the beautiful things he had. Gorgeous, hand woven tapestries hung on his walls and gold goblets and dishes adorned his table. Also on the table was a true feast! He pulled a chair out for me and I sat down. He did not join me. "Aren't you going to eat?" I asked. "There is enough food here for five people!" He said he was not hungry and for me to eat all I wanted. I did not understand his kindness, but with the voracious hunger I had, I would not question it now. I did wonder how this beautiful table had been set while he had been at the temple listening to Jesus. I did not allow my mind to ponder on these things – the food was too good!

He finally sat down across from me and I smiled and thanked him again. I knew I was probably eating like a pig, but it had been two days since I had any real food and the wine had weakened my body. He looked deep in my eyes and began to speak. "I have heard that you and your boyfriend broke up and you don't have a job to buy the necessary things you need. I have a proposition I would like to share with you. We have an important man coming to our city to speak to us at the temple. He has traveled far and we would like to make him as comfortable as possible. His wife had a tragic accident years ago and was left paralyzed. She has been unable to be a wife to him and he has been very lonely. We would like to make his stay memorable by giving him a companion that would keep him comfortable while he is here. We will pay very well for this, Mary. Do you understand what I am saying? "

In the middle of a bite of lamb, I stopped and looked at him. Oh, yes! I understood! He was asking me to be a prostitute! I swallowed hard and nodded that I understood. "We will pay you thirty pieces of silver if you will help us with this." I felt so insulted, but at the same time thought how much money that was, and what I could buy with it.

"Where would I meet him?" I could hardly believe that was my voice, that I was considering this at all! "It would be right here. Only for two days." Thirty pieces of silver for two days! The truth was I had been doing the same thing for free, for years, trying to find someone to want me. To need me. To love me. This man would leave and I would never see him again, and no one would ever know what I had done! And I could put food on the table! This seemed too good to be true! I looked at him. Searched his face. "This will be told to no one? No one else will find out in the temple?" The last thing I wanted was to be known as a prostitute. Or worse, for Jesus to find out. His voice interrupted my thoughts and fears. "I promise you, Mary. No one will know but you and the man we will pay you to accompany." I considered again the consequences of what I was doing and remembered how hungry I had been over the last few days. Was there really any choice to be made? "I'll do it. When does he come?" A slow smile formed on his mouth and he answered, "Tonight. He will be here tonight."

I raced home to clean up and put on my best clothes. The priest had told me the man would be here tonight, and I wanted to look as nice as I could. I had been told frequently, when I was younger, that I was an attractive woman, but at forty-four, I was beginning to look my age. My hair was still beautiful and had not turned gray yet. I would take special care to put it up and I would wear the necklace Mary and Joseph had left at the little house, the day they disappeared. I was amazed I had not lost it! The hurt welled up again when I thought about them leaving me! All these years and the pain still felt so fresh. I thought we were close friends and I had tried to help them. But, how could I think such good, kind people would ever really accept me? I think that is another reason I didn't want Jesus to see me. In my anger, I might say something about his parents that I would regret forever.

I was exhausted so I lay down to sleep for awhile. I slept fitfully, with dreams that seemed to expose all the years of my painful life. When I awoke, the sun was going down and I lay there wondering why I was even considering this man's proposition. I was struggling with what I was about to do, but suddenly decided to not think about it anymore; an ability I had learned at a young age. Our agreement would be fulfilled before I knew it and I would not think about it ever again. I allowed my mind to fantasize about what he looked like and how old he might be. I hoped he would not be disappointed with me. Maybe, if he really liked me, he would come back and get me when his wife died and then

I could be his wife! Maybe, I would finally have someone who loves me! I got lost in this thought for a while until I heard a knock on the door.

Oh, I hope that is not Nathan! It would be my luck for him to show up, full of apologies. I got up to answer the door. It was the priest. "You look very nice, Mary. The man has arrived. When you are ready, just go to the house where we ate. He is waiting for you there." With that he turned and walked away. I blushed at his compliment and went to blow out the candles around my house. I took one last glance at my little home and found myself praying, "God, please forgive me." I put on my shawl and went out into the night.

When I arrived, I knocked at the door several times, but no one came. I slowly opened the door and stuck my head in and said hello. No reply. I said hello again and there was still no reply. I quietly came in and shut the door. There were candles all around the room. A large jar with two goblets sat on the table. I removed my shawl and looked around. I saw him sitting in a large chair in a corner of the room. I thought it odd that he had not answered the door. He stood and came to where I was standing. He was a tall man and actually, quite handsome. He was strong in build and wore very rich looking clothes. He touched my face and hair and said, "Hello, Mary. You are a very beautiful woman." I felt the heat rise to my face as I blushed and thanked him. I was so nervous! I asked if he would like a drink. He said he would and I went to the table and filled both glasses. I picked up my goblet and drank it straight down. "My! You are a thirsty girl. Let me fill it for you again." I didn't like the tone in his voice or the way he referred to me as "girl." As he was filling my goblet, I remembered Jesus' words earlier today about being thirsty and coming to him. What had he meant? And what an odd time for those words to come to my mind! I wasn't thirsty; I was just drowning the last bit of doubt there might be about what I was doing!

I picked up the goblet again and drank it straight down. The familiar, warm feeling was spreading throughout my body and I began to relax. I took off my shawl and looked at him and said, "You have an advantage over me. You know my name, but I do not know yours." He did not answer me, but his eyes lingered on my body as if he were undressing me with his eyes. I felt nervous and asked, "Aren't you going to drink some wine?" He just looked at me and smiled and handed me his glass. "I'm enjoying watching you. I'll catch up." Something about him made me uneasy. He was not being mean. In fact, he had touched me very gently. But something wasn't right. I took the goblet from him and began to drink again. It was going down very smoothly and not until I had drained the glass, did I notice the bitter aftertaste. I looked into the goblet and then looked up at him. I knew that taste! I thought, "Oh, no! Not again!" Then everything in the room began to spin. I thought for a brief moment that I was going to get sick. Before another thought could come, I passed out.

Sometime during the night, I awoke to voices in the next room. My clothes had been removed and I was on a large, padded mat. My head was pounding like someone was repeatedly hitting me with a hammer. The voices I heard belonged to men, maybe three or four of them, from what I could tell. They were speaking softly, but I understood bits and pieces of what they said. "This may be the only way we can trap him! If it works, we can accuse him and be rid of him!" Another voice, "Yes, but we must be careful. He has many followers that could cause problems. It is best to do it early in the morning, before everyone is working and packing up to go home. Most everyone will sleep late because of all the celebrating today." Another, deeper voice, "You are right. Few of the kind that follow him will be near the temple in the morning." I wondered who they were talking about and had a hard time even thinking with my head hurting so badly. I tried to sit up to be able to hear better and as soon as I did, the room began to spin again. I immediately felt like I would be sick and lay back down. As I drifted back to sleep, I heard one of them say, "Tomorrow we will finally be done with him!"

When I woke up the next morning, I was not alone. The man I had come here to be with was lying next to me with his arm across my chest. My clothes had been placed neatly across the chair in the corner of the room. I lay there for several minutes, collecting my thoughts. My head still pounded. I remembered the bitterness of my last swallow; I could still taste it, and wondered why they had given me the powder. I looked over at the man next to me. I had no memory of being with this man. He was naked also, so I must have had another blackout. I couldn't remember what we had done.

As I looked at him, I remembered the uncomfortable feeling I had the night before. Then I recalled the voices I had heard. Had he been one of them? Maybe all that had been a dream. I didn't know for sure. I tried to sit up and when I did, he stirred and opened his eyes. I had not been able to see them well the night before and they were quite striking. I lay back down. I was so nervous and uncertain, I felt I had made a huge mistake in doing this. I began rambling. "Good morning! Did you sleep well? I think *I* did, but I have a terrible headache this morning. Do you know..." He didn't let me finish my sentence. He leaned over and began kissing me. Before I knew it, he was groping me and being so rough! Though most of my bruises had faded, I was still tender in those areas. I tried to slow him down, but he would not stop. I struggled to get up, but he got on top of me and his weight prevented me from moving. He said nothing and I feared another beating so soon after Nathan's. I shut my eyes and tried to go somewhere I had not been in a while. I tried to hide in the big weeping willow tree by the river. But no matter how hard I tried to find it, my safe place remained elusive.

Afterwards, I lay there quietly, barely breathing, hoping he had fallen asleep. If he were, I would get dressed and get out of here. Why did I ever agree to this? At this point, I didn't even care about the money! I had always gotten through tough times; I would survive! Suddenly, I heard the door crash open! There were hands all over me, pulling me from the floor!

They were dressed in robes like the priests wore! In fact, I recognized some of them from the first day I had heard Jesus speak at the temple. These were the ones who had sent for the temple guards! I tried to reach for the sheet to place around me, but they would not let me go. "Please, let me put something around me! Or let me get my clothes and go!" They all ignored me.

The man I had been with said, "I didn't think you would ever get here! What took you so long?" The man who held my left arm was grinning at me and watching my breasts as I tried to free myself. He licked his lips and answered, "We have been here for some time. Watching. We were waiting for Zadok." He turned toward the door and said, "Zadok, are you ready?" I heard a voice from the other room, "Yes, I am ready to go. We have heard he is already at the temple. We must hurry!" Just then, the man they called Zadok walked in. It was the man that brought me here to eat and offered this "job" to me!

I was so confused! "Will someone please tell me what is going on?" I looked at Zadok, who seemed to be in charge and begged, "Please let me go home. I don't care about the money!" He roughly grabbed my face in his hand and the kindness I had seen last night was gone. He squeezed my cheeks hard and said, "You have not fulfilled your purpose yet!" He looked down at my nakedness and grabbed the sheet off the bed and threw it at me. With a loathing look, he ordered, "Put that around you!" They all watched as I wrapped the sheet around my body. I was trembling so hard; I was having a difficult time. I had never felt so much shame.

The man I had been with was also dressing. He was talking to one of the priests and laughing. The priest who had been leering at me handed him a small burlap bag and said, "Thank you for your help." The man chuckled and said, "Easiest money I ever made!" I was so bewildered. What were they paying *him* for?

I still did not know what "purpose" I had to serve! One of them grabbed me and pushed me out the door. Fear overcame me as I realized they were not letting me dress before I went outside! "Wait, I can't go out like this! Please let me put my clothes on!" Again, they ignored me. Zadok said, "Don't leave anything of hers behind."

I saw them pick up the dress I had so carefully chosen the night before, and wad it up in a ball with my shawl. My hand immediately went to my neck. Relief! The necklace was still there! Even if they would give me none of my other things, I had that!

Zadok roughly grabbed my arm and shoved me outside. The morning was very bright and clear. By the coolness of the air, I could tell the sun had only been up a short time. I began to plan a way to get to my house without being seen. I started to walk away when two of them grabbed me. One of them was the man I had been paid to entertain.

"You aren't going anywhere, sweetheart! We have big plans for you." The eyes I had found so attractive earlier had been replaced with evil, leering slits. "By the way, thank you for a good time. It was worth every piece of that silver! I especially liked your trophies!" He roughly squeezed my breasts, chuckled and turned to leave. I spat at him as he walked way and I began to cry. What big plans? What were they going to do with me?

Another grabbed the arm that he had vacated and they began to roughly lead me toward the city. There must have been ten or twelve of them and they were all in their priestly finery. Such beauty and goodness on the outside and such ugliness and evil on the inside! This is who represented the God Mary had told me about? I tried to stop them and ask where they were taking me. The grip tightened on my left arm. "You need to shut up, woman!"

I continued to wrestle as we were beginning to pass houses in the city. The little booths were everywhere. It wasn't bad enough what was happening to me. It had to happen during the Succoth, with all these people staying in their little huts in the streets! And of course, people would be packing up to go home. I prayed they had all celebrated late and would not be up yet. I should have known my luck was not that good. A few were already up, saw me and turned away. Some covered their children's eyes and went back into their homes or booths. I was mortified.

I struggled so much that the sheet fell off, but they would not stop. I became hysterical and began to beg for them to get it. One of them went back and picked it up and handed it to Zadok. He glared at me and said, "Do you promise not to fight anymore?" I could not speak and just nodded my head. "If you do, I promise you will go through Jerusalem naked!" He gave me the sheet and I quickly wrapped it around me.

As we walked, I tried to make some sense of what happened last night and how it played into the events of today. I had been completely fooled by this man named Zadok. I believed everything he had said. *No one will know but you and the man we are paying you to accompany.* Now the whole city of Jerusalem was going to know! I tried to remember what they had said in the bedroom. The man I had been with seemed to be expecting all this and was actually waiting for them to come! I tried to recall all I had heard last night and today.

The realization of the words"we have been here for some time" hit me like stone. Had they been watching us while they waited for Zadok to arrive? I felt so much shame. My parent's words "you are good for nothing" penetrated my heart. They were right! I had become a cheap prostitute and now I was being paraded through the streets of Jerusalem, wrapped in only a sheet, so everyone would be sure to know it. My only prayer was that this would not be a day that Jesus was around. I knew he would not know me, but I could not bear seeing him. I could never face him again.

The two men behind me kept pushing and trying to make me walk faster. They had not given me my shoes and the stones and rocks in the streets were cutting my feet. I dared say nothing for fear of them taking the sheet. I walked as fast as I could. I realized that we were heading toward the temple. What would they be bringing me here for? I contemplated running. I was truly scared of what my "purpose" might turn out to be. We walked into the women's court and I knew I could go no further, so I slowed down. "What are you doing? Keep walking!" I noticed that they had all picked up large stones along the way, and it had not registered in my consciousness what they were going to do with them. I was struggling more with the idea that they wanted me to walk to the inner courts. There was a crowd there and then gradually I began to grasp what was going on. The man I had been with was a married man. And I was still married to Didymus, since he had never given me a bill of divorcement. Adultery was punishable by death! Death by stoning! What had I been thinking? No wonder they had been collecting stones along the way!

Why had I trusted this Zadok? Did I really think I could trust any man? I tried to slow down to give myself time to think. Two more hands grabbed my arms and I was being pulled toward the crowd. I struggled to keep the sheet around me. As we got closer, tears began to sting my eyes again. Was this how it would all end? Was this what my whole life would culminate in? A public stoning as an adulteress?

Sitting by Mary in the stable. Her words were penetrating my soul. "This same God loves you, Mary! I do not know what troubles you so, but I do know that He will help you." After she spoke, the peace had come and I did

252

not feel that I deserved it. But I could not stop it and I had thanked Mary's God for it. There had been similar words in my dream about Mary after I left Didymus. Oh, God! Can you help me now? I know I don't deserve your help. I know that I turned away from you, but I have nowhere else to go! Please, hear my prayer!

As we finished climbing the steps, I saw why the crowd was here. They were listening to someone speaking. Please don't let it be Jesus! Please! I heard one of the men holding me say to the others, "There are people already here. What do we do?" Zadok answered him in disgust, "Follow the plan."

The people were standing around the speaker, who was sitting on a step in the middle of them. When we were within a few yards, I saw a break in the crowd. My heart sank. It was Jesus! I tried to turn and the hands tightened their grip on me. They were pulling me into the center of the group... to where Jesus was. He had stood up and was looking directly at me.

I could not remember ever feeling like this in my life. Not even that night at the inn. I wanted to run. Disappear. Drop dead. Anything to escape this! The men threw me down at Jesus' feet. Many of those that had been listening to him left the temple, anticipating trouble. The sheet was pulled off my upper body as I fell and I reached over and pulled it around me. I slowly rose to my feet without lifting my eyes.

Zadok came up beside me, pointed at me and with a look of total disgust on his face, said, "Teacher, this woman was caught in the act of adultery. In the Law, Moses commanded us to stone such women. Now what do you say?" There was utter silence. I slowly looked up and saw Jesus kneel down and begin to write something on the ground. He was not answering them! They continued to fire questions at him and eventually he slowly rose, looking at me as he did. He said to them, "If any of you is without sin, let him be the first to throw a stone at her." When he finished, he again stooped down and began to write on the ground.

There was much grumbling among the priests. Hushed whispers came from the few remaining crowd. One by one, I heard stones hitting the ground as they were being dropped. I looked up and noticed the older ones leaving first. The younger priests were holding on to their stones and I saw two of them opening and closing their fists, obviously struggling with what they should do. Eventually, they too, dropped the stones and left.

When there was no one left with us, Jesus stood up and walked over to me. I stiffened as he touched my chin and raised it so he could look into my eyes. "Woman, where are they? Has no one condemned you?" His eyes were piercing me, slicing me wide open! All the disgrace and blame that had been buried deep inside me was draining out. Like the huge abscesses I had cut open on some of the women I cared for, the abscess in my soul was being penetrated and drained. I saw love in his eyes. A love I had never seen before! I *felt* love that I had never experienced before! I realized I was weak in my knees and giddy! This was what I had felt in the stable the night he was born - but multiplied a hundred fold! I was tingly and I wanted to scream! Instead, I answered him, "No one, sir." It was all I could manage to get out!

He continued to look into my eyes and said, "Then neither do I condemn you. Go now and leave your life of sin." I just stared at him! Had sweeter words ever been spoken? The Christ does not condemn me! This bringer of peace to my soul does not rebuke me! I wanted to dance and sing! But I wasn't dressed for that! Suddenly, I did not care that I was wrapped in a sheet - in the temple courts - in the heart of Jerusalem! I felt carefree and blissful like the story Mary had told me about King David, dancing and praising God on his way into Jerusalem. I stood there and tried desperately to control all I was feeling. Then I noticed he was looking at the necklace around my neck. I watched as the corners of his mouth began to form a smile. My hand went to the necklace and touched it. He again looked up at my face, smiled and walked away.

I was a changed woman! I would never be the same! I vowed that from this day forward, the people of Jerusalem would see the change that had just taken place and I would tell them Jesus did it! I turned and watched him until he was out of sight, oblivious to the pattering of feet and hushed whispers of those doing their daily, temple routines. I walked over to where he had knelt down to write. In the dirt, he had written words that did not make a lot of sense to me, but I would read them anyway, and hide them away in my heart. If he had written them, they were worth remembering! I knelt down so I could see them better. Since I had turned 40, my eyesight had changed drastically. I slowly followed the words with my finger as I read:

For I know the plans I have for you, plans to prosper you and not to harm you, plans to give you hope and a future. Then you will call upon me and come and pray to me, and I will listen to you. You will seek me and find me when you seek me with all you heart.

I did not know why Jesus had written these words here. I did not even know whom this was written to or whose words they were. But, today I had called upon God and prayed to Him. And He answered me! I had not been stoned and I had certainly deserved it!

I felt such gratitude and admiration for this man... *Jesus!* He had looked at me with so much love! Someone had finally looked at Mary Magdalene with true love in his eyes! No desire. No lust. Just love. I had never felt so free! Free from what, I was not sure. I only knew how I felt! I knew the heaviness in my heart was gone! The heavy burden of unworthiness- gone! The shame and guilt I wore like garments-gone! I felt alive! And my new life would begin today!

14

Forgiven much

My walk back home was a long one. Many people were still in the streets for the greatest day of the Succoth celebration. I clung tightly to the sheet wrapped about me and walked as fast as I could. If my feet had not been so badly cut, I would have run. I tried to ignore the hushed whispers and quiet tittering that came to my ears. I still felt tremendous joy and freedom in my heart, but the reality of my situation had fogged it slightly. I needed to get home so I could block out everything else except that moment I had spent with Jesus. I giggled as I thought about the change in the faces of the men who, with their grand intentions, had thrown me at his feet. Only a few words from his mouth had caused their arrogance to melt away into fear and anger. Some had even looked at Jesus with hatred! His words had pierced them! And they had pierced me.

I finally got to my house and quickly locked my door. I half expected a mob to show up and tell me to leave the city! Even if they did, I would not go! I was going to find a way to see Jesus again, somehow. I looked around my little house and saw many things that reminded me of my pitiful existence since I had been here in Jerusalem. The cheaply made furniture. Certainly not the fine furniture I had when I lived with Didymus. The numerous amphorae that I could never afford to fill. The men who had lived here failed to take them when they left. The thick woven blankets I had hung over the windows to keep the light out and the darkness in. In general, it was unclean and unkempt. Like my life. *Go now and leave your life of sin.* Yes, that would change today.

I got some water and scrubbed my body, until my skin was red. It didn't seem that I could scrub hard enough to remove the years of men touching me. I only knew I needed to try. When I felt satisfied that I was finally clean, I dressed myself and proceeded to clean my house in the same way. I took the blankets down from the windows and was surprised at the brightness of my little home. It immediately felt like new! I threw the amphorae out my back door along with the sleeping mats. I scrubbed the walls and all the furniture. I brushed the dirt floor and even cleaned all the candle-holders and placed fresh candles in each. When I was finally finished, I looked around and thought, "Now this is more like it! Everything is fresh and clean! This is what I want for my life, everything to be fresh and clean!"

I sat down and began to pray. "Oh, mighty God. I don't know how to thank you for what you did for me today. I feel so undeserving—so unworthy—of the mercy you have shown me. I don't know how to receive such mercy! I have turned from you so many times! I have cursed you in my pain and questioned your very existence! Can you ever forgive me? Can I do anything for you that would help pay back my debt? Jesus saved my life today from those horrible men. I want to be able to thank him and tell him how immensely grateful I am. I want to tell him how much I love him. But I don't know where to find him. If I ask where to find him, people will laugh at me! That a person like me is looking for a man of God! But I must tell him! *Neither do I condemn you.* Those words were so beautiful to me! I must tell him how much his words meant to me. Please help me find him.

Thank you again, Jehovah. I used to pray to you and say, 'Thank you, God of Mary.' But now you are my God and my heart is yours and my life is yours. Help me know where I go from here. Help me know what to do."

When I finished, I found myself on the floor, face down, and crying. My prayer had been so intense, I didn't even realize I had gotten on my face. I sat up and wondered how I could possibly find Jesus. There must be someone who knows. Then I heard a knock at my door. Oh, no! They have come to tell me to leave! To tell me I am an embarrassment and that I must go. Again, the knock. It was a gentle knock though, not the knock of an angry mob of disgruntled people. Then I heard a soft voice. "Mary. Mary, are you here?" It was a woman's voice! No women ever came to see me!

I got up and went to the door, hesitated and then opened it. It was a woman about my age and she looked hauntingly familiar. Recognition was knocking at the doorway of my memory, but it wouldn't come in! Then she said. "Hello, Mary. It has been a long time." It was Joanna! She hadn't changed at all! She was as beautiful and sweet as she had always been. I grabbed her and hugged her as hard as I could! Joanna! After all these years! I finally let go and said, "Joanna, come in! Come in! You don't know how wonderful it is to see you!" She stepped in, looked around and then hugged me again before she sat down.

"I'm sorry I don't have a mat for you to sit on, Joanna. I need to get new ones and I know my house is small but..." She stopped me with a warm smile and a gentle squeeze on my arm. "Mary, stop apologizing. Your house is lovely and so are you. You look just like you did the last time I saw you at your father's inn." I felt the heat rising to my face and I blushed deeply. "Thank you Joanna. I thought the same about you. How have you been? Why did you all move without saying goodbye? I found out from a woman who was renting the house where Joseph and Mary lived." Joanna

259

looked down at her lap and when she looked back at me her eyes were sad. "Mother died very suddenly and Father was crushed. I was very worried about him and suggested we go to Bethany where he had family and they could help him through his grief. He felt that was a wonderful idea and we packed up two wagons and we were gone."

I pulled Joanna to me and we cried together for some time. "I deeply loved your mother and I am so sorry for the way I treated you the last time I saw you both. I used to wish, when we were little, that she was my mother, too." Joanna nodded, "She felt the same way about you, Mary. She loved you very much and prayed for you and your safety all the time." We hugged and cried some more. The shame and guilt I felt for having thought such negative things about them was overwhelming. How could I have been so selfish to think they didn't care? All I had been thinking about was how it affected me, not what might be going on with them! There had been many others I did that with, also.

"Joanna, have you ever seen Mary and Joseph? I know Jesus is in Jerusalem, but I didn't hear anything about them." I wasn't about to volunteer how I knew Jesus was here and I hoped she wouldn't ask. "Yes, I have seen Mary, but Joseph died a few years ago. Mary still lives with her other children." I couldn't believe it! Joseph dead. Deborah dead. These had been important people in my life and they died without me even knowing! I remembered the time Thaddeus had ridden up to Joseph and Mary's house and Joseph had been so protective of me. He had modeled what a father should be like and what I had wanted my future husband to be like. And now he was gone and I couldn't tell him how much I respected him. I couldn't tell Deborah how much I had appreciated her. Instead of trying to find them and find answers, I had wallowed in my anger and self-pity.

One thing was puzzling me. "Joanna, how did you know I was here? How long have you known?" Joanna smiled.

"Jesus asked me to come find you. He knew exactly where your house was and gave me directions to find you. He wanted you to know how to find him." The bottom dropped out of my stomach! Two opposite emotions were fighting for first place in my mind and heart and I had to swallow hard to get my thoughts together. First, had Jesus told Joanna what happened this morning? I didn't think I could bear that. And did he know the history of Joanna and me? If he did then he knew who I was and I couldn't bear the thought of that either. These fears struggled with the unbridled joy that I felt, knowing I had just prayed to God that I would find Jesus and here was a messenger telling me how!

Again, I swallowed and carefully attempted to talk. "Joanna, does Jesus know we were friends and that I used to know his mother?" Joanna shook her head. "No, he only said he knew you and knew that you were here. He was aware that we were friends in the past but didn't mention the other details. I wouldn't be surprised though, Mary. He knows things that no one else can fathom! He is such an amazing prophet. I have been following him for some time. There are two women that travel with him everywhere he goes. I follow him when he is in Judea because my husband is also a believer. The women help out financially and we also help prepare meals for Jesus and the disciples. I do not work; my husband Cuza works at the palace and he gives money to help, but the other women are not married and use their talents to provide income and food."

What an awesome opportunity! I would love to help out with Jesus' ministry! I was paid quite well as a midwife and I could help as the other women did. I expressed this to Joanna and also my curiosity about several other things. I had so many questions for her! What were disciples and why was Jesus traveling around? I had heard him speak in the temple and there was a mix of people who admired him and those who jeered him. What was his purpose for these public teachings? I was sure Joanna could help answer my questions. She and her mother had done that when I was little.

Joanna spent most of the afternoon telling me of Jesus' amazing ministry. The miracles and the people healed. The huge following he had in Galilee. She even told me that the man I had seen at the Jordan baptizing people had been Jesus' cousin! He was the son of Mary's cousin, Elizabeth, the barren woman Mary had told me about who had gotten pregnant in her old age. My thoughts drifted back to my friend Elizabeth. What different lives these women lived! I was certain their name was the only thing they had in common. Joanna and I also spent many hours reminiscing about our days in Bethlehem. She helped me prepare dinner for us and we talked until we noticed the sun going down. "Mary, I must leave before it gets too dark. Jesus is staying in Bethany with some friends, two sisters, Mary and Martha and their brother Lazarus. He wants you to come to him. You have no children and are not married, so you could follow him, even into Galilee. Maybe you could find work there and help out."

The idea was tempting and I wanted desperately to see him and thank him, but I felt I really needed to clean up my life first. I needed to be acceptable. I needed to be worthy. "Joanna, I would love to see him, but I need a little time. Could I follow you when you go tomorrow and maybe I could sit at a distance with the rest of the crowd? Eventually I will talk with him."

Joanna looked at me and took my hand. "Jesus wants you just as you are, Mary. You need to change *nothing* to come to him." I held up my hand. "I believe you, Joanna. But I need time. There is a great deal about my life I have not shared with you and, frankly, don't want you to know. I need to feel better about myself. But if you could do just one favor for me? Could you give him a message for me? Tell him I am so grateful for what he did for me. He will know what you mean." Joanna agreed and got up to leave. I had to ask just one more time. "Joanna, did he tell you my name was Mary? Do you know how he knew that?"

Joanna shook her head. "He said, 'There is a woman living in Jerusalem, her name is Mary. I would like her to join us. She used to be a friend of yours when you were very young. She would like to see you, too.' That was all he said. I didn't question him because we all accept that he just knows things. You are the only Mary I had as a friend when I was young so I was excited to do this for him." I nodded and we hugged. She promised to come the next day and pick me up.

In the morning, I bathed again and dressed in my most modest clothes. Joanna arrived early, as promised, and we took her wagon. Bethany was just a short ride, and the house of Jesus' friends was just outside the town. When we arrived at the house, only Lazarus was there. He told Joanna that Jesus had gone to an area called the Mount of Olives, to teach. A large crowd was waiting for him and many had brought their sick family and friends as well as those they thought were filled with evil spirits. He informed Joanna it was only a few miles. She said she was familiar with the area. We got back on the road and headed north. I was filled with anticipation... and fear. I was not ready to see him yet, but I would, at least, get to hear him speak again.

We had no problem locating the crowd. It was huge! They all sat, surrounding Jesus, who was sitting on a large boulder half buried in the hillside. The mass of people seemed to cover the whole side of the hill as far as I could see. Joanna pulled her wagon off the road under some olive trees. We both got down and Joanna started to wade her way through the crowd. She turned back to me and held out her hand. "Mary, come with me. You will be so glad you did." I shook my head vehemently. "No, Joanna! Please, not yet. Soon, I promise." She looked as if she was going to say something else, but stopped and just nodded her head and then proceeded up the hill.

I went around the outside of the crowd until I was close enough to hear and see. People were taking turns standing and bringing their loved ones to him. Blind people, deaf people, lame people—some even looked like they had leprosy! And he healed them! He healed them all! One touch and they received sight! One touch and they could hear! I saw one young woman practically dragging an older woman through the crowd. The older woman was completely wrapped in dirty cloths and even her face was not visible. She fought the younger girl and I could hear her saying over and over, "No, I can't! No, no, unclean." But the other woman would not relent.

The crowd parted as they went with looks of horror on their faces. They finally reached Jesus and when they did the older woman fell to the ground at his feet. He stood and knelt down next to her and removed the covering from her face. I heard the gasp go up from the crowd. Her face was bone white and lumpy from the leprosy. It appeared that her nose was partially missing. She tried to pull the filthy scarf back over her face, but Jesus stopped her. He took her hand and began to unwrap it. Her fingers, below the first joint, were missing. She was crying and then I heard her say, "Please, master, could you heal me? I have never touched the faces of my grandchildren. I lost my husband and have been banished for eight years. My daughter told me about you, but I was afraid to have hope. I was afraid to believe. But I have seen you do great things today. Could you help me, too?" He tenderly looked at her and touched her face and said, "Woman, your faith has healed you. Now go and play with your precious grandchildren and make up for the time you lost!" Immediately her face was smooth. Her nose was renewed! She held up her hands and unwrapped them the rest of the way. Her fingers were whole! Her skin was as smooth as mine! She bowed to him and thanked him and he hugged her and they laughed together. She got up and, with her daughter, ran down the hill rejoicing!

I had never seen anything like this! Lame people were carried to him and they walked away! This went on for what seemed like hours. Finally, the last person had been healed. Jesus started to speak when two men stood up and very tentatively made their way to him. I was curious because they did not seem to have any defect that was noticeable. They kept looking back and forth at each other as if afraid to speak. Jesus flashed them a smile and asked what they needed. Finally, the smaller of the two spoke up, "John the Baptist sent us to you to ask, 'Are you the one who was to come, or should we expect someone else?'" What a strange thing for John to ask! Wasn't this the man who was sent to tell of his cousin's coming ministry? Why would he send these men to ask Jesus if he was the one of whom he spoke? Why didn't he come himself?

Jesus continued to smile patiently and placed his hand on the shoulder of the man who spoke. "Go back and report to John what you have seen and heard: The blind receive sight, the lame walk, the dead are raised, and the good news is preached to the poor. Blessed is the man who does not fall away on account of me." They both nodded and bowed to Jesus and then turned and left very quickly. As soon as they had gone, Jesus began to speak. "What did you go out into the desert to see? A reed swayed by the wind? If not, what did you go out to see? A man dressed in fine clothes? No, those who wear expensive clothes and indulge in luxury are in palaces. But what did you go out to see?"

I looked up and Jesus was looking straight at me. It was almost as if he was asking me that question personally! I had been thinking about the men who had dragged me through the streets and who had come dressed in their finery to hear John, the day he rebuked them. Jesus eyes did not leave mine. I pulled my scarf more tightly over my face and he finally looked away and continued, "What did you go out to see? A prophet? Yes, I tell you, and more than a prophet.

This is the one about whom it is written: 'I will send my messenger ahead of you, who will prepare your way before you.' I tell you, among those born of women there is no one greater than John; yet the one who is least in the kingdom of God is greater than he."

Jesus was saying more but I didn't hear his words. I was back at the Jordan, listening to John, remembering the pull in my heart to go to him. The same pull I was feeling now. Tears were running down my face and I did not even know when they started. The miracles I had seen today only made my gratitude for this marvelous man deepen. My heart felt like it was breaking, but not in sadness—in thankfulness! But there was still this nagging doubt. The people he had healed, all had physical problems. My problems were inside me. How could he help me?

Just then I realized the crowd was breaking up and Joanna was coming toward me. I had missed the rest of what he said and I was not pleased with myself! Joanna was excited. "Mary, can you believe what you saw here today? Isn't he wonderful?" I was nodding my head in agreement and grabbed Joanna and just hugged her. "I do want to speak with him, Joanna! My heart feels like it will explode if I don't!" Joanna nodded in understanding. "Unfortunately for you, he has gone to pray, right now. He always spends many hours praying after a day like this." I was disappointed but thought I could wait till tomorrow. "What if I come with you tomorrow also? Do you think he will see me tomorrow?"

Joanna smiled. "Mary, he will see you anytime. It was his idea that you come! But he just told the disciples to go back to Mary and Martha's house tonight. He has plans of spending time with some of the Pharisees tomorrow, for what reason I do not know!" At that moment she sounded just like her mother. I chuckled and she asked me what I was laughing about. When I told her, it sent her off on another tangent. "Well, I don't know why he would spend time with a bunch of men that do nothing but put him down! Especially that Simon! He is the most outspoken of them all!" I asked her who the Pharisees were and after she explained to me, I realized these were surely the men who had tricked me. They may even have been the men at the Jordan that day. When I asked Joanna, she retorted. "Oh, I would not put it past them! They always are prancing around and looking important. Jesus has had some strong words for them." I told her about John's words the day I saw him. "Yes, but unfortunately, John has been hushed. Herod had him arrested because John was confronting Herod's adulterous relationship with his brother's wife. Herod needed to shut him up. That's why John sent his disciples to ask Jesus that question today. He has been locked up in that dark dungeon so long; he has forgotten who his light is!" She shook her head sadly. "It has been hard on Jesus, but I have been a little help to him by keeping an eye out for John. I told you my husband, Cuza, works at the palace of Herod and so I get all the inside gossip." When she smiled that way, she was a duplicate of her mother!

"Joanna, not to change the subject, but are you telling me I will not be able to see him tomorrow either?" Joanna laughed and hugged me. "I am so glad you want to see him so badly, but it will have to wait one more day. He could be at Simon's house most of the day, Mary, and then he will probably go off by himself again to pray. He will need it after a day with them! Be patient, Mary. Your time will come!" I agreed, knowing it was going to be a lot harder than I was letting on. We walked back to Joanna's wagon and headed back to Jerusalem. Neither of us spoke. I was basking in the joy of seeing him the day after tomorrow. When Joanna dropped me off, she promised to come and get me for her next journey to Bethany. "Thank you for today, Joanna. You don't know how much it meant to me." She looked down at me from the wagon and cocked her head to the side. Another of her mother's characteristics!

"Mary, I can't help but feel that something has already happened between you and Jesus. Your desire to see him goes way past the invitation he gave. You said to thank him—and I did—for helping you. What was it he did for you?" I looked into her eyes and said, "Joanna, I love you dearly, you know that. But there are some things I'm not ready to talk about. Not yet. Please, give me time." She reached over and squeezed my shoulder. "You know I love you, too. You take all the time you need, Mary. All the time you need."

That night, sleep seemed impossible for me. I tossed and turned all night. I didn't want to wait two more days to tell him how I felt. I didn't want to wait to tell him how grateful I was. I cried most of the night just thinking how undeserving I felt to even be in his presence. All the horrible things I had done in my life and he was so perfect! When he smiled, my heart just stopped beating! It happened when I lived in Nazareth and went to his house, it happened at the temple and it happened today. I would probably not even be able to speak when I did finally stand in front of him! Of course, I would not be standing. I would be bowing like those people today. Oh, how I understood that leper woman's tears! I wanted to thank him just as she had. But one thing he must never know. He could never find out that I was the girl that was his mother's friend. He would never understand. I would thank him and follow him, but I must keep that part of my life a secret.

I finally fell asleep as I heard the cocks crowing in the distance. I woke after several hours and when I did it was with Jesus' name on my lips. As I tried to get through my daily routine, I would think about having to wait until tomorrow to tell him what I needed to say and the tears would start. I tried to eat something. I tried to do things to keep busy, but it was hopeless! I would go and find him. I didn't care where he was or whom he was with, I must tell him. Thank him. Touch him. I also needed to take him a gift. But I had nothing of any value. What could I take? Then I remembered an alabaster jar of perfume that a young mother had given me as barter for my services while working with Ruth. She had no money and I told her not to worry about it, but she insisted. I had kept it in my bag all these years and had truly forgotten about it. I found it odd that it had never come to mind until now. I had desperately needed money—even gone without food—and still never remembered the alabaster jar. If I had, I certainly would never have accepted Zadok's awful proposal! I was still not sure what Jesus would do with it, but I felt I needed to take it. Ruth had told me it was quite valuable. And it was the all I had.

I got dressed and thought about who might know where this Pharisee lived. I prayed Simon was not one of the ones who had assisted in my public degradation. I thought about going to the palace and asking Cuza if he could help me locate him. I couldn't ask Joanna because I had forgotten to ask where she lived. I left my home not knowing exactly where I was going. By the placement of the sun, it must be late afternoon. I started walking and planning how I could get the information I needed. My heart was so full; tears seemed to be just on the brink. I needed to keep them at bay if I was going to pull off my plan. I would go to the temple and say I was a servant and had a delivery for Simon. I hated lying but didn't know any other way.

The closer I got to the temple the more scared I became. What if I ran into Zadok? I couldn't be responsible for what I did to him! I stopped and prayed. "Oh my God. Please help me find someone who will be kind to me and who will help me. Please, God." As I walked toward the temple, I saw a man lighting the torches around the outside court. I decided to take a chance. "Excuse me, sir. Could you help me find one of the Pharisee's houses? His name is Simon and I have this jar of perfume to deliver to him." I had my face covered, and hoped he had not seen me earlier in the week. He turned to me and smiled and said, "Of course, I know where he

lives. Do you know where the Gennath Gate is located?" I
nodded. "He lives next to the Tower of Hippicus, near that
gate." He smiled at me again and went on his way. To find
someone that helpful, especially to a woman, was a blessing.
To find someone that friendly, that was a miracle! I turned to
thank him, but he was gone. I turned in the other direction.
He wasn't there either. I looked all around me and there was
no one in sight. That was really strange! There was no place
for him to hide. It was totally open where I stood. I scanned
the area again and shook my head. Very strange, but at least
he had given me the information I needed.

I headed to the west of the city and the closer I got the
more tearful I became. *What if Simon turns me away? What
if he does not let me in to see Jesus? What if I embarrass
Jesus in front of this holy man?* I stopped and thought about
abandoning this idea. Who did I think I was? People in
Jerusalem knew about me! Surely, the other Pharisees that
had so arrogantly paraded me through the streets shared their
antics with the others. And I wasn't even sure that this Simon
was not one of them! I turned to walk back to my house. I
stopped again. Wait a minute! This wasn't about me! This
was about letting Jesus know how much I loved him and to
thank him for what he had done for me! It was about getting
this fullness off my chest so I could breath normally again!
I must tell him! I had to let him know how special he was to
me and that I would do anything for him. Anything.

I turned and began to walk back toward the Gennath
Gate. My chest felt so heavy, it was like someone was sitting
on top of me. There was a knot in my throat that threatened
to suffocate me. As hard as I tried, I could not swallow it. As
I approached the tower, I saw the house that the man at the
temple had described to me. It was a grand house! *Too grand
for you, Mary! What are you thinking? What are you doing?
If you think you have been embarrassed in the past just...*

I put my hands to my ears and cried out "You will not sway me from my mission! Go away and leave me alone! I will not listen to you!" I looked around and there were people coming in the gate to my right. I took my hands down and straightened my clothes. They hurried past me as if afraid of me. I guess my actions looked strange, to say the least. That voice had haunted me all my life and it had been the cause of some of the worst decisions I had ever made. But it would not change this one! No matter how my hands were trembling, how much pressure I felt in my chest or how little air I could breathe, nothing was going to change my course! I closed my eyes and prayed right there in the middle of the street. "Oh God, my God, help my feet make the rest of this journey. Let my heart pour out the intense gratitude and love that I have for him. And please, let him receive it. Thank you."

I began walking again and soon enough my shaky feet had taken me to the door. I stood there for a moment and listened. It sounded as if they were already eating. They were also talking of things I did not understand. It sounded like there were more than just the two of them I had expected. Oh, could anything else go wrong? I prayed again remembering the humiliation I had felt standing in front of Jesus at the temple with only a sheet wrapped around me. Tears stung my eyes and I was helpless to stop the flow. My heart started beating so hard in my chest, I was sure they could hear it inside the house. I tarried for only a moment more. I knew if I knocked they would probably not let me in so I placed my hand on the door and pushed it open. There were five of them reclining at the table in the center of the room. Jesus was directly in front of me, but facing in the opposite direction and unable to see me. However, I was in plain view of the others. They all turned their heads as I walked into the room. I only recognized one of them; he had been the one who lingered at the Jordan River when the other Pharisees left.

I slowly walked to where Jesus was lying and stood at his feet. I could hear the grumbling of the others but refused to look at the hatred I knew was in their faces. I stood there, crying, unsure of what to do next as my tears dropped on his feet. I watched as each tear rolled down leaving trails of clean skin behind. These holy and rich men had not even given him water to wash his feet! I knelt down and as I did, my shawl fell from my face. There was an audible gasp when they realized who I was. Part of me wanted to run, but first I had to do something for Jesus.

When I knelt at his feet, Jesus glanced at me. One look from him...his eyes seemed to melt every cold place in my heart and mend every shattered dream. I was crying even harder as the shame I felt was being replaced with my love for this man. The impact his eyes had forced me to look down. My hair had fallen across his feet, mixing with the tears. I picked up my hair and used it to gently wash the dust from each of his feet using the tears that continued to fall.

My heart was full to bursting and I wanted to pour out my love on this wonderful man. I wanted to do something else for him. I wanted to give something back for what he had done for me, but what thing of worth did I have to give him? Then I remembered the jar of perfume. I pulled it from my bag and thought about handing it to him. I had not once looked at Jesus since I started cleaning his feet. I hesitated because this seemed like such a trivial gift. I feared the others laughing at me, or worse, laughing at him. Then an idea came to me! I would pour out this perfume on his feet just as I desired to pour out my love for him! This would be a symbol of my love! I removed the top from the alabaster jar and slowly poured it all over Jesus' feet and then massaged the rich oil into his skin. The fragrance filled the room and I heard one of the men grunt in disgust. My eyes slowly came up until they rested on Jesus' face. He was smiling at me and I thought I saw a tear slip down his cheek. He reached over and laid his hand on my shoulder as I put my head back down and began to cry again. The men continued to grumble. Then I heard Jesus say, "Simon, I have something to tell you."

The host of this dinner answered him, "Tell me, teacher." Jesus continued. "Two men owed money to a certain money lender. One owed him five hundred dinarii, and the other fifty. Neither of them had the money to pay him back, so he canceled the debts of both. Now which of them will love him more?"

Simon replied, "I suppose the one who had the bigger debt canceled." Jesus answered. "You have judged correctly. Do you see this woman? I came into your house. You did not give me any water for my feet, but she has wet my feet with her tears and wiped them with her hair. You did not put oil on my head, but she has poured perfume on my feet. Therefore, I tell you, her many sins have been forgiven—for she loved much. But he who has been forgiven little loves little."

He removed his hand from my shoulder, placed it under my chin and lifted it so I could look at him…just as he had done at the temple. He waited for me to look into his eyes before he spoke. "Your sins are forgiven." I began to say something… to thank him, but I heard the men saying among themselves, "Who is this who even forgives sins?" I said nothing but thought to myself, "If you only knew! If you only knew!" Jesus smiled at me as if he had heard what I was thinking and said quietly, "Your faith has saved you; go in peace." His eyes were gentle and said more to me than his lips. I whispered, "Thank you," and turned to go. As I walked from the house I noticed one of the men, the one I had seen at the Jordan, smile at me. It was a sincere smile. He didn't seem to be caught up with the others as they ridiculed and grumbled. He was off to himself. I returned the smile and quickly went out the door.

I walked home as if on a cloud. It was nothing like I had anticipated and I felt certain Jesus had received my gift as I had meant it. My heart was troubled, however, because my feelings for him were not entirely pure. My sins had just been forgiven by the Messiah! How could I have these thoughts about him? Oh, I needed a lot of work! I had always dreamed of someone treating me with the kindness that Jesus had just displayed. To be honest, there had been another. Amos. He loved me, but I shunned him.

I would need to talk with Joanna about what happened today. Find out exactly what forgiveness of my sins meant. I knew how it made me feel. There was no more darkness inside. I actually felt like a great weight had been lifted. I felt peace. *I felt peace!* Of all the things I felt, that was the biggest thing! The peace that had drifted in and out of my life at every thought of Jesus or the times I had prayed. I believed, with all my heart that it was finally here to stay! But then there was this struggle with these feelings I had for him. I would not let them steal my peace! Joanna could help me with that. She could guide me.

I arrived home and began to pack my things. Joanna had told me that Jesus and the disciples would head for Galilee in a few days and I should be ready to go with them. Joanna was even going this time because Cuza was on a short trip for Herod. I would find Orpah and tell her I needed work. She had promised it would always be available to me. If I rented out my house and sold what few belongings I had, I could get enough money to help until I began working. Then I could support Jesus' ministry the way the others did. There was a man in Bethlehem who had asked me, on three different occasions, if I would rent my house to him. I would find him tomorrow.

As I cleaned up the house, I found myself singing the way Leah had done. I don't think I had sung since I was a young girl. It felt good. *I felt good!* I finished cleaning as best I could, grateful for the thorough job I had done yesterday. I didn't know what to do so I lay down and tried to sleep. I was too excited! Then I remembered something from my childhood. I allowed my mind to drift back to the first night I had met Jesus in the stable. I had lay on my mat that night and just said his name over and over again until I fell asleep. I decided to try that now. *Jesus. Jesus. Jesus.* And soon I was asleep.

15

Denial

*"A farmer went out to sow his seed. As he was
scattering the seed, some fell along the path;
it was trampled on, and the birds of the air ate it up. Some
fell on rock, and when it came up, the plants withered
because they had no moisture. Other seed fell among
thorns, which grew up with it and choked the plants. Still
other seed fell on good soil. It came up and yielded a crop,
a hundred times more than was sown."*
*The meaning of this parable: "The seed is the word of God.
Those along the path are the ones who hear, and then the
devil comes and takes away the word from their hearts,
so that they may not believe and be saved. Those on the
rock are the ones who receive the word with joy when they
hear it, but they have no root. They believe for a while, but
in time of testing they fall away. The seed that fell among
thorns stands for those who hear, but as they go on their
way they are choked by life's worries, riches and pleasures,
and they do not mature. But the seed on good soil stands
for those with a noble and good heart, who hear the word,
retain it, and by persevering produce a crop."*

A lmost every night this week, Jesus had met with the disciples to prepare them for the opportunity to go out, two by two, and minister in his name. I had only been with the group for a few days and though I had been meeting with Joanna since I saw Jesus at Simon's house, I was nervous about the other women accepting me. Susanna was tall and slim and had a beautiful face. She was very soft spoken and seemed quite innocent. There was another older woman whose name was Mary and I knew little about her. She was more heavy-set and had a plain, but very kind face. She reminded me of Deborah—very loving, but quite loud. Joanna told me there were other women that sometimes joined them, but this was the core group. We all felt strongly that we were to help support Jesus' ministry because we all had the means to do so. The women were friendly to me, but I didn't know how they really felt, so I was cautious. They just seemed so much more worthy to be here than me.

The women sat in on some of the meetings, to give prayer support and help prepare the meals. We would sit in a circle and as night came, the women would build a fire and prepare the dinner. Jesus would keep right on teaching as we ate and even after we had cleaned up and the cool night air had settled in, he would continue, sometimes late into the night.

Tonight they talked about Jairus' daughter and the sick woman. Both of these miracles had taken place today on the heels of another miracle in the region of Gerasenes early this morning. I listened in awe as Peter, James and John took turns sharing about the twelve-year-old girl that Jesus brought back to life. Then the others talked of the woman who had been bleeding for twelve years and with just a touch of his cloak, was healed. They told of their boat trip last night and the sudden squall that meant certain death for them. Thaddaeus shook his head, "I know most of you are used to the water and rough seas, but I had never experienced anything like that! I knew I was going to drown and when I went to wake

278

Jesus," now they all began to shake their heads, "can you believe he was sleeping?" Thaddaeus' eyes sparkled with amazement and then he continued, "When I woke him, he just stood up and rebuked the wind—and it stopped! The sea was completely calm! Then he said we had no faith!"

I heard a chuckle. I looked over at Jesus and his head was down, quietly laughing. "Please, forgive me, Thaddaeus. I do not mean to laugh, but the way you tell the story with such seriousness, well, it just struck me as funny." Then we all began to laugh, but I could not take my eyes from Jesus. He was so handsome and his gentleness only made him that much more appealing. I tried so hard to love him in a pure way, but I was failing miserably. I was in love with him and there seemed to be nothing I could do about it! I tried to censor my feelings when I talked with Joanne for fear of being rejected. My intentions had been good. I was going to share everything. That's what Jesus had wanted. But this was too much, too deep, too sinful. I knew it was wrong, but I didn't want to hear anyone else say it.

When the laughing died down, Jesus said, "I said you have little faith because you have seen so many miracles with your eyes, but it has not reached your hearts. But it will." He looked around at each of us with incredible compassion in his eyes and then with more emphasis than before added, "It will. You are young yet and your faith will grow. When you go out and do miracles in my name, you will begin to build your faith." There was silence for a while and then Andrew told about the healing of the man with many demons. "When I heard the so many different voices coming from one man's mouth, I was afraid! But even more, I was amazed who the demons said you were, 'Son of the Most High God'!" Jesus held up his hand. "We will talk more about what they said later, but tonight I want to prepare you for your journeys."

As he continued, I thought about the marvelous things I had just heard. Oh, how I wish I had been there, but the women had gone into Capernaum to the market and though I desperately wanted to be with Jesus, Joanna felt I needed to go with them. After all, it was our ministry to Jesus and his disciples to help them monetarily and that included buying food for them. Reluctantly, I went. I had so many questions to ask about these and other miracles. But that would have to wait. Right now, Jesus was very focused on his disciples. I would bide my time until he had sent them out and then I would talk with him.

The next day, as Joanna, Susanna and I prepared the morning meal, my thoughts went to James. Jesus called him one of the "sons of thunder." It was easy to see why because of his quick temper, but his good looks offset any negatives in my eyes. I felt he was more handsome than his brother and more outspoken. I had especially enjoyed the times of teaching because I had noticed James looking at me. I would sense him staring and when I returned the gaze, he would quickly look away. I was certain he liked me and it had been such a long time since I felt anyone attracted to me. I knew I couldn't have Jesus, so having someone close to him sounded like the next best thing. I was pretty sure the only reason James had not said anything to me was because he wasn't sure how I felt. I began to think of ways that I could let him know I would be receptive, but I had to be careful. Jesus was very firm about all of us being friends, nothing more. Maybe tonight, after the sun went down, I would sit next to James in the circle. And if we were very discreet about our relation-ship, surely, after a while, Jesus would approve. But we had to be cautious. I would never do something that might make Jesus angry with me.

Later in the afternoon, I took a walk by the water. The sun was low in the sky and had started to hide behind the mountains. I stood for a time and threw rocks into the water, trying to skim the flat ones. I remembered doing this with my father when we lived in Magdala. I was only four or five and he would stand behind me and guide my arm as I threw the rocks. I felt the tears coming and sat down in the sand. What had happened? I had not seen him or my mother for years! My brother had grown up without me! He had been six the last time I saw him. With bitterness, I remembered how they kept him from me. Why had they done that? Did they think I was so bad I was unworthy of even seeing him?

I buried my head in my knees and sobbed. Where were all the victorious feelings of peace and freedom I felt at the temple...and at Simon's house? I did not want to be one of those seeds Jesus talked about, which fell on the rocks or was crowded out by the thorns. What had happened to those feelings? I cried until my throat hurt and there were no tears left. I wiped my face and looked up at the water and listened to its gentle lapping. It was getting dark and I needed to help with the evening meal. I would not think about the past any more today. I would think about James and the possible future we could have together. After all, what better husband could I have than someone who was a disciple of Jesus? I found myself smiling and thinking about my plan for tonight. Yes, tonight I would let James know for sure that I liked him. And Jesus would eventually be happy for us.

Nightfall finally came and Jesus and the disciples were coming back from their evening walk. Every night, Jesus would take them to walk along the Sea of Galilee. Many of the disciples missed their work on the water and I believed Jesus did this for them. I watched carefully as everyone sat down around the fire. I noticed James talking to Peter and John and I patiently waited to see where he would sit. At last they finished their conversation and he found a place next to the one I believe they call Bartholomew. I had not learned all the names yet. Some, I had not even met, like Bartholomew. My thoughts went to my brother again. By now he was the same age as Jesus. I couldn't tell how old this Bartholomew was, it was too dark, but I'm sure they were close in age. I wondered if I would ever see my brother again.

I realized that Jesus was getting ready to start and I had not found a place to sit. I looked across the fire at James and sure enough, there was plenty of space to his right. I made my way to the spot and sat down. My arm brushed his as I sat and I quickly apologized. He smiled at me and then looked over at Jesus. He had such a disarming smile! I was so excited; I could feel my heartbeat quicken!

We listened to Jesus teach us about the plans for the next day. They would leave in pairs. "John, you and Thaddaeus will go together. James, you go with Thomas. Peter, you go with the other James. Matthew, you with Judas Iscariot. Andrew, you and Simon pair up and then Phillip and Bartholomew. I will give to you power and authority to drive out demons and cure diseases in my name. You will preach the kingdom of God and heal the sick. You are to take nothing for the journey—no staff, no bag, no bread, no extra tunic, for the worker is worth his keep. Whatever house you enter, stay there until you leave that town. If people do not welcome you, shake the dust off your feet when you leave their town, as a testimony against them." There was loud murmuring among the disciples, especially the one they called Thomas. Jesus encouraged all of them to express their concerns. And there were many.

Time soon came for dinner and I got up to help the other women. Peter was cleaning the fish they had caught and was preparing it for us to cook. We set all the food in front of Jesus to bless. I was barely listening as he finished teaching, blessed the food and began to pass around the bread. The night was cool, the fire was crackling loudly and the crickets and frogs were singing to us. I stole a glance at James and watched the fire dance on his face. His facial features were chiseled, like they had been cut in stone. He was so handsome, I felt like I would burst at the thought of him liking me.

I returned to where I had been sitting and sidled as close to James as I could get. When he looked over at me, I pretended to be cold. I smiled at him and softly said, "I'm sorry, I was just trying to get close to the fire." I could feel his thigh against mine and I was sure that he probably felt as I did, but didn't want to show it in front of Jesus. Peter finished cooking the fish and we all began to eat. I tried to anticipate every move James made and took advantage of every opportunity to "accidentally" touch him or rub against him. I felt certain, at one point, he had made a furtive move to touch my arm and so I took the chance and gently laid my hand on his knee. It was under my cloak and I knew Jesus couldn't see. I waited for him to respond, but dared not look at him. I felt embarrassed, like a young girl with a new boyfriend. I felt giddy and a bit sneaky which only added to the excitement. I was about to move my hand when James suddenly jumped up and asked Jesus if he could talk with him. I was mortified! While they talked, Jesus turned his gaze from James and his eyes found mine. I immediately looked down.

I lost my appetite and got up and walked the short distance to my sleeping pad under a large olive tree where the other women slept. We were always quite a distance from where the men spent their nights. I saw Joanna get up and she walked over to me. "Mary, is anything wrong? You got up so suddenly and you looked upset." Joanna's concern for me had never wavered over the years. Jesus had suggested I talk with her if I had any problems. He felt it would help me if I were accountable to her, not only for my actions but also my feelings. I wasn't sure I really understood that concept and was often uncomfortable telling anyone the things that went on in my head.

"It's nothing, Joanna. I touched James on the leg. I was cold and trying to get close to the fire and…" Before I could finish, Jesus had walked up to us and placed his hand gently on

Joanna's shoulder. He whispered something to her. I couldn't hear what he said, but she bowed her head and backed away and went back to the fire. There was a little light from the moon shining over us, but not enough for me to read what was in Jesus eyes. He approached me and attempted to touch my shoulder, but I shrugged off his hand.

He looked into my eyes and said, "Mary, let's walk. I need to talk with you." I placed my shawl over my head and partially covered my face before I followed him. It felt like my heart was in my throat and my stomach was turned inside out. I don't remember feeling this way since I was a little girl and my father would tell me he was going to spank me just in case I did something wrong that day. But he wouldn't do it right away. Then I would go through the day not knowing when it was going to happen. That was a nasty memory that this situation was bringing to the surface. I wanted to run and hide.

We walked quite a way before Jesus stopped at some rocks just off the shore. They were large enough to sit on. He sat down on one and waited for me to do the same. "I think you know why I have brought you here, Mary." I rolled my eyes and began to explain away the 'accidental touch.' I felt the anger, mixed with guilt and shame, welling up in me. "If James told you I did that on purpose, he was lying! I was cold and that's all!" I felt indignant, but refused to look at Jesus, knowing what his eyes did to me.

I paced back and forth as I continued my tirade. "He has done things that made me feel that he liked me and I just wanted to get warm. I don't know why he's lying about me!" I sat on the rock and began to cry, hoping to induce some sympathy from him. "I'm just trying to be a good friend to everyone and they take it the wrong way. What's wrong with touching anyway? We aren't doing anything else!" My tone had become sarcastic and I knew I needed to be careful. I also realized I was doing all the talking. I began to cry harder, holding my head in my hands.

I got up off the rock and slowly inched my way toward Jesus, with my eyes covered and then I felt his hand on my shoulder. I let myself fall into his arms and started confessing what I had kept penned up for so long. "It's really you I want, Jesus! No one has ever treated me with so much respect and kindness. I long for you to hold me and make me feel safe in your arms. I love you and I want to be close to you and hold you and…"

He quickly stood and pushed me away at the same time. His voice was loud and firm, "Stop, Mary!" I ignored him and tried to push against him, hoping he would give in to my pain. He pushed me away again, with more authority this time, and held me by my shoulders at arm's length. His voice was gentler as he spoke, but his grip did not relinquish. "Mary, look at me." I felt so humiliated that I didn't want to look at him. Again he said, with even more gentleness in his voice, "Mary, look at me."

I slowly raised my eyes to his face. His eyes were searching mine and they were filled with compassion and understanding. "Mary, sex does not equal love and love does not equal sex!" I looked at him, stunned. What was he thinking? What did he think I was trying to do? He said it again and I opened my mouth to defend myself, but his eyes stopped me. "Stop lying to yourself, Mary. You must recognize this truth so your healing can be complete. It is not your fault that you feel the way you do. It's all you have ever known. At an early age, your father and other men awakened in you feelings that should have stayed dormant until you were married. These men taught you that you could get attention if you were sexual. That it made you a "good girl." At your tender age, you equated those feelings with love and acceptance. If you performed sexually, you would be loved more. If you rejected their sexual advances, they rejected you. When you got older, the other men in your life did the same."

"True love, Mary, agape love, does not need sex to exist. It is unconditional, whole-hearted, and pure. It isn't selfish, self-serving or erotic. Mary, the love I feel for you is this agape love. No matter what you do or don't do, I will still love you. No matter what you have done or not done, I will still love you. No matter who you have been or not been," he paused and then with emphasis on each word, added, "*I will still love you.* But, Mary it is a pure love, not a sexual love. I have no sexual feelings for you and you must have none for me. And also, you must have no sexual feelings for the disciples. They care deeply for you, but only with the purity I have mentioned. Their focus must remain on their ministry."

His words penetrated my soul. I felt so unworthy of the love he described because my thoughts and feelings had been impure. I began to cry and turned away from him. He came to me, turned me around and in his most tender voice said, "Mary, I am not rejecting you, only your advances. You are worthy of the love I offer you because your heart is with me. You have sought forgiveness and you desire to be everything our Father wants you to be. The confusion you feel will last for only a season. For the first time in your life, you are being loved and admired for whom you are, not how you perform. The disciples admire the child-like faith you have and they long to have the same. We love your heart, Mary, and we expect nothing in return."

I collapsed on the rock where I had been sitting. My insides were contorted with the ambiguity of my life. The words I was hearing were contradictory to everything I had ever believed. "I don't know how to receive this kind of love and keep it pure, though. How do I do that?" He tenderly took my hands. "I will teach you, Mary. As you spend time with me, I will teach you. I will teach you how much our Father loves you. And as you believe my words, understanding will come. You will believe and you will begin to change. Do you remember the parable of the sower?" I nodded. That was the first teaching I had heard after Simon's house. "You have been all the seeds I spoke of…at different times in your life. Now you are the good soil, but there is a bit of thatching and tilling left to do and I will be your farmer. It will take time; it took time for you to think the way you do now. It will take time to change those thinking patterns."

Jesus took my hand in his. "And soon, the sexual feelings and longings you experience now, will diminish and be replaced with his love. You will put him first in your life and he will replace the void you have known—with a full heart, a healed heart, a servant heart. He will give you a crown of beauty instead of ashes, the oil of gladness instead of mourning, a garment of praise instead of a spirit of despair. You will be called an oak of righteousness, a planting of the Lord for the display of his splendor."

I looked at him in bewilderment. "I don't understand." Jesus smiled and nodded his head. "You will, Mary, you will. Meet me by the sea, at sunrise, and we will talk some more." He turned to walk away, paused, and then added, "Get some sleep, Mary. You will need it. Tomorrow will be a special day for you." His eyes were tender. "You must trust me, Mary. Trust me." I felt my heart skip a beat. I had heard those words before! But where? I watched him walk away and pondered what he had said. Somewhere in the recesses of my memory, I had heard his voice say those words. *Trust me.* The words he had written in the dirt at the temple came to me. *I know the plans I have for you…*I felt they somehow tied into what he had just said to me. That day had been such a horrific experience and it had ended with such joy. Could I possibly feel that freedom again?

The chill in the air caused me to pull my shawl closer around my neck. As I did, my hand felt the necklace. I grasped it and remembered. The stable…Mary…Joseph… baby Jesus…the incredible peace I felt whenever I was around him…the little house…our friendship…the three kings…how I felt when I found Mary and Joseph gone. Had I misread what happened like I did with Joanna's family? Had the years of bitterness and anger been based on a mistake in perception? Mary had befriended me and taught me about her God. I had trusted someone for the first time in my life. I had told her everything… well, almost everything. That opportunity had been negated. I had been consumed with Mary. Was that the problem? I rubbed the necklace. I wore it like a memorial to her. All the professing I did about loving God was tossed aside with my perceived abandonment by Mary. I chuckled. Oh, no! That's a lie! It wasn't tossed aside, it vanished! How real could my relationship have been with God if I threw it away at the first sign of trouble? I had been a perfect example of the parable of the seeds.

A deep yawn interrupted my thoughts. Jesus was right! I needed to get some sleep. I didn't know what to expect tomorrow, but the thoughts I was having tonight were a new revelation for me. I wanted to ask Jesus these questions. I wanted to ask him how his mother was doing and if I could visit her. Now more than ever, I wanted to share with Jesus who I was. That I had been there when he was born and witnessed angels in the sky announcing his arrival. That I held his little hands while he learned to walk. But the thought of him knowing that the adulterous woman he saved from stoning was the same that his mother had befriended— well, that was just too much. He would never understand how I could have witnessed and experienced all that I had with his family and then allowed my life to become such a mess. I was still trying to figure out that one for myself! As I made my way back to the sleeping area, I thought about it again. Yes, my relationship with him and his family, so many years ago, was something I must keep well hidden from Jesus.

16

Life given

Sitting by the Sea of Galilee as the sun is rising. Flecks of gold and silver sparkle in the water as if alive and dancing for joy that another day was beginning. The opulence of it leaves you mesmerized in wonder. And with the artistry of the sea, you experience the majesty of the mountains and the lushness of the valley below, filled with olive trees. It causes you to wonder what brilliant mind could think up such splendor. Who could paint such an exquisite picture? Such love he must have for us, that he planned this breathtaking beauty just for our enjoyment.

I don't know that I have ever fully enjoyed the wonder of God's creations until recently. I don't know that any person can, unless their mind and heart have been emptied of shame and guilt. I didn't feel that I deserved to enjoy things, even the things of nature. If others had always treated me so badly, then surely something must have been wrong with me. I must have had some defect of character that deserved disrespect and abuse. My past demons haunted me and robbed me of the peace and tranquility that I longed for. I had seven such demons. And it was on these shores, by the Sea of Galilee, that they were eternally banished.

I sat in the sand and listened to the lapping of the water at my feet. Next to me, Jesus sat quietly. He had told me to meet him here. I felt privileged because this was where he met with his disciples. Every morning on these shores, he would gather with them as the sun was rising. He would teach them. Pray with them. Prepare them. But today was my turn. I didn't know what to expect, but I was filled with hope.

We sat quietly for some time before he spoke. "Mary, I know that last night was very hard for you. I want you to know that James did not say anything negative about you, only that he felt the boundaries that I have set for everyone had been breached. He was actually complimented because he does think you are an attractive woman, but his focus is on his ministry and nothing else. He and John have both admired your child-like faith. That will come for them, too. I just wanted you to know that no one feels any negativity towards you. You have done nothing to be ashamed of."

I nodded, not sure of where this was going. "Mary do you know why you were created?" He glanced over at me and I slowly shook my head. "Well, I'm going to tell you because if you understand that, you will be able to understand why you searched so long for the peace that you now possess. You were created to have fellowship with God, for him to love and adore you and for you to do the same in return. He is our Father in heaven. He gets enjoyment every time you talk to him, reach out to him—pray to him—and when you praise and worship him. God is love and he loves you more than you can ever imagine. He loved you before your parents knew they were pregnant with you. He loved you and rejoiced the day you were born, because he already had a plan for your life. 'I know the plans I have you...' Do you remember that, Mary?"

I ecstatically nodded my head! "Yes, I read it and memorized it after you left the temple that day. I didn't know who wrote it or why you wrote it in the dirt, but I knew if you did, it must be important." He chuckled and reached over and patted my shoulder. "Mary, I do love your innocent faith! A great prophet named Jeremiah wrote that. God gave him those words so that everyone who reads them will know God has a plan for their life. Our Father has a plan for each person that is for their good, to give them hope and a future and not to harm them. Part of his perfect plan was that children would have parents that love and adore them—cherish them as a precious jewel—the way God does. His desire was that the parents of each child would know God personally and in turn, raise the child to know him also. He wanted the parents to teach his commands to the children, talking about those commands when they sat at home and when they walked along a road, when they lay down and when they got up. He wanted them written on the doorframe of each house and on their gates, so the days of the parents and their children would be many and he would bless them."

Jesus continued. "But because of sin, this perfect plan is not realized in every family. Some parents don't know God and so they do not raise their children to know him. Some people are not prepared for parenthood because they have not known the love of our Heavenly Father and his loving discipline. They don't realize that he is the role model for all of them. Some of these parents don't make the child feel special at all, certainly not the way God had intended. Without the unconditional love and acceptance of the parents, the child develops a void—a vacancy of the heart—and without knowing God, this vacancy grows and never gets filled even through adulthood. The child tries to find things that fill the vacancy, but nothing works. As she grows, she experiments with different ways to fill the vacancy, but fails miserably and then the feelings of hopelessness and worthlessness begin. So with each passing year, she persists in experimenting with ways to numb the pain that continues to intensify, never realizing that there is one solution that can take away her pain—one answer that can fill her vacancy—and that is God."

I placed my head in my hands and began to weep. He was describing my life! He was spelling out why I had responded to life with so much dysfunction! I felt his hand gently touch my back. And then he said, "You, Mary, have experienced this. You searched your whole life to find ways to fill your vacancy and in the process got yourself in a cycle of guilt and shame. The ways you tried to numb your pain brought more guilt and consequentially, more pain. And all the time you had the answer inside of you. You knew the peace of God. You ran from it because of lack of trust. You believed that your Heavenly Father was like your earthly father, and therefore you could not trust his care for you in times of trouble. You turned away and sought to do things in your own strength. But he never took his eyes from you. Yes, you suffered the consequences of your choices, but things could have been so much worse without the protection of his hand."

The expression on my face made him stop. "Tell me what you're thinking Mary." At first I shook my head. I didn't want to argue my point with him, but he encouraged me to be open. "If his plan was for my good, why did all those bad things happen to me when I was a child? And if he loves all of us, why did my sister have to suffer and die?" I felt no anger or bitterness with these questions, just a sincere desire to understand.

"Mary, God created man with a free will. There are many who use that free will to hurt others. That is not our Father's desire; it just happens." I felt confused so I asked, "But can't God do anything?" This was one of the first things Mary had taught me. Jesus nodded so I continued, "Well, if God can do anything and it isn't his desire to harm us, then why didn't he stop it? Why didn't he protect us?"

Jesus smiled at me and there was great compassion in his eyes. "Mary, you are only aware of the things that actually happened to you. You have no idea of the harm that could have come to you had our Father not protected you. Let me give you some examples. Do you remember the three men that badly hurt your friend?" I nodded, in awe of the details he knew of my life! "You were surrounded by angels that day and the plans the men had for you were thwarted. You both could have easily been killed that day, Mary."

"Another time, you were badly beaten in a tavern and the man you were with planned to beat you even more after he dragged you outside. But someone came to help you and took you home. Do you remember?" Again I nodded, a little bewildered. "But I thought that was my imagination. Leah saw me walking in the street and she said I was alone." Jesus smiled. "That's because she could not see the angel that was helping you to walk home and taking you out of harm's way." I gasped. "That was an angel! I can't believe it!"

Jesus grinned. "Well, believe it, Mary! There was also another time. When you went back to your father's inn and drank so much wine. You had mixed it with the powder you intended for Didymus." I blushed deeply realizing he knew of my shameful plan. "You should have died that night, Mary. But someone was there to help you." I sat straight up. "Was that an angel, too?" Jesus slowly smiled and said, *"Trust me, Mary."*

What did he just say? I felt like I couldn't get my breath! "That was you? You came to help me and paid them to take care of me? That was you! But wait... the angel said trust me, too!" Jesus laughed out loud. "I can send messages, can't I?" Again, I had forgotten who this man truly was. I felt ashamed. "Forgive me, master."

He patted me again. "That's all right Mary. It is for these reasons that I came. To teach you and the others about our Father and why he sent me." I felt confused again. "But it was you, not God, that helped me, wasn't it?" He looked off to the water and when he looked back at me his face was very serious. "If you know me, you know my Father. For I am in the Father and the Father is in me." I had heard Jesus say these words before, but it was still unclear. It seemed that he was telling me that if he had helped me, then God had helped me. I would save my questions on that subject for another time.

Jesus started to speak again. "Now do you see all the times you were protected?" I nodded and without looking at him asked, "But what about my sister?" He looked off toward the water again and then said very slowly, "Mary, these are questions that I can't answer for you right now. Your Heavenly Father's ways are far above your ways and his thoughts far above your thoughts. But I can tell you this: nothing happens that has not been sifted through his hands. He does not desire certain things to take place, but he doesn't always stop them. Do you know the story of Joseph?" I nodded eagerly. That had been one of my favorites. "Well, the way Joseph was treated was not God's plan; it was the plan of the devil. But, our Father had a plan for Joseph and so all the bad things that happened to him, God used for good. His imprisonment led to his high position in Egypt and because of that position, he was able to save the nation of Israel from famine."

I had heard Jesus mention the devil and I was curious about that. "Master, could you tell me more about the devil you mentioned?" Jesus explained. "The devil, or Satan, or Lucifer, as he was known in heaven, was once an angel. A very beautiful and special angel. One of the highest-ranking angels. But he became proud and he wanted to be like God. He had followers—other angels—that felt as he did, and a great war was launched in Heaven. Satan and his followers were thrown out of heaven and they have tormented man ever since. From the temptation of Eve until today, he has been a murderer from the beginning, not holding to the truth. There is no truth in him. He is the father of lies. He speaks lies into peoples' minds. He causes them to doubt the love of the Father. He lies to them about their spiritual condition. He lies about who they are... their position with God. He convinces them they are bad and when they believe it, he laughs at them. When a person hears a message in their head that they are a bad person—that is the devil! He makes a general statement. He tries to make you believe you are *all* bad.

I desperately wanted to understand this truth. "So how do I know if it's Satan in my head? Doesn't God tell us when we are bad, also?" Jesus looked amazed at my question. "That is a great question, Mary! When God convicts a person of something they did wrong, he is specific to the sin. He clearly tells them in their conscience, 'What you did to that person was wrong.' or 'That thing you did was wrong.' It is always specific, so the person does not feel condemnation. This brings repentance that leads to forgiveness of those sins. Satan has spoken to you, Mary. He has lied to you. And then he sent his demons, the angels that were banished with him, to continue taunting you, haunting you, destroying you. And he almost did."

I nodded in agreement. Listening to Jesus talk, I realized for, perhaps the first time in my life, just how close I was to total destruction. "Mary, I'm going to teach you some things that you have never heard before. I want you to listen and learn, and as you do, answers will come. Answers about your past and answers about your future. First, there is a parable I would like to share with you and then a teaching that will free you."

I perked my ears for this! I felt great anticipation as I waited for him to begin. "When an evil spirit comes out of a man, it goes through arid places seeking rest and does not find it. Then it says, 'I will return to the house I left.' When it arrives, it finds the house swept clean and put in order. Then it goes and takes seven other spirits, more wicked than itself, and they go in and live there. And the final condition of that man is worse than the first. Now let me explain."

"Mary, you were introduced to the love of God and you believed for a short time. Original sin, the sin all man was born with because of Adam and Eve, was driven out. The evil spirit was driven out. But, like the seeds that took no root, when a crisis came, you abandoned God." I swallowed hard thinking this is where he tells me that he knows his mother was my teacher.

But he never mentioned Mary. "You refused to talk about God and you refused to allow anyone to talk to you about God. You swept your house clean. As time passed, you began to do things that you thought would relieve you of your pain. The wine, the opium and the people you befriended were all ways for you to escape. And finally you thought that if you physically gave all of yourself, you could win the heart of a man and be married. When none of those worked, you let yourself be led into a lifestyle where lying and stealing were acceptable. There were many opportunities for you to make your way back to our Father, but something always got in the way. When you decided to not let your own children live, you entered into the darkest place you had ever been, accompanied by the worst of the wicked spirits. Murder and suicide were in your thoughts. Mary, your mind has been a playground for Satan. He knew where you were weak and he preyed on that weakness."

This was all very disconcerting to me. How could I ever change? As if he read my mind, Jesus continued. "You must spend lots of time with me, Mary. You must talk about your feelings with Joanna. If you had not been afraid to speak to her about James, she could have guided you in a different direction. Mary, when you keep things inside—when you keep things hidden—then Satan has fertile ground in which to plant his lies and deceptions. And without having the truth spoken into your life, you believe what you hear in your head."

I knew this was supposed to be helping me feel better, but I wasn't there yet! "So is there ever any hope of victory?"

Jesus laid his head back and laughed out loud. A very contagious laugh. "Mary! You have victory right now! You have
been forgiven of your sins! Now, when you fill your house
with the truth of God's love, Satan will have no place to
play!" It sounded so easy when he said it, but I knew after
both times I had felt so free, at the temple and in Simon's
house, the insecurities soon crept back in. Again, as if he
heard my thoughts, Jesus said, "Mary, I told you there was
more thatching and tilling to be done. It will take time. But,
today—the wine, the opium, the sex, the lies, the theft, the
murder and the suicide have been revealed! They have been
brought out of the darkness and into the light! They have no
more power over you! Mary, I know all these things about
you and my love has not changed for you! Neither has the
love of our Father! It does not matter to me what you have
done in the past because your heart has changed. You now
have a repentant heart...a humble heart. That is why you
have been forgiven and set free!"

Tears were running down my face and I looked at him
and tentatively asked, "May I hug you?" He smiled a broad
grin. "Oh, yes, Mary. I would love that." He held me like
that for quite some time while I cried over forty years worth
of tears. But these were not the tears from my past. These
were cleansing tears! Tears that were washing away my past,
like they had washed away the dust from Jesus feet. Holding
him, I felt none of the dichotomy in my emotions I had felt
before. This was pure.

When I had finally calmed down to a few sniffles, I asked
Jesus about the other teaching he had for me. "Ah, yes. You
did not forget and I am proud of you, Mary. I have taught
you many new things today and I feared overloading you,
but you look motivated!" I eagerly nodded my head. He
continued. "This teaching is very important for you and it
may be hard to hear, Mary. But stay with me as I explain it
and you will rejoice in the end."

I nodded again. He smiled at me and began. "Our bodies are meant for God. They are a temple unto him, in which he can dwell. Sexual immorality is the only sin man commits against his own body. Other sins are committed outside the body. The truth of this lies in the words God had for Adam and Eve. He said they would be joined and the two would become one flesh. Mary, you have joined yourself to many men. If you became one flesh with each of them, then you have lost little pieces of yourself to them and they have left little pieces of themselves with you. Your body—and your life—now belong to God. We must make you whole again and remove what has remained. Do you desire that cleansing, Mary?"

I didn't hesitate for a second. "Oh, yes, Master. I want that with all my heart!" Jesus grinned at me and with authority in his voice said, "Then I tell you now, Mary, that it is done. You have been set free and when the Son sets you free, you are free indeed!"

As I sat there I felt it! I really felt it! I jumped up and danced in the sand! I picked up rocks and threw them in the water. Jesus lay back in the sand and chuckled, watching me rejoice. I ran into the water and started throwing it up in the air. Then I threw some on Jesus. He laughed and yelled, "Stop, Mary!" But I wouldn't stop so he leaped to his feet and ran down to the water and started splashing me. We splashed each other until we were both dripping wet. I looked at Jesus and the realization of what he had done for me was so tangible, I began to cry. I sank to my knees, looked him straight in the eyes and in a voice choked with emotion said, "Thank you, Jesus. Thank you so much." I saw tears come to his eyes as he answered, "You are welcome, Mary."

The joy I already felt was magnified a hundred fold! I stayed on my knees and took his hands and thanked him again and then praised our Father! *Our* Father! What a wonderful sound that had! I thanked him and praised him and cried. Then I thanked him and praised him and cried some more!

I finally stood up and we walked back to the shore together. The sun was hot and it felt good. In my excitement, I had not realized how cold the water was. I felt bad for getting Jesus wet, but he didn't seem to mind. He had thrown off his robe before coming in the water and he now had it wrapped around him. We sat in the warm sunshine and listened to the water lapping the shore. I had one other question I needed to ask Jesus, but wasn't sure this was a good time. I was not at all sure I wanted to hear the answer, but I had to know.

As always, I felt that he was reading my thoughts, as he said to me. "Mary, is there anything else you would like to ask me?" I looked down at my hands and then said, "Yes, Master. There was a man that came to my room at night when I was a young girl…was it my father?" He looked at me and then looked away for a moment. When his eyes found mine again, I felt that piercing stare that left me totally vulnerable. "Mary, tell me why you need to know."

That took me by surprise! I stammered my way through my answer. "Well, because I need to know if it was him! My mother said my sister got pregnant by the man she heard shuffling to her door. I heard shuffling at mine. I think it was the same man. I think it was my father." Jesus looked deep into my eyes. "Mary, I think you want to know because it will feed the anger that you have carried for so many years. You have been used to being a victim and that thinking will take time to dispel. You know your father did things that were inappropriate; you can remember them. I realize there are things that you still don't recall. You went to your 'safe place' and as a child that protected you. Our Father provided that escape so you could survive the abuse. But as you grew older, many memories surfaced and confused you, so you reacted the only way you knew. You numbed them! But those choices were not safe."

His eyes were soft and gentle. "The things you still don't remember may come back to you or they may not.

Our Father will never give you more than you can handle. For now, you have enough information about those difficult times. Now you must concentrate on forgiveness for what you do recall. And you must forgive your father for the things he did, as hard as it may be. You must forgive him for what he did to you... and your mother and sister. You also must forgive him for keeping your brother from you. That is a lot of work, Mary." He paused for a moment before continuing. "Forgiveness is a choice, but one that will free you. For your sake, you must forgive him and for the sake of our Father in heaven. God will not forgive those who don't forgive others. When you forgive, Mary, you release the bitterness and anger that drove you to do many of the destructive things you have done in your life."

Forgiving my father? This seemed almost impossible to me. "But, master, is it fair that he just gets away with all he did? If I forgive him, isn't that saying that he is off the hook?" Jesus looked thoughtful and then smiled at me. "Those are excellent questions, Mary. First, you must remember that our Father says, 'Vengeance is mine.' He will decide the punishment that is fair. Our Father does not tolerate evil. But he also loves *all* his children and wants none of them to perish. Your father, no matter how many bad things he has done, is one of his children. Your forgiveness could be the seed that leads him to repentance some day. And if it doesn't, you have no regrets, because *you* did all you could."

Jesus placed his hand on my shoulder. "As for your other question, Mary. Forgiveness does not imply that your father has done no wrong. When I ask you to forgive him, it is a statement of the condition of *your* heart—not his. You are the one that benefits. For some, it is not even safe to return to the abuser to offer forgiveness; it could open the door to more abuse. In those situations, the work must be done in the heart alone. If the abuser has not sought repentance for his sins, it is still not safe to reconcile with him. But you must trust me, Mary. I would not send you if it were not safe. And if your father does not receive your message, that is all right. Your obedience will complete the work needed to be done in your heart—and that is what God sees and blesses."

I wasn't sure I was satisfied with the answer, but if Jesus said it was best for me, I would accept it. But there was one other thing nagging at me. "Well, could I ask you one other question then?" Jesus nodded. I continued. "There was a change in my mother before I turned four. She just seemed to put me on a back shelf. Before that, I felt loved by her and then suddenly, it was gone. Did I do something?"

"No, Mary, your father did something. He paid a great deal of attention to you as a little girl, sometimes in response to arguments they had. He knew it hurt your mother when he lavished love on you at her expense. When you got older, in your teens, his awareness of your developing body, was always a source of concern for your mother. She suspected his feelings were less than pure, but her own insecurities made her powerless to leave. There had been other women in the past, so she viewed you as another betrayal. She became jealous of your relationship. Because she loved you deeply, this caused a conflict within her. It was very difficult for her to see you every day, know what he might be doing to you and live with herself for not protecting you. She wanted to take you and your sister and leave, but she was afraid of being alone."

I was listening intently and Jesus turned to me and with that same powerful look, he asked a question that cut a gaping path through my dysfunctional past. "Does that sound familiar, Mary?" I can't express the emotions that I felt emerging. My mother had loved me! She wanted to protect me! But like myself, compromised the things she knew were right because of her own dysfunction—her need for a man at all costs. This changed my whole outlook! It helped me understand so much! Jesus was still looking at me and said, "For generations, your family has battled these problems,

Mary. Your mother, your grandmother, your great-grand-mother—they have all tried to live without the truth. They didn't have the benefit of God's perfect plan." My thoughts immediately went to my brother. "But, Master, what of my brother? Will he find this truth?"

Jesus nodded. "If he seeks the truth, he will find it. If he seeks God with all his heart, he will find him and then he, too will find the truth and it will set him free. The curses will be broken from his life as well. And when you both have children you will not pass these curses on to them. When you have children, Mary, they will have a healthy mother, one who will teach them about God and his commands."

I laughed out loud. "My brother may be young enough, but I think I'm a little old for children, don't you think?" I saw Jesus gaze back out over the water. His face was serious and I thought I had overstepped my boundaries, but when he looked back at me he was chuckling. I smiled at him. "Did you find that amusing?" He shook his head. "No, it just reminded me of another woman, a long time ago, who laughed when I told her husband she would have a child in her old age. And she was much older than you, Mary!"

I decided I would ask no more questions. Where was my faith? "I am sorry, Master for questioning you. It's just the idea of having a baby at my age seems impossible… and I don't even have a husband!"

Jesus gave me a knowing smile. "Oh, Mary, you will have a husband and I know who it will be!" I blushed deeply and inquired whom, but Jesus shook his head laughing. "Oh, no! I will not make it easy on you. When the time comes, you will know! As for being too old, my mother's cousin was older than you when she had my cousin John. So don't worry about that!"

I nodded in agreement, but I was perplexed that Jesus seemed to know about everything in my life except the time I spent with him and his parents. Well, I didn't know why and I wasn't about to remind him! I was in the middle of thanking him again for the new life he had given me today when we both heard Joanna crying out for Jesus. "Master, Master I must speak to you!" She was weeping and running toward us as fast as she could. Jesus jumped up and started to run to her. When she reached him, she fell to his feet and rocked back and forth, crying and saying over and over, "Master, it is terrible. It is terrible news."

Jesus knelt down and took her by the shoulders and encouraged her to tell him. Joanna looked over at me and then at Jesus and began crying again. "It is John, your cousin. Herod had him beheaded!" I gasped in horror! Jesus put his head down. My heart went out to him. He loved and respected his cousin and to have him die in such a violent way! He slowly stood and helped Joanna to her feet. He walked with her to where I was standing and said to us, "I need to be alone. I need to pray. Please don't wait for me at the evening meal." He turned and walked away and Joanna and I watched until he was out of sight. Why did this wonderful day have to end like this for Jesus? He had freed me from years of bondage! He had shared how important I was to our Father! He had given me back my life. I said to Joanna, "I wish there were something I could do for him!" She solemnly took my hands and said, "There is, Mary. We can pray."

17

Reunited

He has sent me to bind up the brokenhearted,
to proclaim freedom for the captives and release
from darkness for the prisoners,
to proclaim the year of the Lord's favor and
the day of vengeance of our God,
to comfort all who mourn, and provide for those
who grieve in Zion—
to bestow on them a crown of beauty instead of ashes,
the oil of gladness instead of mourning and a garment of
praise instead of a spirit of despair.
They will be called oaks of righteousness, a planting of
the Lord for the display of his splendor. They will rebuild
the ancient ruins and restore the places long devastated...
Isaiah 61:1-4

I t took a few days for Jesus to return to us. The women
prayed for him every day. We were worried about him and
how he would eat and sleep. Joanna assured me his Father
would take care of him in his grief, but I was still concerned.
In his absence, we prayed for the disciples, too. We knew
they were facing a great deal of opposition—both physically

and spiritually. Jesus had told us they would be like lambs among wolves. I certainly understood how that felt!

After Jesus returned, I was willing to put off my teaching until he felt better, but he was insistent that we keep going. He said it was for my welfare and the welfare of the other followers. I wasn't sure how I felt about that comment, but I trusted him, so I let it go. Everyday, except the Sabbath, Jesus met me at the water's edge and we talked. Over the time that we waited for the disciples to return, he taught me many more truths. He told me stories about men and women of God, like Mary had done, and I enjoyed them all. One of my new favorites was about Job. I could relate to Job! Yet, in all our conversations, it remained a mystery to me that he never brought up my relationship with his mother. I was grateful!

I enjoyed our time together, but unfortunately, this private time with Jesus was coming to a close. I had finally found, during the many mornings by the Sea of Galilee, what I had always been seeking. My chains were broken, my heart was full and the peace, that I had only tasted before, was now mine eternally. The struggle with my carnal feelings toward Jesus would take more time, however. My intense gratitude intermingled with the love I felt for him. Jesus had taught me that in my past, the positive emotions I felt, such as love and gratitude, were frequently confused as sexual responses and this had caused me great conflict. But, I had noticed over the last few weeks, they were separating and becoming more appropriate. Still, when he said my name in his gentle, loving way, my heart still melted.

The disciples had started to return, two at a time, filled with excitement and stories of miracles. Jesus received them with open arms and words of praise. After eight of them had returned, Jesus told us we needed to head north, toward Caesarea Philippi, the city where he had sent Phillip and Bartholomew. He said we would join them there. He left Mary and Joanna behind to tell the remaining disciples, Matthew and Judas, where we had gone so they could also join us.

A few days after we arrived in Caesarea Philippi, all the disciples were finally together again. Matthew and Judas came early that morning and the last to join us that evening were Phillip and Bartholomew. Jesus was welcoming them back and listening, with excitement, to their tales of miracles and new believers. The women were busy fixing a large evening meal to accommodate the ravenous hunger of the disciples who had joined us today. After listening to them compare stories, and especially John and James trying their best to outdo some of the others, Jesus began to teach. I tried to get as close as I could so I wouldn't miss a single word.

"Do not judge, and you will not be judged. Do not condemn, and you will not be condemned. Forgive and you will be forgiven. Give, and it will be given to you. A good measure, pressed down, shaken together and running over, will be poured into your lap. For with the measure you use, it will be measured to you. Why do you look at the speck of sawdust in your brother's eye and pay no attention to the plank in your own eye? How can you say to your brother, 'Brother, let me take the speck out of your eye,' when you yourself fail to see the plank in your own eye. If you first take the plank out of your own eye, you will then see clearly to remove the speck from your brother's eye." I had not heard this teaching before, but it was moving my heart. Jesus had spoken of my need to forgive my father, but I did not know how to begin. This was making it clearer. As I continued to clean the fish, I leaned in closer to hear more.

"No good tree bears bad fruit, nor does a bad tree bear good fruit. Each tree is recognized by its own fruit. People do not pick figs from thorn bushes, or grapes from briers. The good man brings good things out of the good stored up in his heart, and the evil man brings evil things out of the evil stored up in his heart. For out of the overflow of his heart his mouth speaks." Jesus finished and looked around at his disciples. Though Peter sat silently, he had been fidgeting and seemed to become increasingly irritated. Jesus focused his attention on him. It took little time for Peter to speak. "Master, I am confused as to why you are going over this again. We covered this teaching some time ago and you seemed satisfied that we understood it and would apply it in our lives. It is a good lesson, but we already know it!" Jesus placed his hand on Peter's shoulder and smiled patiently. "Don't be weary, Peter. I have a purpose for what I do. The meaning will be clear soon enough."

Joanna and I were finished cleaning the fish for the evening meal and then I saw Jesus coming toward us. He gestured for me to follow him. Perplexed, I looked over at Joanna and then back at Jesus. He nodded his head and said, "Yes, both of you can come." We followed him to the fire and he invited us to sit. I felt uncomfortable. I had not sat in the circle with the disciples since the incident with James. "Rabboni, the food is not ready! The disciples have traveled a long way and they are hungry. I could hear you from where I was sitting." I immediately felt awkward when I realized everyone had heard me. I looked down. He came over to me, gently lifted my chin and said, "Mary, I would like you to join us tonight. You need to hear what I have to say." His eyes were so gentle and I could never refuse anything he asked of me. "Of course I will stay. Forgive me for arguing with you." He nodded and walked to the other side of the fire and sat down.

He looked around at each of us and then began to speak, "The night I was born, my parents were in a region far from their home. There was not a room available at the inn, so the innkeeper offered his stable. The innkeeper had a daughter, a young girl of twelve. She helped my parents by getting them food and even finding a place for us to live." My heart felt like it had stopped. My mouth had dropped to my chest and I had to cover it with my hand to keep from gasping! This was my biggest fear! He does know who I am! Why is he talking about me to the disciples? Where was he going with this? His eyes caught mine and he smiled at me. "My mother loved this girl very much and invited her to our house every day. She was like one of the family. For almost two years they were the best of friends." Hot tears had started slipping down my face as I remembered those wonderful years. Mary had been another who had come to my mind as Jesus was talking about judging people…and forgiveness.

"One night my father learned that our lives were in danger and we needed to leave immediately for Egypt. My mother had no time to tell her friend that she had to leave or why… and this broke her heart. The only thing she knew to do was to leave a family heirloom behind, a necklace that her friend had admired." The tears were pouring from my eyes now. I realized all the things I had felt about Mary were wrong and she had never abandoned me at all! My hand went to the necklace. She left this for me hoping I would understand that it was a sign of friendship and I had looked upon it as a tool of punishment. Caught up in my tears of awareness was still the confusion as to why Jesus was telling this story. Surely, he would not tell everyone that I was this girl!

As my trepidation grew, Jesus continued. "This young girl had a little brother whom she would bring to our house and he became my first playmate. He actually learned to walk in our home, with the help of my mother. And I learned to walk with the help of my mother's friend. The girl and boy lived a difficult, abusive life, but she loved her brother very much and protected him every chance she could." I was crying uncontrollably as I allowed the memory of my brother to surface. The promise to protect him had been broken because of my father's unwillingness to let me see him…and my own selfish obsession with men. Sobs of regret shook my body and I was hardly aware of Jesus coming over to me. He put his arms around me and held me tightly, while yet another hidden area of my life was released from its captivity.

I don't know how long he held me like that, but he didn't let go until I began to calm down. When I had quieted, he lifted my chin slowly and looked into my eyes. I was conscious of the tears and slobber that must be covering my face. I knew I needed to blow my nose and wipe my face before I could speak to him. Embarrassed, I tried to clean up with the end of my cloak, but I heard Jesus say, ever so gently, "Mary." I closed my eyes as I felt the leap in my heart, the leap I always felt when he said my name. I opened my eyes and looked into his. His voice was so quiet that only I could hear him. "My mother never stopped praying for you and your brother. She prayed for your safety and she prayed that someday you would meet again. Her prayers have been answered this day. There are two of my disciples that you don't know very well. They were the last to return."

He turned from me and said to the disciples. "The little girl of whom I speak is with us tonight. Most of you know her as a friend of Joanna's who only recently began to follow and support us. But there are two of you who have not really met her or spent time with her. You really have not even had an opportunity to speak to her and I would like you to do that now." My heart dropped to my stomach. What was he doing? He really *did* know who I was and the power of that truth was seeping into my brain. He had known all along! And he still loved me! Unspeakable joy was mixed with uncertainty as I wondered why he was choosing this amazing time of revelation to meet these two disciples. As I continued to consider his reasoning, Jesus gestured for the two to come over to me. Again, I felt self-conscious because I knew my face was a mess from all the crying I had done. My joy of the moment overtook my self-consciousness and I looked up.

As they approached, I noted one was slight of build with lighter colored hair. Jesus introduced us. "This is Phillip."

He looked up at the disciple. "And Phillip, I would like you to meet Mary. She is very special to my family." I could feel the heat rise to my face with Jesus' compliment. I was grateful for the shadows of the evening. Nevertheless, I took Phillip's hand when he offered it. I then noticed the other man standing a little behind Phillip. He was quite handsome and strong of build. Strangely, even in the dim firelight, there was an air of familiarity about him. I thought to myself that I surely hoped this was not someone I have known in my travels! Jesus hand went to my shoulder as if he knew what I was thinking, and gave me a gentle squeeze.

The two men exchanged places in front of me and Jesus looked directly into my eyes. "Mary, this is Bartholomew." As Bartholomew reached his hand toward mine, Jesus said to him, "And Bartholomew... this is your sister, Mary." My extended hand stopped in mid-air! This could not be! I must have heard wrong! I looked at Jesus in total astonishment! My mouth had dropped open and I could not close it! He was smiling and nodding his head. "Yes, Mary. This is your brother." His words finally penetrated and I grabbed Bartholomew's hand as he dropped to his knees. At this level, the firelight flickered in his face. *Of course he looks familiar; he looks just like Mother!*

In the mixture of feelings I was experiencing, I had failed to notice how Bartholomew was reacting. His face looked troubled. He looked at Jesus and said, "Rabbi, do not jest with me about such painful things! I was told my sister was insane and on a secluded island with lepers and others like herself. How can this woman be my sister?" Jesus tenderly placed his hand on Bartholomew's shoulder and said, "Look into her face. The truth is there." Bartholomew did as Jesus said and recognition washed over his face. "You look just like Mother! It is you...Mary!"

My hand touched his face and the tears started to flow again. I grabbed him and we hugged so tight I could barely breathe, but I managed to say, "So many years I wanted to know how you were! The last time I saw our mother and father, it was pretty ugly. You were in Magdala with relatives and I was to go with them to pick you up. But Father sent me away before I could see you. I broke the promise I had made when you were a baby. I promised myself—and you—that I would find a safe place for us and take you away from that awful mess." Bartholomew began to cry. "Oh, Mary I wish you had! Things were terrible. I left home as soon as I was old enough and went to live with our uncle in Bethany."

We both looked at Jesus. Bartholomew asked, "How did you know?" Jesus gazed lovingly at us. I was certain I saw tears in his eyes, too. "My mother never stopped praying for you. Both of you. She recognized your sister's pain and wanted her to know the Father of fathers. Our Father answers prayer." I was speechless! Jesus had known who I was all along! The choosing of Bartholomew as a disciple was not an accident!

For the first time since I had sat down in the circle, I looked around at the other disciples. Their faces were awestruck and they were speaking excitedly among themselves. I saw Jesus look over my shoulder and nod to Joanna. I had completely forgotten she was there. I reached over to hug her and asked if she had known any of this. She shook her head. "No I didn't know everything. Jesus only shared a few things. But there is one more thing." Joanna jumped up and walked away from the fire. I turned back to Jesus and grabbed his hands. "Thank you, Rabboni! Thank you so much!" He squeezed my hands and whispered, "There's more!" I could not imagine that there was anything that could improve this evening! What else could there possibly be?

I watched him walk away from the circle and knew he was going off by himself to pray. He did that a lot. It was his time alone with his Father. His time to replenish. To renew. To share. I looked up at my brother, excitedly talking to the other disciples. His eyes caught mine and he flashed a smile.

He surely looked like Mother! I turned back to where I had seen Jesus walking away and he was gone. Gratitude for him totally consumed me. *Thank you my Jesus, thank you.*

My reverie was interrupted when I felt a hand on my shoulder and I turned. It was Joanna. And standing next to her, smiling down at me was Mary! My heart leaped from my chest! She stooped to hug me and I practically pulled her into my lap! Sobbing, I hugged her and said, over and over, "I'm so sorry, Mary! I thought the very worst of you, even after you left me your treasured family heirloom. Look I have never taken it off!" I pulled it from beneath my tunic. Mary smiled at me as I held it and rubbed my fingers over it, as I had so many times over the past thirty years. "It saved my life one time, Mary! It prevented a knife from cutting my throat!"

Mary looked at me tenderly. "It was not the necklace that saved you, Mary. It was God. He has faithfully watched over you. Yes, you have been through many difficult times, but there were so many more situations that could have been worse and he protected you. But let us talk of those things tomorrow when we are more rested. My trip from Nazareth was tiring."

I hugged her again and said, "I heard about Joseph. I am so sorry, Mary. Ever since I heard, I have been grieving. So many things I would like to have told him; I had the opportunity and didn't take it. You know I lived in Nazareth for a time. I even came by your house, but could not bring myself to go to your door. Jesus and Joseph were working outside." Mary smiled. "I know, Mary. Jesus told me. He knew who you were and told me you had been by the house. But I wanted to respect your decision to keep your distance, so I never came to see you, either. I knew you were not ready. I'm sorry you didn't get a chance to say goodbye to Joseph. He loved you very much and considered you as a daughter."

This news brought more tears to my eyes. *Joseph had loved me like a daughter!* That truly blessed my heart! I remembered what a special man he was and how much he and Mary loved each other. I hugged her again, and then she went off with Joanna to find a place to sleep. What a wonderful woman! Jesus had her come to Caesarea Philippi just for me! I was in awe at his desire to care for our every need and bring relief for our despair. Such love he has for us!

I noticed that all the disciples were up and talking with each other. Bartholomew had come to sit with me after Mary left. He was as amazed as the rest of the disciples that Jesus had known everything about us. He repeated to me the same words I could hear them asking each other, "Who is this man that knows the past and the future?" We listened as the others talked. Some were saying he was a great prophet of old, others that he was a great teacher. The only one not participating in this discussion was Peter. He was quietly sitting by himself away from the fire. He seemed to be in deep thought…troubled. Of all the men here, he was the one I thought would have been saying more than anyone else. He *always* seemed to have more to say than anyone else! This seemed out of character for him.

I heard a noise behind me and turned to see Jesus coming toward us. He walked up to where the disciples were standing and gestured for everyone to sit down. When they had each gotten comfortable, he asked, "Who do the crowds say I am?" Eager, they all started responding at once. "Some say John the Baptist; others say Elijah; some say Jeremiah; and still others say that one of the prophets of long ago has come back to life." Jesus held up his hand and they got quiet. "But what about you?" he asked. "Who do you say I am?" There was total silence except for the crackling of the fire. I did not even hear the frogs or crickets. It seemed everyone and everything was waiting for the answer to his question. Out of the corner of my eye, I saw Peter stand. His face was serious as he walked toward Jesus. He stopped directly in front of him. "You are the Christ, the Son of the Living God."

Some of the other disciples gasped while others just stood in captivated silence. Jesus placed his hand on Peter's shoulder and smiled. "Blessed are you, Simon son of Jonah, for this was not revealed to you by man, but by my Father in heaven. And I tell you that you are Peter, and on this rock I will build my church, and the gates of Hell will not overcome it. I will give you the keys of the kingdom of heaven; whatever you bind on earth will be bound in heaven, and whatever you loose on earth will be loosed in heaven."

Jesus became very serious. "It is imperative that you tell this to no one. The Son of Man must suffer many things and be rejected by the elders, chief priests and teachers of the law, and he must be killed and the third day be raised to life." My breath caught in my throat! What was he saying? This could not be! Peter jumped up and grabbed Jesus' cloak and pulled him near where we were sitting. Whispering, so the others could not hear, he rebuked Jesus, "Never, Lord! This shall never happen to you!" I leaned closer to hear the rest, but Jesus' words shocked me! "Get behind me, Satan! You are a stumbling block to me; you do not have in mind the things of God, but the things of men." Peter looked hurt and Jesus placed his hand on his arm and motioned for him to sit.

"If anyone would come after me, he must deny himself and take up his cross daily and follow me. For whoever wants to save his life will lose it, but whoever loses his life for me will save it. What good is it for a man to gain the whole world, and yet lose or forfeit his very self? If anyone is ashamed of me and my words, the Son of Man will be ashamed of him when he comes in his glory and in the glory of the Father and of the holy angels. I tell you the truth, some who are standing here will not taste death before they see the kingdom of God."

The disciples were whispering among themselves and Jesus said to them, "We have had a long day. It is time for us to rest. You have witnessed the restoration of a family that has been separated for many years. You have been introduced to my childhood friend, a woman some of you had concerns about. Though you envied her child-like faith, her past caused you to wonder if her faith could be genuine. Check your planks! For I came to bind up the brokenhearted."

"You have heard a great truth from the mouth of Peter; words that came directly from our Father in heaven. The full meaning of his words will take time for you to understand. But, eventually, you will grasp them. You will accept this truth. For I came to clothe you with garments of salvation."

"You have heard I must suffer and die and be raised on the third day. This is hard for you to hear for I know your love for me. But I must be pierced for man's transgressions and by my stripes they will be healed. But I will see the light of life again. For I came to bear the sins of many, and make intercession for the transgressors."

Jesus looked around at them. The look on their faces was one of a young child learning a great lesson from their father or mother. I think this was pleasing to Jesus. He smiled at them and said softly, "Follow me; take up your cross daily. Do not deny me or be ashamed of me and all these things will be made clear to you. Go now. Rest and pray about the things you have heard. Be renewed. We will talk more tomorrow."

He walked over to Bartholomew and me and said, "I would guess you two have a great deal to catch up on! I am so happy to see you together again." Bartholomew looked up with tears in his eyes. "Master, do you know what it does for my soul to know I was your playmate when we were babies? I still can't believe it!" Jesus patted his shoulder. "Thank your sister, Bartholomew. She made sure we played together everyday! And thank your heavenly Father for the opportunity to tell her." He also patted my shoulder and then turned and walked off toward the hills. I watched in wonder. What a man! Feelings stirred in my stomach and I was reminded I would always need to be careful of my thoughts about him. Always.

The next morning, I awoke filled with excitement. Mary and Joanna were already gone so I jumped up and dressed as quickly as I could. I couldn't wait to talk with Mary! When I found them, she and Joanna were busy fixing breakfast for us. I volunteered to help and as soon as the disciples had eaten, Jesus took them away. They were going into the town of Caesarea Philippi to spend time with the people there.

Mary and I sat down together. Joanna excused herself to give us time alone. I just stared at Mary not knowing what to say to her. She spoke first. "It is so wonderful to see you again and to see you reunited with your brother. My son has never forgotten you and he planned all of this to restore you to your brother."

I was still overwhelmed by his love for us. "You mean Jesus knew I would follow him? He knew that Bartholomew would become a disciple?" Mary was smiling and nodding. "Yes, Mary. He knew your brother was also hurting and needed healing. Because Bartholomew has been through so many painful situations, it will make him a strong disciple. He will understand the pain and suffering of others that have been hurt as he was. He will be able to speak to them of the hope and healing he has experienced because of my son. As you will, Mary. Your testimony will bring healing to many."

I grabbed her and hugged her as tight as I could. "I was so devastated when you left, Mary. I hated you and I hated God. After that, my life became a never ending search to fill the void." Mary was shaking her head. She took my hand and gently replied, "No, Mary. It was not my absence that caused you to feel that way. It was the absence of God in your life. You felt good when I was with you because I spoke to you of him and taught you of his love. But you put me in God's place. You made an idol of me. Instead of focusing on God, the giver of the peace you experienced, you focused on me. I was only his mouthpiece, Mary. God used me to teach you about himself. But, when I had to leave, it felt like he left with me."

"Do you remember how you used to tell me that every time you were around Jesus you felt that wonderful peace? Well, that was because he is the bringer of peace. But Jesus' peace does not leave you, even when you can't see him or be with him. His peace is permanent. You knew that because you told me whenever your parents were mean to you, you could go to your room and say Jesus' name and the peace would return. The gift of God's love and the peace it brought to you would have remained with you, Mary, even after I left. If only you had not rejected it…if you had not rejected God."

Her words were hard to hear, but I knew they were the truth. That revelation had been placed in my heart the first night I spoke with Jesus. As a child, I was looking for anyone that would give me attention. I found that in Mary. Even though we were close in age, she was far beyond her years and mine, emotionally and spiritually. I had viewed her as my savior, one of many I had tried to substitute for God. Though they were painful, her words brought healing. As did most of the words she spoke into my life. Our friendship deepened and grew and I praised God for his blessing.

I had many conversations over the next two years. Healing conversations… with Mary, Joanna and sometimes, when possible, with Jesus. The insecurity and shame from my past became a distant memory. A memory that I could retrieve and talk about, but no longer held me captive. I became strong and confident. Bold and friendly. I no longer needed a crutch—like the wine—to feel relaxed enough to mingle with people. I didn't need the opium to numb the anguish of unworthiness. I enjoyed following Jesus and meeting those who came to him with physical and emotional pain. Men and women with blindness of the eyes and others with sightlessness of the heart. Those with ears that couldn't hear sounds and many that were deaf to the truth. Those with so much money, they wouldn't give it up and those with so little, they gave it all. Multitudes with much anger and much fear...with little faith and little hope. And he healed them. He healed them all.

One of the most difficult shocks for me to deal with since my healing was learning from Bartholomew about my mother's death. I was devastated. She had spent her last years alone, sent away from those she loved so my father could live with another woman. It was a crushing blow. That my brother had been lied to about my whereabouts so he would never look for me was demoralizing. But there was also the memory of Jesus speaking into my heart the need to forgive. Forgive the man who had caused this pain. Forgive the years of abuse. When I went to Jesus after learning about her, he confirmed I must forgive. It had to be done for *my* sake. He reiterated what he had told me on the shore, by the Sea of Galilee. My inability to forgive would lead to bitterness that would eat away at me. It would prevent me from being the witness for him that he wanted me to be. It would prevent any hope of reconciliation. It would prevent my healing from being complete.

I knew I still harbored unforgiveness in my heart. But as I had become accustomed, Jesus never let me stay where I felt comfortable. He never let me hide. I didn't like it, but always found the pain of it was worth the outcome. Or as he said, the pruning, though painful, made a more beautiful tree. He promised to help me learn to forgive. He said forgiveness was a choice. A choice I had to make and then stand firm, no matter what my feelings said to me. He was right.

We had been staying near Jerusalem since Jesus rode through the city gates on the back of a donkey. Everyone there had been happy and celebrating his arrival. But in the back of the crowd, I saw the men in their fancy robes and I still got a bitter taste in my mouth whenever I saw them. None of them had a smile on their face. *That's all right.*

The people have accepted Jesus as their Messiah! It doesn't matter what those jackals think anymore! But I still did not trust them. I knew I never would.

A few days before the Passover, Jesus suggested I go find my father and offer forgiveness. He also wanted me to seek forgiveness. That was a little harder to swallow. I started to argue with him that I didn't think I had done anything wrong for which I should ask forgiveness. One look from him shut my mouth. "Mary, I can do much with a contrite heart, but a proud heart is not teachable." I nodded in agreement. "Why are you sending me now? We just had this wonderful reception into Jerusalem. Everyone was glorifying your name and singing 'Hosanna.' The people showed their love for you as they laid palm branches before you! It will be a joyous time here in Jerusalem, during this Passover and I want to be here with you." I realized I was sounding like a spoiled, impertinent little girl. "You will be with me Mary, but I feel this is a good time for you to go." Then he smiled at me and placed both hands on my shoulders and said, *"Trust me."*

Those words again. I agreed and went to tell the other women I would be gone for only a short time. Except what I needed to travel, I left all the money I had. I said goodbye to the disciples and then Bartholomew walked with me to the road. He had helped me load what I needed onto the donkey I had borrowed for the journey. He prayed with me for strength and courage. Afterward, he said, "Mary, I must tell you how proud I am of you. You have come so far and Jesus speaks of you with great respect. What you are doing, takes great courage. I am not ready to see Father yet. I can only hope that with time I will also be able to forgive. The last I heard he was in Jericho. Walking, you should be able to get there in a few hours."

I smiled. "If I still had Joshua, I would get there very quickly. But this donkey looks like he can barely carry my food and water. I'm not sure he could handle my weight, too. At times like these, I still miss Joshua very much." Bartholomew gave me hug. "I will be praying that you find Father swiftly and that he does nothing else to hurt you. I will also pray that you will be back to us for the Passover. Jesus told us today, we would be in Jerusalem for the celebration, so meet us there. He is still talking in these riddles about being turned over to the Gentiles and then being raised up. We know he is talking about his death, but we don't understand all of what he says. It's frightening to most of us."

My heart felt troubled. "I know Bartholomew. It scares me when he talks like that, too. I just want us to enjoy this Passover and maybe afterwards he can help us understand more clearly." My brother and I hugged again and I was off with feelings of dread... fused with anticipation.

The trip took much longer than I had hoped. The donkey decided to sit and take a rest more than a dozen times on the road to Jericho. It took even longer to find my father. I learned he had a small tent making business in the city, but had been sick and was not in the market where I had been told I could find him. It still amazed me how talented he was. He could take on any project and master it in no time. He had a way with people that made him successful in any venture. Finally, I found someone who knew where his home was located. He was living with a woman in *her* home. I didn't think it was possible for this to get any harder...

I followed the directions I was given. The house was way outside the city at the foot of the mountains. It was a large house and seemed very nice. I tied my donkey to the post and prayed the whole way to the door. I knocked as hard as I could and a beautiful, dark skinned woman opened the door. She looked like she might be Egyptian. I noticed she was much younger than my father as she asked if she could help me. Her accent was foreign to me. She had a warm smile and I felt a little more relaxed. "Yes, you can. My name is Mary and I have come to see my father, Bartimus."

Immediately the smile melted from her face and it was replaced with disgust. It had been years since I had seen someone look at me like that. "Your father does not want to see you and you are not welcome here. Now take your donkey and go." I was not going to give up. "I have traveled a long way to see him and there are things I need to say." She was getting angrier and her voice was elevating to a higher pitch. "I told you he does not want to see you. You are an embarrassment to him and everyone else who knows you. Now go."

There was a time, when these words would have crushed me. But they had no power over me now. I knew Jesus; and the truth was, Jesus loved me with all his heart! What else could possibly be more important? However, this woman did not know Jesus and she desperately needed to meet him, but I didn't feel that I was the one to offer her this information.

I started to say again how important it was for me to see my father when I heard a voice come from inside of the house. It was Father! "Who is it, Bithiah? Why don't you shut the door?" She yelled back at him, "Your daughter is here and she won't leave." Within a few seconds he was at the door. His face was red and angry. She looked at him and said, "You know you have not been well. Now tell her to leave and come back inside." He nodded to her and told her he just needed a few minutes. She shook her head in dismay as she walked away saying, "Just hurry up and get rid of her!" He almost seemed afraid of her... or maybe afraid of being alone.

I stood in front of a man I hardly recognized. He looked nothing like I remembered him. In the past, he had always had such a demanding presence. He stood tall and proud everywhere he went. Now his body was thin and frail. He was slightly bent over, his hair gray and thinning. I felt pity for him. Not because of his physical presence. Everyone gets old. But there was another presence. One of anger and bitterness. Guilt and shame. Pride and self-righteousness. Hadn't I known these, too? Weren't they once familiar to me? My heart went out to this man and I wanted to share with him that he didn't have to stay this way. He, too, could be free.

I opened my mouth to speak, but he held up his hand. "I don't want to hear anything you have to say, Mary. You need to go back to wherever you came from and leave us alone. The kind of life you have chosen for yourself is just that –your choice! I don't want any part of you!"

I started to feel like I needed to defend myself. "But Father, I have changed. I am not like I used…" He stopped me again by raising his hand and his voice. "You will never change, Mary! Go live your life and let me live mine." I started to say something else when I remembered what Jesus had said. *With a contrite heart, I can do much…* I backed away from the door and as I did I said, "I will leave, Father. But first, I want to ask your forgiveness for anything I did that was wrong or embarrassing to you at anytime in your life." His face changed slightly. It softened, just a little. "I also forgive you for what you did to me. I don't carry the guilt and anger around with me anymore. And I want you to know I love you and will always be here if you need me." His face looked confused; his voice held suspicion. "I don't know what this is all about, Mary! I don't know what you think I've done to you that you should forgive me! You have always made lies up in your head and then believed them!"

My feelings of sympathy grew. "No Father. You know what you did and so do I. It doesn't matter if you admit it, it only matters that I forgive you. And I do. I am sorry if I have caused you and your friend any trouble. I hope you can forgive me." Again he had that confused look, shook his head and slammed the door. I slowly turned and walked toward my donkey. The sun was setting and the day after tomorrow was the Passover. If I were to get back in time, I would need to hurry. I decided to try and ride the donkey and after climbing on his back, turned him toward the road that led to Bethany and then Jerusalem. I could hear Father and

Bithiah arguing inside and it was reminiscent of all the years I had spent with my parents. I was glad those years were over for me. I was glad to be going back to Jerusalem and seeing all the people who loved me. I was glad to be going back to Jesus.

18

Loved Much

Jerusalem at Passover. A sea of bustling Jews, trying to get all of their sacrifices ready and their food prepared. The pilgrimage has been planned for weeks and people have traveled far to see family and friends and offer their first and their best to God. But this Passover is much different from any other. This Passover will be a time that won't celebrate what we give to God. This Passover is about what God will give to us. Today, God also offers His first and His best.

How could it have come to this? Last week, thousands had been here, outside the walls of this city, escorting Jesus as he rode in on a tiny donkey. Laying palm leaves across the path he was taking - some even removing their cloaks and laying them down—dancing, praising and singing, "Hosanna." Welcoming him into the city. Where were they today?

There had also been a few on that day, the ones that stayed at a distance, who were not praising. Not dancing. Not singing. Not even smiling. No, they were not celebrating. They were planning. Many of them I recognized. Some had been those who pulled me from a lover's bed that *they* had paid me to occupy. Others had been in Simon's house that day I came to anoint Jesus' feet and had acted as if I had leprosy for just coming to the door—or worse—for entering their "holy" domain. Yes, they had been there last week - thinking and scheming and devising the evil plan that had led to this day of horror.

And where had I been? Why wasn't I given some inkling of this? Some shred, some hint of the need Jesus had last night! I don't know if I could have helped him, but I would have tried! Why had he sent me away knowing I might not be back in time? I had returned late after traveling most of the night and I was exhausted. That donkey had not let me ride him for more than a mile and that meant walking thirteen miles with him sitting down at every turn.

I remembered the conversation I had with him before I left for Jericho. After I agreed to see my father his face had changed. He seemed troubled. He had looked into my eyes and said, "Mary, the things I have been telling all of you are about to take place. I need you to be strong. My disciples will need to see your strength." I had asked him to stop. He was scaring me! I tried to ask him questions, but he put his finger to my lips and said, "No, Mary. No questions. Just do as I say. And know how much I love you."

When he spoke to me like that, the old feelings would rise in me and I would have to stop and pray for strength. He was pure. He was untouchable. He was my Redeemer and he could never be anything else. No matter how much I wanted him to be. Those last words he spoke to me kept running through me—piercing me—and I wondered if that was why he had sent me away? Because he wanted to protect me from what he knew they would do to him? Had he hoped the trip to see my father would keep me away longer and escape all of this? I would rather have died myself than to have seen him hit. Spit on. Beaten. Laughed at. Humiliated. Scourged.

To see the skin of his back ripped to thin strips of bloody flesh. It would have destroyed me.

Oh, yes. He protected me. But for what? I have no desire to go on without him. How can I possibly face a day on this earth without his tender voice? Have a day go by without being able to look into his gentle eyes—the eyes that totally melt my heart at every glance? I couldn't imagine life without him. It had been a long time since I had thoughts of hopelessness like these. A very long time.

His words came back to me again. He had given me a final directive. Be strong for his disciples. This, I *must* do. How much more they must be feeling right now! He had been with them longer than I had. Why would he ask me to be strong for them? Surely, they had much more strength and courage than I could ever hope to have! They were his best friends. His chosen. They had seen many more miracles, heard many more teachings, and actually performed miracles in his name! But he had wanted *me* to be strong!

Words he had spoken at Simon's house filled my head. "She has been forgiven much - for she loved much. But he, who has been forgiven little, loves little." It was almost as if I was back there and hearing him say the words again.

I would honor his last request of me. I looked toward heaven and began to pray. "Oh, my God. Please give me the strength to go to him now. Help me to be strong for his mother. Help me be strong for him. Let him know that not one minute that he has spent with me, prayed for me or sat teaching me was wasted. Let him know that I soaked him up like a sponge, so that I may never sin against you again. Let him know that the day I fell head over heels in love with him was when he looked into my eyes and said, 'Woman, where are your accusers?'"

That day, his love pierced through me and I was eternally changed. I still remember standing there, with un-thrown stones surrounding me. A memory of another time, another look, another prayer in a stable. Then it was Joseph, looking at my brother, as well as Jesus, with so much love, as they lay in a manger sleeping. The way I had prayed for someone to look at me someday. How could I have known that the look I had prayed for would come from the Christ, the Messiah!

"Let him know, God that I love him with all my heart, soul, mind and strength and always will. I will never let a person cross my path that will not hear about him and what he did for me. I am begging you to help me do the hardest thing I have ever done or ever will do. Please help me stay strong. Thank you, my God and my Father."

I looked out toward the gate of the city that led to Golgotha. He had walked up this narrow path less than an hour ago. I didn't know why Joanna had not come to me before now. She had sent Susanna to wake me and tell me what had happened to him, so very early this morning. I was sure Caiaphas, and those arrogant buzzards he controlled, were responsible for this whole thing! Those cowards! They knew if they did not do their devious work in the middle of the night, an uprising might take place. So many people loved Jesus!

Susanna told me everything had been settled with Pilate almost before the sun had come up! The women, who had followed him for so long, had been there by the side of the road as Jesus passed by. Joanna had alerted all of them after her husband, Cuza, told her that Jesus had been brought to Herod's palace. She did not feel she could leave Jesus to come tell me of all the events that had taken place, so she sent Susanna. I was grateful Joanna stayed with him.

Was this yet another way he protected me from the visual horror that he knew would have destroyed me? As I began the walk up the path, I slipped on a stone and looked down. It was covered with blood. As I allowed my gaze to follow the path, the droplets of blood continued every few steps. My heart felt like it was going to sink to my feet. Tears stung my eyes. I thought I had cried all the tears I could cry! I had been in Jerusalem long enough to know what they did to those who were crucified. This Golgotha was the Roman's chosen place to make examples of the lowest of the low. With a death that was torture at its best. And this is where they were taking my Jesus. As I continued along the path, I saw places where footprints had been made in the blood. I knew they did not belong to the soldiers, who escorted him, because they had leather sandals. These were bare feet – Jesus' feet. They did not even allow him to wear shoes to keep his feet from being cut on the rocks along the way. At one place, I saw where he had slipped down. The blood was smeared across several smooth stones. In the past, I had watched the procession of other condemned men upon this path, carrying a crossbeam on their backs that, by the sheer size of it, must have weighed a great deal! I was certain he had fallen under the weight of the cross.

"Oh, Father, the pain I feel inside! I can't bear it! I can't be strong!" The tears began coming in torrents. I felt like my insides were tied in knots that someone was slowly tightening. Deep sobs wrenched my chest and I could hardly get my breath. I had to stop and lean against a building. I felt drained of all that was within me, dizzy and weak.

"Why, Father! Why does he have to die? He has been my all - my everything. He stepped into my life and I knew love for the first time! Please, don't take him away from me!" My knees became weak and I sank to the ground. I held my head and cried. As I reached for the hem of my dress to wipe my face, I saw a large puddle of blood next to me. His blood. I reached down and touched it. It was still warm. I touched it again.

Words that he had taught me, not so very long ago, came back to me. "Though your sins are as red as scarlet, you will be washed white as snow." I looked at the blood again. Red as scarlet. My sins were as red as scarlet. Just like his blood. *But I have been washed as white as snow. And now, my fingers are washed in his blood. He had told me his blood would have to be shed...*

So many teachings were swimming in my head. But the blood I still had on my fingers mesmerized me. An unusual feeling of courage came over me. A strength that was being summoned up supernaturally was taking captive my emotions. I had to get up and go to him! I stood up and carefully wiped the blood on my shawl. *This* stain I desired to have. I ran the rest of the way to the gate that led out of the city. Out to Golgotha. There was a huge crowd surrounding the three crosses. I fought my way through the people.

Not unlike a young, curious twelve year old had done, so many years ago in a stable. Only then it was with shep-herds. I had wanted to protect him. **They** *wanted to see the Messiah - in the form of a beautiful, newborn baby — and worship him!*

This time was so much different. This time I had come to see a beaten and battered Savior, being crucified. I still longed to protect him, but that honor had been stripped from me. Stripped from all of us who loved him. I gasped as I looked up at the crosses. Even with this newfound strength I felt, nothing had prepared me for this! There he was! Hanging there with the muscles of his arms and legs bulging - as if they were screaming! His skin shredded and laid open. His hands, bloody and his wrists driven back against the wood by the huge nails the Roman soldiers had pounded into them. I thought about how many times those hands had touched people in tenderness, in healing, in love. His feet were also driven into the wood by an even bigger nail. The feet that had walked so many miles, so that his people could be healed and so he could minister to them—to guide them—so that they might know his Father the way he did. *The same feet I had washed with tears of gratitude and anointed with perfume.*

I had to touch him! I went to his cross and began kissing his feet. They were so swollen and dark in color. And cold. Again, I found my tears washing the dirt from his feet, but this time the dirt was mixed with his blood. I looked up at him and said quietly, "Master, I love you. Please do not suffer long." He opened his eyes briefly, but did not open his mouth, his eyes revealing that he had heard me. His face was almost unrecognizable from the swelling and bruising. It was covered in blood, from what looked like a crown of the biggest thorns I had ever seen.

His head hung down, his eyes now shut. I found myself wishing he had already died. I knew it would have hurt me to not be here for him, but I would rather live with that, than the prolonged agony I knew this torture was bringing him. A soldier roughly grabbed me and pushed me away from the cross and said, "Move on! No touching the prisoners!" I stepped back and tried to take in the reality of what I was seeing. There he was, hanging between two other men who seem to be mocking him. How could they do that to him as he hung there? How could they do that to the love of my life? I had to turn away, and as I did, I saw Jesus' mother, Mary, Joanna and two other women. John was standing next to Mary and had his arm protectively around her.

Many people who had followed Jesus were arriving; I'm sure the news of his crucifixion was traveling fast. I saw many of the other women that were faithful followers of his, holding each other and crying. Then, I also saw those familiar faces I had seen the day Jesus made his triumphant entry into Jerusalem. Today, they were having their own triumph! They call themselves chief priests, teachers of the law and elders! What hypocrites! They hurled insults at Jesus. "He saved others, but he can't save himself! Let this Christ, this King of Israel, come down now, from the cross, and we will believe in him. He trusts in God. Let God rescue him, for he said, 'I am the Son of God.' He saved others; let him save himself if he is the Christ of God, the Chosen One."

Others were spitting at Jesus and mocking him, shaking their heads telling him, "Come down off the cross if you are the Son of God! You, who are going to destroy the temple and build it in three days, come down from the cross and save yourself." I had to fight back the desire to jump on them and beat them till they looked as bad as Jesus did! All of them! Instead I went to Mary. She looked her age, for the first time since I had known her. She had so much pain in her eyes.

Another memory of that night in the stable. In light of the events of today, that beautiful, peaceful night now seemed like it had all been a dream. But I remembered Mary had the same look in her eyes that night, as the shepherds talked with her. Could she possibly have known as she suckled her newborn baby that it would end like this? I could not imagine the pain she must feel.

I grabbed her and held her as tight as I could. As I hugged her, I opened my eyes and saw John looking at me. He had also been crying. His eyes were red and swollen and he looked like he was about to break down again. I smiled at him and he touched my hand as it rested on Mary's back and he mouthed the words "thank you." I knew he was grateful to have others here who loved Jesus the way he did. I was shocked to see none of the other disciples here, not even my brother. John being here, however, did not surprise me. He and Jesus had a special bond. I sometimes thought that the others sensed this, but I had never heard anything said. John had also been close to Mary. I often saw him talk to and encourage her. She had seemed sad and quiet for weeks. I think she was the only one of us that believed what Jesus had told us about this day.

I nodded to John and closed my eyes. As I held Mary, so many thoughts floated through my mind. Nothing would ever be the same! Where would Mary live? I certainly did not have the type of home she deserved; it was too small. I knew after Joseph died, she had stayed in her house and visited her other children frequently, but now, after all this, she needed to be cared for and not be alone.

I heard some men talking loudly and I opened my eyes to see the soldiers, who were guarding the crosses, arguing. They were holding in their hands something that looked like clothing. One of them was the man who had pushed me away from Jesus feet. I strained to hear what he was saying. "I say we cut it into four equal shares. It is the only fair thing to do." Another soldier, with a more gentle voice said, "This is beautiful linen. It will bring a good price if we keep it in one piece. If we divide it evenly among us like we did his other things, it will be worthless!" A new voice, "He's right. We shouldn't tear it. Let's decide by lot who will get it." They all agreed except the first soldier. "I still don't think it's fair." He had moved closer to where I stood and I noticed his right hand and arm had dried blood on it. So did his breastplate. I wondered to myself if this was the one who had driven the nails into my Lord.

The softer speaking one, a centurion, put the cloth down in front of them and said again, "Please, let's not divide it. Throw lots for it." I stared down at the cloth and my breath caught in my chest! It was Salome's wedding linen! Jesus had worn it to the cross! Mary must have seen my reaction because she looked at me and said, "Yes, Mary, that is the material you gave me the day after my son was born. I never used it for him as a baby; it was too beautiful— too special. I knew it must have another purpose. I have saved it all these years. He came to me a few weeks ago and told me he was having a very special Passover meal with his disciples and he wanted something special to wear. There was almost urgency in his voice. Somehow I knew it would be the last meal he would ever share with them. I promised him I would have something for him and knew that this was the purpose of your sister's wedding linen."

I looked at Mary in astonishment. "I never told you it had been Salome's! How did you know?" Mary smiled her beautiful, gentle smile at me and said, "Mary, the morning I asked you about the material, you said, 'I promise that my mother never had any intention of using that material as a wedding dress for me.' There was so much pain in your face when you said it, but I did not know why. Until you started telling me about your sister. All the time that we spent together at the little house revealed much to me, Mary. God revealed much to me. Your love for your sister was shadowed by the way your mother bathed her in attention. At your expense. I knew that material had been meant for *someone's* wedding. It just made sense that it was your sister."

I, again, was amazed at her wisdom. I stared down at the linen as the soldiers cast lots. She had known the whole time! I had carried so much guilt, but she had known and it didn't matter! She still loved me! No wonder God had chosen this incredible woman to be Jesus' mother! As I watched the soldiers, I felt sick that they were playing this silly game for Jesus' clothes and even worse that the intended wedding dress of my sister would end up in the clutches of a Roman soldier!

A cry of disgust went up from the three soldiers, who apparently had lost, and I realized the winner had been the soft-spoken centurion. The others got up and began to patrol the area pushing people back and yelling at them in harsh voices. The centurion stood slowly, never taking his eyes from the material and began to walk toward us. I was not sure what to expect from this man, but when I looked at his face, there was sadness. I even thought I saw tears. He approached Mary and handed her the material. His eyes rose to meet hers and he did have tears streaming down, causing lines of clean skin to show through the dust covering his face.

His voice was husky as he said, "I know you don't know who I am, but you don't need to be afraid. I want you to know that my superiors ordered my presence here, to oversee these new soldiers. I had nothing to do with the crucifixion. I would have done anything to stop it, if it were within my power. Your son healed someone very special to me a year ago. I had heard of a great miracle worker that traveled among your people. I learned he was in Capernaum and I went to him to help my servant. Though he was a servant of the family, he had been the only father I had ever known. Jesus had volunteered to come to my house and heal him. That shocked me! He did not care that I was a Roman soldier! I had mixed feelings about his offer. As a centurion in the Roman garrison, I feared someone might see a Jew enter my home. But that was mixed with an overwhelming feeling of not being worthy to have him set foot in the home of a 'pagan'."

"I explained this to him and he healed my servant that very hour. But something else happened also. Something happened to me. I was changed. I do not know how to explain it, but I found myself going anywhere I could to listen to him. I loved it when he taught at night; I could go under cover of darkness. I was afraid of being seen mixing with the people. The Roman leaders would use me as an example if I were discovered. I usually said I was 'keeping the crowds in order' so that I could stand close and listen."

"When I learned that I would be on duty for crucifixions today, I did not know for whom. When I found out, I thought of running. But in Rome, there is not far to go when you are a centurion. As we walked the path here, I stayed as close to your son as I could and when he fell, I had someone carry his cross. I felt that was so little, but he thanked me! He actually thanked me!"

"I knew of the tradition where we divide the clothes of the crucified, and I was determined to try and get his. For you. Especially the undergarment. It was breathtaking! I knew it had cost someone a great deal of money. I wanted so much for you to have this. I even tried praying to your God that I would win the lots so that I could present it to you. I know it is little in light of what he has done for me." Tears ran down his face again. "Please forgive me." Mary looked at him and gently said, "Of course, I forgive you. And thank you for helping my son the way you did. Anyone who has met my son, cannot go forth without being changed. I am aware that sometimes, as today is witness to, the changes are expressed for the worse. But that is only because of blind jealousy. I am glad to know that knowing him has changed you for the better and I know God is aware of your heart. I will pray that the work that has begun in you will be finished soon, so you can live in peace."

He looked down at the ground. When his face met Mary's again, his tears ran freely. Mary's words had touched him deeply. His voice was hoarse and unsteady when he spoke. "I also have a piece of his robe. I want you to have that also." He handed the robe to me. I did not know why at first, but as I took it from him, I felt the dampness. I pulled one of my hands back and it had blood on it. The sick feeling was in my stomach again. I felt like I would throw up. The centurion nodded to both of us and walked away. The blood on my hand was Jesus' blood! Something about it nagged at me. Was there something he taught me about the blood that I had forgotten?

I felt John's hand on my arm as he nodded toward Jesus. "Mary, I think he is trying to say something." I looked up at Jesus and he seemed to be trying to clear his throat. His lips were so dry and he was licking them with a tongue that was swollen and as dry as his lips. He looked at Mary and managed to speak loud enough for us to hear him. "Dear woman, here is your son." He then looked at John. "Here is your mother." It was as if Jesus knew what I had been thinking earlier! I looked over at John and his back was heaving with each breath as he sobbed. Mary touched him and began to comfort him. "John, I will be proud to have you as my son." They both held each other, and I marveled at the love that she could pour out in her own time of need.

One of the criminals who hung next to Jesus suddenly said, "Aren't you the Christ? Save yourself and us!" But the other criminal rebuked him. "Don't you fear God since you are under the same sentence? We are punished justly, for we are getting what our deeds deserve. But this man has done nothing wrong."

He looked at Jesus and there were tears in his eyes. I had noticed nothing but hate earlier; now it was replaced with love...and hope. A change had taken place. But why should that surprise me? After all, was I really any different from this man? No one could be close to Jesus and not be changed! The man then said, "Jesus, remember me when you come into your kingdom." Jesus lifted his head with much difficulty. His physical pain caused even the smallest movement to be difficult. His eyes looked to the man that had spoken kindness to him. One last person that expressed hope in him. A need for him. Someone who had not *earned* anything; only believed. The look was one I knew, and knew well. He opened his mouth and in words that were hardly audible, he said, "I tell you the truth, today you will be with me in paradise."

It was the sixth hour and we noticed the sky becoming very dark and the sun turning black. People were running and screaming, fear covering their faces. I could still see Jesus' face and when I looked up at him he seemed to be praying. I felt if he was making this gesture, surely I should be doing nothing less. I left Mary and John momentarily and went to Joanna. We began to pray together as we had so many times over the last couple of years. I thanked God every day for a prayer partner like her.

Sorrowfully, our prayers were different today. Before we prayed for protection for our Jesus; today we prayed for his swift death. How could I pray for the demise of the lover of my very soul? But could that be worse than what I saw him enduring?

For some strange reason, there was no finality in the thought of his death! I would never speak to or touch him again, yet I felt no sorrow about it! Sorrow for his suffering, yes, but not about his death. The ambivalence of my feelings was troublesome, but not without peace. The peace I had come to know since that day I saw him as a little baby. I had heard him talk to the disciples about a "Counselor, the Holy Spirit" that he would send to comfort them. I wondered if it would feel like this! No matter the circumstances, if I felt this peace, all was in his control. I also wanted him to have peace. We prayed and cried out for a swift end to his suffering.

There had been another day where there had been much mourning, crying and suffering. That day in Bethany, just a little while ago. Everyone was awaiting the arrival of Jesus. A late arrival. Four days late. A loud wailing was being made for Lazarus. The dead man. The man who had been one of Jesus' best friends. Some were saying, "Why did he not come and save his friend?" Even Lazarus' sisters seemed to be questioning Jesus' loyalty to their brother. That is, until they saw his tears. I don't know if he cried because of their doubting and unbelief or his deep sorrow for his friend. Jesus knew he would raise Lazarus; he did not need to mourn him. But I believe the misery that his family and friends were feeling hurt him deeply.

The authority in his voice that day would have made a believer out of anyone! He was questioning where they had placed Lazarus and with each request Jesus made, there seemed to be doubt. They showed him to the burial caves and he asked for the stone to be taken away. Again more doubt from Martha, Lazarus' sister. Jesus looked at her in disbelief and said, "Did I not tell you that if you believed, you would see the glory of God?"

Jesus looked up and prayed to his father. Then he turned to the cave opening and commanded, "Lazarus, come out!" His voice resonated through the arid valley where the tombs were located. There still seemed to be doubt and confusion on the faces of those around him; they were whispering and pointing and shaking their heads. (I remember being glad he had said Lazarus' name! Otherwise, the whole valley may have been filled with people coming out of their graves!)

But, when they saw the walking grave clothes come out of the tomb, there was total silence. Not a soul moved. Well, one was moving. Lazarus' soul had returned. Jesus said to them, "Take off the grave clothes and let him go." A deafening cheer went up from the valley and the celebration began! I don't think I had ever seen Martha set such a feast and without a word of complaint! It was one of the biggest parties I had ever attended, commemorating one of the biggest miracles Jesus had ever performed! None of us knew at the time, that it would be his last.

Joanna's tears brought me out of my nostalgia, and I immediately felt guilty that I had been thinking of other things instead of praying. It was a problem I had even asked Jesus about. I wanted to be more disciplined in my prayer time, so I asked him what I needed to do to improve it.

It had been a beautiful, spring day; cool and quiet as we sat by the Sea of Galilee and watched the sun come up. As I asked him how I could pray more effectively, he had tossed his head back and laughed out loud! "Mary, Mary, Mary! Your thoughts travel faster than the birds of the air! I watch you as you do your daily routines. You amaze me with the number of things that you are able to accomplish in such a short time. And the way you organize your time! Our Father has truly blessed you with a brilliant mind! Don't let your heart be troubled over how to pray. He knows your heart. Even when you do not know how to pray, He helps you!"

I had been so embarrassed by his compliments that I had been unable to respond. He had looked into my eyes, patted my shoulder and said, "Mary, He knows your love for me. Therefore, He knows your love for Him." Then he had gotten up and walked away and left me there to contemplate what he had said. He did that often and I never liked it! I was supposed to figure out what he meant. And as always, the answer would come. Sometimes it took hours - sometimes days. But it would come. And I would run to him and tell him and he would say, "Mary, you have done well. You are wise and discerning about the things of our Father. I am proud of you."

I would be embarrassed again, but the words "of our Father" made me feel wonderful inside. It was as if Jesus shared his Father with me or that we were brother and sister. What a humbling thought. Maybe that is why I never felt proud of the things I learned. But I did feel much gratitude.

Again, Joanna's crying brought me to the present. I had done it again! I reached over and held her. She was saying to me that she wanted to go to the other women. I hugged her and nodded and said that I also needed to get back to Mary and John. We cried together but had no more words. She got up and walked back to the group of women standing on the hill. Susanna put out her arms as she approached. For a brief moment, my heart ached for my mother. I longed to be held like that. Especially now. I got up and walked over to where Mary stood. I noticed John was not with her. She seemed to be praying, so I gently placed my arm around her shoulder and looked for John. He had approached the cross where Jesus' body hung limply. I felt it was *too* limp. I looked at his chest to see if he was still breathing! Yes, there was movement. Shallow breaths still wrenched his body with horrific agony. His face was contorted in pain with each gulp of air. Mary touched my arm and I realized I had been squeezing her shoulder very tightly. I began to apologize when we were both startled by Jesus' cry. Mary's back stiffened under my arm and she began to tremble. Jesus was saying words I did not understand. There was anger mixed with confusion on his face.

"Eloi, Eloi, lama sabachthani?" I looked at John and he looked troubled. I heard people around me saying that he was calling Elijah. One man ran up, filled a sponge with wine vinegar and put it on a stick. He then offered it to Jesus to drink and with a smirk on his face said, "Now leave him alone. Let's see if Elijah comes to take him down!" I moved forward to slap him, but John stopped me. I was filled with so much rage, I could hardly contain myself, but I backed down. "Why should they make him suffer anymore than he already has? Don't they know who he is? Don't they know how much he loves them?" John was looking at me with all the pain in his face that I felt in my heart. "No, Mary, they don't. Remember, he told us they wouldn't."

Yes, I did remember. But I didn't want to. I had felt so much strength earlier. I had been amazed at the peace I felt with all this chaos around me. I had marveled that my sorrow centered more on not being available to help him, than on the finality of his death. Now I just felt anger, mixed with intense pain. These people around me did not realize who this amazing man was! They did not have a clue whom they were crucifying! Why was he letting them? He had done so many miraculous things! How difficult could it be for him to stop this? As I rambled on in my head, the blood I had touched earlier again came back to me. I looked at my shawl and a connection began to take place. But before I could figure out what it was, Mary's loud crying interrupted me.

Mary's face was streaming with tears. I remembered what Jesus had cried out from the cross and wondered if this could be what was upsetting her so much. "What did he say, Mary?" She looked so crushed I didn't know if she was going to be able to answer. "He was crying out to God. To his Father. He said, 'My God, My God why have you forsaken me!'" As she finished speaking, she sank to the ground and wailed loudly. I didn't know how to comfort her.

Early evening in the little house in Bethlehem. They had returned from Jerusalem, the week Jesus had been circumcised. She spoke of a man, Simeon, who had been in the temple. He told her prophetic things about Jesus. One of those things had been that "her soul would also be pierced." I had never understood how the mother of Jesus could possibly feel sorrow about her role. She was the mother of the Messiah! Looking at her now, his words became clear.

I knelt down next to her and she took my hand. John knelt on her other side and we cried with her. Then in a raspy voice we heard Jesus say, "It is finished." His head dropped to his chest and he took in a shallow breath. It came out very slowly, very much like a sigh. I knew there would not be another.

19

Forty days

"But he was pierced for our transgressions; he was crushed for our iniquities; the punishment that brought us peace was upon him, and by his wounds we are healed. We all, like sheep, have gone astray, each of us has turned to his own way; And the Lord has laid on him the iniquity of us all. He was oppressed and afflicted, yet he did not open his mouth; He was led like a lamb to the slaughter, and as a sheep before her shearers is silent, So he did not open his mouth. By oppression and judgment he was taken away. And who can speak of his descendents? For he was cut off from the land of the living; for the transgression of my people he was stricken. He was assigned a grave with the wicked and with the rich in his death, Though he had done no violence, nor was deceit in his mouth. Yet it was the Lord's will to crush him and cause him to suffer, and though the Lord makes his life a guilt offering, He will see his offspring and prolong his days, and the will of the Lord will prosper in his hand. After the suffering of his soul, he will see the light of life, and be satisfied, By his knowledge my righteous servant will justify many, and he will bear their iniquities. Therefore I will give him a portion among the *great, and he will divide the spoils with the strong, Because he poured out his life unto death, and was numbered with the transgressors. For he bore the sin of many, and made intercession for the transgressors. Isaiah 53:5-12 NIV*

The next several hours passed as if I were in a dream, or more appropriately, a nightmare. Even though I was certain that Jesus was dead, the other men who were crucified still cried out in their agony. I noticed the Pharisees getting anxious and talking among themselves. Soon the lot of them headed back toward the gate, except two that I assumed stayed to gawk. Mary was at the foot of the cross weeping and praying. She had asked us to leave her alone for a time. The soldiers were visibly shaken by the three hours of darkness and the tremors in the earth. The centurion, who had returned Jesus' clothing to us, saw Jesus breathe his last and stated, "Surely he was the Son of God." Jesus had truly touched this man's heart!

I went to John and asked if he knew what the Pharisees were up to and he shook his head. "I can't be sure, Mary. It may be that tomorrow is the Sabbath and they don't want the bodies hanging there with so many people visiting the city for Passover. You know the Romans usually leave them here as carrion."

I looked at John in total revulsion. "How could you say something like that, John? That is our Lord hanging there!" He grabbed my hands and held me. "Mary, I'm sorry. That wasn't how I wanted to say it. But you know that's what they do to the other criminals. I'm sure the priests want them to be taken down. And of course, that is what we want...so that his body can be prepared...properly." He broke down in tears and so did I. We stood there and held each other until he saw the Pharisees returning with more Roman soldiers.

"Here they come, Mary. Now we will see what they want." I turned and saw the soldiers walk up to the crosses while the Pharisees stayed back. One of them had a huge hammer and he went to the foot of the first cross and swung it with all his might at the man's legs. I turned away at the awful sound that followed. I felt my stomach turn and thought I was going to be sick. Then the awareness that they would do this to my Jesus struck me. "No, NO! You can't do that to him!" They were already swinging the hammer at the second man's legs and again I heard that splintering sound! John tried to hold me back, but I ran to Jesus' cross. Mary had stood up and I think she was planning to place herself in their way if they approached Jesus. I leaped to her side and pleaded with them, "Please, sir! He is already dead. There is no reason to break his legs!" He looked at the other soldier and then at Jesus and threw down the hammer. The other one picked up his spear and thrust it into Jesus side before I could stop him! Blood and water flowed from the wound and some of it sprayed on Mary and me. We both turned and cried, holding each other.

My emotions felt like a raw wound with salt poured on it. I just could not believe I would never talk to Jesus again…see his smile again…hear him say my name again. I cried out, "Why God did you have to take him from me!" Immediately, I felt horribly selfish. What must Mary be going through? Yet when I looked at her, she seemed calm, almost serene. She was grieving, but in a much different way. I asked her, "What are we going to do, Mary? What will we do without him?" She smiled at me and touched my face. "Now is the time, Mary, you must remember his words to you. You must remember to be strong and do what he asked you to do."

Just then the two Pharisees who had stayed behind approached the guards and handed them something. They nodded and climbed up a small ladder that they placed against Jesus' cross and proceeded to remove the nails from his hands. While they did that, the two priests introduced themselves to us as Joseph of Arimathea and Nicodemus.

I recognized the second man as the one who had smiled at me in Simon's house. I was puzzled as to why they wanted Jesus' body. They told us they had been believers in Jesus, but feared retaliation from the other Pharisees. There was such sincerity in their voices, I did not question their motives.

Joseph turned to Mary and took her hands in his. "I know this is a difficult time for you and I would like to help in a small way by offering a new tomb for your son, in a garden nearby. No one has ever lain in this tomb. It is the least I can do." Mary consented. "Thank you for your kindness to my son. It means a great deal to me." I noticed Joseph had brought clean linen with him and Nicodemus had a large jar. I asked Nicodemus what was in the jar. He opened it and told me, "It is a mixture of myrrh and aloes. We will wrap his body in the linen, with the spices. It is a custom of our people." I leaned over and smelled the spices. The name had been familiar to me and the smell was even more familiar. This was the spice that one of the three kings had brought to Mary in Bethlehem! He had told her Jesus would die a young man. I looked at Mary and she nodded. She remembered the scent, too. Tears fell down her cheeks. I realized she had lived with this knowledge the many years she watched him grow. It must have haunted her with each passing year, knowing he was getting closer to his purpose.

The soldiers loosened the nails and Joseph and Nicodemus took Jesus down from the cross and laid him across Mary's lap. She held and rocked him like a baby...caressing his bloodstained face. Her tears fell onto his skin and left streaks in the dust and blood.

It seemed just a short time ago; we were in Simon's house. As my tears fell, they left streaks in the dust on his feet. I was appalled that they had not given him water to wash. After cleaning his feet with my hair, I had looked into his beautiful eyes. There are no words to describe what it felt like to have his eyes fall upon me. They had melted my heart...and I would never see them again.

The two men went to work very quickly. It was getting late on this Preparation Day. They must be finished before the sun went down, marking the beginning of the Sabbath. They skillfully ripped the linen into strips and after covering his body in the spices, they carefully wrapped him from his head to his feet in the linen. Nicodemus looked at us and said they would take the body and lay it in the tomb. "It is not necessary for you to follow us. You all need to go home and prepare for tomorrow."

John nodded and hugged both Mary and me, then went to find his own mother, who was standing at a distance with the other women who had followed Jesus. Mary and I watched Joseph carefully cradle Jesus' head and shoulders as Nicodemus did the same with his feet and legs. They nodded to us and began the short walk to the garden. Mary and I exchanged glances and followed them. Sitting across from the hillside where the tomb had been cut, we watched as they laid his body inside. Joseph rolled a huge stone across the entrance; then the two of them went away. Mary and I stared at the rock and then she turned to me and said, "Let us pray, Mary. Let us pray for the power and glory of our Lord to be known to all the earth." We prayed for some time and then as the sun began to set, we headed home. On the way, we agreed to meet early, on the morning after the Sabbath, to take spices and anoint Jesus body. I offered to let Mary stay with me but she felt she needed to be alone.

The walk back to my house was long and lonely. When I finally lay on my mat that evening, the events of the day seemed as if they were in a cloud...like a dream. I raised my arm and looked at Jesus' blood streaked across it and said to myself, "No, it wasn't a dream. I can only wish that it were." Seeing the blood that had splattered on my arm reminded me of the thoughts I had while making my way to Golgotha.

This was the connection I kept trying to make! I was washed in his blood for the forgiveness of my sins! And that made me white as snow! Tears began to flow and I hugged his robe that I had carefully placed by my head. I could smell his scent in the cloth. I closed my eyes and breathed in deeply. Yes, I could smell him! I cried out into the darkness, "Master, why did you leave me? I loved you so much! What will I ever do without you? If I could just hear you say my name one more time! If I could just look into your eyes again! I love you, I love you... I love you." I cried until the lack of sleep from the last two days caught up with me.

I slept through most of the next day. When I finally awoke, the sun was going down. I thought I'd better hurry and gather up the spices I needed to take with me the next morning. After I had everything I needed, I came back home and ate a small dinner and then lay back down. I expected to toss and turn most of night, since I had slept so long, but to my surprise sleep came quickly. I awoke before the cocks crowed and dressed. This was a day I would honor Jesus. It would not be easy to touch his body, cold and discolored. But I needed to do it to honor him. I put all my spices in a small basket and left my house to meet Mary. She was to be staying at John's home and I guess from Jesus' words, she would be moving there soon.

Mary was already outside waiting and told me a few other women would join us. "Salome and Joanna will meet us by the gate. We will all go together." Neither of us talked on the way there. Joanna was waiting when we arrived and she hugged me. "Oh, Mary. I know he told us, but I didn't think it would really happen." Her eyes and face were swollen from crying. I took her hand, "I know, Joanna. I don't think any of us really believed it would happen, except her." I nodded in Mary's direction. We saw Salome approach and hug Mary. I had only met Salome once before and I remembered wishing she had a different name. *Memories.* She seemed a quiet and kind person.

We saw the first shades of light in the sky and we headed out of the gate together. Mary and I walked ahead, with Joanna and Salome behind us. On the way, Joanna asked, "Who will roll the stone away from the entrance of the tomb?" None of us had even thought about that! I turned around and said to her, "If all of us push, I think we can do it." Mary agreed and we continued on until we reached the garden.

Joanna was the first to gasp, "Look, the stone has been rolled away!" Then we all stopped in fear. Joanna and Salome stayed back and Mary and I ventured into the tomb. Suddenly, there were two men with clothes that gleamed like lightening! Mary and I bowed down, not understanding what was happening here or what had happened to Jesus! Then one of them spoke, "Why do you look for the living among the dead? The Son of Man must be delivered into the hands of sinful men, be crucified and on the third day be raised again." Then the other angel spoke, "Do not be afraid, for I know that you are looking for Jesus the Nazarene, who was crucified. He is not here; he has risen, just as he said. Come and see the place where he lay. Then go quickly and tell his disciples and Peter: 'He has risen from the dead and is going ahead of you into Galilee. There you will see him.' Now I have told you."

Mary and I got up, saw the folded grave clothes and went outside, filled with wonder. I felt apprehensive, because I didn't know where they had placed his risen body. Joanna was sitting across from the tomb, alone. She had lost most of the color in her face and I bent over to ask her what was wrong. She looked up at me and said in a voice barely audible, "What happened in there? We heard this loud noise like thunder and saw a very bright light. We thought you both were dead! Salome got up and ran!" I helped Joanna to her feet and told her what had happened. "We need to go to the disciples and give them the message. They are to meet Jesus in Galilee."

All three of us practically ran to the house where John had told us they would be hiding. Since Jesus died, they feared the same happening to them. Breathlessly, we burst into the little house, startling the disciples. Mary conveyed everything the angels had told us. I then turned to Peter and said, "They have taken the Lord out of the tomb, and we don't know where they have put him!" Peter jumped up. "No, you speak nonsense, Mary! He can't be gone!" He looked on the verge of tears and then John grabbed his arm. "Come, Peter. Let's go see for ourselves."

They both ran out of the house and I left the others and followed behind them. John reached the tomb first and I saw him hesitate as Peter approached. As soon as Peter reached the opening, he went straight in. John followed him. I stayed across from the tomb and waited. Soon they both came out and their faces looked troubled. I stood and approached them. "Did you see the strips of linen and the folded cloth? Where have they put him?" John took my hand and looked at me. "Mary, we don't know. We have to try and remember everything he told us and then maybe we will have answers. We must meet with the others and tell them." The two of them walked away and left me there alone.

I stood there for a long time and cried. When would this nightmare ever end? John and Peter had not mentioned seeing the two angels. Had they gone? I walked over to the tomb to see if they were still there. I bent over to look inside and there they were! This time they were sitting at the place where Jesus' body had lain. One at the head and one at the foot. They said to me, "Woman, why are you crying?" That seemed like a silly question to come from an angel! Surely he knows! "They have taken my Lord away and I don't know where they have put him." I started crying even harder and backed away from the tomb, then turned around. I gasped in alarm! There was a man standing there! I wanted to run, but felt no strength in my legs. He gazed at me and said, "Woman, why are you crying?"

How many times would I be asked this question? I felt irritation at first and then I thought this might be the gardener. Maybe he saw something or maybe he was the one who took Jesus' body. I collapsed at his feet and begged. "Sir, if you have carried him away, tell me where you have put him, and I will get him."

As I cried, my tears fell on his feet. My heart wrenched in pain as I remembered Simon's house. *Where is my Jesus?* Then I felt the man's hand reach down and pull my chin up to look at him and as he did, I heard the gentle voice I had come to know so intimately, "Mary." I had tried to turn my head away, but when I heard that voice say my name, I cried out with joy, "Rabboni!" I reached up to hold him, but he stopped me. "Do not hold on to me, for I have not yet returned to the Father. Go instead to my brothers and tell them, 'I am returning to my Father and your Father, to my God and your God.'"

It was Jesus! He was alive! I ached to touch him! My eyes pleaded with him, but he just shook his head. "I told you I needed you to be strong, Mary. This is the time of which I spoke. Now go and do as I said. You will see me again." I ran all the way to the house where the disciples were staying. I was so out of breath when I arrived, I could hardly speak. I cried out when I got to the door, "I have seen the Lord! I have seen the Lord!" John opened the door and helped me inside. I needed to sit and get my breath. Peter sat next to me and asked me what I was saying. "I have seen him, Peter! And he gave me a message for all of you."

I relayed the message exactly as I had heard it. The disciples were in an uproar! They were taking turns questioning these recent events. I listened for some time and felt my impatience building. "What you need to do is get yourselves together and head for Galilee. He told you he would meet you there!" John came to me. "It is not that easy, Mary. We are terrified of being seen! Many people knew that we followed Jesus and we don't know if his enemies are looking for us, too." I looked into John's face and there was real fear there! I looked around the room and saw it in all of their faces! "What is wrong with you men? Have you forgotten who Jesus is? Have you forgotten all the miracles he performed? Don't you remember Lazarus? Dead for four days—his soul should have been gone—and Jesus merely said, 'Lazarus, come out!' and he did! Everything he told us has come to pass! He has risen! He is alive! Where is your faith?"

Thomas looked angry. "You didn't believe either, Mary! You were worried about where the body had been placed!" Bartholomew spoke up. "Take it easy, Thomas. She is speaking the truth and we all know it. My sister's faith has always amazed us." I felt humbled by my brother's words. Looking around the room, I felt great compassion for them. "I am not trying to rebuke you. I'm trying to help you. He is alive and he wants to meet with all of you. Would he tell you to do something that would hurt you?" They slowly shook their heads. "Jesus will protect you. He promised to meet you in Galilee and he will be there. But the question is… will you?"

No one said anything and only Bartholomew would look at me. I stood up and said to them. "I am going home to get packed. I am going to eat a good meal and rest for the rest of the day. Then I am going to leave in the morning for Galilee. My prayer is that you will join me." I turned and gave my brother a hug and kiss, and then I left. On the way home, I worried that I had been too harsh. After all, their hearts were as broken as mine. But I truly didn't understand their lack of faith. *You did well, Mary!* I stopped. I had not heard "the voice" in years! What was this? *You were strong and bold, as I had told you to be for them. You did well!* It was Jesus voice! I should have known! It was still and small instead of loud and accusing. I started walking again. "Thank you, Rabboni."

The next morning I was awakened with loud knocking on my door. It was my brother and he was very excited. "Mary, Jesus appeared to us last night! He showed us his hands and feet and ate with us! It was amazing! He opened our eyes to understand why all of this happened! It was all foretold in the scriptures! He will be meeting us in Galilee just as you said he would and we are preparing to leave. Are you leaving soon?"

I was so happy that they had seen him! I was anxious to see him, too. "Yes, I did all my packing last night. All I need to do is load the things on the wagon." I still had Father's wagon. He probably would never believe that it had lasted this long! Bartholomew offered to help me and while he loaded the last water jug, he said, "Mary, we all want to thank you for last night. I know some of the disciples were angry with you, but we needed to hear what you had to say. You helped us remember who Jesus really is and what he means to each of us. Thank you, so much." I hugged him. "You're welcome, Bartholomew. I'm just happy that you've seen him!"

Bartholomew helped me into the wagon. At 46, my knees weren't what they used to be. Bartholomew looked concerned. "Mary, aren't you worried about taking this long trip by yourself? If you wait until this afternoon, you can go with us." I reached down to touch his sweet face. "Brother, I have traveled more on these roads than you could ever imagine! God has always protected me. He will protect me on this journey, as well. He is the same yesterday, today and forever. Jesus taught me that!"

He smiled at me and said, "I'm so glad we have found each other, Mary. I only regret the time we missed." I nodded. "It is all right, Bartholomew. We have plenty of time to make up for it. Have a good trip and I will see you in Galilee." I clucked to the ox and we were on our way. I turned as I steered onto the road that led out of the city, and saw my brother waving to me. "Thank you Jesus, for my brother. Thank you for all you have done for me. Thank you so much."

I arrived in Galilee after three days of travel. I wasn't in a great hurry and had hope along the way that Jesus might show up. But he didn't. I wasn't sure where to go, but felt drawn to Magdala. It had been so many years since I had been there. All the years I lived in Tiberias, I never went to my hometown. As I pulled the wagon into the city, I realized how very much it had changed. Many more people were living here now and it seemed like a thriving fishing town. I made my way down to the Sea of Galilee and continued along the shore until I found an unpopulated area. There were many large rocks and boulders at the waters' edge, so it would not be conducive to good fishing. This would be a good place to stop.

I got down from my wagon and released the ox from his yoke. I walked him down to the water to drink. He was a faithful fellow, left behind by the man who rented my house in Jerusalem. He had lost his business and had no money to pay me. So he just moved out and left the ox behind. I patted his back and remembered Joshua. Someday, I knew I would have another horse, but he would never replace Joshua. I sat there for a long time watching the sun as it was setting. It was such a beautiful sky! The sunlight etched muted shades of purple, pink and gold into the clouds. I realized I had better get a room before it got too dark. I hitched up the ox and headed back to the inn.

The next morning I was up before dawn. I wanted to get down to the water and watch the sun come up. I quickly dressed and walked the short distance to the shore. Light was just beginning to show on the horizon when I arrived. I skimmed rocks for a while and then sat down in the sand. There was not a sound anywhere except a few cocks crowing in the distance. The gentle lapping of the water took me back to the days spent with Jesus. A smile came to my face. They had been such wonderful days! I had learned so much from him. Things that had certainly prepared me for the painful time we had just spent in Jerusalem.

I stood and started skimming rocks again. I had not lost my touch! Every one bounced five or six times. I was throwing my last stone when I saw another stone skim the water next to mine! I looked to my left and standing there with a huge grin on his face—was Jesus! I ran to him and then hesitated. "Am I still not able to touch you?" He laughed and grabbed me, hugging me! Tears of joy ran down my face! It was really Jesus! I pulled back and looked into his eyes. "Master, I have missed you so much! How long will you be here with me?"

We sat down in the sand and he explained he could stay for the rest of the day, but he still had a lot of work to do with the disciples. "They really need me right now, Mary." I felt sad and a little cheated— no, jealous! "Well, I need you, too, Rabboni! Will I see you anymore after today?" He smiled patiently at me. "Mary, I know you need me, but I am with you. I am right here." He pointed to my chest. "I am in your heart, I am wholly with you. The disciples are not there yet. When the Holy Spirit comes upon them, that will change, but for now, I need to be with them. And, yes you can see me again. I need you to come to Bethany, to the Mount of Olives. In thirty-six days, I will meet you there. That is where I will say goodbye to everyone." I looked down at my hands. Quietly, almost in a whisper, I asked, "Then we will never see you again, will we?" He placed his hand on my shoulder and said, "No, Mary. Not like this. But I will always be with you; you know that."

We sat quietly for some time as I pondered these things. I knew Jesus words were true, but accepting his permanent departure was hard to swallow. He gave me time to let it sink in. Then the peace came. He moved closer to me and put his arm around my shoulder. "Mary, after you have come to

Bethany to say goodbye to me, I want you to seek out some people from your past. Those that may need your forgiveness and those from who you need to seek forgiveness. I especially want you to seek out Amos. Would you promise me you'll do that, Mary?"

I blushed. Stammering, I asked, "Are you...telling me... he is the one that will ...be ... my husband?" Jesus laughed out loud. "Oh, no, Mary! You will not trick me into telling you who he is, even with that coy little act of yours." He threw both arms around me and hugged me. "I love you, Mary!" My heart sank at the thought that this would be the last time I got to hold him. "I love you, too, Jesus." I closed my eyes and basked in the moment. My Lord and my redeemer, was holding me. I felt the warmth of his body...and his love... and wondered what I would do without him. Tears began to slip down my face as I felt the first rays of sunshine. I opened my eyes and saw Jesus looking at the sun as it rose over the water. He seemed thoughtful and I wondered if he would miss these times with us. We both sat and watched the sun continue to brighten the sky. I cherished this moment with Jesus... and the peace that was forever mine.

20

Wounded Healer

All praise to the God and Father of our Master, Jesus the Messiah! Father of all mercy! God of all healing counsel! He comes alongside us when we go through hard times, and before you know it, he brings us alongside someone else who is going through hard times so that we can be there for that person just as God was there for us.
II Corinthians 1:3-4 (The Message)

Two months have passed since we stood on the Mount of Olives and watched Jesus ascend into the sky. I watched until he was hidden from my sight in the clouds. He had been right! After our day in Magdala, I didn't see him again until I traveled to Bethany to meet with the disciples. After spending only a few hours with them, I could see the changes he had made in their lives... and their faith. It was worth my sacrifice.

I had been struggling, since Jesus' ascension, with the mission he had assigned me. I had promised him I would find people from my past and forgive them and in turn, ask for forgiveness. But I was having a really hard time keeping my promise. The people I was struggling with the most were the ones involved, in some way, with my lost babies. I just didn't see how I could forgive them. I realized after a lot of prayer, that I had made the final choice and no one had forced me into it. But I still held malice in my heart. I decided I would—again—commit this to prayer and try to apply the teachings Jesus had given me. He had said it was a choice to forgive. He said I needed to do it for *my* benefit and I needed to do it for God. With these in mind, I got on my knees and prayed for help, so I could keep my promise to Jesus.

That night, I tossed and turned a lot before I fell asleep. I kept wondering what my babies would be like right now if they had lived. Would they be boys or girls—or both? I calculated that their ages would be six and fourteen. Would I have been a good mother? I think I already knew the answer to that one! How different would my life have been if I had both of them? The questions kept spinning in my head until I thought it would drive me mad. Finally, I fell into a fitful sleep.

I'm walking on a path surrounded by beautiful flowers and baby animals. The animals are all so friendly! They let me pet them and don't run in fear. Up ahead I see a brook gently sliding over the smooth rocks that make up its bed. Then I see a weeping willow tree! This is just like the safe place from my childhood. I hear sounds. Unusual sounds in this setting. It is the sound of children playing. I walk a little faster and I see them. There are two of them and they are playing together. They look to be close in age to my children...had they lived. I walk faster. They see me and wave and then begin to run away from me. I run after them, and then I see someone sitting under a tree up ahead. They have gone to that person and have sat with him—one in his lap and the older next to him. As I get closer to them, I slow down to a walk.

Soon, I am close enough to recognize the man. "Hello, Mary." It is Jesus! I stop in front of him and he invites me to sit down. I am very confused and ask him, "Jesus, where am I? I knew this place at first, the safe place where I used to hide, but I don't know where I am now." He smiles his most loving smile. "Mary, this is heaven. I want you to meet your children!" Both children run to me and sit in my lap. I hug them as tight as I can. My children! The older is a girl; she looks like my sister, Salome! The younger one is a boy. After I hug them, they run off and begin to play again. Jesus takes my hand. "Mary, on the days you chose to not let your children live, they each came here to live with us. They prayed for you, Mary. They prayed unceasingly that their mother would find her way back to God, so they could meet her someday." My tears were falling like rain. "You see, Mary, your faith in me has given you everlasting life here in Heaven. When it is your time to die, your body will perish, but you will come here and live with your children and me. Don't struggle with forgiveness of others, Mary. Remember what has been done for you and pass it on." I look up to see the children, but they are gone. I look back to Jesus and he is gone, but his voice remains...Trust me, Mary. Trust me.

I sat straight up in the bed! I looked around my little house and slowly remembered where I was. Did I really dream that? I could still hear Jesus' voice...*Trust me.* I had seen my children, only briefly, *but I had seen them!* And they had prayed for me! I knew I would have no problem heading to Galilee now. In fact I would do it tomorrow! I got on my knees and began to pray. "Oh, my Father. Thank you for taking such good care of my babies. Thank you for letting me get a glimpse of them... and a glimpse of my future home! To know they are waiting for me is such a blessing to my soul! I am humbled by your kindness and thank you from the bottom of my heart. Thank you, Father...and thank you, Jesus."

It took me several days to travel to Galilee and I enjoyed it. This was a mission. There were many memories along these roads and most of them were not good, but there was no pain attached anymore. I was truly free. There were many people along the way, from whom I needed to ask forgiveness. Methodically, I traced my past relationships and then stopped in each town to find that person.

First, I went south to Bethlehem and found Leah and her sister. I shared how much I appreciated them making me leave, because it eventually had led me to Jesus. They were very curious about him and I spent many hours telling them of the many miracles he had performed. They were genuinely happy for me and offered me work any time I wanted it. As I was leaving, Leah said, "Mary, you were the best midwife I have ever had work with me. It would be a shame for you to give it up." I smiled at her and replied. "I may go back some day, but right now, I feel I have a different purpose for my life. Time will tell."

I drove a little further south to my father's inn. I did not know their names, but that wasn't the important thing. I drove into the courtyard and came to a stop at the well. I drew some water for the ox and then went to the innkeeper's quarters. I knocked and the same woman came to the door. "Do you need a room for tonight?" She did not seem to recognize me and I said, "No, I have come to ask you to forgive me for something I did here a few years ago." She looked skeptical, but after giving her a few details, she remembered. "You seem very different from the woman you were." I nodded. "I am different. A special man changed my life." She still seemed guarded, but replied, "Well, of course we forgive you. I am glad you got your life straightened up." I thanked her and got back in my wagon. Now I could head toward Galilee. There were just a few more stops along the way.

I traveled through until I reached Sychar. This had been Thomas' home. I stopped at the inn and got a room for the night. The next morning, I set out to find someone who might know him. It didn't take long. He was in the local tavern. I waited outside until he came out. It was still early in the morning and I hoped he would not be too drunk. He wasn't staggering, at least. He walked right up to my wagon and said, "Hi, beautiful! What is your name?" I chuckled as I remembered the first night we met. I got down from the wagon and said, "My name is Mary and we have already gone down this road." Slowly, I saw recognition bloom on his face. "Mary, how are you?" He grabbed me and hugged me and it was all I could do to push him away. "I just came to ask you to forgive me for my part in the failure of our relationship. I should never have lived with you without being married and I realize I was half the problem." His face looked bewildered and he cautiously answered, "Well, of course...I forgive you." I had planned to tell him about the baby, so I could ask forgiveness for that, but standing here looking at him; I realized it was a bad idea. I turned to get in the wagon when he grabbed my shoulder. "Hey, is that it? After all this time, how about having a drink with me?" He looked so desperate for company. *A look that I frequently wore during those days, so long ago.* I shook my head and replied, "No, Thomas. I don't need that anymore." I turned again and got up into the wagon. I saw loneliness in his face and recognized the longing in his soul. I was amazed by the great compassion I felt for this man who had hurt me so badly. "You know, Thomas, you don't have to live like this. There is another way. If you ever want to hear about it, come to Jerusalem and find me." I turned the ox north and waved to Thomas. His face seemed sad. Maybe I had planted a seed.

And that is how it went until I had found everyone I could. Some receptions were better than others, but even those who weren't interested in what I had to say—like Didymus—still heard about who had changed my life. Ruth was very happy for me and had already become a believer in Jesus. I stayed with her for two days before heading home. When I shared with her that my last stop was Gadara, she told me that Sarah had died this year. The news was heartbreaking because, though she would have been the hardest for me to forgive, Sarah needed Jesus. The desire to forgive her was my main focus, but I had also been excited at the idea of sharing with her the hope I had found in Jesus.

The next morning I prepared to go home. Ruth hugged me and asked what I was going to do now. She told me she would love to have me back and I was always welcome to come here to work. I was thoughtful. "I really don't know for sure, Ruth. I feel that there is something on the horizon. I'm just waiting to discover what it is."

On my way home to Jerusalem, I passed the road leading to Nazareth. There was one stop I hadn't made. This was probably the most important one because Jesus specified that I should talk with Amos. I tarried for only a few minutes before turning the wagon to the east. Maybe Sarah was not the toughest one after all.

I arrived in Nazareth in late afternoon. Not too much had changed here and I found many memories sprouting up. I drove by Mary and Joseph's house and remembered Joseph and Jesus in the front yard waving to me. I could almost see them. A little further and I came to the house where Orpah used to live. She had gotten married and moved about six months ago. She had been good to her promise and let me work for her when I was in Galilee following Jesus. She only gave me the deliveries on the outskirts of the city because I had not been ready to come back into Nazareth yet.

I kept going until I reached Amos' parents house at the end of the road. There were still very few houses here. I pulled into the yard and two little children came out to greet me. They were beautiful little boys! The older boy went running into the house yelling, "Abba, Abba! We have company! It is a woman!" I blushed and was wondering if Amos still lived here. As I got down from the wagon, I noticed the yard still had the look of a carpenter's dwelling. There were tools in the yard and what looked like a new table project near the workshop. I waited patiently for the father of these children to appear so I could ask where Amos might be.

In a few minutes, a man walked out. His hair was almost entirely gray and so was his beard. As he got closer I realized this was Amos! I couldn't believe it! I guess God had blessed me because I still had my long black hair and only a very few gray hairs were beginning to show. He walked toward me with partially squinted eyes, trying to see who I was. When he reached me, his face lit up! "Mary is that you? Praise Jehovah, I never thought I would see you again! How have you been?" He was so glad to see me! We hugged briefly and I replied, "I am better than I have ever been, Amos. I have changed a lot of things in my life. That is part of the reason I am here. But first, introduce me to these handsome boys. Are they yours?"

Amos blushed. "Yes, they are mine! The older one is Nathaniel, and the younger one is Simeon." I introduced myself to them and was charmed by their good manners. "You have done a very good job with them, Amos. With boys like this, you must have an amazing wife! Is she home?" I was a little nervous that she might get the wrong impression if this wasn't handled delicately. Amos looked down at the ground. It was a few seconds before he answered. "No, she died last year. First, my mother died and then my father. They coughed all the time and then my wife started. We don't know what it was and the physicians were not able to help. One morning she just didn't wake up. It was truly a miracle that the boys and I stayed well."

I touched his arm. "I am sorry, Amos. I know how much you loved your parents. I'm also sure you made a wonderful husband and that your wife was very happy." He nodded. "We were happy. It took me a long time to accept the fact that you weren't coming back, Mary. I finally realized I had to get on with my life. She was the daughter of my parents' best friends and Mother liked her very much. I'm sorry, Mary, I really didn't think I would ever see you again."

I shook my head. "No, Amos, you have nothing to apologize for. I came here to ask your forgiveness for the way I treated you and your parents. I would really like you to forgive me, Amos, if you can." He had a similar expression as the others I had seen on this journey. Surprise, with a little skepticism mixed in. For a moment, Amos seemed to be at a loss of words. "Mary, of course I forgive you." He paused and studied me for a moment. "You know, there is something very different about you. You have changed... you have changed a lot!"

It was my turn to blush. "Yes, I have Amos and I would love the opportunity to tell you about it." He grinned. "And I would love to hear about it! Can you come in and stay awhile?" He turned to his boys. "Nathaniel, Simeon, get some fresh water and bring it in the house for our guest to wash up." I followed him into the house and shared the story of my life since he had last seen me. I held nothing back. I felt safe and I knew he would not judge me. In fact, this was the safest I had felt since the days I spent with Jesus on the Sea of Galilee.

I ended up staying three days with Amos. Every evening I slept at the inn and then would return to his house in the morning. The idiosyncrasies that had bothered me so much before seemed to be gone. He had changed. Or maybe I had changed. We had long talks that I enjoyed immensely. He was a fabulous cook and I enjoyed that, also. But what I enjoyed the most was tucking his boys in at night...and I could tell they liked it. It would be hard for me to leave, but there was that nagging feeling that there was still something I needed to do.

The morning of the fourth day, I came to say goodbye. He was making breakfast for us and seemed sad that I was going. "Mary, you don't have to leave. I could let you stay here and I could sleep in the workshop." I gave him a hug. "No, Amos that would not honor your parents. You can't compromise your standards. I have a house in Jerusalem. You can come visit me and I will come visit you." He looked like he desperately wanted to say something, but was afraid to. "Amos what is it, what's on your mind?" He was almost wringing his hands. "Mary, would you consider marrying me? I have always loved you. I loved my wife when we were married and I didn't think I would ever love anyone else again. But then you walked back into my life and I realized the feelings are still alive. Would you, Mary?"

This caught me by surprise. Not that the same thing hadn't occurred to me. The whole time I was here I had been praying that if he was the one Jesus had been talking about, that there would be some kind of sign. Everything had been so positive, but I didn't know if he would want me as his wife after hearing all I had shared with him. I knew he would be my friend, but marrying me was entirely different. Even his interest in learning everything there was to know about Jesus was such an encouragement. But first, I had to find out what it was that was nagging at me. I took Amos hands in mine and looked him in the eyes. "I would be honored to be your wife, Amos. But I need a little more time. There is something I feel I need to do first. It's like a missing piece. But I am certain it won't take long to discover what it is. Then we can talk more about this." He nodded. "That sounds fair, Mary. You know, I am truly amazed at how much you have changed." I hugged him again and then we ate the breakfast he had prepared.

The boys gave me big hugs and begged me to come back soon. Amos helped me into the wagon. I chuckled. "I'm getting old, Amos. Are you sure you want to marry an old woman like me?" He took my hand in his and looked at me with intense love in his eyes. "Mary, you are as beautiful as the day I first met you. I would be the luckiest man on the earth if you would become my bride!" I blushed deeply and squeezed his hand and waved to the boys with the other. "I will see you soon, Amos. I feel very sure of that. Until then, take care of yourself and those wonderful boys."

He nodded. "I will Mary. They will miss you a lot. You know you are going to be a wonderful mother." Tears immediately came to my eyes. I didn't think he could have paid me a higher compliment. I turned the wagon toward the road and said a last farewell. Goodbye was too permanent. I would be back. Of that I was quite certain.

Back in Jerusalem, I prayed every night for God to show me what direction to take. I still had quite a bit of money saved that I could live on for several more months. So, I wasn't in a rush to get back to being a midwife. I just wanted to know what I was to do. My curiosity was killing me!

One day, I was sitting by my window and sewing some patches on my older tunics. My mind went back to the days I used to watch my mother sew. Memories from different points on the timeline of my life drifted in and out of my mind, some pleasurable and some sad. Then they seemed to stop at the time when I was staying with my parents in Cana. Father had come home and heard me talking with Mother and threw a cup at the wall. I acutely remembered the sound it made as the pieces hit the floor. I recalled thinking what a mess that would be to clean up. Wait…something was connecting for me! I put down my sewing and closed my eyes.

My life had been like the clay cup my father had thrown at the wall. Smashed. Broken. Shattered. Ruined. Destroyed. But like a master potter, Jesus had taken all the pieces and carefully placed them back together. He didn't make the cracks disappear. Those damaged areas—my wounds—were the very parts that helped me understand damaged people. Those who were walking through life, feeling the way I had felt. Because of my wounds, I could now help others. I could help them because I understood them. I could guide them, because Jesus had guided me. He had told me to 'pass it on.' This was the missing piece!

The next evening, I needed to get water. As I walked down the path that led to the well, I passed a familiar intersection in the road. A memory returned to me. I had passed this way many times and had not thought about it, until today. It felt so distant now, still retrievable, but no longer associated with pain...or guilt... or shame. The chains had been broken. I stopped and looked down the road to my left and visualized it, as if I were an onlooker watching from a distance. Disconnected, as if I were watching someone else.

Wrapped in a sheet with hands roughly pushing and pulling her. Being paraded through the streets for the purpose of tricking Jesus. "You haven't served your purpose yet!" The sight of Zadok squeezing her face gave me chills. The thought of him touching her at all nauseated me. I knew he was instrumental in the crucifixion of my Lord. That they tried to use her to succeed in their devious plot! "Don't try to escape again! If you do, I promise, you will go through Jerusalem naked!" Oh, how I recognized the feeling of shame on her face. Standing naked, in the middle of Jerusalem, where all the people visiting for the Festival were camping out. Jesus had used everything that happened that day to convict the hearts of his adversaries and bring glory to himself. And, more importantly for me, he had used that incident to change my life. To bring me to himself.

I turned my gaze from the road and began to walk again. I was truly not that person anymore.

I chuckled as I continued on to the well. So many times he had said just a word or phrase and it would shut the mouths of the Pharisees. I wondered what they were thinking now! During the forty days following his crucifixion, many people had seen him. The Pharisees could not deny what had been witnessed. I immediately found myself praying for the scales to be removed from their eyes. Jesus would have wanted me to do that. *"Love your enemies,"* he had said, *"it is easy to love those who love you, but it takes agape love to love those who hate you.*" Some of the things he had asked of us were not easy, and this was one of them. But I would do it. What other means could cause the Pharisees to change? Didn't they need to be shown the truth? Jesus had said they truly knew the scriptures, but did not understand the truth they revealed. I would pray for them instead of having thoughts of vindication. Even though I knew, if they saw me in the street, they would turn and walk the other way, I would still pray for them. They also need to love the unlovable, reach out to the unlovely and have compassion on the wounded.

As I approached the well, I saw a woman, sitting near one of the buildings, with a bowl in front of her where people had dropped coins. Her face was covered and she leaned forward over the bowl, shadowing it, as if protecting it. As I approached, I reached under my mantle to the little cloth bag where I kept some of the money I had managed to save. I thought how dejected she looked and how humiliating it must be to have to do what she was doing. Most of the beggars were made to stay by the gates so as not to "embarrass" anyone. Somehow she had slipped through.

I pulled out my hand with some of the coins and leaned over to place them in her bowl. When I did, I pulled my hand back in disgust! Someone had placed a small piece of sheep or donkey dung in the bowl! I didn't know people could be this cruel! *Oh, but you do know, Mary. And this child of mine needs my love revealed to her as it was revealed to you. This is my call on your life, Mary. You know what to do.*

I leaned over and removed the nasty substance from her bowl and replaced it with my coins. She looked up at me and I saw gratitude in her eyes. I knelt down and touched her arm. She didn't pull away. I saw tears forming. There was something very familiar about her eyes and the sadness that seemed so comfortable there. I tried to quickly sift through the years to determine how I might know her when she said, "Mary! Mary, is it really you?" Her hand reached up and slowly pulled down the scarf around her face. She was smiling as the tears now poured from her eyes. I still did not recognize her, but she definitely knew who I was! The eyes were old and sad, her face wrinkled and pale. I had a hunch that her lifestyle had aged her face, more than the sun or her years.

Again she spoke. "Mary, it is you, isn't it?" I nodded my head and gently wiped her tears. "Yes, but though you are familiar to me, I can't place you." Her eyes looked down. I heard a soft laugh and then she looked up at me again. "The years have not been as kind to me as they have to you, Mary. There is little difference in you from when we pulled water from the well together at your father's inn." I gasped. "It can't be!" She was nodding her head. "Oh, yes, Mary. I am Elizabeth. I bet you thought I was dead."

I grabbed her and hugged her as tight as I could. It alarmed me how thin and frail she had become. "Elizabeth, it is so good to see you! I have prayed for you so many times." She laughed out loud. "You, Mary? Praying? And you were praying for me? Maybe I have made a mistake!" She laughed heartily. At first I was hurt and then I realized she had only known the former Mary, the one I had seen in the street earlier. I began to laugh with her. "You are right, Elizabeth. I am very different now." She suddenly stopped laughing and grabbed me with both hands. "You found a man, Mary! That is what has kept you so beautiful and happy! You finally found that man you were searching for! I am happy for you! Obviously, I wasn't so lucky."

I stared into her eyes. They were so sad. So rejected. So alone. I held her face in both of my hands and said, "Yes, Elizabeth. I did find the man I was always looking for. Or I should say that he found me. And he is truly the most wonderful man who ever lived." She began to cry again. "Tell me Mary. What is his name? From what family does he come? Is he rich?"

I hugged her again. "Do you have a place to live, Elizabeth?" She shook her head. "No, I was in Cana for a time, but had to leave quickly. I would have been stoned had I stayed. I guess I don't need to tell you the details." I shook my head and thought to myself. *No, Elizabeth, those are details I am very familiar with!* She continued, "I've been here for only a few weeks and hoped to collect enough to rent a small house. But you keep avoiding my question, Mary. Who is this man?"

I helped her to her feet and noticed that it had been some time since she had bathed. "I will take you home with me and fix you some dinner. You can stay with me until we get you on your feet again." I bent over to pick up her bowl and when I stood up, she was crying again. "I can't believe you are helping me, Mary. I left you and never even said goodbye and now you want to give me a place to live? Your husband may not approve, Mary! Or is that the reason you won't answer me? Are you not married to this man?"

I stood up straight and hugged her again. When I pulled away, I, too, was crying. Not from sadness, but from the joy that was emerging inside me and almost taking my breath! Knowing that I was doing for someone else what Jesus had done for me! And there was an understanding in my heart and mind, that she was only the first. I wiped her tears and then my own, and helped her as we began to walk back to my house. She smiled at me and said, "Mary, you are really avoiding my question about this man! Now tell me about him, please!"

I wasn't sure where to start and then remembered Mary's words to me the night I met her in the stable. Those would be good words for Elizabeth. "He is a special person to everyone who meets him, Elizabeth. No one will ever forget him… or his name. I want you to meet him, too. His name is *Jesus*."

Epilogue

I hope during this time we have spent together, that you, too, have discovered the love of your life. He is the lover of your soul and His love is unconditional; no matter what you have done or how many times you have done it. Nothing can separate you from His love.

Beyond any doubt, He is the *Way* - only through Him, will you find the peace that goes beyond man's understanding. Only through Him will your chains be broken, for *He came to set the captives free.*

Beyond any doubt, He is the *Truth* - every single word He says about you in the Bible is true. You have been chosen. You are His child because He adopted you into His family. You are a saint. You are forgiven, redeemed, adored and cherished. You are held in the palm of His hand as a precious gem.

Beyond any doubt, He is the *Life* - Only through Him can you find everlasting life. A life where you can meet Him, talk with Him and ask Him all the questions that never had answers. And most important, worship Him in gratitude and love for an eternity, because you know that He is the reason you are there.

I wonder, if you have not yet fallen in love with Jesus, is it because the baggage you carry is too heavy? Or maybe you have carried it for so long that you are afraid to put it down? Take heart! He will find you in those "safe places" where you run and hide. He will take you by the hand and lead you out. But *you* must let Him! Don't hesitate to go! No matter how comfortable you may feel in your safety net. Trust Him. This is one time—I promise—you will not be hurt. And when He takes your hand, look down at His and be sure to notice the scar that it carries. It is there for you.

You see, I understand those "safe places" very well. He called them *demons*. Some became idols in my life. Things that I turned to, instead of turning to him. I called them *addictions*. All I knew is that they gave me a temporary anesthesia from the intense pain I carried. He told me that during those extremely painful times, I needed to turn to Him and receive comfort and forgiveness. And most of all I needed to forgive those who had hurt me.

Yes, I truly understand the safe places. I still have one. Only recently have I allowed Him to take my hand and lead me out. This one is going to take a lot of time, I'm afraid. Someday, I would love to share *that* journey with you also, but that is another book.

To close our time together, I would like to reminisce a little and take you back to the poem I wrote so many years ago. When I felt deserted. Abandoned. Forsaken. Rejected. Discarded. Hopeless. I felt every one of those feelings and many more. Do they sound familiar to you? Are you feeling them now? Do you wear them like garments? Be encouraged. Read with me:

Most things can be broken only once.
Some can be mended.
The heart is an exception to this rule.
The difference is, the heart can't be mended,
It just goes on breaking into smaller and smaller pieces,
Until nothing is left,
But some remnants of love...

And then came Jesus.

If you or someone you know is in pain and have questions or comments that you would like to share with Leslie, please feel free to e-mail her at <u>somemoresfor6@yahoo. com</u>. She would love to hear from you.

CPSIA information can be obtained at www.ICGtesting.com
Printed in the USA
LVOW062324191011

251240LV00001B/126/A